BBC

DOCTOR WHO

TIME TRIPS

BBC

DOCTOR WHO

TIME TRIPS

A.L. Kennedy

Jenny T. Colgan

Nick Harkaway

Trudi Canavan

Jake Arnott

Cecelia Ahern

Joanne Harris

Stella Duffy

BBC
BOOKS

1 2 3 4 5 6 7 8 9 10

BBC Books, an imprint of Ebury Publishing
20 Vauxhall Bridge Road, London SW1V 2SA

BBC Books is part of the Penguin Random House group of companies whose addresses can
be found at global.penguinrandomhouse.com

Penguin
Random House
UK

This book is published to accompany the television series entitled *Doctor Who*, broadcast on
BBC One. *Doctor Who* is a BBC Wales production.
Executive producers: Steven Moffat and Brian Minchin

This print edition published in 2015 by BBC Books, an imprint of Ebury Publishing.
First published as ebooks in 2013 and 2014 by BBC Books.

www.eburypublishing.co.uk

A CIP catalogue record for this book is available from the British Library

ISBN 978 1 849 90771 2

Editorial director: Albert DePetrillo
Series consultant: Justin Richards
Project editor: Steve Tribe
Illustrations by Ben Morris © Woodlands Books Ltd, 2015
Cover design: Two Associates © Woodlands Books Ltd, 2015
Production: Alex Goddard

Printed and bound by Clays Ltd, St Ives PLC

Penguin Random House is committed to a sustainable future for our business, our readers
and our planet. This book is made from Forest Stewardship Council® certified paper.

MIX
Paper from
responsible sources
FSC
www.fsc.org   FSC® C018179

CONTENTS

Paul Harris was dying. This wasn't something his afternoon's schedule was meant to include. Death, as far as Paul was concerned, was one of the many unpleasant things which only happened to other people. He'd never even attended a funeral – *all those miserable relatives*. He'd also avoided weddings – *all those smug relatives*. And he'd skipped every christening to which underlings in his firm had thought they should invite him – *all those sticky, noisy babies… all those sticky, noisy underlings…*

Mr Harris's death was particularly surprising to him as it involved being eaten alive by a golf bunker. At least, he could only assume that something *under* the bunker was actually what was eating him alive – now he'd sunk down past his knees into the thing – and he could only assume that it wasn't going to stop eating him because… it wasn't stopping.

First he'd been gripped around his ankles while he eyed a tricky shot for the 13th green. The process had involved an initial pressure, combined with a slight, but very disturbing, pain and then a type of numbness had set in. Next, he'd sunk into the sand by a few inches, before another – he tried not to think of the word *bite*, but couldn't help it – before another *bite* was taken with a little more gentle pain and then more numbness and another tug downwards. Paul liked to think of himself as powerful and unstoppable and there was huge power and a definitely unstoppable will at work here and he would certainly have admired them both had they not been ruining his very nice pair of lime green golfing trousers and his very nice legs inside them.

Paul was surprised to discover that he was completely unable to scream for assistance and there was no one about to even notice his rather unusual situation, never mind save him from it. His golfing partner, David Agnew, had unfortunately flounced off towards the clubhouse a short while ago. As Paul was jerked further into the sand, he reflected that Agnew had proved himself as bad a loser as he was a really irritating man. Still, it would have been helpful if Agnew had stuck around because then maybe he could have pulled Paul out of the bunker, or written down a few last requests, or got eaten too. Paul imagined that seeing David Agnew get eaten by a golf bunker would have been highly satisfying, because people like David Agnew were pretty much ideal golf bunker food, in Paul's opinion, although he was prepared to admit that he knew nothing about bunkers which ate people and what they might prefer. If he'd had any information on them, perhaps provided by his loyal secretary Glenda, then he might not be plunged to his waist in one right now.

The list of things that Mr Harris knew nothing about was extensive. He had never been at all curious about those aspects of the world which didn't benefit him directly.

Nevertheless, the most inquisitive human alive on Earth at that time still wouldn't have known Paul was being consumed by a creature so old and so mythical the universe had almost completely forgotten it ever was. The thing had passed beyond legend and was now simply a vague anxiety at the edge of reality's nightmares.

In a way, it was quite wonderful that such a being should still exist. Although, of course, it wasn't wonderful for Paul Harris, whose abilities to communicate – by signalling, crying out, or extending a subtle and sophisticated telepathic field, should he have been able to do so – had all been suppressed by his attacker. His attacker didn't like to be interrupted when it was feeding and fortunately evolution had allowed it to develop an ability to prevent its meals from attracting any kinds of aid. Unless, that was, the beast wanted dessert to arrive in one big arm-waving, or feeler-waving, or tentacle-waving, or slave excrescence-waving, or tendril-waving crowd of would-be rescuers, all panicky and delicious. In which case screaming, pleading and pretty much anything else along those lines was permitted.

Evolution also meant that although Paul was being injured horribly he was feeling only mild distress. Eating a struggling meal was potentially dangerous and tiring, so the creature had developed many complex and fascinating mechanisms which meant that each bite it took of its prey released soothing analgesics and sedatives into – taking this afternoon as an example – Paul's ravaged circulatory and nervous systems.

By this point Paul's arms were flopping gently on the bunker's surface and his torso was locked into the sand as far as his armpits. He wasn't a stupid man and he was fairly sure that as much of his body as he could still peer down at and see was about as much as was still available for board meetings and games of squash or, for that matter, golf. (Although he was definitely beginning to go off golf.) It seemed strange to him that he couldn't seem to be too upset about any of this. He was, in fact, increasingly docile and happy in a way that reminded him of once being a quite pleasant child with many exciting and generous prospects ahead, every one of which he had ignored or wasted later.

As Paul's head was tugged down beneath the surface of the bunker, he could still feel the gentle summer breeze tickling at the palms of his hands which were raised and therefore still vaguely free. He experienced a brief regret that he hadn't kept up his piano lessons and that he'd gone on holiday to the Turks and Caicos Islands instead of attending his own grandmother's funeral. Paul then thought, 'Is that breathing? I seem to be able to hear breathing... A bit like a cow's, or a horse's breathing... some very big animal. I wonder what it is.'

At which point Mr Harris stopped wondering anything.

Anyone who had passed by the bunker at that exact moment

would have seen two well-manicured hands apparently being sucked into the bunker and disappearing. They could then have watched the sand tremble and shiver until it presented a perfectly smooth and harmless surface again.

Bryony Mailer was quite possibly the most inquisitive human alive on Earth at that time, which was 11.26 a.m. on 4 June 1978. She was a slim but wiry 24-year-old female human with a great sense of humour, huge reserves of ingenuity and a degree in European History. None of these things was helping her enjoy what she had once hoped was a temporary position as Junior Day Receptionist at the Fetch Brothers Golf Spa Hotel. There wasn't a Senior Day Receptionist, because that would have involved Mr Mangold, the hotel's manager, in paying Senior kind of rates. So Bryony was Junior and would stay that way for as long as she was here, stuck in perhaps the most tedious place on Earth. Lately, a couple of guests had even checked in and then simply given up on the place, leaving their luggage and running away. Their accommodation had been paid for in advance – it wasn't as if they were trying to dodge their bills – and she could only assume the sheer boredom of the Fetch had driven them out. And the wallpaper in the bedrooms was quite offensive – she didn't think she'd want to sleep inside it, either.

When Bryony wasn't folding away other peoples' abandoned pyjamas and storing their unwanted spongebags (in case they came back for them), she was dealing with the health and beauty requirements of golfers' bored wives, coordinating the coaching and playing and post-game massage and bar lunch requirements of the golfers and generally fielding every bizarre request and complaint that an old hotel full of petulant people can generate on any given day. She didn't get a lot of down time.

But she'd been having a quiet spell lately. For as long as six minutes, she'd been able to ponder whether she'd have her tea with or without a biscuit and whether the biscuit would be a Mint Yo Yo or an Abbey Crunch. It wasn't so long ago that she'd been able to tease apart all the convolutions of French foreign policy under Cardinal Richelieu, but now even a choice between two biscuits was likely to give her a headache. And Mangold would probably have eaten them in the meantime, even though they were her biscuits…

She decided to take the risk of leaving the slightly scuffed reception desk unattended and propped a small handwritten card next to the brass counter bell – PLEASE PRESS FOR ASSISTANCE – before she slipped off through the door next to the scruffy room-key pigeonholes and along the narrow passageway that led to the Staff Office.

Bryony had never liked this passageway. It was too narrow and its wallpaper was dreadful – worse than in the bedrooms – a claustrophobic pattern of purple and red swirls which almost seemed to wriggle when you looked at them. And it was always either overly cold in here or – like today – much hotter than was pleasant. She tended to rush the journey.

As she rushed – it wasn't far and would take less than a minute – she wasn't aware that behind her the wallpaper not only wriggled, but swelled in two places, heaving and stretching until it seemed there were two figures caught behind it and fighting to get out. Had she turned and seen this happening it would have made her very frightened and also slightly nauseous, but she kept on walking, hurrying, simply aware of an odd taste in her mouth, as if she'd been sucking pennies.

When Bryony reached the office doorway she saw that both her packets of biscuits had disappeared and there was a little gathering of crumbs on the shelf where she'd left them.

She didn't see – because her back was turned and anyway why on earth should anyone be on the alert for such a thing? – that two figures had detached themselves stickily from the nasty wallpaper and were now padding along towards her. Each of them seemed unfinished, like rough models of small human beings made out of purple and red meat. Their outlines shifted and rippled horribly. Eyes and teeth emerged to the front of the two rudimentary heads; they showed white and shining and clever against the shifting masses of glistening flesh.

And there was no way out for Bryony. The Staff Office was a dead end in every sense, as she'd often told herself.

'Oh, bum.' Bryony sighed. This was going to be another awful day. And she had the very distinct feeling she was being watched. There was a tingling against her neck. She was filled with an impulse to turn round and also an idea that if she did she might not like what she discovered.

As they walked – now very close to Bryony – the figures kept altering, their outlines firming, features coming into focus and solidifying. Then four arms stretched out towards her and, as they lifted, were sheathed in fresh skin. Four hands became completely hand-like, with four thumbs and sixteen fingers and twenty fingernails, just as they reached to clutch her.

As Bryony finally did begin to spin round she felt herself being held by both her wrists and heard the word, 'Boo!' being shouted by two very similar voices.

'Oh, for goodness' sake.' It was the Fetch twins, Honor and Xavier, looking up at her and giggling while they squeezed her wrists. 'You two nearly scared the life out of me.'

'That would be bad. Your life should be in you,' said Xavier, the boy twin. The Fetch twins weren't absolutely identical, as they liked to tell everyone. They were a boy and a girl, very alike, but not the same. 'We're very sorry.' Xavier didn't currently look sorry at all.

Neither did Honor. 'We didn't want to scare you… only sort of worry you a bit. To be exciting.' She smiled and looked very sweet. 'Excitement is nice, isn't it?'

Bryony forgave the little girl, as she always did. She always forgave both twins – they were just extremely… forgivable. Even though they did seem to turn up suddenly more often than not, as if they were creeping about and planning something only they understood. And it wasn't as if Bryony didn't need some excitement. She longed for it, in fact.

Xavier squeezed her hand between his, tugging. 'Grandmother says she would like you to come and visit her for tea.'

This was sort of good news – the twins' grandmother was Julia Fetch, the reclusive widow who owned the hotel. If she had decided to like Bryony that might make life much easier for the Permanently Junior Day Receptionist and maybe even mean Mangold didn't eat Bryony's biscuits. Then again, she really didn't want to work here for much longer. Possibly it would mean she got a good reference when she resigned, though…

The twins peered up at her, identically expectant and cute with their willowy limbs, perfect complexions and sun-bleached hair: Xavier in a blue and white striped T-shirt and blue shorts, Honor in a red and white striped T-shirt and red shorts. They were both barefoot, as usual. Bryony thought maybe she might mention to Mrs Fetch that running around with no shoes on wasn't terribly hygienic. Then again, maybe Mrs Fetch ran around in bare feet, too. No one ever saw her and she was incredibly wealthy – she could do whatever she liked. She could just not wear anything at all, ever, if she felt like it, or dress as a pirate. Of the two choices, Bryony was strongly in favour of the pirate option.

Honor squeezed Bryony's hand this time. 'Do say yes. We'd be ever so pleased and have cucumber sandwiches.' Both twins spoke like children out of an old-fashioned story book. 'Truly we would.' And maybe incredibly wealthy people talked like that all the time – Bryony had no idea, being what she might have called *incredibly not wealthy* if it wouldn't have depressed her to do so.

Bryony nodded at the twins – while thinking *pleasepirate-costumepleasepiratecostume* – and both kids gave a cheer. 'Thank your grandmother very much. When I have a break I will come over.'

'This afternoon! This afternoon!' The twins skipped and chanted as they scampered away up the passage and out of sight.

'Weird little people.' Bryony shook her head and, in the absence of biscuits, pottered back out to the reception desk. There was no sign of the twins and the grandfather clock was, as usual, not ticking. As far as Bryony was concerned, life was dusty and hot and dull, dull, dull.

Out on the golf course, now shimmering with heat under the June sun, a peculiar person struggled with his golf bag, which seemed to be much larger than was necessary. It was almost taller than him. But then, he was on the small side. Once again, his putter fell to the grass and once again a fellow golfer spotted him flailing about just where he shouldn't be and yelled, 'Get out of the bloody way, man! Fore, for heaven's sake! Fore!'

As he picked up his putter, only to watch several woods clatter onto the carefully manicured turf in a heap, the figure sighed and wondered, 'Four of what? I don't think I even have one of them… I don't think…' He was out of his depth, as he usually was, and felt distinctly hot and uncomfortable in his black woollen unsuitable suit. He peered in the direction of the Fetch Hotel and the Fetch Hotel front entrance and the Fetch Hotel reception desk and the area near to the reception desk and the precise spot – which he could only guess at longingly – where Bryony Mailer was standing at that very moment.

He sighed again, this time from the soles of his feet, right up to the ends of each hair on his head. It was horrible being in love. It was considerably more horrible being in love with someone too beautiful for you to even look at properly – unless you knew they were looking somewhere else and you wouldn't have to meet their eyes and blush and then want to burst into flames or evaporate or something. It was more horrible still when you understood completely that the person you loved clearly found you far less interesting than watching a pebble. It was most horrible when your love could never be, not in any way, not ever.

He sighed again until he felt completely hollowed out and didn't even flinch when a golf ball sliced past him, close enough for him to hear the way its tiny dimples disturbed the air.

'Fore, you *moron*! *Fore!*' An irate voice screamed away to his left.

He really would have to work out this four thing. He bent to gather up his clubs with a heavy and tragically romantic heart.

As a golf ball landed much further away from the 12th green than its owner had intended, Bryony thumbed through her stack of pending reservation slips while deciding – yet again – that she hated golf, hated golfers, hated golfers' wives (did they have no lives of their own?) and that she really hated her ex-boyfriend Mick (a non-golfer) for having sapped her confidence, just when she'd been making postgraduate career decisions. A year ago, she'd thought working here would be relaxing and give her a taste of real life, and maybe she could write a book about… something… something to do with history… in her evenings off before becoming a stunningly attractive and popular young professor somewhere. Now she knew she was bored out of her mind, was never going to write anything if she didn't get away from the horrible Fetch premises and horrible Fetch guests and the horrible Mr Mangold. Bryony was equally certain that she had no idea what came next. Her lack of clarity about what came next was scary and why she hadn't left yet.

'Oh, I wouldn't worry terribly much about that, you know,' said a friendly, velvety kind of voice.

Bryony glanced up to see a very tall man studying her from the doorway. He grinned with rather more teeth than one person should have. He appeared to have been dressed by a committee, possibly a drunk committee: wing collar and something that might once have been a cravat, baggy checked trousers, brown checked waistcoat, long purple velvet frock coat with bulging pockets, raddled shoes… an immense and disreputable scarf with a life of its own…

'These things quite often work themselves out in highly unpredictable ways. Luck has a lot to do with it. Although one can make one's own luck, I always think. At least I think I think that. Or else someone told me that. Probably someone lucky.' He made his way across the foyer towards her, half loping and half tiptoeing with a general air of being highly delighted to see everything around him including the dust on the broken grandfather clock. Bryony thought she'd never encountered anyone so remarkable in her life.

She was right.

As the man toped, or liptoed, up to Bryony's desk he continued amiably: 'Quite possibly you'll discover you're a creature of infinite resource. It's very warm for January, isn't it? Or then again I may have missed January and I'm definitely not in Chicago. Am I?'

Bryony heard herself say, 'Arbroath.'

'Well, that's quite close. I degaussed the Mackenzie Trench circuit before I set off. Which sometimes works. But mostly not.' And he smiled again, even more largely. 'Hello, I'm the Doctor.' He seemed somehow like her oldest friend, like a wonderful relative she'd heard a lot about but never met.

Bryony, while wondering how any human being could have that much hair – this kind of dense, lolloping head of wildly curly hair – fumbled through all the possible replies she could make to this Doctor person. Among them were, 'Who on earth are you really, though?' and 'How did you know what I was thinking?' and '*What?*' and 'Do you ever wash that scarf? Or can't you because it would object? Would it be like trying to wash a cat…?'

While she *urred* and *ahed*, the Doctor nodded patiently, even slightly annoyingly, as if he were coaxing a dim child through a really easy sum. On the one hand he was clearly the type of person who should make anyone sensible very nervous, but on the other he filled her with the deepest sense of trust she'd ever experienced. Which took her right back to supposing she ought to be nervous.

Eventually, she managed, 'Do you have a reservation?' Which was a completely boring thing to say and made him look gently disappointed.

'A reservation? Well, no, I don't believe I do. When I travel I generally bring my own accommodation.' The Doctor's very large and very curious eyes lifted to ponder the ceiling while his monologue ambled along both gently and unpreventably. 'I might be due for a holiday, of course. I always forget to take them. Usually someone reminds me, but there's no one to do that for me at the moment.'

Bryony wondered if he was just some weirdo who was camped in the scrub by the lake – they'd had that kind of problem before. He smelled a bit peculiar – but it was a clean kind of smell, more like the way the air smelled right before a thunderstorm with a trace of added icing sugar than someone who woke up in a tent.

He continued, while apparently trying not to grin. 'I was lost in a virtual jungle for a while quite recently. Have you ever been lost in a virtual jungle? Takes it out of you. Perhaps I should have a holiday?' He eyed her name tag. 'Bryony Mailer, do you think I need a holiday, should I stay here?' Then he looked straight at her the way an extremely bright boy might if he were expecting ice cream.

And Bryony Mailer thought – *This is it. This is what's next.*

Then she told the Doctor. 'Yes. I think you should stay. You should stay here.'

*

At the most secluded edge of the Fetch Estate in a small, but dazzlingly well-equipped cottage, Miss Julia Fetch – she had never got around to marrying – rearranged her extensive collection of glass octopuses. (Or octopodes.) She had them made in Venice by an increasingly elderly team of master glass blowers, lamp workers and glass artists. She softly ran her – she had to admit – increasingly elderly fingers across the rounded head of an *Octopus rubescens* and gently waved at the perfectly modelled tentacles of a red-spot night octopus, or *Octopus dierythraeus*. She smiled.

As the years had passed, she'd found that she had become slightly forgetful, perhaps even very forgetful, but she had perfect recall when it came to the names of octopus species. She had always been fond of octopodes (or octopuses) and she was using a tiny fraction of her monumental cash reserves to have every variety of octopus modelled in glass. There were over a hundred to reproduce and each exquisitely delicate sculpture took nearly a year of the craftsmen's work. It was very possible that she wouldn't quite manage to see the collection completed. She was also sole patron and very generous supporter of the Julia Fetch Foundation for the Care and Support of Octopuses (or Octopodes). These were really her only two remaining indulgences, apart from the cottage's fantastic kitchen – which she hardly used – and the marble-lined bathroom and generously proportioned bath in which she soaked her sometimes rather achy limbs, while wishing that she had more legs. Or more arms. Or both.

When she was younger Miss Fetch had enjoyed the usual toys and treats of the ultra-rich: buying sports cars and villas on sun-kissed coastlines, owning a London townhouse and a moderately sized castle (with village attached) quite near Folkestone, running stables full of racehorses, and country estates, all of which were seething with fat, juicy, slow-moving game birds and succulent deer. But she didn't really enjoy driving and paying other people to drive her Bugattis and Duesenbergs and Alfa Romeos had seemed silly. Filling her villas (and the townhouse and the castle) with loud strangers hadn't been nearly as much fun as she'd expected and filling them with friends was very difficult because having friends when you're vastly rich just gets quite *complicated*. Rattling around next to her swimmerless swimming pools, or wandering alone across her dusty ballrooms had been depressing. She'd caught herself talking to the geckos in one place and half expecting them to answer. Her racehorses were beautiful, but had never seemed that fond of her – they tended to be slightly highly strung. And she had never been able to bring herself to kill anything on her estates. In fact, she'd been vegetarian for at least twenty years, if not forty, or sixty... Eventually, she'd given away all her homes apart from the cottage. They'd been turned into community centres and octopus research facilities. She'd sold her sports cars and horses and let her estates go back to nature and be overrun by un-shot-at animals and, by now, some quite rare plants, which nobody shot at either.

Or that was the past which she currently remembered. She sometimes had the feeling that she had previously remembered other pasts, but she couldn't be sure. Being this old was slightly confusing. Then again – as the twins often told her – it was very reasonable to be confused when she knew so much and had been to so many places and done so many things, occasionally in diving gear. (But never dressed as a pirate.)

And as long as she had the twins – her beautiful, kind and charming Honor, her handsome, kind and charming Xavier – she knew that everything would be all right. That was something she didn't forget.

She never left her cottage these days. She didn't need to. A dedicated geostationary satellite poured a constant flow of information into her personal media hub – located in what used to be the pantry – and she could spend all day, if she wanted, learning more about octopus camouflage techniques, or the cunning ways in which they could impersonate other sea creatures, or reading her Foundation's latest test results on octopus intelligence. From the hub, she could also keep an eye on the stock market and watch her money quietly making more money.

But she did feel the need for a little company now and then. She did think – perhaps regularly, perhaps only once a month, she wasn't entirely certain – that it would be nice to invite some pleasant people to take tea with her. Nothing grand, or fussy – just tea with small sandwiches and perhaps slices of fruit cake and maybe scones.

She did sometimes tell the twins about arranging to have tea and they did promise to go and find her suitable guests, but she couldn't – if she was honest – absolutely recall how often this happened, or if she had ever served anybody tea, or discussed the mating rituals of squid while buttering very thin toast and handing out napkins. Occasionally she dreamed that the inside of her mind was somehow becoming occupied by a being much cleverer than she was, something with dark tendrils, or tentacles reaching into her personality and softly wriggling about across her memories in a way that made them jumble and fade.

Still, it didn't matter. She was entirely happy and probably had forgotten her last tea party in the usual old lady type of way. Probably, if she concentrated, she could say how many cucumber sandwiches this or that visitor had eaten and whether there had been enough jam. And there was no reason to worry if she couldn't. As she stared out through her window at the well-groomed trees and glossy shrubs bordering her golf course, she nodded to herself and smiled again. She had a good life. And sixty-eight perfectly lovely Venetian glass octopodes. Or octopuses.

*

David Agnew was a man who purposely ate octopus whenever he could. He was currently sitting in the Fetch Hotel's Sweet Spot Bar and wishing he was, instead, lolling by the pool at his Greek island villa, tucking into some fresh octopus legs and shooting geckos with his air pistol. These were the kind of things he enjoyed.

He was not enjoying his vodka and orange, which was warmish and rather unpleasant and definitely hadn't involved fresh orange juice, even though he'd asked for it specifically. Some chance of proper service in a dump like this. Still, Fetch Brothers had a fabulous golf course and he could usually get round it in 86. Or 90. Definitely in 98.

Agnew considered complaining, but he couldn't be bothered because at present he felt extremely good about life. He'd showered after he left the course, changed into his new, rather dashing, safari suit and he wasn't due back at the office for another two hours. That gave him more than enough time for a spot of lunch. He snapped his fingers to summon the barman and ordered a prawn cocktail and a basket of scampi and chips. And a glass of Liebfraumilch.

While he waited for his bar meal, he glanced round at the golfing prints, the photos of men in large caps and plus fours, the little shelf of donated trophies and the Challenge Cup. This year, he had a real chance of winning the Cup. There had been ten players who were better than him on paper, but seven of them weren't competing this time round.

Actually – he corrected himself – *eight* of them wouldn't be competing. Yes, he was sure of that. He was absolutely sure that Paul Harris wouldn't be trying for the Challenge Cup this year. Or any other year. David Agnew tugged at his beige jacket to smooth it and grinned. The world was a very satisfactory place.

Then it became significantly less satisfactory as a grassy, shabby, scrawny, sweaty man clattered into the bar with a golf bag he seemed quite unable to control. Knocking over a number of stools as he proceeded, he then sank to a halt at the table next to Agnew's and flopped the bag messily down beside him. Its ancient clubs emerged like a rusty threat and disfigured the carpet.

Agnew gave the newcomer his best withering stare and pointed to a large sign which read GOLF BAGS AND GOLF ATTIRE ARE NOT PERMITTED BEYOND THE CLUBHOUSE.

At this, the dreadful interloper flinched and said, 'Oh. Oh, dear... I... but I'm... well, I thought that as I was... I'm a resident... guest... that is... oh, dear... I am very...' He fumbled at the bag's shoulder strap, which had come adrift, and stood up rapidly in a way that produced a shower of tees, grass tufts and dried mud. Then he reached into his bag and pulled out – Agnew couldn't begin to guess why – its last remaining club, a battered putter, and waved it around as if he was conducting some type of interior orchestra.

'Careful! You nearly had my head off with that. What's wrong with you?'

The putter crashed down across Agnew's table while the ghastly little man mumbled, 'Wrong...? No, it's just me... me, you see... people always seem to find that me being me is wrong... I don't mean it to be...'

Agnew bellowed, 'Sit down!'

At this, the stranger squeaked, 'OK.'

Agnew announced, 'I have a headache and would like to finish my lunch in peace.' Which was a confusing thing to say as his lunch hadn't arrived yet, but he was too annoyed to make sense. Agnew frowned while the man peered at him.

'Well, I... Sorry for speaking... but I won't interrupt. That is... I'm Mr Ian Patterson.' The grubby man recited his name as if it was something he'd had to memorise recently. 'And I... being here without golfing was... it would have seemed... but I don't play golf... and...' He shoved the fallen clubs back into his bag distractedly. 'They loaned me these... things... and

I already had the… the putter thingy…' Then he started to thump at his clothing in a doomed effort to remove the layer of muddy dust under which he was now operating. This simply spread the dust further.

'Mr Patterson!'

'Ah!' Patterson ducked warily for an instant and stopped thumping. 'Yes?'

'Why don't I give you a golf lesson?' Agnew smiled like a crocodile approaching a fat gnu he'd caught out paddling by itself. 'Would you like that? Eighteen holes? Ideal, I'd say… I'm David Agnew. Allow me to be…' He clearly found it difficult to say the next word. '… Helpful.'

Before Patterson could even think about how unlikely this was, he found himself suddenly having his golf bag thrust into his confused arms and being propelled out of the bar while Agnew shouted to the barman, 'No lunch for me. Busy. Cancel it all. Back in fifteen minutes.'

This puzzled Patterson because even he knew fifteen minutes wouldn't give them enough time for a full round of golf, not that Patterson wanted a full round or really anything more to do with golf. It seemed a ridiculous game and – *oh, dear* – he was being badgered along towards the front entrance and – *oh, no* – here was Bryony, lovely Bryony, talking to a bizarre-looking guest and apparently getting on extremely well with him – *it was the curly hair, women loved curly hair* – Patterson's hair was as flat and lifeless as his hopes – and it was ginger – and…

'Good afternoon, Mr Agnew.' Bryony had lifted her head. Her extremely attractive head. And because of the whole attractiveness thing it was horribly impossible not to look at her, while she then said, 'Good afternoon, Mr Patterson.' And the whole looking at her thing meant that Patterson was completely, supernaturally, aware that she was looking at him in return. This caused a kind of searing pain to dart straight into his chest and then bang right out again through his back.

It was such a real sensation that he worried about his jacket and whether it had been singed.

'Oh, I'm… sorry… covered in mud… and grass… and… trying some, er, golf…' And the last thing he saw of her as he was bundled down the steps and outside was a smile. It was a slightly confused, if not dismayed smile, but it had been for him.

She'd smiled at him.

That was wonderful.

As the golf-related chaos receded, the Doctor continued talking to Bryony while also thinking a great many things at once. He was aware that the ability to do this was an indication of genius. He was a genius, after all, and what kind of genius would he be if he didn't know that?

Currently, he was wondering why the TARDIS had deposited him here. Even at her most random, the TARDIS always worked within her own kind of personal logic, so his arrival must have some kind of reason behind it. Unless it didn't. Why Arbroath now, as opposed to Chicago in a snowstorm several months ago when the Chicago Area Computer Hobbyists' Exchange was going to develop its MODEM work and create an inadvertent danger to all life on Earth? Which he'd just have to deal with later. Or rather, earlier… As his friend Robert Louis Stevenson had often told him, there did usually need to be an extremely pressing reason for someone to be in Arbroath, so what was it? And simultaneously the Doctor was finding it odd and worth considering that ever since he'd materialised his mouth had tasted of Maillindian Fever Beans, when he hadn't eaten any in years – dreadful things, just like chewing on old Earth pennies. That needed an explanation. *Metallic taste, metallic taste…* He searched his immense and extremely disorderly memory for dreadful, or marvellous, or significant events which having a metallic taste in his mouth could indicate were on the way. The words *Telepathic Clamp* flittered past for his consideration and he dismissed them. No one on Earth would have such a thing for hundreds of years. And there were very few creatures who could generate anything like one – each of them so staggeringly horrible that they would be bound to have already caused the kind of chaos that leaves definite traces: arm-waving, screaming, running about, the telling of wild stories... And meanwhile he looked at Bryony Mailer and thought what a splendid girl she was, really promising for a human being, and wondered why that very untidy fellow who'd just left hadn't mentioned being in love with her before he was pushed outside, because the chap clearly did adore her. The Doctor reflected, not for the first time, that it was a miracle human beings ever reproduced, given the way they seemed to make the whole process so *difficult*. When they weren't running about being scared and trying to kill each other, they were being *shy*. It was ridiculous.

At which point, what the Doctor could only understand as the most massive **THOUGHT** he had ever encountered battered into his consciousness and overloaded every one of his remarkably agile and adaptable neurons.

As he fell over, his mind had just enough room to reach out for the single word *fascinating* before everything went blank.

Moments after the Doctor fell, Julia Fetch pottered across her cottage kitchen and set out a stack of doilies and side plates on the table, just in case they might be needed to slip under cakes later at tea. *You never knew when people might drop round.* Then she wondered if she actually had any cakes...

Meanwhile – and much more helpfully – Bryony Mailer rushed round from behind the reception desk just in time to not catch the Doctor as he crumpled up into a multicoloured heap on the foyer floor. 'Oh goodness. Doctor? Doctor?' He looked quite serene, but was completely unconscious. 'Doctor whoever you are?' When she took his pulse it seemed very strong, which was good. It also had a kind of built-in echo which surely was much less good.

As Bryony knelt beside the large, horizontal, almost-guest and wondered if she should call an ambulance or just fetch a glass of water, she heard distinctive slithery footsteps approaching. Kevin Mangold, hotel manager and biscuit thief, had arrived to make an awkward situation worse. He always did.

'Miss Mailer, I hope you haven't knocked out one of our guests…?' Mangold snorted wetly and then waited for Bryony to appreciate what he obviously thought had been an impressive joke. She ignored him, so he stared through his dandruff-flecked glasses at the Doctor's highly personalised choice of clothes and then asked dubiously, '*Is* he a guest…?'

Bryony stood up, partly because she was several inches taller than Mangold and knew this annoyed him. 'He was going to be a guest. He was telling me a story about Charles Darwin and then he just turned very pale and collapsed.'

'Well, we can't have that.' Mangold tutted at Bryony as if having people collapse in the foyer was some crazy new scheme of hers to welcome tourists. 'Not at all. Other guests won't like it… Perhaps if we dragged him out of the way. He could fit in the Office, or the linen cupboard…'

'We can't just put him in a cupboard. He might be ill. We need to call a… another doctor.'

'Another doctor? Have you already called a doctor?' Mangold was clearly remembering that the hotel's official physician, Dr Porteous, was over 70 and more likely to steal towels and bread rolls than be of any help in a medical emergency.

'No, no, the towels are safe… That is, I mean, *he's* a doctor.' Bryony pointed at the Doctor and saw his feet twitch as if he was a big dog dreaming of rabbits.

'Well, he can't be a very good doctor – look at him.'

Bryony found she was feeling protective towards the now

faintly groaning stranger. 'I don't think that really follows.'

The Doctor flopped over onto his back, opened his eyes and declared, 'I told them the Dymaxion House would never catch on. Far too shiny.' Before passing out again.

Mangold swayed on his creaking shoes and sucked his teeth. 'Oh, I don't like the sound of that.' Bryony could have sworn a tiny shower of fresh dandruff rose and then fell as Mangold shook his head. 'You're Junior Day Receptionist. It's your responsibility to prevent outbreaks of this kind, Miss Mailer.'

Bryony was about to make a cutting remark about unfunny idiots and biscuits when the whining sound of the Fetch Resort's one golf cart interrupted her and Xavier ran in, holding a tartan rug and shouting, 'Someone is ill. Isn't it frightful? Someone is ill.'

A number of things then happened simultaneously: the rug was dropped over the Doctor's legs, Mangold sneaked backwards in case he was associated with anything troublesome while any member of the Fetch family was around, Honor ran in and took Bryony's hand and then the Doctor lurched up into a sitting position and sneezed, surprising everyone – apparently himself most of all.

'Now where was I?'

He seemed remarkably unsurprised to be on the floor, surrounded by people and partially covered in Royal Stuart tartan. But there was a clear flicker of worry at the back of his eyes. And that made Bryony worry, too. She also asked herself, 'But how did the twins know that someone was ill?'

Out on the golf course, David Agnew was marching his irritating companion along the path that snaked through the little stretches of woodland and scrub surrounding the fairways and greens. It was pleasant here and cool because of the shade from the trees and the small and picturesque stream that ran into the course's central lake. Agnew whistled as he marched and was in excellent spirits, but not because of his surroundings. He was, in fact, almost giggling because soon he would reach that especially deep and tricky bunker south of the 13th green and soon he would tell Mr Patterson to step down into it and practise using a sand wedge and soon after that Mr Patterson would be gone, gone, gone. The buffoon probably didn't even have a sand wedge, but Agnew didn't care – every time he left someone he hated in what he privately called Unlucky Bunker 13, they never came back. And he really, really hated this Patterson chap – the man was untidy, he didn't know how to behave and he was making a joke of everything David Agnew believed should matter. And what David Agnew believed should matter was important. In fact, he'd recently become sure that what he thought was right should be the only thing that *was* right and should therefore govern everything worthwhile. Just lately, it had seemed clearer and clearer that if the world was run along the lines that he, and only he, could imagine for it, then it would be a much better and more orderly place.

It seemed to Mr Agnew that making two people disappear in one day would be perfectly reasonable and convenient. Then he could have his lunch in peace, or maybe a spa session first to unwind. Why not? Keeping the world as it should be was tiring and he truly couldn't see why he shouldn't have some time to pamper himself now and then.

Also out on the golf course was the Doctor, now striding along in the sunshine next to the golf cart as it trundled joltingly forwards. 'I love machines that trundle, don't you? I think I should get one… or make one… If it would like to trundle…' He smiled down at Bryony, who was riding in the cart with Xavier. 'How are you feeling?'

'How am *I* feeling?' Bryony snapped. She'd been really worried about the Doctor and didn't appreciate that her worry hadn't been appreciated. 'How am *I* feeling?'

The Doctor nodded encouragingly, 'Yes, that's what I just said. But you might not remember, you've had a nasty shock.'

Bryony was exasperated. She jumped out of the cart, 'Doctor, you were the one who fainted. I'm perfectly all right.'

Xavier patted her with sympathy. 'You looked awfully wobbly, though, old girl.'

And Honor, trotting along and holding the Doctor's hand, chipped in: 'Yes, seeing a fainted person must be a dreadful thing.'

Bryony heard herself growl out loud with frustration before beginning, 'You saw him being a fainted person, too. Why isn't everyone treating *you* like an invalid? And the Doctor *was* the fainted person. He should be riding on the cart. He should be *lying down*.'

The Doctor tried to calm her, 'But I *was* lying down. On the floor. That's what upset you.' Bryony slapped his arm and he suppressed a grin, because he was indeed teasing her. 'Oh, quite. Quite.' Annoying Bryony – and she liked being annoyed, the Doctor could tell – was distracting him slightly from the incredible pain in his head and neck and the tiny, unaccountable gap he kept running across when he checked his recent memories. Right at the back of today's record so far, there was a numb area. It was disturbing. There were very few things that could interfere with the Doctor's mind, even superficially, and the technologies powerful enough to intrude on him were all both dark and extremely unpleasant. He really wouldn't want to be around if any of them had been unleashed. Except he was around and it seemed highly likely that one of them had been unleashed. Or had unleashed itself… telepathic and psychic energies were so unpredictable and so likely to colonise other available consciousnesses and then magnify… or even to generate rudimentary sentience in awkward places… Whatever it was, it was a whole lot worse than what now seemed the friendly and welcoming possibilities of a vast telepathic clamp, squeezing the free will out of every brain it afflicted…

Bryony turned to the Doctor and actually stamped her feet, which she hadn't done since she was Honor's age and which immediately made her feel foolish. 'I'm so tired of people talking down to me, just because I'm a woman! And I'm not a Junior Day Receptionist, I'm the Only Day Receptionist! And it's him you should be taking care of!' She waved her arms at the Doctor and then the twins. 'He's scared of something and trying to hide it and I don't think there are many things that scare him and I really…'

Bryony stopped and immediately regretted all of this so strongly that the Doctor was dimly aware of the precise trains of thought she was moving through. He understood that no one had ever wanted to hear Bryony discussing the role of women in the workplace and so even considering this now made her feel bullied and a bit stupid and as if she was weird and also she would rather be on the golf course with Mr Patterson just now because she thought he was sweet and not sexist and basically unlike almost every other Fetch Hotel golfer she'd met. Not that he really was a golfer… and…

Bryony, unaware she was thinking *really quite loudly*, was pondering the fact that her last sentence had made the Doctor look genuinely worried for a second or two. She hadn't been mistaken. He really was frightened. And the Doctor being frightened didn't seem like good news.

The Doctor looked at her, completely serious, and said very kindly and softly, 'Oh, I'm incredibly scared most of the time, you know. No one with even a basic knowledge of the universe wouldn't be – it's a completely terrifying place. And enormous. But it's also wonderful and lovely and more interesting than you could possibly imagine. Even than I could possibly imagine. It never lets me down. And I get to be alive in it all and to be scared and amazed and delighted and… I wouldn't be without it.' Then he adjusted his hat and grinned, playing the fool again. 'I've been without me and before me and after me, but I wouldn't be without the universe.'

Bryony wondered if she was absolutely happy she now knew someone who could casually consider being without the universe.

The Doctor turned to Honor. 'And where are we going?' He'd forgotten their destination again. All his thoughts seemed a bit sticky, or clumped, or hairy, like boiled sweets left in a jacket pocket.

Honor explained again. 'To see Grandmother and be in her house and take tea and get better. Grandmother's teas make everyone better.'

While Julia Fetch carefully put away her side plates and doilies, mildly under the impression that a very fine tea had just been enjoyed by a number of fascinating people, the Doctor nodded and discovered this made his brain feel as if his Lateral Interpositus Nucleus had been prodded with a sonic probe, and the only time that had actually happened he hadn't enjoyed it one bit. Something in there definitely wasn't as it should be. It was almost as if a new engram had been forced into his memories – a fake recollection. And the fake was there to make him believe there hadn't already been another alteration, it had been inserted to make him forget there was a gap. If he couldn't get control of the process, eventually it would all just heal over and then where would he be? A genius with a bit missing who couldn't recall there *was* a bit missing and maybe some added ends and odds which absolutely shouldn't be there – that would never do… Plus, he was starting to feel a little peculiar again. He put his hands in his pockets and whistled a fragment of the 'Song of the Arcanian System Exploration Corps', which was quite pretty and had lots of twiddly bits. Whistling twiddly bits often cheered him, although not so much today. He felt increasingly as if he wasn't walking on grass, but on green fur, annoyed green fur.

David Agnew was chuckling and peering down at the tricky bunker south of the 13th green. At the bunker's deepest point, the pathetic figure of Ian Patterson hacked an ancient-looking sand wedge into its blinding white surface for something like the 100th time. And for something like the 100th time his golf ball stayed exactly where it was while a great deal of hot sand went all over the place.

'You're doing incredibly well,' Agnew called, rubbing his hands together in anticipation. *Not long now.* 'I will have to nip off in a minute, but I think you should stay right there and enjoy yourself.' Agnew was waiting for the unmistakable sensation he got just before It started, this tingling in the soles of his feet and a feeling of immense sort of… Doom.

When the Doom got too bad he just ran. He'd never looked back. He was a man who didn't like to dwell on details – he preferred to just focus on results.

'I'm not sure about that, really.' Patterson swiped the head of his club wildly, producing another sand shower that reached as far as Agnew. 'I seem to be getting worse. Maybe if I took up swimming, or snooker…' He swung again and the sand wedge flew out of his hand, landing near Agnew's ankles.

Patterson was hot and miserable and wanted to lie under a tree with some lemonade and the memory of Bryony's smile. 'I'll just climb out…' He firmly believed that if at first you didn't succeed, you should maybe try once more, but then give up completely if you failed again.

'No!' Agnew handed back the club rather forcefully. 'You're really improving.' He smiled like someone who loathed everything he was smiling at and wanted to do it harm. 'Practice makes perfect if you want to be a top golfer.' He then adjusted his expression until it seemed only furious and painful. He didn't have a face designed for happiness.

Patterson dodged the new incoming smile by studying his sand-filled shoes. 'But I don't want to be a top golfer.'

'Then you should practise until you do.'

Patterson sighed and wondered if he was getting sunstroke, because he was beginning to feel unsteady. Either that or the bunker was beginning to feel unsteady, which wasn't exactly likely. Up above him, he heard Agnew giggle and then say, 'Wonderful. Oh, wonderful!'

'I beg your pardon? I haven't even hit it yet.'

Agnew was suddenly furious. 'Well, if you're not going to make an effort, I'm leaving!' Then he burst out laughing – which was very peculiar for someone who apparently intended to seem angry. 'Yes! Off I go!' And then Agnew was suddenly running – quite fast – away from the bunker and back along the path to the Fetch Hotel. 'It's a trip to the spa for me. You've left me quite exhausted, Mr Patterson.' Agnew guffawed weirdly. 'But don't you worry. The fun is on its way,' he yelled over his shoulder as he pelted into the cover of the trees. 'Goodbye, Mr Patterson. Absolutely goodbye.'

Ian Patterson frowned. Then he felt unsteady again. Then he wiggled his sand wedge, set it down and reached into his golf bag for his putter. When he looked at the bag he could have sworn it moved slightly. Then, as he gingerly pulled out the putter, he had the distinct impression that something hot and wet had grabbed hold of his feet.

'Jelly baby?' The Doctor was feeling enormously hungry. He offered round the crumpled white paper sweet bag more out of habit than because he didn't currently want to eat every one of them at once, followed by a big roast dinner and a full Maori hangi all to himself. His headache had got worse and also felt as if it belonged to someone else, or maybe something else. Bryony didn't seem to want a jelly baby, but he tried encouraging her.

'Go on. Have a purple one – they taste of Zarnith.' It seemed that sharing a jelly baby might make him feel less lonely.

LONELY

The vast thought swiped in at him and, although it didn't knock him out this time, he did stumble and he was aware that Bryony was staring at him with concern.

'No need to worry,' he told her. 'The world's my lobster. Honestly, I couldn't feel better.' Like all good youngsters on Gallifrey, the Doctor had been brought up with a strong awareness of how little other species knew about, well… anything and how they usually shouldn't be told about, well… anything, because most of the information a Time Lord might be able to offer them would at least make them retire to the country and keep bees – should their planet have bees, or similar life forms – if not actually drive them irreversibly insane. 'Everything's absolutely fine.'

Just for an instant, the Doctor contemplated what would happen if he were to become irreversibly insane.

And then someone not very far away screamed horribly, which was a great relief, somehow. The Doctor knew exactly what to do when he heard horrible screaming – run towards it and help.

So while David Agnew slipped his safari suit into a locker at the Fetch Hotel Spa and wondered whether he should have a massage first or sit in the hydrotherapy pool, the Doctor was loping across well-groomed turf towards continuing sounds of horror and repeated dull thuds.

Bryony found that she, too, was running as if this was just the right thing to do and, although she was scared silly, she was also completely exhilarated and – despite his hugely long strides – almost keeping up with the Doctor.

'What are you doing? Grandmother's this way…' Xavier called.

But Bryony and the Doctor left the golf cart and the bemused twins behind, coming rapidly to the top of a gentle rise. From there they were able to see the 13th green quite far off with its pretty flag and manicured grass, along with a small flight of crows lifting away out of the trees and croaking in alarm. They could also see a deep bunker with Patterson at the bottom of it. He was flailing about in the pit like someone who had just found out a great deal of new and unpleasant information about life, and he was yelling. He was screaming. In his hand he had what was left of his putter which was – as Bryony stared – both flaring and melting away with a cherry-red glow. The club head had already gone and the metal shaft was disappearing. As glowing droplets of what Bryony could only think of *redness* fell into the sand, they landed with odd thumps and very clearly made it shudder. Each impact was producing thin trails of gently green vapour.

Like many humans when presented with a reality too strange to digest, she found herself saying something absurd, just to prove she was still there and could hear her own voice. So – as she continued to run forwards – she remarked, breathlessly, 'Well, that's unusual for this time of year.'

The Doctor half turned his head back towards her with a huge grin. 'Splendid. You really are. I knew you would be.'

By the time the Doctor had reached the edge of the bunker, he had already assessed the situation, in as far as he could. There was obviously something under the bunker's surface – something large and carnivorous, perhaps a sandmaster, which shouldn't be anywhere near this solar system, but never mind about that. Or else something worse...

'Take my hand.' There had, by now, been arm-waving, screaming and running about and the Doctor was sure that the telling of a wild story was just around the corner... 'My hand, take it!' The Doctor reached forward and held out his arm as the chap continued to fire – if you could call it firing –

what seemed to be a very rudimentary fusion lance at the area around his own feet. 'Take my hand!' The man shouldn't have a fusion lance on twentieth-century Earth. No one should.

Patterson did as he was told as the last of what was indeed his fusion lance's fissile core sputtered and got actually much too hot to hold, although there was no way he was letting go of it while it was still any defence at all. 'Oh, thank you. Thank you.' He felt his free hand being grasped in remarkably strong fingers and found himself looking into precisely the type of reliable, experienced face he might have wanted a rescuer to have. 'Thank you.'

Just then he noticed Bryony arriving and shouted, 'No, keep back, darling!' And he was suddenly very angry that whoever his rescuer was had put the most wonderful human being on Earth in danger by bringing her along. Although it was lovely to see her. Even though he was mortified that he'd called her 'darling'. And then Patterson felt an altogether different strong grip close back in around his ankles and this time there was a definite tug downwards.

Bryony watched, horrified, as Patterson's feet seemed to sink and jerk unnaturally backward and the rest of him fell forward towards the sand, then jerked to a halt, suspended lopsidedly by the one wrist the Doctor was gripping. Whatever device he'd been holding, dropped out of his grasp and he windmilled his free arm to try and catch at the Doctor with both hands. It was as if Patterson was drowning and clutching up towards his only hope. The Doctor himself was wrenched over the lip of the bunker when Patterson fell and was left hanging down into the pit, only his legs and waist still on the grass. The glowing, steaming, rippling sand waited below with a kind of dreadful appetite. Both men were clinging to each other desperately by this point, but it seemed certain that Patterson was very likely to drag the Doctor into whatever trouble he was facing, rather than the Doctor being able to haul him out.

So Bryony, without pausing for a second, raced down to grab the Doctor's ankles.

The Doctor managed, 'Just keep calm. Everything's perfectly all right.'

'No it's not!' chorused Bryony and Patterson.

'No… True…' The Doctor clung on with steely certainty to Patterson's hands while deciding that whatever was under the bunker might not be a sandmaster. It wasn't behaving like a sandmaster… and that metallic taste was very strong, along with a sense of true, primordial horror. 'Very true…' With relief, he felt Bryony working out exactly the most sensible thing to do and taking hold of his feet. She really was a wonderful girl. 'Everything is immensely dangerous, but I do feel we're managing terribly well under the circumstances.' And if he'd had the spare energy, he would have laughed. This was, after all, why one became a rogue Time Lord, wandering the universe… to be right on the spot when somebody needed rescuing from a glowing green death pit… a pit infested with something he was sure he should be able to remember…

Then the Doctor slipped a few inches nearer the position beyond which he would inevitably topple into the glowing green death pit himself. Which he guessed would be unpleasant. So he decided to stop raising everyone's morale and concentrate on keeping everyone alive by holding very tight and trusting Bryony.

Bryony wasn't that big or powerful, but she did know that her strongest muscles were in her legs. If she'd sat or lain down and hoped her weight would act as an anchor on the Doctor, she would very probably have been pulled over into the bunker when the Doctor finally slipped forward past his tipping point. Instead, she lifted the Doctor's feet – it was a risk and he did find he was drawn even nearer the bunker as she did so, letting poor Patterson hang ever closer to the shining, oozy, hungry sand. But next she was able to crouch and then slowly stand, leaning back and letting her weight and her legs do the work of pulling. If she both tugged on his ankles and then fell backwards, still gripping the Doctor, they might be OK. She concentrated all her will and strength into saving both her new friends.

Whatever was holding Patterson fast seemed utterly immoveable, but finally it did give way a bit, then a bit more and then, just when the Doctor gave a long and pained shout, it gave up entirely.

SAD

Another plunging, metallic word battered into the Doctor's mind.

Bryony landed suddenly on her back. The Doctor's legs were tangled in her own and then she was scrambling free as the Doctor was finally able to yank Patterson up and away from danger, Bryony hurrying to reach down and help with the last hard tug.

For a long space, the three of them lay in a breathless heap, the turf beneath them shaking, and sand – hot, steaming sand – raining down.

But gently, unmistakably, the turf calmed, settled, the sand stopped falling and all was peaceful.

The Doctor was the first to gather his senses, sit up and study his two companions. The girl was… an excellent girl… but the man was – of course – not a man, in the Earth sense… clearly not from round here. Not from anywhere near here… More like someone from Yinzill… In fact, exactly like someone from the planet Yinzill, which the Doctor should have noticed at once… It wasn't something a massive intellect should *just miss*…

He rubbed his face, found his hat – it had rolled to a safe distance and was calmly waiting for him – and dusted it to give himself something to do. This was all very bad.

BAD

The alien thought was slightly gentler this time and seemed

to be leaving, somehow. The Doctor felt as if a large hand was being opened inside his skull and then withdrawn. His headache was back. He also wished that so much of rescuing activity didn't involve arm strain. Beings were always dangling off building, or cliffs, or into evil-minded pools, or bunkers and they always did need to be hauled back to somewhere less risky. There was a lot of hauling, generally.

HURT

BADHURT

After which everything was back to normal, expect for this renewed feeling that more bits and pieces had sort of been vanished away from his mind.

He didn't have any time to worry about this, because Bryony – human beings were wonderfully insane – then also sat up, stood up and went to lean over into the bunker and fetch out what was left of the lance. It looked like the blackened stump of a golf club handle. Although it surely wasn't.

As she bent and reached forward into the sand both the Doctor and Patterson yelled, 'No!'

But it was too late.

Or, at least, it would have been, if rummaging about a bit with her fingers, lifting up the lance and then turning round with a puzzled expression had still been dangerous activities to try. In fact, they were perfectly safe and meant Bryony could stare down into her hand, examine what she'd found and say to Patterson, 'It's very small.'

Patterson was dishevelled and defensive. 'It was quite big when I started.'

Bryony peered at it with distaste, 'Well, it's not big now. But it is ruined. Do you want it back?' She wagged it in Patterson's direction.

'Not… well, no, it won't work now. It's…' Patterson rubbed his sore wrists and stood up, blushing.

'I'll chuck it back, then.' And Bryony slung it back into the bunker where it landed with a thump while another 'No!' rang out across the golf course. The Doctor and Patterson flinched.

But nothing happened. 'What?' Bryony turned to them and frowned at the Doctor. 'You were pulling him out of the bunker and onto the grass – obviously you think it's safe on the grass… We're all on the grass… I'm on the grass… So we're safe, right?'

'Well, I wouldn't say—'

'And how is it you know about these kinds of things? Doctor? People being dragged underground by a golf bunker kinds of things…?'

She waited while the Doctor wondered why she was sounding cross. He'd saved the day, after all. Again. That was cause for thanks and congratulations and maybe that tea he'd been promised.

Bryony folded her arms as significantly as she could and frowned more, 'Do you want to explain what on earth is going on?'

The Doctor opened his mouth, but seemed unable to let any words emerge – Bryony was a little bit unnerving when she was angry – and so she turned to Patterson.

'And who are you, Mr Patterson, and where are you from and what were you firing, or burning, or… what was that, exactly? And don't tell me it was a big sparkler, or an experimental… umbrella… or that you got struck by lightning, or something else unbelievable, because I'm not a complete idiot.' Patterson looked so bewildered at this and was so clearly on the verge of crying – Bryony could genuinely be quite fierce – that she softened a little and patted his arm. 'My dad always used to say that to me – "Bryony, you're not a complete idiot. I think we lost some of the bits."'

Usually people found this funny, even if it was a very old joke, but Patterson just swallowed hard and said, all in a rush, 'My broodfather hated me. He said I was a waste of perfectly good cloning equipment and I agree, I do, I really agree, but…'

He stared from the bunker to Bryony and then to the Doctor and then took a deep breath, but before he could say anything, the twins appeared over the hill, Xavier driving the golf cart. They both waved tranquilly and shouted, 'Hello! Hello!'

Honor gambolled delightedly down the slope as if dishevelled strangers and steaming pits were all part of enjoying a normal and lovely summer's afternoon. 'We wondered if anyone would like a lift back in the golf cart again.' She didn't even glance at the plume of greenish vapour still hanging above the bunker. 'We're sorry there's only one cart, which really isn't big enough to fit five passengers. Grandmother did talk about having more, but she thinks that walking is good for people and should be encouraged and no sitting about unless you're incredibly old – grandmother is incredibly old – or you can sit if you've had to look at somebody who's fainted, or had to be somebody who's fainted. Good afternoon, Mr Patterson.'

Patterson watched his hand being shaken solemnly by the little girl and then Honor led him up the hill as if she was the adult and he was the child.

The Doctor and Bryony followed on, Bryony noticing that she felt sore all over from the recent struggle. As they went, she asked, 'Doctor, do you get the impression those children are a little unusual?'

The Doctor laughed. It was marvellous that the one thing she chose to mention as unusual was the children. Everything else that had just happened had simply made her inquisitive and cross. *Magnificent.* He took off his hat and waved it at Xavier. 'I suppose twins are often slightly remarkable…' Xavier waved back. 'But yes…' He racked his brain, trying to recall where he'd read about adorable barefoot pairs of creatures. There was nothing like reading to prepare you for life, but if all the words were slipping and going dim… if everything you'd read was going to be taken away soon…

He felt a spasm of true panic.

Clearly an alien entity – or Patterson – was flooding this area with telepathic energy at immensely high levels, thousands of psychons, maybe tens of thousands… what could do that? And also lie in wait to devour other beings, just eat them up? Or rather, eat them down? He should know the answer to that. He almost knew that he *did* know, or *had* known a very good answer… And clearly the energy was already animating matter… Sand would be quite easy to form into shapes, limbs, silicon support structures, jaws… It didn't bear thinking about what might come next, but he definitely felt relieved that he *was* still thinking… even with gaps…

And the Doctor was a determined individual, he didn't give up easily, if at all. As long as he could think, there was hope. He looked up at the perfectly blue 1978 sky – not too radioactive, not too toxic, a gorgeous pearly dab of light when viewed from outer space – and he thumbed through recollections: the perfectly umber skies of Gallifrey, the first time he'd smelt a dew-laden Earth dawn in seventeenth-century France, swimming in the thick silky waters of Praxus Minor – and it seemed that his head was still stuffed with every kind of this and that. Maybe he'd just misplaced an occasional item, made filing errors due to telepathic shock.

Nothing to fret about.

The Doctor glanced down and noticed he was holding Bryony's hand. As if he needed to know someone was there to help him. It was extremely unlikely that a solitary Earth girl with almost no effective technology and not a clue about the space-time continuum, psychon dynamics or transchronic psychology would be of any help to him in any way. He didn't let go, though. He held on tighter than ever.

Back at the Fetch Spa, David Agnew was disgruntled and tense. He hadn't enjoyed his massage. And when he'd shouted at Brian the masseur, two very strong elbows had been pressed very hard up and down his back in a way that probably wasn't strictly necessary.

He'd taken a shower – which wasn't the right temperature, somehow – and now, as a last resort, he was going to sit in the hydrotherapy pool. No matter what, a nice dip in the pool never failed to relax him. He attempted to feel content.

Agnew flip-flopped along the relentlessly calming corridor with its tranquilly scented incense burner, its photographs of placid lakes and its speakers softly playing the songs of whales who, if he could have understood them, were actually having a quite heated argument with each other. He despised everything about this imposed serenity, but told himself that the idiots and women who were usually in here must find it reassuring. He didn't need this kind of nonsense to help him relax – he just needed to focus on really, properly hating someone and then imagining them being devoured, bit by bit. After he had relaxed, he would run through his plans for the future – the future of everywhere and everything and everyone.

Emerging into the Hydro Room, Agnew came as close as he ever did to happy. He stepped out of his flip-flops and bath robe, revealing his strangely hairy feet and his checked polyester swimming trucks. Soft lights played on the bubbling surface of the large, warm pool – the room was currently green, the next shade would be blue, then red, then there would be a soft and flattering white light and then the coloured filters would cycle round all over again. A nice soak for a couple of cycles would be more than long enough to cheer him up. There was no one else around – no silly wives gossiping and flapping their hands, no morons boasting about their golf scores – there was only the wonder and the glory that was David Agnew, enjoying the presence of none other than David Agnew. Something told him – loud and clear – that he was the jewel at the centre of the universe.

*

In her deluxe cottage Julia Fetch stopped reading a thrilling article about the way an octopus tastes with its arms. She thought this would be inconvenient for humans, because then everything would taste of blouse. Which would be boring – even though her blouses were of a very fine quality and handmade by Markham & Lancet of Jermyn Street. She decided she was slightly peckish and probably that meant it was time for tea… Or had she taken tea already? It was so hard to tell.

Out on the course, Bryony was riding in the golf cart beside Patterson who was, as a result, practically writhing with joy and at the same time more depressed that he had ever been during a quite remarkably depressing life. She nudged him in the ribs, which meant he discovered a new bruise in one of the few places where he hadn't noticed he was sore, but was also enormously delighted. He stared down at his mangled shoes – they were covered in vicious scrapes and something which looked suspiciously like greenish-purplish saliva – and gave himself time to be very, very delighted indeed. This would probably be the last time she would want to be anywhere near him, but for now – *being delighted*.

She nudged him again. 'Don't thank me for saving your life, then.'

'But I did, I mean I have, I mean… Didn't I? I thought I thanked you both.' He gulped down a breath. 'I am grateful.' He said this with the tone and facial expression of a person who thought that saving him would always be a terribly bad idea. 'I just…' He took the plunge. 'I'm not called Ian Patterson. I'm called Putta Pattershaun 5, because I'm the fifth Putta Pattershaun – we were a batch of ten – and I'm… all the others have *done* things, and *invented* things and… I was going to head off into the universe and *achieve*… Only then I met you and… I got distracted… not that meeting you hasn't been an achievement, it's been the best…' He made a noise like a ferret being held underwater and not liking it. 'No, that's not as important as me being from another planet. You should know that. I am. From another planet.' He waited for her to scream. Or hit him. Or call out whatever Earth force dealt with alien threats, possibly by dissecting them and freeze-drying their bits for snacking later.

'Yeah.' She shrugged. 'What I thought. OK.'

'OK!?'

'Yeah.' Bryony had worked this all out already – this or something very like this – because she *wasn't* a complete idiot. She *was* completely certain it was the coolest thing she'd ever heard of. Nevertheless, she was trying to look unimpressed and managing well, even though she wanted to leap up and down and yell – *A space man, I've met a space man. I am sitting next to a space man. I fancy a space man. And I think he fancies me. Take that, Mangold. Take that, Cardinal Richelieu.* She shrugged again, nonchalant. 'And…?' She wanted to seem like a sophisticated woman of the galaxy and also needed to appear stern, because she didn't like being lied to, or having things hidden from her by a potential boyfriend.

'And? I don't… that is…' The golf cart juddered slightly less than Putta, but only slightly.

Potential boyfriend? Where did that come from? Bryony tried not to look happy, or surprised, or whatever it was that she was starting to feel – she wasn't quite clear right now, but whatever the feeling was it felt pleasant. 'Yes. And…?' Thinking of Patterson, or Putta or whoever he was as a boyfriend suddenly made Bryony realise she ought to consider him in more detail… He was cute. In a mangled way. And he seemed scared of her, which could be fun. And maybe the solution to having found Earth men so disappointing was to choose someone from well outside the neighbourhood. She realised that Putta was staring at her with a kind of adoring horror.

Putta waved his hands despairingly, '*And*… you're an Earth person, a human being, and human beings are famous all over the… well, you would call it the Pisces-Cetus Supercluster Complex – famous for being…' He sighed and then blurted out, 'You kill everything you don't understand and then sometimes you eat it. You don't even like people from other continents on your own planet, you…' He faltered, while the Doctor chuckled audibly.

The Doctor was strolling easily next to the cart, covering the ground in that particularly light-footed, long-striding, tiptoeing way he had. 'They also have very promising features. And there's always evolution. They could improve endlessly. Almost endlessly.' The Doctor's large eyes shone benevolently. 'If the black tip sharks and fruit flies don't get there first.'

But Putta wasn't paying any attention to the Doctor, he was meeting Bryony's eyes and blushing, 'I'm so sorry. I didn't intend to be rude about you.'

'Not just rude about me, rude about my entire species… that's a first.'

'Sorry.' Putta squirmed visibly.

'Then next time maybe mention that we do…' Bryony tried to think of anything human beings were good at. The 1970s hadn't been inspiring so far – starvation in Biafra, nuclear testing, terrorist attacks and hijackings, Nixon being Nixon… at least the war in Vietnam was over, but things in Cambodia didn't look good… 'We do make a lovely shepherd's pie. For example. Sometimes. Some of us. By which I mean we kill things we don't understand and put them into pies… I don't mean we would make good pies by being put into them as a filling, although I suppose we could… By a superior alien race…' While Putta desperately tried not to look superior and absolutely managed, Bryony grinned, 'We are a bit disappointing… And shepherd's pie isn't even a pie – no pastry.' She nudged him on an especially tender bruise. 'You're from outer space. How great is that? That's just…' And she thought about kissing him, but then reconsidered and acted cool again.

'While I am glad that we're all friends...' The Doctor leaned in under the golf cart's gaily striped canopy as they progressed across the turf and fixed Putta with an icy look. 'Apart from the multiple treaties and byelaws you're transgressing... Explain yourself, young Putta. What are you doing here so far from Yinzill? It is Yinzill, isn't it? Your home world? Yinzill in the Ochre Period.'

Bryony interrupted. 'Never mind that – what happened to him?'

'Which is also a good question,' the Doctor admitted.

Bryony continued, 'And what happened to the bunker? I'm not a big fan of golf, but I do know bunkers aren't supposed to reach up and grab people's feet. Or Yinzillites' feet.'

Putta was, of course, aware that the proper word for a being from Yinzill was a *Yakt*, but thought it was sweet of her to make the effort and didn't like to correct her in case she punched him. She seemed to be a very physical kind of Earth person and was quite possibly stronger than he was.

'Well?' And she was glowering at him in expectation of an answer.

Putta tried to organise his information in a logical stream, 'Well, I... that is... My family... several of the other Puttas have done very well as... I mean...' He sort of knew this wasn't going to go well. 'I am a bountykiller.'

'*Wha-at!?*' The Doctor made the word sound much longer and more threatening than usual and suddenly looked completely furious. 'Barging round the universe, collecting trophies for ultra-millionaires? Making the shells of barber sylphs into finger bowls...!?'

'But I never—'

'You criticise human beings and you're throwing stun canisters into bandan nests!? *Of all the idiotic...!?*'

'I haven't... I like bandans... And sylphs... We only target predator species.'

48

The Doctor's whole frame was bristling with outrage and suddenly he didn't look at all like an amiable fool, more like a formidable enemy of injustice and wasteful harm. 'And who decides which species is a predator? You? You think you have the right?'

'There's a list…' Putta scrabbled in his inside pocket, then in each of his pockets… with increasing levels of despair… 'They give us a list.' He couldn't find the list. It was gone, along with his fusion lance. (His lance not-very-cunningly disguised as a golf club, given that he couldn't play golf – he'd somehow put his name in the Form section of the formatting instructions and ended up with a putter…) And he no longer had his Model G50 Threat Detector, which started leaking psy fluid after he dropped it on a hard surface – which you weren't supposed to – so he'd had to throw it away before it dissolved his control panel, and his hands for that matter, it was appalling stuff, psy fluid…

The Doctor raged on. 'Is *she* a predator?' He pointed at Bryony who couldn't help being slightly alarmed. She'd never seen him like this. 'Is everyone who eats shepherd's pie a predator? Shouldn't they be?'

'I don't… I'm not sure… That is, I've never…'

'So many lives, so delicately balanced, so close to the abyss, so full of hope, and some greedy squad of imbeciles classifies them as a predator, as a resource, and you and your kind of destructive idiots come along and harvest them until they're gone.' The Doctor looked both furious and implacably sad.

He seemed so alone in his grief that Bryony touched his arm. 'I don't think he meant any harm.'

'His kind never mean any harm – they still do it!' The Doctor stopped himself, quietened. 'Very few species truly understand that actions have consequences. When you destroy something, that isn't an isolated act.' And for a second or so he looked like someone who had understood far too many consequences and who had been made very tired by that. Then he patted Bryony's shoulder. 'Our lives are connected. And other lives are connected to those lives and on and on. We are even connected… to Putta Pattershaun 5.' He glowered at Putta.

Putta responded with an apologetic babble. 'I thought it would be a good idea, I mean I don't like it, haven't liked it, haven't done it, not properly… I've never killed anything. I took aim at a Parthian mind wasp and I couldn't fire. And they're terrible. They can eat your whole personality and then lay their eggs in your face. But they have wonderful wings. There were colours in the wings that I'd never seen on any planet… I just couldn't…'

Bryony kept on with what she thought was a promising line of enquiry which would be much more use than additional shouting. 'Patter- Putter, whatever your name is. Never mind all that – what happened to you? Did you do something? Did you bring some alien thing with you that ended up in the bunker? A whatsit, sense wasp? Something else? Or do your people have a problem with sand? Does it usually eat you?'

'Which is what I would have asked. Roughly. What I would have asked if you hadn't kept interrupting,' nodded the Doctor. 'Except for the sand part.'

'Sand? No, we like sand,' Putta bleated miserably. 'Unless it gets into our shoes, or… elsewhere… Oh… I don't know. I thought… My detector, just before it broke it showed this, this signal that couldn't even have been true, but I landed here to look for – no one has even heard of them, not for millennia, and I didn't expect to find… but then maybe the detector was broken already, giving a false reading before I dropped it… and I was left, anyway, with no more detector, no more signal, no more…' Bryony was glowering at him with such impatience that he gulped and steered himself round to the events of the afternoon. 'There was this man, this human man and I met him in the bar.' Bryony snorted with derision which would have made her seem slightly unattractive to anyone but Putta. He continued, 'The man definitely… he *lured* me into that sandpit. I'd never even seen him before.'

'Did you do something to him?' Bryony asked, with a hurtful level of suspicion.

'You are quite annoying you know,' confided the Doctor. 'That could rub people up the wrong way. Not to mention your profession. Did you mention your profession – Bountykiller Putta?' He pronounced the last two words as if they were a disease.

'I didn't mention anything,' whined Putta. 'I was being as human as possible and that appears to involve golf and sandpits.'

'Bunkers,' corrected Bryony and then disliked herself for it.

'Bunkers. He was very angry all the time. I mean, so angry I could feel it on my skin somehow…' Putta wrung his hands.

'Can you usually feel other people's mental states?' the Doctor asked sharply. 'And did you have a strange taste in your mouth?'

Putta nodded and looked calmer, as if he now had the resident expert on his side. 'Yes, a funny taste and, no, I can't usually feel… well, my own feelings are a bit of a problem without anyone else's…' He caught sight of Bryony's frown and got back to the main issue. 'The man… Mr Agnew… I think he knew about the bunker and he got angrier and angrier as he walked me over here and then he made me play golf and got angrier still – only in a nasty, happy kind of way – and then the bunker got angry and then he left as soon as… once it started trying to eat me… he ran away.' He looked a bit sickly as he remembered. 'It grabbed my feet. If I hadn't already got out my fusion lance…' And then he didn't want to finish the sentence.

The Doctor tsked. 'Running around showing off advanced technology to a less developed and very… emotional species…' As if he'd never do such a thing himself. 'You ought to be ashamed.'

'Thank you for saving me.'

'Well, it's all part of a day's work, really, I—' The Doctor broke off when he saw Putta smiling carefully at Bryony and nodding.

Bryony wasn't currently that interested in gratitude. She thought she was on to something. 'If he laid the trap… If Mr Agnew laid the trap, he must know how it operates and what it is. It must be his trap.'

'Yes, you know, if you think about it, whoever laid the trap would understand what it is and be the one to use it,' the Doctor added. In case anyone had forgotten he was a genius. He was already hypothesising about how a telepathic bond would react if it were partially corporeal and suffered pain, because – for example – someone had repeatedly fired a fusion lance at it… if the mild psychic abilities of a sandmaster had been somehow magnified and tamed… and if its governing consciousness had run away and abandoned it while it was injured… A feedback loop in that kind of situation could be extremely bad news for everyone concerned.

Bryony burst in with, 'Then we have to find Agnew!' and looked pleased with herself. 'I mean, shouldn't we?'

The Doctor nodded absently, murmuring to himself. 'My tracking skills are a bit rusty. I studied with the Miccosukee people for a while…' He began to stare significantly at the grass. 'It will take great skill…'

'Or we could look in the spa,' suggested Putta.

'Don't be ridiculous.'

'He mentioned he was going back to the spa.' Putta blinked. There was a pause.

The Doctor boomed, 'Why on earth didn't you say so?'

'But you didn't ask.'

'Turn that thing round at once and back to the hotel!'

As Putta and Bryony swung the golf cart unsteadily round to follow the Doctor, the twins trotted swiftly into their path and stood.

Xavier told them, firmly, 'I don't think you should. Grandmother is expecting you.'

'Yes. And you shouldn't disappoint Grandmother.' Honor looked sad, but also very determined. 'She likes tea. A lot.'

The Doctor adopted his most persuasive voice, 'Oh, but we can come back. Yes, we can. Immediately. We have this one thing we must do together by ourselves in the Spa and then we'll be back and then absolutely tea with Grandmother will happen. I look forward to it, I do.' He wondered how a powerful effusion of psychons might affect the malleable minds of children. Probably quite badly.

The twins stared at him and suddenly didn't seem even slightly adorable. Their limbs stiffened and their faces hardened. It was possible to think that they might be dangerous in a fight – very swift and unforgiving.

Bryony found herself thinking they should just abandon the golf cart and run – it would be faster, even with Putta's badly bruised ankles. She also suddenly felt certain the twins would turn out to be much faster than anyone else running and that their speed might not be a comforting or unthreatening thing.

'It isn't four o'clock yet, you know. And four o'clock is tea time,' the Doctor wheedled. He very carefully pretended to be someone who didn't feel scared in any way. 'We all promise we'll be back here by four. If you wait for us. And then we'll have fun, which I always enjoy, there's nothing as much fun as fun, I find. Don't you find?' He wagged his hands and shrugged like someone who wasn't rapidly calculating and puzzling and trying to get back to the hotel *fast* and to work out the twins' real nature, while soothing them with unstoppable courtesy. Soothing with unstoppable courtesy often worked on most planets. It was one of the many reasons why the Doctor didn't carry a gun.

And then, as if the sun had come out – or as if they had finished their own calculations – the twins giggled and stood aside and Honor said, 'Yes, we'll see you later then. That will be terribly nice. And fun.'

And Xavier patted Bryony on her arm and said, 'Good luck, old girl.'

This felt just a little bit creepy, so Bryony put her foot down and the cart zoomed – in as far as it could zoom – back towards the spa with the Doctor loping alongside as though what he loved most in whole the universe was rushing towards dangerous situations without having a proper plan. Or any plan at all.

The three arrived at the Fetch Hotel to see that the foyer was full of dissatisfied guests. Mr Mangold was just saying, 'I am doing my best, sir. Miss Mailer, my receptionist, has disappeared…' So he didn't call her Junior when she wasn't around, Bryony noted as she hurried past, shouting, 'Guest emergency! Can't stop!'

By the time they'd reached the Spa Section, they had all realised that they certainly did look in need of relaxation and therapy. At the very least. Putta was covered in sand, grass, mud, vapour stains, fissile backwash and a layer of anxiety. In places his suit looked as if something had recently tried to eat it, because something had. Bryony's own business suit had several small rips in it, was grass-stained, her tights were ruined and her name badge was missing, along with her shoes, she now noticed – she'd taken them off when she had helped wrestle Putta out of the pit. Or bunker. And her hair was alarming. The Doctor – he looked like the Doctor, which was always vaguely alarming to people like the Spa Manageress (who habitually patronised Bryony, because of her poor skincare, obvious split ends and Junior status).

'Can I help you?' There was a blatant sneer in the question.

The Doctor paced up to the Spa Welcome Desk like a jolly tiger in a maroon jacket. 'Indeed you can. How splendid that you're here. Just who we need.' He fished a weirdly pristine piece of paper out of his pocket and unfolded it for the Manageress to inspect. Whatever she read on it made her immediately attentive and slightly flirtatious. She gladly showed the Doctor that day's register and David Agnew's signature – he'd definitely signed in and hadn't signed out yet. He must be inside.

The Manageress then insisted on giving each of them gift bags and free swimming costumes. It took all Bryony's powers of persuasion to get them into the spa without having to accept a guided tour, free sauna and beating with twigs.

Far across the Fetch Estate, the golf cart had been parked neatly in its charging bay behind Julia Fetch's cottage. The twins were standing near it. Slowly, Honor pressed the palms of her hands against Xavier's and he pressed back.

Honor asked Xavier, 'Shall we go and speak to Grandmother?'

And Xavier told Honor, 'No. Let's not. Not yet. Let's do this instead.'

So they stood and pressed their hands together while the birds sang and little breezes pushed about amongst the rose bushes in Julia Fetch's garden.

The Doctor and his companions rendezvoused in the Tranquillity Lounge, which instantly became less tranquil. In fact, its two occupants – sisters Sylvia and Rosemary Hindle from High Wycombe – decided they might just head off somewhere else. Right away.

As several firmly worded signs said they must when in the Therapy Areas, Putta and Bryony wore their new, slightly ill-fitting, swimming costumes, Fetch Spa issue flip-flops and bathrobes. Putta was absolutely certain that he was never taking his bathrobe off, not even if it killed him. Bryony was never going to see him in swimming trunks. It was bad enough that his gingery-haired shins and monster-bitten ankles were so horribly visible.

The Doctor had managed to pass through the changing rooms without changing a bit – apart from having folded his hat into his jacket pocket and having donned a gift-bag shower cap instead. His hair was fighting the shower cap. And winning.

'Now stay with me.' It was very hard to take him seriously in the cap. 'I mean it. No good will come from our splitting up and I can't be everywhere and…' His sentence trailed off and he seemed to become unfocused for a few breaths. But then he stalked off with immense energy and they began their hunt for Agnew.

The woody heat of the sauna, the foggy depths of the Turkish baths, the bad-tempered massage rooms, even the towel cupboard were searched before they all – staying together, just as the Doctor had said they must – walked along the corridor to the Hydro Room.

As he pressed on, the Doctor felt that metallic taste in his mouth again and began to think that having a plan at this point might have been a good idea. There was something dreadfully uninviting about the warm, thick, damp air slowly oozing from the pool. And wouldn't it maybe have been safer to split up, to let his companions wander off and not run the same risks as he was about to?

The Hydro Room lighting was on the red part of its cycle and the wide, round pool was bubbling and seething dramatically. Agnew was lolling back in it as if he was having the time of his life – eyes closed and a slight smile on his lips.

The Doctor understood at once that many things were terrifyingly wrong and he regretted absolutely having brought the others with him. He said, very quietly, 'Perhaps you two should go outside.' His head throbbed and his ears seemed filled with the roiling of the pool waters. His tongue and lips were coppery.

Putta stared at the red, restless liquid and at Agnew. And he was annoyed. Really as annoyed as he'd ever allowed himself to be. 'It's no use pretending to be asleep!' he shouted. 'You left me out there. With that thing! Now, what is it? Tell us what it is! Tell us what you are!'

The Doctor said, even more quietly, 'He can't tell us.'

'Of course he can!' Putta was enjoying being angry. Other people had always been angry with him and this time it was going to be his turn. 'You! Wake up!' He leaned right over the edge of the pool and shouted with all his might across the water to Agnew: 'Wake up!'

Which was when the colour of the lights changed to soft and flattering white and yet the water and Agnew's face were still thickly red and patches of damp on the floor were red and Bryony felt sick and then she *was* sick and the Doctor seemed to be walking over to comfort her, but then he cried out, holding his head and dropped to the red-spattered tiles, kneeling and rocking, apparently in torment.

As Bryony rushed to him she heard Putta call, 'Bryony! Bryony! Get out! Leave us! Bryony! Run!'

And when she looked up she saw the thin, funny, little man called Putta trying to rush away from the pool, but what looked like ropes, like purple-red muscular ropes, were undulating and rushing out of the water and they caught at the hem of his red-stained bathrobe, snaked into its loose sleeves and wrapped around him, dragging him slithering and fighting back towards the water.

Bryony met his eyes and thought that he was a very brave man, or being, or whatever, and a good one and that it was a shame he'd never realise it. She thought he would have liked himself more if he had.

The Doctor yelled to her, 'It's a feedback loop – the pain drove it back here. Get out now! With no mind to control the creature, it will devour everything it can find! I should have known! Quickly! It doesn't know what else to do!'

And then a huge thought swept through him again.

BLOOD

He'd led them all into the same trap that had just turned on Agnew, its creator.

'Run!'

Bryony wavered, as the Doctor convulsed and Putta battled the swift, repulsive arms swarming around him. Clearly it would be sensible to run… She paused for a breath.

'Go!' Putta was fighting desperately to get out of the bathrobe that might very well kill him, as the pulsing tentacles slithered over his body, scraping his skin like gluey sand as they went. 'Please!'

But Bryony couldn't run.

'It was feeding on his rage!' The Doctor, was holding his head in both hands. 'I can feel it… this… fury… magnifying. It's so angry… so… scared…'

BLOOD

'Then don't be furious! And don't be scared!' Bryony was yelling herself now. 'Relax!' Putta looked at her in utter bewilderment. 'Relax, Putta. Trust me. You can trust me, can't you, you stupid space man!'

And she said this with such affection that Putta did relax. The arms immediately drew him right against the low wall that contained the pool, knocking the breath out of him, but then they too relaxed slightly. They seemed indecisive. The ends of a few tentacles twitched, shivered.

'Pat them!'

'What?' Putta looked at her as if she was insane.

But the Doctor, still pale and wincing, nodded. 'Yes. Of course! Of course! The field is still operational. It will magnify whatever we feel.' He focused on thinking clearly, gently, willed the agony in his skull to retreat a little. 'If we can't dissipate it, we can change its orientation and bring it back under control. Well done, Bryony. Well done.' He trembled, frowned, but also managed to nod encouragingly. 'You're terribly good at this.'

'Then let's blooming well get on with it!' Bryony yelled again.

Putta just stared, locked with fear. He was in danger of quite literally terrifying himself to death. The Doctor knew that if Putta made the creature too frightened it would defend itself – by killing Putta.

The Doctor tried to help, 'Imagine it's a big... like a giant...'

BBBBB...

He tried to imagine something huge but loveable with lots of arms, and couldn't bring anything to mind apart from an immense and fluffy tarantula – which very few beings would find that adorable – so he just suggested. 'Tickle it. Go on, Putta. Tickle it.'

Bbbb...

Putta reached out gingerly – in as far as he could while the tentacles were tight round him – and patted and then did tickle the muscular bond fastening his other arm to his side. He was wrapped in an immense, clammy strength, but it was no longer contracting. It no longer felt quite as horrifying. He tickled some more. He patted the flesh he'd been trying to keep away from his throat.

'That's it.' Bryony nodded. 'It's working. At least, it's stopped.'

'Of course it's working!' The Doctor was still clearly in pain, but looked less grey. 'And we have to... we have to think calmly, we have to be friendly towards it. We have to love it. I think. If we...' He broke off for a few seconds as his headache peaked. 'We need to love it. We need to be very, very fond of it indeed.'

'Are you out of your mind!?'

'Just do it, Putta!' both Bryony and the Doctor bellowed.

So he tried.

Aaabbb...

Bryony concentrated on attempting to find anything endearing about the heaving red and purple mass which had almost overwhelmed Putta. As she did so, the creature seemed to shudder and lose definition. Putta started to be able to gasp in complete breaths – much to his relief – and could move a little more.

As soon as he did move, the beast tightened around him again, but he tried not to panic, tried to let his limbs flop, relax, relax, relax, and to encourage the grating, sliding pressure to release again. It made his skin crawl. Which was because it was crawling over his skin. But that was fine. If it would just let him go that would be fine. Even if it simply didn't eat him, but kept a hold of him for the rest of his life and he just had to get used to wearing some kind of immense purplish slime and grit monster that would be fine… it would all be fine… he could be calm…

The Doctor filled his consciousness with the faces of all the companions he had enjoyed knowing – their faces and the times when they had helped him, the times when they had been amazed by the universe along with him. He thought about the universe: the light-producing microbes that danced on the walls of the Delling Caves, the Great Library, the Song Towers of Und, the unlikeliness of life existing anywhere in the first place and yet the way it blossomed and flourished and celebrated itself and was so beautiful.

A

A

a

a

b

c

d

And finally Putta found himself dumped onto the floor as the creature trapping him simply collapsed into sand, warm sand, warm wet clinging sand and a kind of rush of dissipating motion.

He looked up at the two beings he would most want to nearly be killed with – if he had to be nearly killed – as they came cautiously towards him. His bathrobe was several feet away, partly obscured by a sand drift – which meant that Bryony had seen him in his trunks. And being nearly crushed to death. And covered in slime. And sand. Which was also inside his swimming trunks. Oh, but things could be so much worse. They really could.

The Doctor set out his arm to keep Bryony back and advanced slowly, but with an increasingly enormous smile. 'Not so tricky, really once the problem was fully understood.' He kicked gently at the sand heaped around Putta. 'I had my suspicions, naturally.'

Bryony, punched his arm. 'Your suspicions…'

'Naturally.' He winked. 'And we would undoubtedly all be dead without you. It was incredibly prescient of me to have chosen you. A sign of true genius.'

'I beg your pardon.' Bryony couldn't help smiling, too. '*You* chose *me*?'

'I just said that. Do keep up.' The Doctor grinned.

Back at Julia Fetch's cottage the twins were still leaning against each other, palm to palm with arms outstretched.

Slowly their hands melted and melded and reformed, looking for a while like a reddish pink ball of dense fluid, caught spinning and writhing at the ends of their arms. Their enchanting faces blurred and their eyes blinked unnaturally open.

There seemed to be a vibration in the air around them and, had anyone been looking at them, it would have been difficult to see them clearly. Even the grass around their feet became almost liquid. Reality itself seemed willing to melt and pour away

But then – slowly, delicately, the grass blades solidified, the air stopped shimmering and the twins' faces became suddenly very clear, peaceful, loveable and their hands became only the usual kind of hands, with the usual kind of fingers. Everything, everywhere seemed to be held in suspension – as if the universe was a sleeping cat, just about to stretch, but not yet – and if Julia had looked out of her window, she would have noticed that the area around the cottage seemed impossibly bright and perfectly formed.

And then Honor and Xavier – slightly as if they had been dreaming for a while – shook their heads and laughed and the universe stretched and settled back into place and they shouted together, 'Tea! Tea! It must be time for tea!' and scampered towards the cottage door.

The Doctor had thought it best to lead his two companions out of the spa through the fire exit. None of them remotely resembled individuals who had been through a sublimely tranquil and restorative experience of balanced wholeness. They looked if they been buried at sea. And that might have alarmed the Spa Manageress. Who would eventually discover the scene of horror they were leaving behind. The Doctor found that leaving behind scenes of horror was usually wise, particularly if you might be likely to get the blame for them.

Their unconventional route out – which hadn't passed the changing rooms – meant that Putta now had to cope with being outdoors in a sand- and slime-covered bathrobe (without flip-flops) in the presence of Bryony. Who had saved his life. Again. He was unsure about whether he wanted to burst into song, or make a break for his Type F378a Abrischooner, fire up the engines and never be seen again. At least he had discovered that it wasn't actually possible to die of shame. Which, in a day of hideous shocks, had still come as something of a surprise.

Bryony herself was sporting a marginally less grubby bathrobe. She was, Putta thought, looking quite graceful as they set off back towards the golf course. Trotting barefoot next to the Doctor, she peppered him with questions. Putta had never seen anyone trot barefoot more beautifully. Actually, he'd never seen anyone trot barefoot – but that didn't make her any less monumentally lovely.

Lovely and frustrated. 'But I don't understand—'

'Naturally, you don't,' the Doctor interrupted. 'You have no experience of what would happen if a completely reckless interplanetary vandal managed to both spill psy fluid on a planet where it didn't belong and accidentally introduce a sandmaster larva to the perfect environment to hyper-accelerate its developmental cycle. *Beings who shall remain nameless should remember to decontaminate their hulls before they make planetfall... You...*' He growled at Putta as if he was only letting him remain nameless because he couldn't bear to pronounce his name and shot him a glance that made him huddle deeper into his oversized, but tattered robe. 'You, *Putta*, came much closer to wiping out every life form on Earth than anyone should on their first visit. Or on any visit. Do you intend to destroy *every* civilisation you encounter?' He continued to glare and then seemed to find further scolding impossible and lapsed back into explaining how cleverly he had worked things out, despite being subjected to a massive psychon dose.

'I had the largest available consciousness, you see... So it attacked me the most.'

'But where has it gone? Where's the monster?' Bryony still wasn't satisfied and she didn't think this was because she hadn't got enough experience of sandthings. She thought it was most likely because the Doctor was extremely bad at explaining and possibly because he was improvising and still unsure of what had really happened himself. 'Doctor, one minute, it's eating everyone it can get a hold of and the next it's a heap of muck. Which there will be complaints about. And... oh, lord...' Bryony remembered the body in the pool – Agnew's ghastly, bloodless face above the bubbling, crimson water... She felt chilled and bewildered, and the Doctor put his arm around her to keep her steady.

He gently distracted her with information. 'The sandmaster's life cycle was advancing so rapidly that, while it was highly aggressive, it probably only had a few hours left before it would either join a mating stream – which it couldn't because we'd surely know if there was more than one around here – or… well, they tend to either explode or dissolve. We seemed to speed up its decomposition—'

'Explode? You didn't tell us it might explode!'

'Would you have been happier if I had?'

'No, but—'

'Then I made a terribly wise decision by not mentioning it. And they don't *often* explode. Then again, they don't often come into contact with psy fluid and have their psychic abilities massively magnified so that they can control matter, interfere with minds…' The Doctor made a noise somewhere between a snarl and a sigh. 'Those twins seemed quite perceptive, didn't they. And not a little odd. I suspect they were affected by the psychic field, though I doubt for a moment that they noticed.'

Putta winced, expecting to be shouted again. But instead he felt the strong and heavy thump of the Doctor's free arm hugging his bruised shoulders. 'Putta. Let's go and have tea. Don't you think that would be a good idea? Tea, anyone?'

'Oh, well…' Putta gulped and felt mildly tearful. 'Um, tea. I think I've had that before. It was nice. It didn't try to kill me.'

And Bryony found herself making the decision unanimous. 'Tea.' Because tea might be what you should have after vanquishing an alien, emotionally sensitive carnivorous golf bunker monster. As far as she could tell.

'Yes. The cottage is this way, isn't it?' The Doctor released them both and paced languidly ahead across the grass, accompanied by his scarf and his new excellent friends.

But then he stopped, turned.

'By the way, Bryony. Thank you so much for saving my life.' And he looked at her, his eyes quickly serious, frighteningly intelligent, a quality in them that seemed to *know* her right down to her bare feet. 'I would have been completely done for without you.'

Then he rubbed his face and looked more playful, seemed to be waiting for a compliment. Bryony duly delivered one. 'Well, but you were the expert.'

'Yes, I was, wasn't I?' The Doctor nodded without a trace of modesty. 'I almost always am.' And he unleashed a startlingly huge smile.

'As long as the thing's gone...'

'Oh, I'm sure it is. Either that or I'm completely wrong and we're all still in horrible and increasing danger.' He chuckled and dodged from foot to foot. 'Only time will tell.'

And then the Doctor turned back and headed off again, calling over his shoulder. 'You didn't do so badly either, Putta. There may be hope for you yet.' His long form loping over the grass as if he liked nothing better than walking across strange planets full of promising people with tea and perhaps cake at the end of his journey. Tea and cake or horrible and increasing danger. Either one would do.

A cold poisonous wind blew across the abandoned wasteland. Some loose gravel, leached of colour, rattled across the barren ground. Above, an ever-moving, angry sky with roiling clouds fretted across the empty landscape.

Or not quite empty. Bleached by the wind, rubbed dry by the sand and stone, skeletons littered the earth as far as the eye could see, a jumble of femurs, knobbly spines, toes. A hank of colourless hair, here and there; a glint of something on the ground that might once have meant something to someone; and the skulls, everywhere, endless, all laughing the rictus of death under the grey and purple sky.

The little piece of gravel had stopped bouncing down the hill of scree, but after a long moment of silence, a tapping noise occurred. Then silence, then another one. At first it was simply a tap-tap-tap. Then it was joined by a low rattle, here and there. Almost indistinguishable from the little stones being tossed by the wind. Almost.

The bones were on the move again.

'Where are we?' said Clara, squinting at the screen.

There was a long silence. This was unusual. Clara looked around the console room.

'We appear to be in the TARDIS but the Doctor isn't talking' said Clara to herself. 'This extraordinarily rare phenomenon is believed by some observers to be the result of his gob being immersed in a black hole… actually what are you doing? Have you got addicted to *Home and Away* again? Are you hungry? I have issues with people who never get hungry.'

The Doctor didn't even lift his head.

Clara jumped round the other side of the red-flashing

console to where the Doctor was craning his neck at a large screen. On it, and replicated on the other monitor, was a sight far from unusual: a planet, orbiting a dull sun.

'Where are we?' she asked again.

At this the Doctor let out a sigh.

'What is *wrong* with you?' said Clara. 'Are you missing that dog thing again? You talk about that dog thing a lot.'

'Yes,' said the Doctor finally. 'But that's not it.' He stabbed a long finger at the planet on the screen. 'I don't like it,' he said crossly.

'It looks harmless,' said Clara. Storm patterns whorled around its surface.

'I'm sure it is,' said the Doctor. 'But still. I don't like it. Let's go somewhere else.' He started tinkering with a large lever.

'Hang on,' said Clara, a smile playing on her lips. 'Where is it? I mean, what's it called?'

The Doctor carried on tinkering.

'Ha! You don't know! That's why you're cross. You actually don't know something. Are we lost?'

'No! Absolutely not. Anyway, we never get lost. We occasionally... get fruitfully diverted.'

He patted the TARDIS fondly with his hand.

'Good' said Clara, putting her hand over his to stop him moving the dial. 'So, just tell me what this planet's called then we can get on our way.'

'Um... it's called... it's called...' The Doctor cast around the room for inspiration. 'It's called Hatstandia,' he said, then screwed up his face at the choice.

'Hatstandia?' said Clara. She pushed a button, which lit up red and glowered at her. 'Hush,' she said. 'I'm just checking.' She looked up. 'The TARDIS doesn't think it's called Hatstandia.' She stood back and folded her arms. 'Do *neither* of you know what it's called? *Now* it's getting interesting.'

'It's not on *any* maps,' said the Doctor crossly. 'It's not referenced anywhere. It's not in any of the literature.'

He threw a hand-sized item covered in buttons with a 'D' and a 'P' just visible on the cover across the control room, then checked to make sure it had had a safe landing.

'Normally if I don't recognise a planet then the TARDIS knows, or something knows, or I can find out somewhere,' he said, rubbing the back of his hair. 'This one, though… It's just nowhere. *Nowhere.*'

'Maybe it's just too dull to bother giving it a name,' said Clara.

'They named Clom,' said the Doctor. 'No, it would have a name. Or at the very least, it would still have coordinates and references. But this… It's like it's just appeared from nothing.'

'Oh, a *mysterious* planet,' said Clara. 'Well in that case we'd better leave it alone, don't you think? Just head off and never think about it again. Yup that will be best…'

They had already landed.

'Ugh! I hate this planet, it's rubbish. Look at all these rocks! Rubbish!' The Doctor hurled a stone far away into a crater. It bounced then skidded to a halt. There was a rattling noise.

'Not Gallifrey, then?'

The Doctor silenced her with a look.

Clara cast her eyes around to quickly change the subject. 'Did you hear something?' she said.

'No. Nothing.'

'Stop grumping,' said Clara, pulling her red cloak around her. She still felt the novelty of stepping out onto the ground of a completely different world. She looked up in the sky. There was a mouldy-looking burnt-orange old sun which gave out an ominously low sickly light. 'It's like travelling the universe with Alan Sugar. Anyway, I think you're being world-ist. Somebody must love this place; it's their home. You know, like Croydon.'

The Doctor gave her a look. 'Don't be daft, Croydon's got a

tram museum. Croydon is *ace. Where's your tram museum, planet?'*

'What's that smell?' Clara asked, looking round in vain for any kind of interesting thing to fixate on.

The Doctor took a deep sniff. 'It's 78.09 per cent nitrogen, 20.95 per cent oxygen, 0.039 per cent carbon dioxide, 0.871 per cent argon, and 0.05 per cent sulphur, hence the *rotten eggy smell*, planet.'

'All right,' said Clara. 'OK, you win, let's go.' She turned back to the TARDIS

'Well I can't, can I?' said the Doctor sulkily, hurling another pebble into the middle distance. Once again, Clara thought she heard it rattle for longer that it ought to have done. 'Planet with its own atmosphere, not on any star charts, not recorded, not in the TARDIS data banks. Well, that's not right, is it?'

'You don't have to find out. You're not the policeman of the universe,' said Clara. 'No, wait, that's exactly what you are, isn't it? You've got the box and everything.'

The skeleton quivered as it lay on the ground; in order now, the bones having managed, slowly, to assemble themselves in the correct shape. Now it looked more like a body correctly laid out for burial. For a moment under the congealing sky all was still. Then slowly, carefully, a toe bone began to flex.

The Doctor strode forward. 'So now we just have to walk about until we find something. I'm hoping for an engraved plaque that says, "Oh, sorry, this is Planet Anthony, we forgot to mention it to anyone, not to worry, we peacefully ceased reproducing six billion years ago and it was all fine, have a nice day."'

'Planet *Anthony*?'

The Doctor sniffed, but said nothing.

'Well,' said Clara, setting off determinedly for the horizon. She mounted a small rocky bank. 'Maybe we could just say it's a pleasant constitutional.'

'Why are you going that way? I think we could do with a bit of colour. Can I wear my fez?'

'No,' said Clara, desperately trying not to lose her patience with him. 'And we can go the other way if you aaaaaaaah…'

The Doctor charged up the bank, then, carefully, back again, hopping as he felt his boots sink immediately. 'Argh, quicksand!' he shouted, throwing himself on the ground. 'Clara! Clara! Get out! We've landed in quicksand!'

But he was too late. Clara was already stuck in: hemmed in by a whirlpool of sand that was swirling round like water in a sink, sucking her down. The more she struggled, the more it was pulling her under. Her large dark eyes were full of terror.

'Doctor!'

'Try not to panic!'

'The sand is *eating me*! So, you know – *panic!*'

The sand was closing in on Clara. She could barely see the Doctor over the top of the ridge. Her body and chest felt entirely constrained, pushed in; her ribs couldn't move to breathe against the sheer weight of all the earth. She couldn't bear the thought of the sand reaching her mouth, but the more she tried to get her head free, the more it sucked her down, the sand whirling round and round her, the scent of old dust in her throat and in her nose, choking her. She pushed her head back as the sand reached her ears, the feeling revolting, the noise a roar: one hand now had been pushed back and was trapped behind her, wrenching and immobile.

Then the sand was in her mouth. One grain, then more, dry, dusty, choking.

'No!' she screamed, her throat raw, clenching and spitting at the muck. 'Doc—'

But then she was forced to close her mouth.

The Doctor was cursing his slow progress crawling over the side of the dune, tugging off the front buttons of his braces.

'This would probably have worked better with the fez!'

he shouted, tying one end of the braces to a dead root that protruded from the dry earth, kept the other on, and dived in towards the sand, headfirst, reaching down. He forced himself down into the earth, groping downwards until he felt a hand, and quickly tied the final side of the braces to it, then forced himself upwards through pure will up against the cascading whirlwind of sand that was still pouring down like a huge draining sink.

Then he buttressed himself against the slope and began the agonising feat of dragging her out, as the elastic stretched and stretched and the Doctor feared it would not hold, as he pulled with all his might, shouting out with the exertion, as finally, slowly, emerged Clara, coughing and choking and covered in fine pale chalky sand. Once her arms were free, she could help herself and moved upwards more quickly.

They both scrambled up the bank, dusting themselves down.

'That was *disgusting*,' said Clara, finally, spitting sand out of her mouth.

'Yes, and—'

'Stop going on about a fez not being elastic,' said Clara, wiping out her mouth with her red cloak, thoroughly shaken up.

They turned round to look back the way they had come. Now, the quicksand seemed obvious – the entire landscape practically undulated all the way back to the TARDIS. The dark and light patches of sand and rubble now appeared ominous in the dull and purple tinged light, the TARDIS listing slightly to one side.

To their left were great mountain peaks, grey and forbidding. To their right, stretching out far, was a thick wood.

'Can you summon the TARDIS to come and get us?'

The Doctor rolled his eyes. 'Yes, Clara, and I've been keeping that from you all this time.' He looked at the TARDIS regretfully. 'She's not a dog.'

'Again with the dog,' said Clara, poking the last bits of sand out of the corners of her eyes.

The Doctor looked around the landscape suddenly.

'What are you looking for?'

'Nothing. Um. Discarded ladder?'

'Oh yes, it's just over there by the handy pile of rope,' said Clara. She too took in their surroundings.

They looked again at the dead and wintry-looking forest of bare trees, their crooked gnarled branches reaching towards the miserable sky at an angle, as if in supplication. They seemed to curve on for ever.

'Shall we try the trees?' said Clara. 'Maybe find a long way round?'

The Doctor was looking the other way, at the mountainous horizon. 'Hmmm...'

They both heard it this time.

A low, distinct rattle sounded, just audible above the howling wind. The Doctor spun around again, confirming the direction of the noise. 'Spooky woods?' he asked Clara.

'Definitely,' said Clara. 'We can climb the desolate mountains as a treat afterwards.'

They inched their way carefully along the stone ledge towards the trees. Despite her cloak, Clara was cold, and the sky threatened rain. Noise was travelling strangely and she was still shaken up by the awful feeling of being nearly buried alive. Of course, there was absolutely no way she was going to admit that to the tall figure cheerfully striding on ahead, his bad mood quite forgotten now there was a mystery to solve, looking for all the world as if he was having a Sunday stroll in the park.

'Hullloo!' he shouted as they approached the woods. 'Anyone here, rattling about? Rattling about, that's a joke, you see? It will disarm and intrigue them.'

He took out his sonic screwdriver and lit it up to give it a steady glow, but in fact, as the day had grown darker, this served rather to bring the immediate ground into sharp relief, whilst plunging everything else into shadow. Clara liked it distinctly less. The trees stretched out their gnarled empty branches likes arthritic arms. There wasn't a leaf or a speck of green to be seen on them anywhere, they were blasted black.

'Maybe it was just the wind whistling through the trees,' she said hopefully.

The rattling continued. It sounded nothing like trees. The Doctor shone his light on the ground ahead of them, and they both stopped, and gasped.

'That wasn't there before,' blurted out Clara.

'Maybe we've got a little confused,' said the Doctor, looking round. The trees on all sides looked exactly the same. It was much darker in the forest than he'd anticipated. But down on the ground, clear as day, there was a spelled out message in ash, like the remains of a bonfire, resting on the blackened twigs.

'K-N-O-W.'

Immediately Clara whipped her head round, but couldn't see anything.

'Well, now we're getting somewhere,' said the Doctor cheerily. 'Come and say hello. What should we know?'

Suddenly the two end letters were blown away by the wind, leaving behind only the N and the O.

Clara suddenly felt rather nervous. 'I'm not sure I want them to come and find us,' she said. 'What are they?'

'Dunno!' said the Doctor, marching on.

Clara bit her lip. She would have liked to have taken his hand, or even just held on to his coat. Sometimes his belief that everyone was as fearless as himself was encouraging and inspiring. Sometimes… it wasn't. She glanced behind her. Already, the ash message on the ground had been blown away by the noisy, ever-swirling wind.

They seemed to be getting deeper and deeper into a forest

that had seemed little more than a thicket when they'd approached. But the normal sounds of a forest – birdsong, squirrels scampering – were all absent. It was like nothing lived there at all.

But they knew that something did.

'So, this is peculiar,' said the Doctor, shaking his sonic screwdriver.

'What's up?'

'Well, I've been heading directly for the TARDIS – I have a perfect sense of direction.'

Clara gave him a Hard Stare, but the Doctor didn't notice.

'We really ought to be there by now.'

'What do you mean?'

'I'm not sure,' he said. 'Unless there's something odd about the dimensions of this place… It's almost like the lost planet wants us to be lost too. But why?'

Suddenly, something caught the corner of Clara's eye and she started a little; she couldn't help it. It was just the faintest brush of something vanishing at speed through the trees; a white flash she wasn't even sure she had seen. But left behind, right there it was outlined on the ground; another message.

'NO.'

They looked at it for a moment.

'What do you reckon?' said Clara. 'Warning us off a delicious gingerbread house?'

'I think the trees are getting thicker,' said the Doctor. 'Like the forest is trying to keep us out.'

Clara glanced around. He was right. 'Do you mean… are those trees closer together than they were before?' she said, her heart starting to pound in her chest.

The Doctor looked behind them. 'Now you mention it.'

As he said this, behind them the way they had come appeared to have closed over completely in a tangle of dead, wiry branches, blocking their retreat. It was getting darker and darker overhead.

'Uh-oh,' said Clara.

'"The best way out is always through,"' mused the Doctor. 'Do you know, I think this calls for a bit of the old you-know-what.'

Clara knew they were not imagining it, even though as they ran it felt like a panicky dream from which she could not awaken.

The trees were moving in the wind as if they were alive; they were twisting towards her; stretching out ancient gnarled fingers, trapping in her hair, clutching at her dress, ripping her clothes. Her heart was pounding in her ears and she could feel her own breath tearing at her throat.

Twisted vines shot up from nowhere, branches appeared, separating them, until she could no longer see the Doctor, could see nothing except the next gap or the next hole in the twisted, splitting wall of nightmarish rotting branches and black encroaching trees.

She was completely lost now, her mind blind to anything but the call to flee. She could not tell one way from another, had no sense of where the TARDIS or even the Doctor might be or might once have been, as the forest swelled to fill her entire world. Half of her red cloak was gone, torn off on a persistent branch, her hair had escaped its bun and had fallen all round her face, and still she ran on.

At last she saw a light glinting ahead through the black thicket of trees and the heavy grey of the sky, and she pounded on towards it.

'Clara!'

The Doctor was calling her, but she couldn't hear, as the blood crashed around her head and all she could feel was branches pulling at her. He snatched up her red cloak.

'Clara!'

Still he could not get through, even as he started to run

towards her, confounded as to how she could be charging so hard towards it.

'*Clara!*' He was running at full pelt now, astonished she had not seen the danger, incredulous she had not stopped. '*Clara!!!!!*'

At the last instant, she heard him. Heard something. She turned her head – and immediately a branch shot out and knocked her to the ground. The last thing she saw was the light opening up in front of her; a huge pit of fire that was consuming the trees and heading towards them.

How had she not smelt the burning, felt the force of the licking flames, the indescribable heat? He scooped her up and glanced around the burning wood, searching for an exit, any way out. The flames were coming faster and faster. Behind him, the woods had closed up against him; the trees were now a solid wall of wood, completely entwined with each other, already starting to smoulder. To the side of the clearing too, the trees were too thick.

'Alors,' said the Doctor to himself, then, looking down at Clara's unconscious face in her arms, took a deep breath, then covered her entirely with the red cloak and picked her up. He turned up the collar of his jacket and quickly smoothed down his eyebrows. Then he blinked rapidly twice, took a deep breath, put the collar up over his mouth, and ran straight into the wall of flame.

He had taken a long run-up and stretched out his legs as far as they could go to get as much clearance on the other side as possible, and he made it. He felt his hair scorch, the smell of burning in his nostrils as he took a huge leap through the raging walls of flame, one which caught the trail of Clara's cloak. He rolled her briskly on the ground to beat out the flames, muttering briefly, 'Please don't wake up right now' as he did so, then blinked the smoke out of his eyes and looked ahead.

'Gah,' he said, as his eyes took in the horrifying vista. 'Naughty Planet Anthony, why do I think you're doing this on purpose?'

They were perched right on the edge of an impossibly vertiginous cliff, over which he had very nearly rolled them both, scree scattering below. The fire was still raging right behind them, cutting off their escape route, but the precipice was perilously high.

The Doctor went to peer over the top of it. It was so steep he had to bend his head out quite far to see the bottom of the vast mountain. Ugly grey tufts were floating beneath them; they were higher than the clouds.

At the bottom of the cliff, at least a kilometre down, was something that at first the Doctor took for a white, foaming river. As he looked closer, however, he saw that it was something – no, many things – moving. Alive. A squirming, writing mass of… something. He couldn't tell what. Beasts of some kind. They looked like impossibly large churning maggots. He arched an eyebrow and sat back, no longer able to pretend to himself that their bad luck was coincidental.

Behind him, Clara was sitting up, rubbing her head and trying to remember where she was. When she saw the Doctor, her face broke into a relieved smile.

'Oh, thank goodness,' she said, sitting up carefully, clutching her head. 'We're safe!'

'Ye-es…' said the Doctor. He frowned and looked over to the far side of the abyss. 'I wish I'd packed a flask.'

He looked up to the other side. Slowly, out of the chilly mists on the far side, a figure was approaching, dressed in a faded cloak with the hood up. It moved slowly and seemed both human and not at the same time. The Doctor moved nearer to watch the figure approach, as Clara gradually pulled herself to her feet, looking in fear at the fire still blazing behind them.

'You're too close to the edge,' she shouted.

'My favourite spot,' said the Doctor, still concentrating hard on the opposite cliff side.

The figure stood there, and its cloak hood fell back. It was not a person; or rather, it was no longer a person. It was an empty, gleaming skull, picked and polished white, and the odd, human-esque figure beneath the cloak was also skeletal; it was made entirely of bone. A walking skeleton.

The Doctor blinked rapidly. 'Well, that's unusual,' he said.

'*Unusual?*' said Clara, beside him. 'He's not a new chair.'

The Doctor ignored her, lifted up his hands to his mouth and hollered across the abyss. 'Hallo there! Nice to meet you!'

'Politeness,' muttered Clara to herself. 'Always important to politely introduce yourself to a *hideous death skeleton*.'

'Who are you? I'm the Doctor, this is—'

'Don't tell him my name!' said Clara. 'What if it's Death, come to claim us? I don't want him to find me.'

'Nah,' said the Doctor. 'Death rides a skeletal horse, too. I'm kidding, I'm kidding.'

The skeleton stared at them, then lifted its bony left arm, one long white finger raw and gleaming, as if pointing at them.

It then raised its right hand, which contained a long, slim, very sharp knife. Then it leant its hand over the side of the canyon, above a grassy outcrop, and started, with delicate movements, to shave off tiny fractions of the bone. They fell onto the gorse, and formed immediately into letters. Clara winced.

'KNOW,' the letters spelled in white powder, the 'K' and the 'W' fading away with the wind, just as they'd seen inside the forest.

'Well, yes, we got that one,' said the Doctor. 'I will say, this isn't the most welcoming spot we've ever visited.'

'That's disgusting,' said Clara.

The Doctor looked along the cliff edge. To the left there was another clump of trees past were the fire had burned out, thick and dense with black, but Clara thought she saw something glinting in the twisted branches; something that made her instinctively flinch.

Ahead was the canyon, and the scorched wasteland ahead showed the skeletal figure silhouetted in the gathering dust. The other side was not far, but it was too far to jump, and the precipice was horribly steep.

'I want to go and chat to him,' said the Doctor decisively. 'I wish I could reach him on the telebone. Ha! Telebone!'

Clara gave him a look.

'Excuse me!' hollered the Doctor. 'Is there a bridge? Can we come and talk to you?'

The figure stayed completely still, then slowly turned and began walking away.

'After him,' said the Doctor. 'There has to be a way across somewhere.'

But to their right, there was nothing as the cliff sheered off. And to the left, they plunged head first into the newest copse of trees.

Clara caught sight of it again out of the corner of her eye. Just a sense of movement, a flicker she could not pin down, but that sent a cold-fingered shudder down her spine that wasn't just the chilling wind. She slowed a little.

'Hmm,' said the Doctor. 'There must be a bridge somewhere round here. Impossible physical skeletons can't fly.'

The next time the Doctor saw it too.

'Hey! There's something up those trees.'

'I was considering pretending I hadn't seen it,' said Clara, 'in the hope that it might go away.' She wrapped her arms in the remnant of the red cloak, and briefly considered putting it over her head, so she wouldn't have to look.

As they approached, Clara saw the movement more clearly: an intense, muscular writhing; brown and copper scales glinting in the half-light, great heavy coils hanging down from branches.

'Well, aren't you beautiful,' breathed the Doctor. 'How on earth do you survive here? What do you eat?'

'*Doctor!*' screamed Clara.

The huge head of the enormous snake shot out with extraordinary speed, its massive jaws impossibly wide, a loud hiss of furious expelled air. The Doctor lurched back, startled, as the hideous creature missed him by inches, then retreated its massive body in preparation for a second strike, its ghastly pink maw wide apart.

'Us!' said Clara. 'It's going to eat *us*!'

'Extraordinary animal,' whispered the Doctor in awe. 'Pure predator.'

They were backing away when Clara heard another malevolent hiss from right behind her. She jumped. The Doctor took out his sonic screwdriver and held it up.

'Now,' he said calmly to Clara. 'The thing about a really big snake is, much as I would hate to hurt her, it pays to be prepared, just in case you ever have to cut your way out from the inside.'

The huge head veered at them again; Clara could see more writhing in the trees around them and found herself backing towards the edge of the cliff. A rattle of scree tumbled down as her foot slipped back on the very edge. Clara was trying to do the odds in her panicking brain; would she rather tumble down a cliff side or be eaten by a snake?

The huge brown snake was rearing again, preparing for another strike, the branch was right above their head, and there was no time left now to think at all. She grasped the Doctor's coat, faintly, for comfort. But he was busy, darting right and left, the snake following, weaving its massive body, its slitted eyes fixed on the Doctor's.

'Can it hypnotise you?' said Clara, her breath stopping in her throat.

'It can try!' said the Doctor gleefully. 'But fortunately my Parseltongue is excellent... I'll talk her out of it somehow – Aha!'

He fumbled with a setting on his sonic screwdriver, which started to vibrate in his hand, glowing a faint blue and, to Clara's utter astonishment, bravely stuck his hand straight up in the air in front of the snake's face and beamed the light into its eyes.

She waited for the creature to devour him fingers first, but instead, the snake hesitated then caught the light with its gaze. Gently, the Doctor waggled his screwdriver from side to side, and the snake followed, weaving its massive head from side to side.

'Ha!' said the Doctor. 'And also: phew!'

He slowed his arm motion down and gently moved his hand from side to side as if conducting an orchestra. As he did so, the snake slowly closed its jaws and started to undulate itself, huge shivers passing along its elongated body. Gradually, the coils relaxed and the huge long tail unfurled and drooped to the ground.

'OK,' said the Doctor in a low voice, not taking his eyes off the snake, or slowing the relentless hypnotic movement of his hand. 'We are almost certainly only going to get one shot at this.'

Clara moved quietly too. The snake's head followed the Doctor's hand, as he carefully inched around.

'Now,' he said, quickly indicating with his eyes and speaking very quietly.

'You are joking,' said Clara.

'No,' said the Doctor, eyes on the snake. 'Because normally my jokes are brilliant, and this, right now, would be a terrible joke, don't you think? I think I would lose my reputation for my wonderful jokes. You know, like that one about the telebone?'

'Yes, that one,' said Clara. She looked ahead at what he was indicating. It was the ravine, the cliff's edge. And, hanging off the tree, the long, long tale of a snake, looking very like a rope.

'Won't we just pull down the snake?'

The Doctor shook his head. 'No, her instincts will make

her grip on. Might hurt a bit, pulling her tail, but that can't be helped.' The hissing from the other trees grew louder and the Doctor frowned. 'They're asking what she's doing. They're getting suspicious. So, are you ready?'

'Am I ready to swing over a precipice by snake's tail?' said Clara.

'Yeah! I know, new thing!' said the Doctor gleefully.

He speeded his hand up momentarily, as the snake looked as if it was settling down to sleep, its tail waving lazily in the wind. They backed away as far as they could without coming up against one of the snake's friends in the other trees.

'1... 2... 3...'

Then they both ran and jumped and swung, the forward momentum carrying them forward straight out over the cliff's edge. A fierce wind blew right through them. Clara clung with one arm to the Doctor, one to the surprisingly warm, smooth body of the beast. She felt it tighten from the top, obviously clinging on to the tree and was only conscious of the Doctor shouting *'Jump!'* before the snake's tail slithered out of their grasp and she felt herself thudding into the other side of the cliff, bumping her head and getting a mouthful of rock and dirt, taking the skin off her hands and knees, grazing her cheeks but clinging on; clinging on for dear life. She risked a look down then regretted it instantly, and instead concentrated on hauling herself up and over the ledge, grabbing the strong arm that reached down for her.

'You know, my old mate Tarzan used to do this all the time,' confided the Doctor. 'He said it was vines, but we knew the truth.'

Clara wasn't listening. She had stopped short, staring straight ahead. Then she let out a sharp cry of surprise and relief.

'*Clara!*'

But Clara had already torn away, dashed over to the sight she was so desperate to see: the TARDIS was there, the familiar blue box that was, impossibly, standing completely by itself on the flat rocky plain this side of the abyss. Clara ran with her arms outstretched as if to embrace it.

The Doctor watched, sadly, as she reached the mirage TARDIS, as she carried on, ran through it, the fake blue light shimmering, rendering the box nothing more than the illusion it was.

He had known straight away, of course. He could recognise his own TARDIS, and he knew this wasn't it; rather a foul trick. But Clara's face, as she turned, put her hand through the blue light image, waved it around, then sank to the ground, was completely desolate and wretched.

'What?' said the Doctor, wandering over. He marched right through the fake TARDIS. 'You've gone a really weird white colour.'

'Because obviously I am having a *really bad day*!' Clara stood up, launched herself at him and buried her face in his jacket.

'You're all wobbly!'

'I'm *shaking*.'

'Really? Teeth and everything? Let me see your teeth, that's my favourite bit.'

She showed him her chattering mouth.

'Ha. Excellent. You can nibble your way out of trouble.'

Tenderly, he took out his handkerchief and wiped away the tiny beads of blood from her forehead. Night was falling fast on the vast inhospitable landscape and it was terribly cold.

'I thought it was quite fun, me rescuing you for a change.'

'Well, how about I don't want anyone to be rescuing anyone?' said Clara, drawing back.

She knew she sounded sulky, but she couldn't help herself. Sometimes, when travelling with the Doctor, she felt... it was hard to explain, even to herself. It was if her true feelings were buried under so many layers that sometimes it was hard to tell what was real and what was just a dream.

Clara pouted. Then she pouted again, because if you didn't make it really clear to the Doctor that you were sulking, he was simply incapable of noticing. Even now he was scanning the horizon, plotting their next course.

He turned round and finally clocked her face.

'Ah. Clara. You're… you're not happy are you?'

'Apart from the quicksand and the moving forest and the fire and the fact that I have *snake* on me? No. I'm great!'

There was a very long pause between them. Then finally the Doctor sighed. 'Look. The thing is…'

She could tell he was trying to be tactful, which she appreciated, because she knew he absolutely did not have the knack.

'The thing is, most people who come travelling with me…'

A faint look of weariness passed over his face.

'Most people… they love it. They love it. And I get to experience a universe I know too well; I get to experience it through their eyes, through fresh eyes. And I need that.'

Clara nodded, feeling suddenly rather tearful.

'What I mean is, I can't promise everything will be all right, I can only promise that it will be interesting. And fun, and wonderful and cool and amazing. But you have to open your eyes.'

'To the beauty of snakes,' said Clara quietly.

'The beauty of snakes,' said the Doctor, nodding his head vehemently. 'Exactly.'

Clara nodded too. *But I'm not*, she suddenly found herself thinking, a voice from deep within her. *I'm not one of your other innocent chums, your buddies you go yomping around with, who 'love' adventures, because they have never learned the cost.*

She wondered what she meant. Her head hurt suddenly.

The odd voice inside her piped up again: *I have known it*, it said. *As deep in my bones as the skeletons who walk here: what it feels like and what it costs me, and I do not think that snakes are beautiful.*

Did they say they would, all those others? Did they say they would die for you and suffer for you and live life as an open wound for you? And did they? Or do they go to sleep at night safe and warm in their beds?

But as quickly as the thought crossed her mind, it rippled away, like shaking off the dust of a fast-fading morning dream. Clara shook her head, which cleared instantly, and blinked away the tears that had somehow started to form in her eyes. 'You're right,' she said, pulling herself together. 'Of course you're right. I'm fine. Again?' she said, indicating left, the purple mountains, the weakening, barely noticeable sun going down, rattlings coming right and left, night coming in on this horrible planet filled with monsters.

The Doctor gave her a wink. 'Once more unto the breach, dear friend?'

'Once more,' said Clara, a sweet smile spreading across her face, as she once again suppressed and forgot the tumult within.

'Who would build this torture garden?'

For that, as the Doctor looked around, was clearly what it was. In the distance he could see lines and lines of barbed wire – landmines? It made no sense. They were being watched, but why the multitude of ways to kill or horribly injure yourself? He and Clara only just skirted a massive mantrap, set up outside a small cave, obviously there to trap the sleepy and unwary.

The chill wind blew right through them as they walked on without speaking, Clara gathering the cloak around herself, her face set against the weather. Finally, across the landscape, the figure they were both following and dreading to see revealed itself; first a dot on the horizon, moving slowly, looking, from this distance, once more like a man. It was only as they grew closer that the hideous skeletal form revealed itself, the pale white bone glinting in the watery moonlight of the two pale moons.

'Ahoy!' shouted the Doctor. 'Where are you off to, matey?'

The skeleton wore its rictus grin, but the slumped posture and weary walk made it seem defeated. Clara, oddly, had the very strong impression that it was sad.

'Where are you going?' said the Doctor.

The skeleton held up his scalpel again, and Clara looked away. The shavings of bone formed on the ground.

'*Le Roi des Os*,' it spelled on the ground. Everything except the 'O's quickly scattered.

'Le Roi des Os,' said the Doctor. 'Oh, you're French.'

Clara stared at it too. 'The King of Bones,' she read.

'You belong to the King of Bones?' said the Doctor.

The skeleton's sightless eyes were still pointing in the direction of the far horizon as it nodded.

'Who is he?' The Doctor circled him, looking closely. The rattling head followed them wherever they went, the scalpel held high. Then he saw it. 'Cor!' he said suddenly. 'They did a right job on you. Come and have a look, Clara.'

'Must I?'

'Look!' The Doctor pointed out near invisible, very thin pale wires that connected the bones to each other.

'Carnutium filaments. Practically undetectable, but send signals at nearly the speed of light. You, my friend are the most astonishing thing, look at you.'

The skeleton turned its head very slowly to look at the Doctor, who was standing behind him.

'Human bones held with electro-stimulating filaments. You are the weirdest robots ever. Why can't you talk?'

The skeleton held up the scalpel again.

'No,' said the Doctor. 'Don't do that. Does it hurt you?'

The skeleton did not move.

'He doesn't want you to talk, does he? The King of Bones? He wants you to do his bidding silently. Is that it?'

'Is there a person in there?' said Clara in horror.

'Y-o-u-a-r-e-n-o-t-a-f-r-a-i-d-o-f-u-s,' spelled the skeleton slowly on the ground.

The Doctor looked at him aghast. 'How could I be?' he said, his voice breaking with pity.

The skeleton stood still for a moment.

'C-O-M-E,' he spelled on the ground, and he trudged on.

They followed a strange path, sometimes veering wildly to the right, sometimes doubling back. The Doctor inferred, correctly, that the skeleton was avoiding deadly traps in the dark of the night, and was grateful, but worried about where they were being led. If the King of Bones did not want them dead, what did he want with them?

All the way he talked non-stop to the skeleton, telling him silly French jokes and singing songs and trying to get a reaction from him that wasn't a scalpel.

'Does he,' he said finally, 'does he make you do things you don't want to do, the Roi des Os? Does he make you? Ooh, Boney! Like that other French bloke, Napoleon. Now, as you know, I like everyone…'

The figure suddenly stopped, and the great empty pits of eyeholes trained themselves on the Doctor. There was an uncharacteristically long pause.

'Um, OK, carry on,' said the Doctor finally, clearing his throat.

Just as he did so, a crackle of light raced up the filaments that bound the skeleton together and it jerked backwards as if shocked. Then it turned to face forwards again, and the party continued.

Although later Clara realised it was only a few hours, that cold and exhausting journey, across the ruined world, dotted here and there with blast craters and the occasional howl, seemed to her to take forever.

Finally, over the crest of a crumbled hill, they saw it, eerily gleaming by the light of the pallid moons. The only building on, it seemed, the entire world. It was built of white marble, Clara thought at first, and was beautiful in the manner of the Taj Mahal but, as she grew closer, swallowing madly, she realised that it was in fact constructed of bones: thousands, hundreds of thousands of bones, like planking on the huge structure. It had rows of windows, the knobbly extrusions of femurs all lined up neatly; smaller crossed bones making decorative patterns around the arched doorframes.

Clara felt the breath catch in her throat. The awful beauty of the palace was undeniable, built though it was on a slaughterhouse. Silent skeletons stood in rows as sentries; there were hundreds of them. She gasped and nudged the Doctor. Over to the side, standing like the others, its head ridiculously large in comparison to its body, standing with the rest, was the unmistakeable skeleton of a child.

The Doctor blinked twice, rapidly, and marched up to the front door. 'Thank you,' he said to the skeleton who had led them there so silently. '*Courage, mon brave.*'

And he looked at the doorknocker, comprised of finger bones, and left it behind, rapping instead with his knuckles, but there was no reply.

He pushed at the door and it opened, slowly. Inside, it was dark, musty smelling, oppressively warm. There was not a sound to be heard.

Clara could hear the blood pounding in her head, the rhythm of her own heart.

The Doctor turned to her with a sudden wink. 'I don't know about you,' he said, quietly. 'But I haven't met many goodies who live in houses like this.'

The first room they entered was covered in weaponry: scores of swords, guns, lasers and axes hanging on the bone walls. Next they passed a stairwell, leading downwards into the dark. Clara thought she could see a faint light coming from the basement, but the Doctor stalked on.

'Watch out for booby traps,' he said, which wasn't helpful as the house was dusty and gloomy, and Clara fully expected the floor to give way with every step.

Moving further in – still they had seen no one, heard nothing – the walls were hung with red woven tapestries that deadened the sound of their footsteps. Dust lay thickly everywhere, under an oppressive layer of heat, and the air was heavy with the scent of decay.

Suddenly Clara stopped. 'Listen,' she said.

They did. It sounded like… it was… music. Definitely music. Strange and complex, and played on instruments that Clara didn't recognise, but it was music. They headed for one of the many doors in that direction, getting closer to it. One of the arched doors was swinging slightly open. That was the room where the music was playing loudly. It was rather beautiful.

The Doctor cleared his throat and knocked loudly on the side of the archway. 'Hullo?'

Again, there was no response, and they made their way slowly forwards.

It was so dark in the room it took a couple of seconds for Clara's eyes to focus; she could barely make out what she was looking at. It couldn't possibly, she thought at first, be a living person, a real one. But, as her eyes adjusted, she realised it was: in fact, it was a young man, but he was also incredibly, grotesquely fat, so fat he could barely move.

His skin was pitted with huge red spots, angry and infected-looking. He wore glasses, which were stretched out either side of his head, and his unwieldy mass was perched on some kind of a cushion arrangement that moulded to his distorted limbs.

The man was wearing a huge, dirty shirt with a row of what looked like pens in the top pocket. Everywhere around him were plates of dirty and discarded food piled up; a large hookah, empty bottles, crumpled up paper, screens. It looked, Clara thought with some astonishment, like the world's messiest teenage bedroom, with the world's largest teenager. It smelled like it too. Rows of screens displaying different areas they had already been through lit up and flashed, and the man's fingers played rapidly over the tops of them, as if it were a fast action video game. There was also a large white-glowing console in his other hand.

Everyone held their breath for a beat.

'Oh yeah, hi,' came a breathy, nasal voice finally, faux casually. 'So, well done for getting this far, yeah? Most people don't.' He pulled a 'what can you do?' face, before picking something up off one of the dirty plates, sniffing it, then eating it and wiping his hands on the large undergarment he was wearing.

'*You're* the King of Bones?' said the Doctor.

The man raised his eyebrows. 'Wow, very good, you got them to talk to you.' His face turned stern. 'I told them not to do that. I stopped them talking, stopped them signing, stopped them writing in sand, and now this. Waste of good bone. Stupid robots.'

His eyes blinked behind the thick-lensed glasses. Clara had the very clear impression he didn't need them; that they were not his, but a trophy.

'Who are you? You guys seem a bit cool about the whole thing,' he said, sounding disappointed. 'Normally everyone is gibbering by the time they get here. Vomit, wet pants, the lot.'

Clara swallowed crossly. 'He's the Doctor and I'm Clara. We don't scare easily,' she said, in her strongest voice.

He just stared at them. 'He doesn't,' he said, not taking his eyes off Clara.

'I don't like your house,' said the Doctor.

'I don't like your jacket,' said the man. 'But I'm far too polite to mention it.'

'Did you build this place?'

'I did,' said the man. 'With blood, sweat, tears. And some bones.' He barked an awkward laugh at his own joke.

The Doctor squinted at him. 'But why? What reason?'

The man shrugged huge beefy shoulders and said the last thing the Doctor had expected to hear. 'It's my job, mate.'

Clara leaned forward. Sure enough, he had a faded, encrusted nametag clipped onto his shirt pocket. It looked completely incongruous in the hideous room. 'Etienne Boyce,' she read aloud.

The man smiled. His teeth were blackened and ghastly, his gums so pink they looked blood red. Clara could smell the decay from clear across the room.

'What kind of job is this?' said the Doctor, struggling to hold on to his temper.

The man blinked very rapidly. 'Security,' he said. 'I'm in computer security.' He indicated the bank of monitors surrounding him. 'Well, I was. Bit more of a freelance these days.'

Clara gasped 'This is a computer simulation?'

The man laughed. 'No! Please. I'm not some ruddy amateur.' He put his hands over his belly in satisfaction. 'Everything here is real. With a few modifications.'

'You've gone rogue?' said the Doctor.

'Best analyst in my division,' said Etienne proudly. 'Was just too good. Don't know how they thought they'd keep tabs on me.'

'Are you a hacker?' asked Clara timidly.

'The best. Hacked the Nestene Consciousness when I was 14. Resting Consciousness more like. Nestene Semi-consciousness, I call it.'

Again came the peculiar barking laugh of someone who didn't spend a lot of time conversing with other human beings. The man took another large bite of something he had found on a plate beside him and belched loudly.

The Doctor look around, nodding. 'So you're keeping this place secure?' he said. 'You were sent to hide this planet. And you did – even from the people who sent you?'

The man sighed. 'Well, yes. I am brilliant. But I still get the odd adventurer turning up. The odd person who won't take a telling. Plenty of crashes of course – that's a hazard of not turning up on navigational equipment. Still got to stop you all. That's my job. Was my job.'

'So, just to get this straight in my head,' said the Doctor, 'you're not here to protect us from the dangers of this planet.'

Etienne laughed again. It was a horrible barking sound. 'No, mate.'

'You made it this way.'

The man wiped his greasy fingers on a filthy napkin.

'It is unspeakable,' said the Doctor, 'what you have done to the people who landed here.'

'Come on, are you joking? Carnutium filament? It's brilliant! And it's not like I *kill* them. They die, and I just use the leftovers.'

'But there's a million things here that can kill you!' burst in Clara.

'Yes, because I have to protect the planet,' said Etienne, as if explaining things to a slow child.

'But those are people!' Clara was still horrified.

'*Were*,' said Etienne. He checked his console. 'Oooh, acid rainstorm coming up. You don't wanna be out in that. You know, I've got the Carnutium machine downstairs. Would be jumping the gun a bit, but it's totally painless, probably.' He looked at Clara. 'Or you can stay a bit, if you like.'

'But why?' said the Doctor, almost to himself. 'Who wanted a whole planet hidden? Who wanted something off the map so badly they would send a nutcase like you to do it? Why not just blow it up?'

Clara leant forward. The old photograph on the ID card was of a much slimmer, very young man – a teenager, really, all Adam's apple and awkwardness, the bare whisper of a moustache on his top lip, in a neat white shirt, looking for all the world completely and utterly normal.

Etienne shrugged. 'Job's a job, innit. Then they started complaining about my methods, so…' He blew on his fingers and opened them up.

'You disappeared for good,' said the Doctor.

'And I want to stay that way,' said Etienne. 'Guards, take them downstairs!' he screamed suddenly, in a startling contrast to his laidback speaking voice, and immediately four skeletons came to the door.

Once again, Clara flinched as the ghostly shapes emerged, their feet clacking on the floor. Then she saw the little one was with them, the child.

Overcome, Clara forgot everything: her fear, her exhaustion, her surroundings; forgot absolutely everything, except the many children over the years and centuries who had been in her care; some she remembered, some who were nothing more than dreams: the new and certain knowledge that these too had been people once, even if they were only robot-operated bones now; even if, whatever the Doctor thought, nothing of them remained except the hideous mechanisation of this man who animated the dead.

On pure instinct alone, she knelt down and opened her arms.

There was a moment's pause in the hideous, stinking, oppressive cavernous room built of the bones of the dead and the lost, the fat discontented king on his dead throne in his charnel house, ruling an empty wasteland.

Unsure it wasn't the last thing she'd ever do, she held her arms wide, shaking once more. And with a rattling and a clicking, its oversized pale white skull, the bones as smooth and cool as a snake's, breaking free of its programming, the skeleton child ran into her arms.

Clara knelt there waiting for a blow to fall, her eyes closed once again, but it did not. She glanced up. The Doctor and Etienne were both staring at her.

'That's new,' said Etienne, still chewing. 'Huh. Hey, insensate matter!' He held up the white shining console, menacingly. 'Seize her! Down below!'

There was a long pause. Then another skeleton, shorter than the other two, stepped towards Clara, foot bones rattling on the floor. Here it comes, thought Clara.

Instead, the skeleton moved towards her – then knelt down next to her, and took the smaller skeleton in its arms, cradling it like a baby.

'Aha!' shouted the Doctor in delight. 'Clara, you're amazing! Look at that. There is something left behind! Which makes *you* a monster,' he said, turning to Etienne.

'They can't feel a thing,' groused Etienne. 'Sometimes I have to readjust the mechanism, you know, bit of a shock just to keep 'em in position, that kind of a thing. But they're just... it's just bones I find lying about. Did the same thing with the trees, and they didn't mind.'

The Doctor looked at him, shaking his head, and turned to address the skeletons. 'You don't have to move for him, you know.'

'Oh yes they do,' said Etienne, sweat popping out on his vast forehead.

He pressed down a white button in the middle of the console, and instantly the crackle of white light pervaded the skeletons, causing them to stiffen and throw their heads back in what was clearly pain.

'No!' said the Doctor, whipping out his screwdriver and pressing another button, making both devices squeal with feedback. 'No, you don't.'

The remote exploded in Etienne's hand and he dropped it rapidly, swearing. He then looked up, his eyes full of fear, as he gazed at the wall of white in front of him.

The Doctor advanced. 'Tell me,' he said sternly. 'Tell me what it is you're protecting that's so special.'

Etienne gave them a twisted smile. 'Make me.'

'You're a child,' said the Doctor, dismayed. 'How old are you, anyway?'

The ruin of a man looked down. 'Dunno,' he said quietly, inching towards the remote control. 'But I am so good at my job.'

The Doctor scowled, grabbed the remote from the floor and stuck it in his top pocket. 'Stay there,' he said. 'Skeletons, can you watch him?'

One held up his finger.

'No, don't do that! Just nod!'

The largest of them nodded.

'Come on,' said the Doctor to Clara. 'Let's figure this out.'

Etienne cringed back a bit then sneered, grabbed one of his screen consoles and started typing feverishly on it.

The Doctor took Clara out into the corridor, and told her to stay where she was. Then he went down to the basement. When he returned, his face was grim, and Clara knew better than to ever ask him about it.

'Now,' he said. 'To business.'

They explored the entire palace, each room more shocking that the one before it. One contained endless boxes of pre-prepared food in cardboard boxes, with a huge hole carved out of it, dirty containers and utensils thrown and scattered about knee-deep, new ones grabbed at will. The smell was unholy. Another was filled with boxes and boxes of seeds, fruit, vegetables, flowers, fertilisers, geodesic domes and water filters, all of it untouched.

There was a room with a weather console, which as far as Clara could see didn't just tell you the weather; it created it.

One room had a huge loom, which had never been used and was clearly falling apart. There was a thrumming cold-storage facility that contained frozen specimens of animals and plants. In one vast workshop, cannibalised parts of spaceships had been put together – beautifully, intricately – into new, sinister-looking machines. One room was full of old spacesuits from different planets and ages; personal documents tossed in as if a huge trash can; hundreds, thousands of them.

One room had fresh linen, faded now and thick with dust: one had books, a huge library, everything one could ever need in any language, sitting in long, untouched rows except here and there, where one had been dragged out and thrown or despoiled or a batch had been burnt for whatever reason.

At this, the Doctor's mouth turned into a thin straight line and he turned abruptly and marched back into Etienne's stateroom. Etienne was typing furiously in the corner, his fleshy mouth pouting, grunting as he heaved himself up. Sweat was dripping from his forehead, and he was drinking something from a long container. The skeletons lined the far wall, blocking his exit. They appeared frozen.

'You could have built a paradise here,' said the Doctor furiously. 'You could have done anything and you have rendered this entire planet a blasted heath.'

Etienne suddenly started to laugh a wheezing laugh. His vast belly heaved and wobbled with the effort. 'A *paradise*?' he roared. 'Ha! The one thing they are here to prevent. A paradise. Oh, Doctor, my only job is to not long for paradise.'

The Doctor stared at him for a long time, his mind working furiously. 'Who sent you?'

Etienne shrugged. 'Can't remember. It was a lifetime ago. A different life. A lot of these.' He held up a bottle.

The Doctor strode forward and attempted to read the faded nametag on his filthy shirt.

Etienne laughed in his face. 'Now you're getting desperate,' he said, his breath foul. 'Doncha wanna know? Oh, I cut them loose. They were no use at all. But you really want what you came here to find? What my job – my *job* – is to keep hidden? You really want it?' Etienne stared into the Doctor's eyes for a long time. 'No way,' he said. 'I can see it. I can see it in your eyes. You've been here before. Ha! You *do* know where you are. Well, well.'

You would have had to have been studying the Doctor's face at very close quarters just then to see the tiny flash of understanding that passed across it. He immediately straightened up and backed away.

'Oh, there it is,' leered Etienne. 'You do know. Well then. Ha. No point in torturing you. You're there already. I thought we'd finally passed into myth. Well, well, well. There aren't many left like you these days.'

'There aren't,' growled the Doctor.

'Well, why don't I show the pretty one? That's why you've brought her back, right?'

'No!'

But Etienne had grabbed another device from the clutter around his chair, a tiny one this time, and pressed a button. Instantly there came the clanging and groaning of an ancient set of chains.

'Don't, Etienne,' said the Doctor, his tone quite different. 'We'll go. We'll turn around and we'll go. Right now.'

Clara shot round to look at him in amazement.

'Hang on, where's the conquering robot-freeing hero now?' said Etienne, looking amused. 'Where's the liberator of this planet, huh? Where's the person who's come to tell off naughty Etienne for his naughty behaviour?'

'Doctor?' said Clara, puzzled. The rattling noise continued.

'Leave!' the Doctor shouted at Clara. 'Get out! Get out of here!' He tried to grab the tiny button from Etienne, who raised his eyebrows and, laughing, hurled it in his mouth.

'Oh, for crying out loud,' said the Doctor, launching himself at Etienne and trying to pinch his nose. 'Clara, *go!*'

But it was too late. Slowly at first, a door in the wall of the house of bones had started to lower itself, drawbridge-style, into the open air. Clara expected of course to see into the dark, cold and storm-ridden night of the Nowhere planet.

Instead, a piercing shaft of glorious sunlight suddenly penetrated the mote-ridden fustiness of the shut-up scarlet room. A draft of fresh, clean, sweet air invaded the space. It was the kind of freshness you get on the first day after a long rainy spell, when it feels as if the earth has been washed clean. It was like waking up on a mountainside, or flying somewhere warm after a long winter.

They heard something else, too, for the first time: the silvering tones of birdsong, the type of spring morning song that makes the heart clench. As the drawbridge drew down inch by inch, tiny wisps of cloud could be seen, floating across a Wedgewood blue sky; the golden light was soft and the sweet wind was scented with lotus flowers and apple. Beneath the birdsong, a fountain could be heard somewhere bubbling away merrily.

'Clara, ignore it. It's a force field. You can't go out there, it's a trap.'

'Oh no, there's no more traps left, mate,' giggled Etienne. His odd glasses had turned completely black, protecting his eyes, but even wearing them he still kept his gaze averted from the trapdoor. 'No one gets this far. I can't believe you missed the crocodile swamp. Anyone who's got a way off this place generally takes it at the writhing maggots.'

'Put that thing down,' said the Doctor. 'Put it down. I… I beg you.'

'Well, I would have begged you not to try and cause a robot revolution, but you wouldn't have listened,' said Etienne, indistinctly as he continued to crunch through the plastic shell of the remote.

The Doctor turned away from him in disgust and ran towards Clara. She was already walking out of the door into the space beyond as if sleepwalking. Etienne's barking laughter echoed in the Doctor's ears, but Clara heard none of it.

Outside, the sunlight was golden like honey, the grass lusciously green and thick. They were on a path, looking ahead at a hill at the top of which was an vibrant orchard, with a wrought-iron fence around it. There was a gate, but it was open.

Clara ran towards it at full pelt, light of foot and joyous of heart. Inside were apple trees, but the apples were silver and gold. Their scent filled the air; Clara had never in her life felt such utter thirst, such terrible hunger. She ran, the Doctor arriving behind her, just as she stretched out her hand.

'Cla—'

The snake in this tree was green.

'Don't you *see* what this is?'

Small, jade-coloured, like a slithering jewel, the snake raised its head. Clara jumped back, but not for long. Her hunger drove her forwards. The Doctor shook his head and grabbed her shoulders. She struggled against him.

'Why on earth are you taking that form?' the Doctor shouted towards the snake.

The snake flickered its tongue at him. 'Hello again,' it said. 'Yes, well, rather. I got it from the human. Between that and your documented fondness for the species, I thought it might rather work.'

The Doctor looked wounded. 'Well, don't get me wrong, I like them and everything, but I've just spent thirty-five years working with the Sculptor Dwarves, and nobody ever mentions that.'

The snake indicated Clara. 'Well, anyway, it's in her head. Got it off the psychic wavelength that's running those poor robots.'

'People,' said the Doctor quickly.

'Something about… "Sunday school"?' said the snake. 'A little church room, a nice lady teacher, the smell of oak polish and the felt-tip colouring on the wall. She loved it.'

It coiled sinuously round a branch, rustling the thick, luxurious leaves.

The Doctor looked at Clara in surprise, then redoubled his grip as she kept trying to pull away from him.

'Nonetheless,' said the snake, stretching its neck in the sunlight. 'It is a rather beguiling look, don't you think? If only I could smell.'

'You're not having her,' said the Doctor, clinging on to Clara for dear life. She struggled against him, her feet trying to move of their own accord. 'You're not.'

The snake shimmered, its scales lost in the light. 'But would you deny her everything? Come, my daughter. Come, taste it all. Every single thing, every last delight, everything there ever was to know or to understand; the fruit of knowledge, of everything. Doesn't that sound delicious? You will love it.'

'It is not what he promises,' hissed the Doctor in Clara's ear, but she could not hear him.

'I want it,' she said. 'I am naked without it.'

'You aren't naked.' The Doctor tugged her again, but she didn't listen to him or even look at him.

'He doesn't know everything about you, does he?' said the snake. 'He doesn't really know you at all, does he? Doesn't know how you bleed for him. But what would he do for you? Does he bleed for you, pretty maid?'

'Clara,' the Doctor said. He glared at the snake, whose mouth was open, as if it were laughing. In desperation, the Doctor spun Clara round to face him, till she was forced to look at him, although her eyes strayed over his shoulder, her feet continued to move.

'I want it,' she said.

'But you have to work for it,' said the Doctor in anguish. 'You have to earn it.'

She shook her head. 'I *want* it.'

'You hate snakes, remember?'

Her eyes were glassy as she stared at him in confusion. It was as if she barely recognised him.

The snake reared and hissed crossly.

'Argh,' said the Doctor.

He held her by the shoulders, her eyes still desperately searching out the apples, her feet still leading her closer and closer to the orchard. The scent on the air now was completely soporific, lulling. It was very hard to think clearly.

With a huge effort, he spun her round to face him again, pushing them both fiercely back from the fence they were drifting towards, their feet not obeying their heads. With a massive effort of will, the Doctor shoved them away from the sharp iron posts so hard he tore both his hands in the process

'I have it,' he said, fast and intent. 'You know I do. I have it already. You can have it. You can have it. Just…' He glanced at the snake. 'Just, please. Take it from me.'

'He doesn't even care for you!' screamed the snake. 'He lets you bleed and you don't even know it! Will he bleed for you?'

The Doctor lifted his injured hands instinctively, and let the wounds show.

She hadn't even known his blood was red.

'Always,' he said simply.

They both watched as the drops fell, vivid on the bright green grass, forming a 'C'.

The second the first drop hit the ground, she snapped back to him.

'Stop that,' she said, looking directly at him at last. 'Stop it immediately.'

The Doctor reached out, gently, his fingers weaving into her dark hair. He had forgotten how small she was; she barely came up to his chest. 'Look at me,' he ordered sternly

Reluctantly Clara focused her eyes on his.

'It is what you want, I promise.'

This was not quite a lie. He would show her the temptation and fruits of that knowledge; everything he had. But he would also show her what it cost and what it really meant and how, afterwards, the rest of her life would be like a dark, spoiled fruit. She could not do this. She was not capable; it would kill her. Or worse.

Etienne had been quite wrong. He had never tasted the fruit. He had never had to.

Her focus wavered.

'Clara! Look at me. Look at me. You have to let me in. You have to let me. You have to say yes.'

Finally, slowly, she blinked her assent and breathed 'Yes', and he pushed his fingers a little more firmly on the side of her head. A golden light started to flow between them as he moulded their selves together, concentrating on pushing to her an awareness of what was there, what he lived with, what the cost would be; how she must resist the temptation; she must.

Just as he was concentrating on the flow from his brain to hers, however, he stopped, and his eyes flicked open suddenly in surprise as, suddenly, he felt her: felt her self-knowledge buried so deeply underneath, so deep in her subconscious; but that showed what the snake had said was true.

She remembered so little, but it was there, deep in the bone; her frustration and her fear and her pain at being around him, all of it buried so far beneath the surface that she did not understand it herself.

Abruptly, shocked and startled, he jumped back as if electrified, and their connection instantly ceased, far too sharply. Clara crumpled underneath him like a paper doll.

The Doctor stared down at her, horrified, then instantly made use of the situation, grabbing her up in his arms and running for all his life, the sunlight softly glinting in his hair, the deep, corrupt, sweet scent of apples in the air, the shrieking, furious scream of the bright green snake. He tore back to the house of skulls, his heart in his mouth, his shock and incredible regret cluttering up his mind.

'Shut the door!' he yelled at Etienne as he entered.

But Etienne simply laughed and said, 'I thought I wasn't in charge any more,' and did not move his vast limbs away from where he was reprogramming the skeletons.

'*Shut it!*' The deadly sunlight was still streaming in. The Doctor look around for a hanging, a coat, anything, that could cover it, as Clara started to stir in his arms. The light lit up every dark corridor, every grim corner flushing out its secrets to the bright golden glorious flood of tempting rays.

'There it is!' said Etienne, raising his fingers from the screen. 'The robots are all fixed. I am a genius. Guards! Take them!'

There was a rattling noise. The tallest of the skeletons, the one they had first seen on the cliff's edge, came marching into the room, followed by another, then another, then another. The Doctor stood up, carefully. Etienne laughed in triumph.

But instead of seizing the Doctor and Clara, the skeleton did something quite different: he led them up to the door's edge, and slowly laid himself down. Etienne pressed a button on the console and the skeleton spasmed as the white light flashed up and down, but it did not stop what it was doing. Another lay down on top of him, then another and another even as they were shocked, again and again, and Etienne screamed at them, until gradually they filled up the space, every chink, and the light died down and down until it vanished completely.

Clara lay on the floor, her eyes flickering. Eventually she came to, blinking. She looked around the room. 'What happened here?' she asked, gazing at the pile of bones.

Etienne and the Doctor stared at her. Then Etienne turned his attention to the Doctor.

'Those worthless bits of bone,' he growled. 'You utter idiot.'

'They're not worthless bits of bone!' said the Doctor furiously. 'Do you know they even try and warn people who land here? Leave them messages?'

Etienne shrugged. 'They're *robots*.'

'You tell yourself that.'

Etienne shook his head. 'But you came back to this place.'

The Doctor stared at the floor. 'I didn't know what it was then, either,' he said. 'It wasn't protected.'

'Chuh.' Etienne stood up, wheezing slightly. He was not tall. 'How do you stop it?' he asked, suddenly serious. 'How do you stop all that knowledge and that power from making you take over the galaxy? From making you destroy it all? From making you an eater of worlds? How do you stop it?'

The Doctor was still staring quietly at the ground. 'I work at it. Very, very hard. All the time. Every day. And I don't always.'

Etienne gave that maddening grin again. 'But you told the Shadow Proclamation it was here?'

The Doctor nodded.

'And then they "hired" me. Or they thought they did. To protect everybody else.'

The Doctor nodded again, very, very wearily.

Etienne watched him as he moved things into the room; much of the packet food, the water filter, every bit of computer equipment.

'What are you doing, man?' he said, nervous. 'You guys are leaving, right? I mean, you'll need me, right? You'll never get back alone, you'll need me to guide you – there's stuff out there you haven't even seen yet. There's stuff out there I don't even remember making. You gotta watch for that zombie ravine, it's hideous. They've got rakes for hands. Boy, I was out of it that night.'

At that, the Doctor marched forward without saying a word,

took every handset and controller he could find, and crushed them under the heel of his boot. Then he went back to working quietly, saying nothing.

Etienne tried to leave the room, but more skeletons came to block his way. Sweating heavily, he turned round to try and reach his remote control, only to remember that the Doctor had it and it was now sticking out of his top pocket. His manifest unfitness made any attempt to launch himself at the Doctor or Clara laughably feeble, the heavy atmosphere in the room growing increasingly unpleasant. He gave up, and started to whine again.

'They're not real people! I didn't know they were! I just thought—'

The Doctor set down a final pile of blankets, apparently satisfied that was enough. 'You know,' he said, in a voice of great weariness and near infinite sorrow. 'You know I cannot let you free. To sit here, and wait for the deaths of others, and use their remains for your own ends… You have proven yourself too dangerous to be let loose on the universe.'

'They let *you* out,' said Etienne sourly.

'Here is everything you need. You will protect the drawbridge: the skeletons have done their duty well. You may build your little worlds, Etienne, on your computers; you can play in a virtual world till your heart's content, but you must never see sunlight again. I will deadlock seal this room.'

'Nooo!' said Etienne, tears now mingling with the sweat pouring down his face, his eyes darting all around looking for an escape route.

'You can take the drawbridge of course…'

Etienne shook his head frantically. 'No. No no no no.'

'Then we understand each other,' said the Doctor. 'Build virtual worlds of suffering. This one can no longer contain you.'

He moved over and spoke quietly to the skeletons piled by the drawbridge. They rattled once, twice. The Doctor understood.

He took out the remote control and, with a consoling hand on the uppermost skull, gently powered it down until they were, once more, simple piles of bones. Etienne, screaming in disbelief, followed it with his eyes, and the rest of them as they filed out, leaving him alone.

Outside, it didn't take much; a simple act of the sonic screwdriver to deadlock the door for ever. They could hear Etienne inside, cursing and yelling and screaming and banging on it; a toddler in a rage.

'But what about the… the tree,' said Clara, whose memories of exactly what had gone on were hazy and muddled. 'Isn't it round the back of the house?'

'Go look,' said the Doctor, and Clara did, even though it was dark and freezing and once more the empty, horrible windswept plain of before – and remained so, all the way around.

'Where is it?' she asked.

'Through his drawbridge, in that room,' said the Doctor. 'He always controlled the portal.'

'And won't he go through it?'

'He knows exactly what will happen if he does,' said the Doctor. 'The instant he takes a bite of that apple, the cold wind will blow and the sun will disappear and his mind will be full of the knowledge of a universe of pain and suffering and death, and he will have to live inside that mind a long, long time.'

He picked up one of the many loose pebbles then, and hurled it with some force at the horizon. This time, nothing rattled.

'Is that what you have?' Clara asked timidly.

He turned to her with a half-smile. 'Not quite,' he said. 'When you gain knowledge for yourself… when you see the universe and learn about its good and its bad… you get the fairy in the bottom of the box too. You see the whole picture, not just… the entropic chronicle of perpetuity.'

Clara was still thoughtful as they stepped out in the

moonlight. 'Doctor...' she said nervously. 'What are you going to do with him?'

'Oh, I expect the Shadow Proclamation have been looking for him for a long time.' He stared back at the house, shaking his head.

'And, er, how are we going to get off this planet?'

The Doctor gave her a gentle smile. 'Very, very slowly and with great care.'

The Doctor was true to his word. First he gathered all of the remaining skeletons together. Then he sent them out with all the seedlings, to disseminate throughout the planet. He brought the bees and birds out of hyper-sleep and sent them forward to pollinate the seed, and recalibrated the weather centre to give them hyper-fast growing seasons, which meant it was rainy and sunny every five minutes it seemed to Clara, mostly wet.

Every time he emptied out a room, they dismantled the bones and buried them far and wide so they could fertilise the earth, until there were only two rooms left standing; Etienne's, which they gave a wide berth (it had gone very quiet: the Doctor suspected that Etienne had gone straight back into eating and playing with computers and wasn't necessarily having a much different experience to his life before, except now he was doing it virtually), and the library, tidied up, as a shelter from the rainfall.

The rain washed away the scree, and extraordinarily fast the plants began to sprout and take hold, spread about like a desert after rain. They grew up thick and fast. Some Clara had seen before: huge, sprawling bushes of bougainvillea, in thick pinks and purples, bright and popping against the pale blue sky between showers; willows that followed the rivulets of water; sunflowers that sprang up overnight and followed the path of the sun, a banana plantation the Doctor had insisted on. And others she didn't recognise; great yawning bushes that looked like sea anemones; flame-coloured trees in bright red. Every day the landscaped changed; the scents strong on the gentle morning breeze. Vines grew up and wrapped themselves around the two remaining rooms, almost concealing their grisly origins.

Clara sat shelling peas and glanced over at the Doctor, who had taken off his jacket in the sunshine, turned up his sleeves, and was whittling. He was humming a cheerful song of contentment as he did so. A light breeze was ruffling his hair, and she smiled involuntarily as she watched him. He looked up just at that moment and caught her eye and smiled back.

'What?'

Clara shook her head. 'It's just... I can't believe how peaceful it is here now.'

He held her gaze for a long moment. 'I know,' he said. 'But we have to move on.'

She nodded.

'And you...' he said. 'When I was in your head...'

Even though her memories were confused, she remembered glimpses; her inexplicable fury at the ravine, and her sense of him: of pity and of shame.

'Do you still feel like that?' he persisted, obviously uncomfortable with the conversation. 'About me, you know. About what we do. I mean, because, for me. Well. You know. Surprise! Ha!'

Clara picked her words carefully. 'I don't know,' she said, truthfully. 'Sometimes I feel that things are too hard. And sometimes I feel brave as a lion. But I don't know why. It's like a dream I had once, that's just out of reach... but it's always with me.'

'Because I can't... I can't be a *burden*.'

Clara looked at him in surprise. 'But burdens can be shared,' she said gently. 'And I am... I am...'

They were interrupted suddenly by one of the taller skeletons. The Doctor had found old identity passes and names scattered about one of the rooms, but there were so many, so many, and they had not been able to give anyone a name, or a grave.

The adult skeleton before them held up his finger to indicate that he wanted to talk, and the Doctor nodded. Clara came over to watch, as the ash scattered on the ground.

'O-N-E-T-H-I-N-G,' it said. 'T-H-E-N-G-O.'

The Doctor nodded respectfully. 'Of course,' he said. He took the skeleton's claw in his and held it carefully. 'Thank you.'

The skull nodded.

'What?' said Clara.

'Time to leave,' said the Doctor.

The Doctor made final adjustments to the weather station to set it on a smooth path; tidied up carefully, glanced not even once at the locked bone room sitting solitary.

'Why didn't they destroy this planet?' said Clara, as they started to move, following the long marching line of remaining skeletons, who travelled ahead. 'To have all the knowledge in the universe concentrated in such a small way. It's *so* dangerous. Any life form that takes it… it's dangerous for everyone. Wouldn't it be better just to destroy it?'

The Doctor shrugged. 'I don't know,' he said quietly. 'There may come a day when the universe needs that knowledge, when everybody needs it.'

'Who put it there?' said Clara.

'Oh, it has always been there,' said the Doctor. 'And I was just the unutterable, awful fool who told somebody.'

Clara patted his hand. 'But look at it now,' she said, indicating around them. The fresh earth and new moss was soft under her bare feet. The tangle of growth meant the world was a riot of green and cherry blossom; long avenues of new fruit trees, some flowering, some already dropping fruit, like all the seasons come at once.

'This you can have,' said the Doctor, handing her an apple, green and red. It was sweet and sharp all at once and its juices ran down her chin. 'Anyone that lands here now... I hope there will be so many orchards, they won't find that one in a hurry.'

'That's amazing,' she said, looking round. 'But what about all the monsters?'

The Doctor took Etienne's controller from his pocket. 'Quite handy having monsters you can turn on and off at will,' he said. 'Wish they were all like that. But there was only one monster, really.'

'And the big snakes?'

'Oh, they're real,' said the Doctor. 'But hopefully now we've established an ecosystem, they'll be able to survive in it without being half-starved to death and furious.'

'*Hopefully*,' said Clara, still eyeing the trees with some nervousness. But all she could see were brilliant parrots flitting from branch to branch and, from far off, something that sounded a little like the chattering of a monkey.

'You brought *monkeys*?'

'Come on,' said the Doctor. 'You don't grow this many bananas without letting in a few monkeys. That'd just be selfish.'

Finally they reached the large crevasse again that split the world in two, but it was unrecognisable. Now, a massive waterfall, formed from all the rainfall, fell over the side, a rainbow prism dancing off it. Below were fresh waters churning and bouncing, and Clara thought she saw a trout leap high in the sunlight.

The Doctor nodded to the skeleton, who moved forward and, with one superhuman jump, the white lights of the Carnutium filament flickering up and down his frame, landed on the other side. Then another, and another. And they joined hand to foot, and on the near side, the other skeletons joined, hand to foot, then, astonishingly, one figure staying on either side as an anchor, the two sides swung like trapeze artists, until they caught and held hands, and made a bridge.

'Oh my,' said Clara.

'Amazing stuff, Carnutium filament,' said the Doctor. 'He was a clever, clever chap indeed. Such a waste. But this is their last gift to us. And then we must set them free.'

The littlest skeleton was on the far side of the abyss, as the Doctor and Clara carefully picked their way across it. As he usually did, he ran to Clara for a cuddle, his mother not far behind.

Clara held him for a long time in her lap then stood up. 'This is what you all want?' she said.

The figures nodded, and those left behind on the far bank waved.

'To return to the earth,' said the Doctor. 'Where good can be done.'

Clara bestowed one last kiss on the bare white skull. 'Au revoir, mon bout-chou.'

Then the Doctor took the remote from his pocket, still glowing bright white, and hurled it with all his strength into the abyss. It fell so far that no one heard it hit the bottom, but instantly, as if someone had cut the strings, the bones all collapsed to the ground, and were still.

'Thank you,' said the Doctor, and Clara, too, nodded.

They covered what they could in fresh flowers as a burial mound, then continued on, through a beautiful avenue that now opened up through the forest, daisies and mushrooms and snowdrops flourishing at the roots, fresh green leaves on every twig and branch. Clara felt a movement in the branches to her right, but she did not turn her head. She did, though, take the Doctor's hand.

The great expanses of sand had gone; instead, when they emerged from the forest, she saw they had been replaced by a wildflower meadow. Rabbits hopped through meadowsweet, sweet peas and waving daffodils. And straight across the plain, under a bower, Clara saw it, the TARDIS – the real, solid TARDIS; not an illusion this time, ringed round with newly sprung pink roses. She ran to it with a happy gasp, the Doctor very close behind her.

The Doctor plucked one of the beautiful blooms entwined around the door and, carefully, put it behind her ear. She flushed at his touch, then smiled.

'Senorita!' he said. 'Shall we go somewhere awesome? With a name and everything?'

'Heh. We should name this place.'

'No,' said the Doctor. 'We should not.'

Clara immediately plucked a rose of her own and, stretching up, tucked it behind his ear, then put her hands on her hips and regarded the results with a disappointed expression.

'Stick to hats?' said the Doctor.

'Definitely.'

'Just as well I look so good in all the hats,' he yelled, as he vanished inside the TARDIS.

Several minutes later he came back, with a small, heavy narrow replica of the TARDIS, about waist height, with a real telephone attached to it. Next to it was a sign that could be read in any language.

'If you have crash-landed here, call this number. Advice and Assistance Obtainable Immediately.'

It looked incongruous in the beautiful meadow. But also somehow quite right. He disappeared back inside.

Clara peered after him, then turned around and glanced one last time at the buzzing, green, sunlit world around her, as a butterfly passed her by on its merry way, its cream wings fluttering happily.

'I am… going to be fine,' she said to herself. And she briefly touched once more the rose in her hair, then slipped inside the TARDIS herself as the butterfly rose on a zephyr in the suddenly empty air, and flew up again and again, higher than the greenest treetops.

He was in the Hungarian Bathroom when it happened, brushing his teeth. He didn't actually need to brush his teeth – his body didn't allow the sort of decay toothbrushes were supposed to prevent – but he liked to do it anyway because he enjoyed the mintiness frothing over his tongue and out of his mouth. It was like a carwash for the tonsils. Occasionally he pretended to be a dragon while he did his incisors, scowling appallingly into the Rococo mirror and blowing menacing bubbles until either he or the image was cowed into surrender. He was fairly sure, at that moment, that he had the enemy on the run.

'Aaaaaarrrrrrrrgggggh!' he told his reflection. He did some hand gestures, too, because after all a lot of communication was non-verbal. The reflection tried the same tactic, but couldn't pull it off. *Hah! Take that, you scoundrel!*

He had to acknowledge that he got like this when he travelled alone. He tended to be a bit distracted, a bit wibbly. He began thinking about people he'd left behind, people he didn't see any more for very good reasons. People like Donna. The Doctor-Donna, who had known him absolutely, for a little while, and who didn't know any more who he was. And Martha Jones. Martha Jones who'd left him, rather than the other way around. Had to respect that.

Had to love it.

And then, yes, all right: he'd spent the last two weeks growing oak trees in a park the TARDIS had apparently generated at some point for reasons of its own. He'd caught himself using the artificial sun to make the branches grow into the word 'Rose', and hurriedly decided it was time to move on.

On the upside, he was pretty sure the guy in the mirror was

ready to throw in the towel. Which would be ideal, because he needed a towel.

'Aaaaaarrggggh!' he said again. 'Aaarghaahahrhgh!'

Then there was a really, really loud bang. He hadn't known a bang like it in…

It was a very, very long time. There had been a Cro Magnon alpha once who was killed by a falling mammoth. For some reason no one entirely understood, it was a fixed point in time. You couldn't do anything about it. Young Time Lords were shown recordings as a sort of learning experience. Sometimes, they were told, this is the universe, and that's it. The mammoth got caught in a scree-slide and went off an overhanging cliff, trumpeting sadly all the way down – and it was a long way – and there below him there was the alpha roaring his defiance at an enemy troop and beating his chest: 'I am mighty! Fear me! Raaaawr.' Lots of raaawr. Then there was this great, awful, hugely significant moment where he looked up and saw the mammoth and you could almost swear he said 'oh, dear', and the mammoth seemed to be looking down and saying very much the same thing. And then both of them were definitely extinct.

Bang.

And now, in the Hungarian Bathroom, with the TARDIS ringing around him like a huge cast iron bell and the Rococo mirror (Giorgio Innocenti of Venice, genius, loved cinnamon buns, drank too much and sang rude songs about the duke; bad idea, long prison sentence, very sad) now in pieces in the sink, he was pretty sure he knew how that felt. To be hit by a mammoth. To be a mammoth hit by a planet. Either, really.

Fifteen seconds later he was staring at the displays in the console room. He squinted through his glasses at the lambent tachyonic visualiser. And then he said quite a lot of bad words one after another in just under a hundred distinct languages.

He'd hit a temporal mine, or, to put it less technically, a big ugly imploding timey-wimey blowy-uppy thing. A BUIT-

WB-UT. Acronyms sometimes made things sound better. He conceded that this one didn't.

The bad news was that temporal mines were on the very short list of things which could actually damage a TARDIS. Destroy one, even. Certainly hurt it. And the really bad news was that there weren't any of them left in the entire universe, anywhere, because they were supposed to be timelocked with the rest of the war, except that this one evidently wasn't. Oh, no, this one was here and it was behaving very oddly indeed, and now it was doing something with really a lot of transtachyonic sheer, something which was frankly a bit impossible, and that was just rude. That much torsion could actually decalibrate the capacitance smoothifier and pop the seams of the TARDIS like a bag full of soup. Splat. Splatter. Splunch. Except not, because the soup would go into the bag and take the kitchen with it. Oh, wait, that was even odder –

He just had time to say something which would get you arrested on the Omogan Planet of Rain.

All the lights went out, and he heard a triple impact, like an alien heart or the footstep of something huge walking on three legs.

Pah pah POM.

He stood in the darkness listening, and hoping it was still outside. It must be, though. The TARDIS wouldn't let anything inside.

The longer he stood there, the more he wasn't sure.

Christina was a respectable sort of widow. There was another sort, all dancing on tables and keeping late hours with poets, but she didn't hold with any of that. She might have been forgiven if, being made single at her relatively young age – she was 35 – she had gone a little mad and done a lot of regrettable things. Oh, not that she was dull. There might well come a day when she would unbutton a little, even be said to cut loose.

Time would heal all wounds, no doubt.

If only it didn't move so slowly about its business, leaden and deadly bread-and-butter and no cake. Every day she could remember was exactly like every other, stretching back to the moment she had opened her doors to paying customers after her husband had passed away.

But that wasn't quite true. The telephone was coming to Jonestown: the mayor had announced it. He would have one on his desk for calling to the Parish Council, and another for London, though he didn't see the point of that, and the police station would have one, and the firehouse, too, and Mr Heidt who had bought the big house at the edge the park, the old Lord's manor, he was so rich – apparently – that he would have one, too.

Hers was a good life. She interfered with no one, and no one interfered with her.

She smiled at this happy thought, and went to clean the Reading Room. She had guests coming, day after tomorrow, and the reading room was always popular at teatime. She opened the door, and stopped.

There was a man.

He did not look like a murderer or a villain, but she knew you could not always tell by the looking. He was reading, evidently, and this was reassuring because even if he was in the wrong place by definition, this being her house and she having no idea who he might be, he was also doing the right thing in this place, reading in the Reading Room, and that was a point in his favour. All the same, before speaking, she stepped to the fireplace so that the poker was within easy reach. She could smell damp in the stones, mould growing in the chimney. She must get someone in to deal with it, or guests would complain. The books would suffer.

Irrelevant landlady detail. She shut her eyes briefly for focus, then gave a stern cough.

'Excuse me.'

She didn't want to be excused at all. She wanted him to give an account of his presence, and that right speedily or she'd bash him with the poker.

If she had set off a bomb under his chair she could hardly have achieved a more spectacular reaction. He jerked up and out of the recliner, arms windmilling and legs abruptly about six inches too long for his trousers. The book – not one of hers, full of technical drawings and the like, he must have brought it with him – went spiralling up in the air and came down with curious neatness on the seat he had left behind, and he gaped at her for a longish while as if she was the first woman he'd ever seen, and then his mouth opened to let out an incredulous:

'What?!'

His amazement was so palpable that she dismissed the poker for the moment, and carried on speaking. 'I said, "Excuse me",' she said, still stern but allowing for the possibility that it was all a comical misunderstanding. Perhaps she'd left the front door open after going to the grocer – the latch was a little soft – and he'd come in here to wait for her return. Or something. There were explanations, thousands of them. Tens of thousands. Numbers larger than that, numbers you'd need new ways of writing down...

He said 'What?' again.

'This is my house,' she said, feeling a little guilty now at having given him such a shock. 'My Reading Room. What can I do for you?'

'Your house?'

'Yes. My house.' She hoped he wasn't going to say surely it was her husband's house. She might have to go for the poker after all, and claim he'd made an inappropriate advance.

'Your house!' he said instead, in the tones of one coming to terms with the idea.

'Yes.'

'Your house!' No doubt about it. The light had dawned. He

smiled. Beamed, even. 'Your house. Of course it is. Where are my manners? I'm with The Library, we're just looking for lost books.' He produced a wallet, showed her a piece of paper. 'And there's one. They get everywhere, don't they, books? Little scamps.' He nodded to himself, gathered up the manual he had been reading and shoved it in his pocket.

She peered at the paper. She said, blankly, 'It's blank.'

He stared at her again, looked at it. 'So it is! Wrong wallet, my mistake. Must have left the card in my other trousers. Lovely house. Lovely library. Really amazing. Oooh, look, there's a copy of *Great Expectations* up there, I've never read that one, I hear it's awful. "Do a comedy," I told him. "Everyone loves *Christmas Carol*."'

She didn't bother to comment on this ridiculous statement; she just waited with what her husband had called her organist's look, because he said church organists always knew how to silence wayward young men and so did she. It worked. He wilted a bit.

'This is my library,' she said. 'In my house. So for the last time: what are you doing here?'

He stroked his chin. It was a fine chin, she thought. No doubt many young women – and, yes, some not so young – had made fools of themselves over this man. Simon had been dead for three years and more. It wasn't a crime to notice.

She stamped hard on that thought, and waited.

'Paying guest,' he suggested.

'Fifty pounds a week, in advance, plus breakfast. How long will you be here?'

'Indefinitely. Hang on, fifty quid?'

'Plus breakfast!'

'That's a bit steep, even for...' He stopped. 'Where are we, anyway?'

Fifty pounds was fifty pounds, even if the customer was a lunatic. 'Wales,' she told him staunchly.

He sighed. 'Yes,' he said. 'Of course. In all the universe, space and time, it turns out however far you go there's mostly Wales.'

He stared off into space – literally into space, she was fairly sure, his gaze seemed to fix on a horizon so far beyond her damasked wall that she was almost a little envious – and when the silence became a little awkward she asked for his name, for the visitor's book. She was fairly sure he was about to say 'Smith' when something stopped him. His mouth – a good mouth, lean and twitching upwards at the corners – started to form the letter 'S', but then a shadow crossed his face and he changed his mind. 'J… Jer- Jah- Juh- Jo… J-J-oooones,' he said. 'Definitely. Jones. John Jones. With a "J". My name,' in case it hadn't been clear enough that it wasn't, 'is John J-ones.'

'Well,' she replied, 'you'll fit right in, then,' and took his hand because he had it stuck out there for her to shake and if she didn't she would seem rude. 'Welcome to Jonestown.'

'Jonestown,' he repeated. 'Of course. Very nice!'

She wondered if he had somehow not known where he was.

The handshake lasted an uncomfortable moment and he said 'John Jones' a couple more times while he waggled her arm up and down, stretching his lips around the second part to get used to it. To escape, she asked if he would like a full breakfast. He beamed.

'Eggs! Bacon! Tomatoes! Fried bread! That'll kill you, fried bread. Clogs up the arteries. Well, it would. I've got tiny… things… in my blood, sluice it out again. So pile it up, *allons-y*—' he broke off. 'I'm sorry, we haven't been formally introduced.'

She felt curiously that it mattered to him very much what she said. 'Christina,' she answered.

'Yes. Christina. Of course, you are. Hello, Christina! Very nice to meet you, I'm—'

'John Jones,' she said, saving him the trouble.

He smiled again, and it was like the sun coming up.

'Welcome,' she said, and he smiled again as if that was a

pleasant surprise as well.

When he'd eaten his eggs, he announced his intention of going out for a walk. 'Unless there's a bus?'

'No, no bus.'

'No big red bus? They go like the clappers, buses. Sometimes it seems they're just flying. Through the traffic, obviously. Bus lanes.'

She shook her head, thinking again that he was a very odd person.

At the door, he turned. 'Thank you, Christina de Souza,' he said.

While she was washing the plates, she suddenly wondered how he had known her unmarried name. But it was unsettling, so she consigned it to the place where she kept all unsettling thoughts, the enormous dark lake in her mind's eye. It was a lonely spot, green and bare and silent, and she let things slip below the oily waters and then they didn't bother her again.

Still, it was odd.

He left the inexplicable house and its unbelievable occupant and went for a walk along the implausible street, peering at unfeasible doorknockers and improbable geraniums, and above all at the impossible people: here, there and everywhere. This was, indisputably, the TARDIS. He could feel it, knew it the way you know you're wearing shoes, and the wind was sweet with the faintest scent of coral and anti-polarised neutrons – and something else, like peat or wet wallpaper, the smell of Jonestown.

The TARDIS contained any number of things – literally, any number, think of a number and that was the right number, then think of another number which was astronomically different and that was the right number too, because that was what a TARDIS was, a place where ordinary numbers broke down and conventional notions did not apply – but it emphatically did not contain a thriving market town with really good bacon and eggs and Christina de Souza running a boarding house. Lady Christina, cat burglar to the aristocracy, thief of museum pieces – well, all right, they had that in common – a woman who could barely look at something beautiful without pinching it. She would have been perfect, just perfect if she'd been born a couple centuries earlier. All those English queens… they'd have loved her. And Catharine of Aragon. Ooh, and Reinette de Pompadour. Now those two could have made some trouble… Christina de Souza on the TARDIS. That was something he would have noticed. Probably when things started to go missing.

Except that here he was, in the TARDIS, in the main street, and it was all physically real. Except again, if it was real, where was the flying bus? And why didn't she know who he was?

And, rather more important: was the whole thing about to implode into a final and appalling nothingness which would devour him and the TARDIS and leave a gaping hole in the universe which nothing would ever entirely fill? That had seemed to be what the temporal mine was aiming for. Which did not explain what he was doing here, not even a bit.

He couldn't hear the noise from all that temporal sheer any more – assuming that was what he'd been hearing when he was back out there in the console room and not in here in Jonestown – but that didn't mean the TARDIS wasn't still under attack. So, the agenda: find the problem, fix the problem, don't get imploded. Did we tick the box marked 'Yes, please, the deadly time-space catastrophe'? Not in the slightest. *Allons* not even a little bit *y* in that direction, at all.

But the agenda would have to include making sure Jonestown didn't get imploded either. He didn't let other people pay for his salvation. Not ever again.

So he wandered and peered at things. He peered at the fishmonger's – the old lady behind the counter gave him a happy smile and whispered something approving he didn't quite hear but which got a lot of giggles from the other old ladies in a queue for kippers. He thought he recognised one of them from somewhere, but he felt that about lots of people. It was a consequence of spending hundreds of years drifting through time: faces got a bit recurrent. There'd been a flautist in Basingstoke who was the spitting image of Ivan the Terrible. But still, Jonestown seemed very full of echoes, of people he almost knew. Christina de Souza and all.

He saluted the jellied eel counter and wandered out. Ooh, there was a pub. Nice pub. It was roomy, dim, and rather comfy. He lolled on a chair, feeling the wood and the cushion. Very nice. Great smell: wood and detergent and fresh flowers and old cloth. Varnish and polish. There was a box of games by the window, games he didn't know how to play. He knew how to play pretty much every game ever made. But these, no. They were by Heidt & Co of Jonestown. Puzzles. He experimented with one for a while. It puzzled him for longer than he would have expected, until he realised it had two halves and you had to solve them at the same time, and then the pieces came apart in his hands. Lovely. He looked around.

He suspected the old men at the bar belonged to the women in the fishmonger's. The publican called them Old Owen and Young Dai, and Old Owen was – inevitably – just a little bit younger than Young Dai. They eyed his suit with a weary sort of irritation, the sort of disregard old men everywhere reserve for younger men – or at least for men who appear to be younger – and when he ordered a lemonade and sat in the corner sucking noisily through a straw they didn't seem to think much more about him. They were rather busy, actually, disparaging the newly arrived Mr Heidt, who was evidently hot stuff in Jonestown and had a weather station on his lawn. Neither Young Dai nor Old Owen, it seemed, had much truck with meteorology. They had a good friendship, he thought. Old friends together, and doubtless their wives were like that too and the four of them gabbed and grumbled and no one was lonely. Wouldn't do to get old and lonely.

Stone walls, dark wood, horse brasses. No jukebox, no television, not even a pool table. Just places to sit and a bar and somewhere what seemed like a pretty good kitchen. That was something he liked about the twentieth century. Quite a few other bits of it were pretty awful, but pubs were properly pubby, with pub grub and chunky glasses to drink out of, and whole families came in on Sundays for lunch. He pondered. Jonestown. People. TARDIS. Pub. Lemons. He liked lemons. They made you make funny faces when you bit them, and a very, very long way in the future there was a really amazing planet where they'd evolved into people and lived in harmony with a variety of hyper-intelligent bee. Evolution. Thousands and thousands of years of tiny changes could turn little burning sparks of chemistry into people, into monsters and angels and even human beings. It happened everywhere. You went to an empty planet, took your eye off it for a billion years, came back and, boom, there it was: life. Stinky, slooshy, complex, amazing life. It always found ways to surprise you. Or maybe that was because it happened in time, and he didn't always pay much attention to how time looked from the inside.

The universe was brilliant. Every last, ridiculous nook and corner. He loved it. Even this bit, although this bit was slightly alarming because, well, there was a leftover war machine trying to open the TARDIS like a bag of soup. Or an oyster. Or a tin of golden syrup. Amazing how sticky those got. Lemon and golden syrup, though, there was a combination which could blow your socks off. Taste supernova. He –

And then, for no reason at all, everything changed.

Over by the fireplace was a metal silhouette of a chicken, technically a cockerel. He had dismissed it at first as a bit of ordinary pub bric-a-brac, but now he saw that it wasn't and it riveted his attention. It was a weathervane, or, rather, it was part of one. Affixed to the feet of the cockerel – he was a proud enough sort of fellow, strutting his two-dimensional stuff across a cast-iron cornfield – were a set of metal gears, and a drive shaft went off at right angles and then, presumably, up the chimney. Very unusual arrangement. Unique, even. And now there was a creaking and groaning and the shaft started to turn, yawing one way and then the other, and the cockerel spun around and around, and the grumbling and joshing in the pub faded away.

The man calling himself Jones looked at them: grave, unhappy faces and concealed fear. They'd built the weathervane to tell them something, and they didn't enjoy seeing it work. Bad news, then. Bad enough that they didn't complain about it. No one said anything at all.

Everyone watched the cockerel go around and around as if it was really important. And he was pretty sure they were right. Never underestimate the value of local knowledge – especially when the locality in question is a Welsh village in a polydimensional quasi-space in the fractal layers of a time machine. Old Time Lord proverb. Aeons old, if he remembered to pop back to the early days of the universe and say it out loud once this was all over, and he was definitely going to make a mental note about that. He might go and say it to that Cro Magnon alpha.

He could feel a funny sort of pressure all around him, knew the TARDIS was letting him know she wasn't happy, that she was under attack. *This is what it feels like to be her.*

The chicken slowed, wobbled, and then pointed firmly east.

'Storm coming, then,' Owen said into the quiet.

'Likely,' Dai agreed.

The publican looked up from the till. 'Good storm?' he asked hesitantly. 'Proper storm, I mean?'

There was a longish pause.

'Likely not,' Dai said.

The publican swallowed and sighed. 'No, I suppose not.'

The old men looked at one another. 'Could be it's time to take the girls home,' Owen said.

Dai nodded. 'Could be.'

They waved to the publican and shuffled out, and with them, discreetly, the rest of the pub. The man calling himself John Jones blew air into his cheeks.

'Nice puzzles,' he called to the publican. 'This one really had me going for a bit.'

'Oh, those. We got them free. Mr Heidt's just come, you see. Wants to make an impression. Glad someone likes them. Most of my regulars are a bit less sure, I'm afraid.'

'Well, new ideas.'

'Quite so, sir. Begging your pardon, but I might close up, sir, pretty soon, if it's all the same to you,' the publican said hopefully to him when they were alone in the saloon bar. 'Don't want to be a bother. I expect you've got somewhere to stay close by, have you?'

'Oh, yes. Of course. Wouldn't do to be out in a storm, would it?'

'No, sir,' the publican agreed. 'No, it wouldn't. Very wise, I must say.'

'Mind you, I quite like a wander in the rain. Thunder and lightning, even. Exciting. Move slowly, don't build up a charge, it's perfectly safe, isn't it?'

The publican looked away. 'I gather it might be, under normal circumstances, yes. Very nice. Romantic, even.'

'But?'

'But I can't say as these are exactly normal circumstances, sir. Not precisely.'

'But you'd rather not explain.'

'No, sir.'

'You look like a bloke I used to know. Soldier. I never explained anything to him, either. Now I see why he always found it so annoying. Really not going to tell me anything at all?'

'I can't say as I'd know how to begin.'

'As a matter of interest: which direction is your Mr Heidt's house? Just wondering, I won't bother him.'

The publican glanced eastwards. 'I don't know as it would be right to say, sir. Irresponsible, you see. You should get home.'

'But if I said I was going for a stroll, didn't need an umbrella…'

'I'd heartily urge you not to dally, sir. I really would.'

'Oh, I never dally,' he said. 'I wander, I deviate, I go off on tangents and sometimes circumambulate; I occasionally shilly-shally, dawdle or potter. I procrastinate, ratiocinate, and from time to time I do actually get lost. But I never dally. Bad for the brain.'

And he walked out into the gathering storm.

There was indeed a dark cloud looming out towards the east, a pendulous monster grumbling and growling to itself, and he could feel the psychic backwash already. Your average rainstorm tasted of mountains and seas, of the anticipation of drenched laundry and of crops raised and eaten. It was a real old lifecycle smorgasbord. The right sort of storm could make you feel alive and perky and even frisky. And soggy, obviously. But this one had none of that easy nature, no goodwill, no lightness. It reeked of smashing things flat, of pounding them into nothingness.

Say one thing for Dai and Owen, say this: they knew a bad'un when they saw it.

The first bolt of lightning flickered, stark nacreous white cracking from cloud to cloud. Then another, and a moment later the thunder from the first. But no rain. No water. Nothing which would nurture, just a warm, gritty wind and the prickle of electricity – and a boiling, metallic fury he could feel in his gums.

He smacked his lips and ran his tongue over his teeth, then walked across the cobbles towards it. The storm seemed to be over the town and yet it was right here, in the street. There was a shape in it, in the dust and the clouds and the roiling shadows. A man-shape, if a man kept blowing himself out like the flame of a candle.

'There you are,' he murmured, into the wind. 'But what are you?'

The answer, when it came, was very loud and blew him all the way back down the street.

Christina de Souza could hear the storm blowing up outside her windows, and she smiled and hunkered down in her chair. There was nothing more pleasant than being inside when the weather outside was bad, hearing the rattle of the casements and knowing that however rotten it got out there it was safe in here.

There were no more tasks left in the day. She could sit and read her book – a most disreputable detective story – and later she would make herself dinner and enjoy some music on the radio. Solitude was not loneliness, and she never really felt alone, anyway. She turned the page. She was reasonably sure that Aaron Catton would survive his latest encounter with the Iron Fist Gang, but at the moment his situation definitely seemed perilous. She wondered what his family thought about his line of work, and whether his parents ever wished he'd just marry the curvaceous Jessica Jarvis who worked on the news desk at the City Paper and choose a less perilous profession. Surely, they must. She turned the page.

The front door slammed open – really slammed, she could hear the doorknob crunch the plaster of her hallway wall – and then the wind roared in, a real gale force like nothing she'd ever known. The geegaws on her mantelpiece shuddered, toppled and flew off. The china dog shattered on the floor. She heard windows banging elsewhere in the house, shattering, and bangs and crashes as more of her possessions fell destructively to Earth, and then John Jones was staggering into her parlour, barrelled along by a vicious torrent of air which seemed almost to be just for him. The house shook as if struck, and she realised as all the lights went out that it had been, that her home had actually been struck by lightning, and then it was struck again and she could smell burning, then and again and again.

PAH! PAH! POMMMM!

A windowpane cracked, and then another, and Jones shouted 'Run!'

'My house!' she objected, as he grabbed for her hand. She batted him off.

He dropped down beside her, spoke fast and very earnestly. 'It's on fire and in a minute it will be more on fire and then so will we. Really, Christina: you need to run!'

'It's all I have!'

'I'll get you another one!'

He hauled her out of the chair, and abruptly she was flying down the corridor to the back door, almost literally flying, and behind her the chair was lit actinic white and then it was gone, burned to ash by lightning, and she could see – it was impossible, and absurd, but she could see the actual storm inside her house and chasing them down the corridor, a faceless, twisting snarl of hateful energy reaching out like an arm.

She could feel her hair lifting on her body, felt her clothes spark, and knew that was what happened just before you were hit.

They were nearly at the garden door. She couldn't imagine how it would do them any good.

She wondered whether what happened next would hurt. She thought, probably, that it would.

Jones – and she was pretty sure this was somehow all his fault – reached into his jacket and produced a short, glowing stick of metal and pointed it at the door. She heard the lock click, saw him reach out for the handle.

She looked back, and saw a snake of white light reach out for her, but strangely slowly, as if time was stopping and she could just step outside.

He opened the door.

And drew her through into somewhere which was not her garden. It was... big. She felt an eerie sense of space and scale. The walls were segmented like a circus tent, and each segment was bordered by buttresses of metal or of something else, something which looked as if it had grown there. Coral? Was there a giant coral reef in her garden now? What about planning permission? There'd be the most terrible row.

He closed the door smartly, and she heard the howl of the storm, the dull impact against the other side of the door, and knew with absolute certainty that there was no way it was coming in here. Not through that door. She reached out and touched it. Cool and metallic. There were discs on it, or shields, which buzzed under her fingertips.

She looked around, and there he was, ruffled but composed, sprawled on a pile of hats. Not just a pile. A dune, she thought, like in the desert. There were modern hats in the most rakish style, Scotch bonnets and metal helmets which ought to be on a knight, and some strange hats which were only hats because they clearly went on your head.

On his head.

'Who are you, really?' she said.

He smiled brightly. 'I'm the Doctor,' he said, as if that explained everything.

They climbed across a small mountain of shoes. The air smelled of salt water, and she thought about coral again. 'Where are we?' she asked.

'The TARDIS,' he said. 'Storeroom 90. Well, we were always in the TARDIS. But this is where I keep all my old clothes.'

'Right,' she said, patiently, 'and where is my garden?'

He looked back at her, helped her up onto a stack of brogues.

'My garden?' she persisted. 'Which is what is usually behind that door.'

'It's where it always is. Which isn't quite as simple as you might think.'

She didn't think any of this was simple. There was a door over the next rise, though, and she slid down behind him. 'If you open that, is there going to be a storm on the other side? Will we die?'

'No.' He hesitated. 'Well, probably not. Well, I don't think so. Well.' He frowned, whipped out the metal thing again. 'Sonic screwdriver.' He pointed it at the door, peered at it. 'No,' he said more confidently. 'No.'

'And what was that back there?'

'Storm. Nasty one.'

'Which came into my house.' She scowled at him. 'I'd like the truth, please.'

'All right. Mobile discorporate mechanico-temporal intelligence manifesting in a semi-stable combat aspect with limited power reserves.' He opened the door, and stepped through. 'You don't get many of those to the pound. A lot like your bacon and eggs, by the way.'

She understood the words, most of them, but the combination made no sense at all.

'Limited?' she demanded.

'Yes. Well, everything's limited. Almost everything. But this is more limited than most things. As in, limited energy. Comprehensibly so. A few days, maybe, at this rate.'

'Well, that must be good.'

He looked dubious. She realised she could hear a sort of endless, low-level groaning, as if she were in an old submarine, far below the surface of the sea. Too far below. And then the noise again, without the fury but with a sort of patient inevitability which was almost worse.

Pah pah pom.

He looked up abruptly with a sort of awful anticipation, then shook his head when the sound died away, as if he was being silly. 'Not the storm. Temporal sheer. For now, anyway.'

'Oh, good.'

'Hmm? No. That's disastrous.' He hesitated, rubbed his ribs. 'Ow. We just lost navigation. And the first-floor kitchen. Well. There goes Christmas dinner.'

She was about to point out that she had no idea what that meant, that Christmas was months away, that his ribs couldn't possibly tell him anything of the kind. And then, as she saw what was in the next room, she said, 'Oh.'

'On the upside,' he said, 'if it hadn't been a limited construction, I could never have used the TARDIS safety system to get us back into the central phase nexus. On the downside, temporal sheer inside and outside the TARDIS. Well, that and... Are you all right?'

She was staring at the room. The floor. The walls. Technically it was a lot like the last one, with the same alarmingly unfamiliar curves and colours. But it was also not the same at all, because it did not contain clothes.

'What... what's this?'

'Storeroom 89.'

'And these are really... diamonds?'

'Mm. Yes. I did say I'd get you another house.' He filled one pocket. Millions of pounds, she thought. Millions and millions and millions and... She folded her arms so as not to reach out and grab a great handful. He looked at her curiously, and she flinched as he poked the screwdriver thing in her direction. It tickled. 'It's all right,' he said. 'Harmless.' She wondered if he meant her. 'Hmm. Come on. Just through here.'

He led the way, and she followed in his steps, absurdly worried about crushing the shining points of light beneath her feet.

The next door opened into a metal corridor, and he led her unerringly left, right, down, up some stairs and then they were in an arched, circular room with a strange central machine, and he seemed to relax.

'Console room,' he said. 'We're safe here. For now, anyway.'

'Who are you?' she demanded again.

'Actually, that's not the question,' he replied. 'The real question is: who are you? Because you're not Christina de Souza, I know that.'

'I certainly am!'

'Not so much. I've met Christina de Souza. Saved the world with her. And she kissed me.' She jolted up, outraged. He raised a hand. 'That's exactly what I mean! You're not her. She'd have gone all sultry and pouty when I said that. And a room full of diamonds? The Christina I know would be asking if she could borrow a sack. Well, she'd have nicked a sack, if I had a sack. Which I do. Thousands of them. Storeroom 104.' He watched her.

She didn't say 'Where's that?' and knew he'd been wondering if she would.

The woman who certainly wasn't Christina de Souza was taking all this rather quietly, he thought. He had given her the basic class in time travel, the TARDIS, and himself, and she had just nodded as if each new idea just explained something she'd always wondered about. When something came along which would really worry someone else, she just dropped it into some sort of silence in her mind and it went down and away and that was that.

It was a useful trait, he supposed, but it made her a bit less satisfying to be around. He rather liked having people shriek and goggle when they saw the TARDIS. Granted, she hadn't seen the outside and then the inside, which was the real shocker for most of his passengers, but the console room itself was still worth a goggle. More than one. The last TARDIS, bounded but infinite, travelling through time and space with the last of the Time Lords. It's got to be worth a second look, surely.

So if she wasn't Christina de Souza, who was she? The scans from the sonic had been a bit vague. Yes, she was human, in that she was human-shaped and made up of tiny bits of biological material working in close cooperation to produce a functioning organism, and she wasn't a clone or a memory, but she was also not Earth-human, she didn't have all the muck from red meat and burned fossil fuels and really dodgy nuclear technology. So why did she look like Christina, who had never actually been inside the TARDIS? And why did she think she was Christina? That wasn't biological. And then again, she seemed to be a lot younger than she appeared. A lot a lot, if you believed the sonic – which he did, because sonics don't lie – but only sort of, because time was a bit compressed and messy in the TARDIS at the moment, and one man's week was another man's millennium.

She was talking. Oh, and he was answering. Multitasking. Very fashionable, but he probably ought to pay attention to his mouth in case it said anything it shouldn't.

'So you're a time traveller.' She was still getting her head around that.

'Time Lord. Lord of Time. Yes.'

'How can you be a Lord of Time?'

'Well. How can you be a Lord of anything?'

'You conquer it and stand on top of it waving a stick,' she said tartly.

'Right. Yes. That's… clearly we didn't do that. At all. That's primitive mammalian behaviour, and we were the most advanced race in the universe.'

'So who did you go to war with? Who could possibly stand up to you?'

'Oh, the Daleks. They were technologically advanced but really… nasty.'

'And the Time Lords were nice?'

He thought about that. 'On balance, no.'

'But the Daleks made this thing, this temporal mine. Because it tried to destroy you.'

'Um.' She was giving him that look again, the one which said he wasn't fooling her, the one she had dished out when he tried the psychic notepaper and she just saw... paper. He sighed. 'I don't know. They might have. Or not. By the end of the war... well, we'd stolen so much of their technology and they'd stolen so much of ours, there wasn't much to choose between us, science wise. And half of these things got captured and subverted and put back out there, then recaptured and deprogrammed and put somewhere else, even the mine probably doesn't know what side it's on any more. And it shouldn't be here at all. Look,' he pointed at the display above the zoomifier, realising belatedly that she couldn't read it. 'Here,' he said, 'this is the temporal substrate. Think of it as being like an Emmental cheese. Lots of holes. And we took a single hole and we put it somewhere else and locked it there for ever.'

'Another cheese?'

That was a ridiculous way of looking at it. He rather approved. 'Yes. A very small, perfectly isolated cheese which can never be eaten, and which will exist in its own perfect moment after this universe and the next one and the one after that have boiled away into dust.'

She nodded.

He went on. 'This thing has somehow escaped from that cheese and ended up back in ours, and now it's broken, and it's trying to do what it's programmed to do. Sort of.'

'Can you stop it?'

'Definitely. Probably definitely. I'm the Doctor.'

'How?'

'Thhhhhat sometimes takes a bit longer. Comes to me in flashes.'

'And what about Jonestown?'

'Yes,' he said. 'What about Jonestown? What is it? Where did it come from? The mine's broken. Well, old. Old and bit weird. It's supposed to suck the TARDIS into a decohering singularity and shut the door for ever.'

'Make another cheese and keep you there.'

'No. Cheese. No, it's… Yes, all right. A really nasty, terrifying cheese which is slowly consuming itself and everything around it until even the rind just boils away you're left with nothing, not even the space where a cheese used to be. But that's not what it's doing. It's trying to tear the TARDIS apart and implode her. You can't do that with a TARDIS. There are safety features. Because if you did, you'd take about four per cent of the observable universe with you. So it's like trying to open a jam jar with blancmange… except if you could get the interior space of a jam jar to start filling up with blancmange… sooner or later that would make a big bang.' An actual Big Bang, but there was no point going into that. 'So the question is, is Jonestown part of the attack? Which is why who you are is really important. Because if Jonestown is part of the mine, then so are you.'

He peered at her, and wondered whether she'd suddenly turn into something strange and terrifying.

She didn't.

Still didn't.

Didn't.

Didn't.

Apparently wasn't going to.

Well, that was a relief.

And definitely not a disappointment, at all.

Of course she was the real Christina de Souza. She knew her own life perfectly. She had been born in this town, grown up, gone elsewhere and fallen unwisely and gloriously in love, lost her husband, and come home to be small and calm and to live through her days of sorrow.

Except that she couldn't really remember any of it. She knew it, but she knew it like something she had read, and she was increasingly uncertain if it had ever happened, or happened to her. It didn't feel real the way the Doctor did, the way today did. It felt... flat.

But if she was some part of an artificial intelligence, or a terrible time weapon, or something from his world... shouldn't she understand what was going on? What if she'd just popped into existence somehow, and any moment she was just going to pop out, never knowing? Would he save her from that, at least? Would he fetch her back again? Could he?

She glanced over at him. He was pacing and muttering. He seemed to need to talk, not just to himself but to someone else, so every so often she asked a question. It evidently wasn't important what she said so long as it was open-ended. If she said something blatantly irrelevant, he went off on a tangent. At the moment, because she'd wondered aloud if she'd ever see her goose-down duvet again, he was talking about the sectional structure of feathers and its relationship to something called Jaffey Curvation. She looked at the dial nearest to her, then the screen over to one side.

'Is this a map of the town?' she asked, looking at it.

'Mm? Yes.'

'Then it's growing.'

He scampered over. 'Growing?' Took his glasses off, put them on again. 'Yes! It is. Growing. How is it growing? That would mean that time in Jonestown... Of course! The TARDIS is functioning like a supersaturated liquid and the sheer is causing the formation of temporal crystals! Jonestown is a precipitate! That means time flows differently in there from out here. Very differently. Evolutionarily and unpredictably differently. In which case, that would probably mean...' He glanced at her, stopped. 'Never mind, no. Speculation, always dangerous, I never indulge. Right! Come on!'

141

'Where are we going?'

'Back to Jonestown to save the day. Chop chop.' He paused. 'It may be a bit different.'

'How different?'

'Well... Newer. Modern. Future-y. Time's passed. What year is it?'

She told him.

He winced, sucked air through his teeth. 'Not any more. Well, nothing for it. Gadewch i ni wneud hyn, eh?'

She peered at him. 'Is that some sort of Time Lord expression?'

'Yes. Absolutely. My mother tongue, that is. The pure form of the most perfect language in the universe.'

'What is it, really?'

He sighed. 'It's Welsh, Christina.'

But now she wasn't sure that was her name after all.

He pulled open a door, and behind it she could see the main street, thronging with people. They went through.

The centre of Jonestown was exactly the same: a small place with small dreams and a hint of quiet sorrow, as if it was built out of the knowledge that all good things must pass. Sash windows and wooden doors opened onto flagged streets, and people still wore the same clothes with the same patches. She recognised faces and smiles, saw them all smile back. No one said 'Where have you been?' No one seemed to think it was remarkable that she'd been away. Her house was still burning, and the fire brigade were just turning up now in a shiny new engine. She looked around sharply, ready to run, but the storm was gone. He must have been mistaken, all the same. No time had passed at all.

Then she raised her eyes, and saw the silver spears of the skyscrapers, the perfect gleaming bridges and the cable cars connecting them all like beetles climbing from branch to branch in a forest made of glass. Or diamond. She wondered if the Doctor would really buy her a new house. She wondered if she wanted him to. She wondered how she would explain a fortune in diamonds to Mr Epley Jones the bank manager.

She saw a woman she didn't know – oh, wait, it was Arwen Jones the fire chief, tall and whipcord lean – directing the fire crew, and that wasn't a hose, it was a great big... thing. It was familiar, somehow. They pointed it at the fire, threw a switch, and the flames dwindled and guttered. Arwen nodded, well done all, good effort, now let's make the building safe. And in they went, and the charred structure was stone cold. Their uniforms relaxed, turned into ordinary clothes.

She was in the future.

But that meant her house had been on fire for years. Decades. It was impossible. She was getting a headache.

The Doctor looked absolutely delighted. 'Morning, Fire Chief! I'm the Doctor. Don't worry, I won't get in the way. Very nice work, though. Top notch.' He was shaking Arwen's hand with that same ridiculous enthusiasm, and Arwen seemed not at all averse.

'If you like,' Arwen looked over at Christina: is this man yours? He's a bit in the way. Not that he isn't picturesque, I will say.

'When did you stop using water, may I ask?' the Doctor wanted to know.

'These are new,' Arwen said, and she was warming to him, of course she was, she loved to talk shop. 'Sonic firefighting. Developed locally, I'll have you know, and now the higher-ups taking an interest. Rolled out nationally in the spring, and good for Mr Heidt, I say.'

'Sonic?'

'That's what they tell me. Well, to be honest, it's point and shoot, isn't it?' She indicated the fire engines, and he saw the Heidt symbol, a broken tablet seemingly held together by a tangle of lines twisting amongst one another like a bramble snarl.

'And the uniforms?'

'Psychic response weave. The cloth knows what you need it to be. Reads your mind. They're his as well.'

'His?'

'Heidt. Brilliant man, but shy. Not everyone's keen. Well, he's not local, see?'

'Brilliant, is he? Well, yes, I should say. And I know brilliant. If I think it's brilliant then it's really glow-in-the-dark, Einstein on his best day, flying cars and jetpacks brilliant. And this is brilliant. Just by the way: have you still got a hose, just in case?'

She smiled. 'Belt and braces, that's the fire service. Mind you, better for Christina's house to use the sonic, eh?'

'Oh, yes. I love health and safety, I really do. Do you two know each other, then?'

'Only in passing, Doctor, as they say. But it's a small town here, even if it is bigger than it was. We keep up.'

'Indeed, you do! The only thing you need to be the perfect fire crew is a time machine!'

Arwen chuckled. 'Yes, that would be handy. I'll talk to the engineers, see what they come up with. Temporal and reactive deflammablisation inductive suppression. Right! *Allons-y*, as they say in Tokyo. Just my little joke; that's French, that is.'

She trotted off, and a moment later they were gone.

'Sonic firefighters,' the Doctor said. He paused. 'Well, all right, then.'

'What?' Christina hated herself for saying 'what?' She felt she was filling a role, doing what people always did around him, as if his personal gravity was so enormous that you just went into orbit around him until he chose to let you go again.

His personal gravity.

That didn't sound like her at all. It sounded like him. She didn't have thoughts like that. She should have thought 'charm'. But she hadn't, and this was the world. Perhaps she was just adapting very well.

*

Sonic firefighters were brilliant. And impressive. Adapting the technology of his screwdriver to achieve a fire suppression field was a teensie bit genius. It would have taken him days. Probably hours, at least. More than twenty minutes, anyway. And how had they got a look at his screwdriver in the first place? Because this was, in the best possible way, a derivative technology. As for psychic jackets – why didn't he have a psychic jacket? He was exactly the sort of person who'd look great in a psychic jacket. He should have a psychic jacket.

Well, all right, he did have a psychic jacket, from Spurrier's of Jermyn Street, and he never wore it because it babbled like a lunatic, and when it wasn't just endlessly wittering away it was telling people things he didn't want them to know.

But psychic firefighter jackets were brilliant, and the firefighters themselves must be more than a little bit psychic to project strongly enough to change the physical make-up of the cloth. Psychic firefighters! Marvellous. And as for time-travelling psychic firefighters… that would be even more brilliant. Not that it would happen. Cracking time travel was hard. Cracking time travel inside an operating time machine? Really very, very, extremely, completely impossible. You can't travel in something you can't touch properly in the first place.

He looked around. Not-Christina was watching him. She was like that. She watched. He wondered if he should call her 'Not' for short. Then he wondered if she was psychic, too. Could she hear him calling her 'Not-Christina'? He frowned and thought hard about things which would really annoy her. She didn't react. Which didn't prove anything, really, because she might have heard him wondering if she could hear him and then she might have heard him planning to zap her with annoyances and she…

Focus.

Focus, focus, focus.

He looked around at the new Jonestown, at the familiar people and the old houses, and at the soaring city beyond, and humphed. 'What we need,' he said, 'is a local data repository. Somewhere you can access everything that's happening anywhere. Where information is in the air.'

Not-Christina pondered. 'There's a library on Glyndwr Street,' she said. 'They have terminals there.'

Terminals. Ten minutes ago she had been from the time before telephones, but now she knew there were terminals in the library. She probably knew how to use the internet, too. Little bit psychic, or he was an Ood. That was a thought: maybe they were all human-like Ood. Although they didn't seem very Ood-y. They were a bit chatty. Out of the Ood-inary.

He sighed. No one here would see why that was funny. What a waste.

Focus.

He looked across the road, getting his bearings. 'Town hall.' He nodded. 'Fishmonger.' He nodded again. 'Bus stop. Post Office. Newsagent. Aaand… there!'

She followed his pointing finger. 'That's the pub.'

'Yes! Beating heart of the community. Receiving and transmitting station for all the important news of the day! Last time I went there I learned all kinds of interesting things. And, look, they do afternoon tea. I like tea.'

He did. Tea was great. But gossip was even better.

The pub was the same as it had been last time he was here, down to the stains on the old wooden boards. He looked around the little, low-ceilinged room, and sat at the table next to a lady with a dog in a handbag, because he'd always found that fascinating.

She'd realised she was going to have to pay for tea, because he wasn't carrying any money. She wasn't sure how she knew that, but he wasn't. He had his psychic notepaper – which hadn't worked on her and wouldn't work here either – and he had a pocket full of diamonds which would almost certainly cause a bit of a stir. On the other hand, he had a pocket full of diamonds and he was going to give them to her to buy a new house, so she could afford to be a bit generous about tea.

When she got back to the table, he was talking to the old woman with the dog, and he had established that his new friend preferred Regency furniture, hated Italian food, and wasn't fond of the new girl in the butcher who was too cheeky by half. And she was going home soon because the streets weren't safe after dark.

'I don't hold with this new fellow, I must say,' she was saying, 'this Mr Heidt. Not a proper name, really, is it?'

'Not like Jones.'

'No! Exactly. Not like Jones, at all. If Jones was good enough for my late husband, why not for this outlandish fellow who wants to develop the place? Wants to come and put those tall towers in the middle of the square, I shouldn't wonder, and here we are after all these years having kept that sort out. There'll be supermarkets and unpleasantness, no doubt.'

'Wouldn't want that. Best to keep to the old ways.'

'I don't say progress isn't very fine,' she said sharply. 'There are gizmos and what all making life better, no question. But in their place. And this person with the Teutonic name is out of his. Well, perhaps he's a good enough sort, I'm sure I've not a notion. But just since he's been it's all wrong, is what I say.'

'Not safe after dark.'

'No, indeed, not. Not safe, at all.'

'Bad weather?'

'Oh!' Her small, dark eyes peered out from beneath flabby brows. She looked like a blackbird scouting for worms. 'I know what you mean. Clever boy. No, not that. Not for years. No, it's different now.'

'Different how?'

Her face set stubbornly. 'It's just not safe. Not safe at all. And I hold it's all this new thinking is the problem.'

'Mr Heidt.'

'I didn't say that, did I? Naming no names. But he's very modern. I don't think we need modern, here.'

The Doctor pressed, but she either wouldn't or couldn't say any more. He escorted her to the door and garnered an introduction to the two crones by the door, both of whom were on Christina's list of Nasty Old Women because they'd been unkind about her after Simon had died. They didn't approve of going out in the evening, or new people, or modern things. They also didn't take much to the Doctor. One of them called him a Fancy London Boy. He retreated.

'That went well,' Christina murmured to him.

'Pffaww,' he agreed. 'They're a pair! They don't like anything. They don't even like the dachshund. Who doesn't like dachshunds? They're little parcels of dog-shaped goodness. I've known Jalabite Hegemon ships give up conquest and start little farmsteads just so they can have happy dachshunds. Everyone likes dachshunds, everywhere in the universe. Well, except on Bithmorency. People there got into a war with a refugee column of evolutionarily advanced dachshund supersoldiers fleeing the destruction of their homeworld. The wire-haired marines took out an entire town – two hundred thousand dead. And it was a tragic misunderstanding. The dachshunds only stopped to ask for some biscuits, automated defence systems fired on them. There's a lesson: never give control of your space weapons to an unsupervised machine.' He shrugged, and she found herself nodding: *schoolboy error.*

She reclaimed control of her head, and they sat and ate scones. The pub began to empty out.

'That's interesting,' he said.

'What is?'

'Well, it's a pub, isn't it? Steak and kidney pie, ploughman's lunch, pint of your finest. The evening crowd should be coming in. But they're not. They're staying home.'

She felt a prickle between her shoulder blades, as if she was being watched by an unfamiliar cat. 'What, everyone?'

'Even him.' He pointed. There was no one behind the bar. 'Popped upstairs and never came back down. It was like this last time, as well.'

'Last time?' She glared at him.

'Yes. I came here just before your house burned down.'

She glared at him. 'You mean this is where the cloud monster limited combat thing found you? Are you looking for trouble?'

'No. Yes.' She kept glaring until he explained. 'No, the cloud thing was in the street. Yes, I am slightly looking for trouble because that's always where the answers are. Aaaand I've found it.' He pointed.

She looked over towards the fireplace. There was a weathervane on the mantle, old and made of iron. It must have been there since the village was built. Town. City. Whatever. She wondered what a weathervane could possibly tell you in a tiny suburb of a great city, surrounded by tall buildings. 'What about it?'

'Well, it's moving, which is what it did before.'

'When you burned my house down.'

'That was the cloud.'

'Which was chasing you.'

'Shsh! Watch!'

'It's a weathervane. There must be a top bit on the roof.'

'Yeah. But before it was just a weathervane. Now it's got that little man on top of it.'

She peered at the wrought iron. Sure enough, one end of the arrow was topped by a tiny, running figure making a gangling escape.

'Doctor,' she said.

'And the question is, what's he running from? What's at the other end of the arrow?'

She couldn't see. The far end of the vane was still in shadow.

But she knew something he apparently didn't.

'Doctor—'

'Because if we knew that, we might know what's about to happen. Mind you, where would be the fun in—'

She heard the wind sigh, felt the change in the air. He must have felt it just before somehow. The weathervane twitched, creaked.

'Doctor!' she slammed her hand down on the table.

'What?' he looked startled that she'd interrupted.

'The little man!'

'What about him?'

The weathervane swung sharply around, and at the far end of the arrow was a vast, hulking shape in black iron, a silhouette from a bad dream, twisted and horrible. Then it swivelled back again, and the little man stood out against the light of a candle.

'It's you!' she told him, and saw, halfway along the length of the vane at the hinge point, the tiny figure of a woman caught between, and knew it was herself.

The first footstep shuddered through the silence, heavy enough to shake the floor and the walls.

Pah pah POM.

The Doctor gave a cry and buckled sharply over his stomach, then gritted his teeth and surged to his feet, pulled her along with him. 'Christina, run!'

The footsteps were impossibly enormous. They seemed to shake everything, even the sky. She didn't move.

Pah pah POM.

'It must be huge!' she said.

'The vibration isn't physical,' he said, 'it's temporal. Each impact is transmitted through time. That thing out there isn't just walking. It's banging on the door. Or maybe the roof. Of the TARDIS, which from in here is the entirety of creation. She can't tell me the way she usually would so she's sharing her pain. That was the entire aquarium level vaporised. I can feel dead fish in my gall bladder. All right? So, yes, it's a very loud noise. Now, did I say "run"?'

The door exploded into pieces, and she just had time to recognise the figure from the weathervane. She'd been right. It was huge.

She ran.

He threw himself forward just as a terrible hand flattened the table where they'd been sitting, and said 'Run!' again, because people very often didn't unless you reminded them. Not-Christina ran. So did he. He felt something touch his shoulder, like a puff of air, and knew his suit would need sewing, heard the fabric part as razors plucked, missed his skin by just that much.

'Back door!' he shouted. Everywhere had a back door. That was a given. In some places it could be rather hard to find, but in a pub, generally speaking, it was through the kitchen and out into the –

There was no back door in the kitchen, just a white wall. He turned, thinking hard.

Christina grabbed hold of a butcher's trolley by the door, a thick wooden block for the Sunday roast on thick rubber wheels so it could go from table to table, and dragged him down onto it, then kicked them off from the sink unit with both feet.

The monster bellowed furiously as they skidded past beneath a grasping arm. For an instant, he looked up into its ugly, misshapen face. Stared into vast, mad eyes.

It said, very clearly: 'Time Lord.'

He wasn't sure if it was an accusation or a plea.

The butcher's block hit the frame of the kitchen door hard and tumbled over, spilling them to the floor, and they ran back into the saloon and out of the pub.

'Where do we go?' Christina demanded.

'It's your town!'

'It's your monster!'

They almost fell around the corner, up the street and away.

'How is it my monster?'

'It said, "Time Lord"!'

'Maybe it's just well informed!'

She didn't have time to argue with that, no doubt the thing would come out of the pub very shortly and try to eat them or whatever it had in mind. She wondered if he ever thought there wasn't time to argue. He seemed to overthink everything, all the time, to argue it out like –

It was infectious. It was insane and infectious and now she was doing it, just like him. No, no, no, and absolutely: no. She ran on, leading the way.

'Where are you going?' he shouted after her, and when she didn't answer he followed, as she had known he would. He had to assume she knew what she was doing because she lived here, and if she didn't he still had to go with her in order to save her. She felt footfalls behind her, knew the thing was coming after them, and she derived a brief moment of satisfaction from the thought that at least he was following her rather than the other way around; the sinister weathervane had been wrong about that.

The footfalls were uneven, as if the thing was limping and dropping to one hand to pull itself along. *Pah pah POM. Pah pah POM.* Run, run, run. She wondered what that room looked like now, the one he had called the console room. Alarms and red lights, she thought, and tortured metal, the way she imagined a submarine at too great a depth. *Pah pah POMMM.*

Behind her the Doctor was pointing the sonic screwdriver, making adjustments and muttering: 'Complex structure derived from the same basic components, electron physiognomy – ooh, you beauty! Partially stabilised matrix attached to—' and then he had to stop, and duck, and roll in the gutter to get away from a clutching hand. He was mad. Mad and dangerous to know. She looked around, saw a car, went to it. She had no idea how it worked, she'd never driven one. The window was open a crack and that was enough to get in, then she found her hands weaving wires together. It was an old model and not very secure – old? Not 1959 old, not as old as her – and the engine started. She stamped down, the car lurched, hurtled forwards. She flung open the passenger door.

'Get in!' she yelled, and was moving again before he was properly seated, felt something land on the roof, a fist driving the back left corner of the car flat against the rear seat.

'What is that thing?' she demanded, shouting over the sound of the car's engine.

'Same as the storm,' he shouted back. 'Lower energy configuration, more sophisticated, still only semi-stable. Where are you going?'

'Away!'

'Good for starters. After that we need a plan.'

'I don't have one! Do you?'

'No. Yes, always. Plan. Plan plan plan. We need a probabilistic confinement system, pin it down and ask it questions.'

'I'll settle for killing it!'

His face changed, and for a moment she could hear him perfectly, as if the wind stopped, as if everything stopped for his response. 'I don't kill things.'

'Of course you do! You said you did.'

'I said I had. I have. And, all right, yes, I do when I can't think of anything else, but that's my failure. That's when I get it so badly wrong I don't have any other options! I'm not doing it any more. Not here. Not today. Today I'm going to get it right. I'm going to win one clean. All right?'

'All right.'

'Will you help me? Will you help me make this be all right?'

'Yes! Fine! Whatever! How?'

He clenched his teeth. 'Don't know.'

'Well, think! What about whatever you did last time? Can you get us away?'

'Yes. Maybe. It might be able to follow. But if it didn't it would still be here. The people wouldn't be safe. And it might change again by the time we got back, into something more dangerous.'

'Last time it was a storm! Now it has a body. You said it was a lower energy thingummy!'

'Yes. Don't you see? It's less physically destructive because it's more intelligent. It doesn't need to be a storm any more. It can think. Well, a bit. It's not just an energy form any longer, not just an electrical anomaly, it's got a—' He stopped. 'Where's the fire station?'

'What?'

'You're a genius. In the dictionary, under "genius", little picture of you.'

'What?'

'Not so much under "quick on the uptake", though.'

'Oi!'

'Well!'

'Oi!'

'All right, I'm sorry! Fire station?'

'That way!'

'Then that's where we're going!' He reached over and grabbed the wheel, spun the car, and they careered through the narrow streets. 'Have you got a phone?'

'How would I possibly have a phone in a car?' she said, then understood. 'Oh, you mean a mobile one. No.' But there was one in a side pocket of the car. He gave another of those funny looks as if she'd done something strange, then dialled.

'Arwen Jones? It's the Doctor. Yes. Yes, we met this morning. I'm fine, how are you? Well, that would be lovely. I – Yes. Yes, I would absolutely love a tour. In fact, we're on our way over now. Well, yes, there was something – Yes. Sort of an emergency, actually. Yes. Yes. Well, no, not a fire. But if you've got the old hoses – yes. Yes, exactly. Well, I'm a bit – Well, no, I – Well, that would be lovely – Yes. Great.'

He took the phone away from his ear, stared at it. 'She says I owe her dinner.'

Christina couldn't help it. She sniggered.

As they rounded the corner and saw the fire station, she was sure everything was going to be all right. She slowed the car and the Doctor jumped out, heading for the main doors, where three old-style fire engines were already growling into life beside the new Heidt Industries sonics. She felt the glow of a job well done. And then she heard – felt – the vast, impossible vibration of the monster's tread, and even from this distance she saw his face twist in alarm.

She turned in her seat and there it was, man-shaped but warped and seeming to inflate, features rippling with fury, and she knew – knew, this time, not hoped or feared but absolutely understood – that it would catch him before he got to the fire station and put whatever plan he had into action. So she shoved her right foot down on the accelerator pedal and turned the wheel and locked the handbrake at the same time, slewed the car round on the spot and charged it directly towards the thing as it galloped forwards. Behind her, the Doctor was shouting and running after her, and she thought: 'Idiot.'

And then there was a strange, weightless moment and the world rotated and twirled. She saw the monster, and the ground, and both of them were getting further away, and then she understood that she had been picked up, flung like a toy across the square. She was not weightless, but her weight kept shifting. It was odd. Disorientating. Interesting. And she knew she was about to land again. That would probably be bad. It would hurt. She tried to remember if it was best to tense to protect your spine or go slack and let the safety restraints do their job. Couldn't. Saw the ground coming up very fast.

The impact arrived and it was so much bigger than anything had ever been before. She saw the dashboard crumpling, saw the engine burst up towards her, felt a strange, pinching impact in her chest.

The Doctor watched it happen. He stared at the monster and at Arwen Jones and the firemen, and was somehow caught in a timeless space between. Not timeless in any way he could engineer. Just timeless because it was so, so bad. Only a few seconds earlier, he had told her: *Today I'm going to win one clean.*

He felt like a fool.

He ran to the car, and saw, and looked away. Saw the monster, saw it seeing him. It didn't seem to be celebrating. He was glad about that, because he knew if it had been he would have destroyed it utterly, would have taken it out of the world at any cost. But it just stood there. It looked almost embarrassed. Then the moment passed and it sneered.

He called back to Arwen Jones. 'Get ready,' he said. 'When it's close enough, turn on the hoses. Make a triangle like a sheep pen. Then bring them inwards and soak it!'

The monster charged. The Doctor turned on his heel and sprinted back towards the fire station. It was close behind him, huge hand reaching down, the same hand which had lifted Christina's car like a balsa wood model. He wondered if today was that day, if he'd wake up different, wake up someone else who remembered him fondly. A new Doctor. He wondered if he'd approve. Would he be more gentle? That might not be so bad. More vengeful? He hoped not. Maybe he'd be a girl. That was distantly possible. Never been a girl. The Corsair had been a girl for a while. New perspective. Confuse people. Keep life interesting.

He slowed, and saw the fire crews staring, knew it was right behind him, right at his back. He felt it lean down, breathe on his neck. It said, 'Doctor.' He heard the huge mouth open and realised it was actually going to swallow him. Not entirely sure how well regeneration would work in that situation. Never tried it. Doubt it would be enjoyable.

A straight white line shot over his head and took the monster in the face, and then another, and another: the hoses. He was close enough. Modern pumping systems. Ice cold water, like a laser. The outermost jet yawed across to strike a claw as it plunged toward him, warding it off, and he had to slide under the stream to avoid being blasted back towards his enemy. He arrived at Arwen Jones's feet in a heap.

'I told you not to do that!' he said. 'I told you to wait!'

'Yes,' she said. 'Notice how I didn't listen to you?' She broke off, shouted to the right-hand crew. 'Bring it around! Fence it!' And then back to him: 'I don't take orders, least of all from random men who are about to be eaten. In general, I give orders, you see, in so far as I believe in them at all. Does that bother you?'

'No, ma'am,' he said, and she grinned.

There was a bright blue flash, and a rich, searing crackle, and he jumped up. He had not been wrong about this, at least: the monster was still electrical enough, malleable and nebulous enough, that a relentless deluge of water was enough to scramble it, destroy the coherent field which held it together.

It was melting.

He watched as it bubbled and screamed, electricity snapping around its legs and arms, and when it was small enough the jets of water knocked it clean over on its back. It looked like nothing so much as a tiny, angry old man with an ugly face.

'Stop!' he shouted.

'Why?'

'Because otherwise it could die.'

'And that's a bad thing because?'

'It's a new thing in the universe. It's special and strange and it's growing. It's trying to be something different from what it is.'

Arwen Jones peered at him, then nodded. She raised her hand, and the flow of water slacked, then stopped.

He glared at the thing on the ground, then pointed back at the car.

'Don't do that again,' he said. 'And don't make me come and stop you. Because I will.'

It glowered up at him, skittered backwards on long-fingered hands and elbows, dragging one leg. Then it got up, and ran, awkwardly, back the way it had come.

'Oi!' Chief Jones shouted. 'It's getting away!'

'Yes,' he said.

'Shouldn't we stop it?'

'We'd probably have to kill it.'

She nodded. 'Yes! And look what it did!'

'And if you kill it now, all broken and running away, how would that be different?'

She shrugged. 'Justice, maybe.'

'But you don't think so.'

'No, I don't suppose I do. But Christina…'

'Oh, well. Revenge is something else. You want to do revenge, be my guest. But I won't. It's a bad place to live, revenge.'

He went to look again at Christina's body and say he was sorry, even though she wouldn't hear him because it was far too late for that. She opened her eyes. Which was completely impossible. Impossible impossible impossible, unless –

'Oh, you beauty,' he said.

'Don't be familiar,' she told him sharply. 'We don't know one another that well.'

He squinted at her, and realised she had no idea. 'You're brilliant.'

'Shut up.'

He was, she thought, slightly less annoying when he was being serious. Only slightly. But there was a germ of sensibleness in him which he hid and ignored. He could really accomplish things if he'd just let it out.

'Christina, listen to me,' he said now, very seriously. 'There is a piece of very sharp wreckage directly beneath your chin. If you look down, it will kill you. So don't. Just move towards me very slowly. Your clothes are stuck on some sharp edges so they may drag a bit, you'll just have to borrow a coat once you're out. Hang on –' he reached down, tore a fragment from her coat – 'gear stick, sorry.' He put the cloth absently into his pocket.

She glowered at him. 'Well?'

'Well what?'

'If my clothes are going to have holes in, you'll need to look the other way.'

He held up his hands defensively and turned his head. She moved. He was right, she was well and truly stuck. She could feel the fabric tearing. These were nice clothes, damn it. He was the most expensive man she'd ever met, positively everything she owned got destroyed around him. Mentally adding another diamond to her bill, she pushed. Something grated against her rib cage. No doubt that would hurt later. The skin felt numb, and she suspected that meant some pretty serious bruising, or maybe shock. She fell out of the wrecked car onto the street, and he helped her up. She looked down at herself hastily. Yes, her clothes were torn, but no, they were not indecent. Good. He tried to walk her away, then, but she looked back into the car.

And stopped.

'Oh,' she said, eventually. She thought about it. And then she slapped him.

'What?' he said, and when she hit him again he ducked away. 'What? What? How is this my fault? You're alive, that's got to be a good thing!'

She slapped him again.

'What?'

But he must know what. The world was upside down. She wasn't Christina de Souza. A huge piece of the wrecked engine had passed entirely through the driver's seat, along with the axel. There was nowhere she could have been sitting, no position she could have been in, which would have preserved her. She should be dead. She looked down at her stomach. Her clothes were whole again.

'I blame you entirely,' she said crossly. 'Everything was ordinary until you came. And now this!'

She wasn't Christina de Souza. She wasn't even human. And that meant, probably, that everything she had ever known was a lie, and that everyone she knew was also an alien who didn't know they were an alien, and she would either have to tell them, which would be extremely awkward and probably mean they thought she was mad, or not tell them and keep secret from them something they had every right to know.

She tried to hit him again, but this time he ducked.

A short while later, they were standing in a room which was either a hotel room or a distant part of the TARDIS and he seemed unable to say for certain which. Surely he should know? But apparently the TARDIS was big and he didn't always keep track, and obviously the whole of Jonestown was inside the TARDIS anyway. When she asked, he said something about how the temporal crystal was expanding and the phase differential between coterminous realities was diminishing in line with the stasis paradigm, and then refused to explain. She still thought he should be able to tell where they were, and she thought he thought so too. She worried that while they were away – if they were – Jonestown would change again, and the monster would change too.

She was worried that the Doctor was losing control of his machine.

More immediately, he was wiggling the sonic thing at her.

Again. Again and again and for the thousandth time. And now he was peering at it and peering at her and making thoughtful noises and she was really wishing she had some sort of appalling destructive power, so that she could zap him into behaving like a human being.

'I thought you might be a multiform,' he said, 'one of the nice ones. A Prestolian Shift-sailor, or an Adumbrated Boon. But you aren't.'

She scowled. 'As soon as I figure out how to turn them on, I am going to zap you with my laser eye beams.'

'Hm. Maybe don't say things like that, just in case your weapons systems are voice activated.'

She hadn't considered that. 'I won't, really,' she said hastily. No gun-sight appeared in her vision, so if she was a walking munition she was either broken or that wasn't how she worked. She told him so.

'Hang on,' he said. 'Laser eye beams? Did they talk a lot about laser eye beams in your day?'

'In comic books.' Not really her scene.

'And you knew what a mobile phone was. Come to think of it, when did you learn to do a handbrake turn?'

'I can't drive,' she said automatically.

'But you can. And you know everything about Jonestown, even though you haven't been here for decades. You're a psychic not-really-a-human-person person. A Pnarap.' He raised his eyebrows for her approval. She shook her head. 'Well, suit yourself. Anyway... Where are the police? Eh? Shouldn't we be surrounded by Jonestown's finest demanding to know what's going on? But we're not, are we? Because you know what's going on, and they know because you know. They may not know that they know because you know, but they do. It's not like they're listening in now –' he waved the sonic screwdriver vaguely – 'because I'd know about that. But your memory and theirs is all... overlappy. Overlappy-mnemonic-psychic-not-really-a-human-person person. Ompnarap. That's a proper alien name, that is. What, still no? All right. Anyway—'

She waved him into silence. To her amazement, he actually shut up.

'What do we do?' It came out rather more desperate than she had intended.

'Well, normally at this point I like to go and talk to whoever's trying to destroy the universe and ask them not to.'

She wanted to say that was absurd, that he should just go straight to whatever terrible thing he did instead when the answer was given, because she was afraid. She could see it was terrible. He hated it. He *obliterates* things, she realised. He shatters them. They think they've won because he's a bit vague and he waffles, but that only goes so far. It's his shell, like a tortoise, if a tortoise was soft on the outside and dangerous on the inside. That's how the Time War ended: he got to the bottom of his patience, and he took two entire civilisations out of the universe and locked them away, and one of them was his own. That's how sharp his sense of obligation is.

And he lives like that. He does it all the time.

She really hoped Jonestown wasn't that sort of threat. That she wasn't. 'So why don't we do that? Let's go and ask nicely.'

'Because I don't know where to go.'

'I thought this Mr Heidt…' she said.

He nodded. 'Oh, me too. But what I don't know is: do I go after him – it – in here, or back to the TARDIS and try to get into the mine outside?'

She shrugged. 'If you can't tell where we are now, does it matter any more?'

'Yes, because one's in here and one's out there. That one is where the mine started out, but its operating intelligence could be in here. It could be Heidt. Or all this could just be a reflection and I'd be talking to the air. The whole point of Jonestown could be so that I waste time in here when I should be out there.'

'But you said that this thing is twisting space and time and trying to tear everything apart, even though that's not how it's supposed to work.'

'Yes.'

'And the TARDIS is a time machine, it tunnels...' She screwed up her face in thought. 'The bubbles are bigger than the cheese. It makes one bubble after another around itself.' She stopped again.

'I never told you that.'

She brushed this aside. 'But is it true?'

'Yes.'

She had the distinct impression that he was getting flustered. 'And the temporal mine is the same thing. A TARDIS without a heart. All rage and no poetry.'

He was definitely staring at her now. 'Yes,' he said. 'Exactly.'

'So with the TARDIS fighting the mine... what makes you think there's any difference any more between what's in here and what's out there?'

She had the immensely satisfying experience of seeing his mouth drop open as if she'd smacked him with a kipper.

Heidt House stood on a pinnacle of stone jutting straight up from the middle of a vast chasm. It was absurd, a half-mile across, and the bottom was a very, very long way below.

Not-Christina was looking out of the window and seemed to be thinking very hard. The Doctor frowned. She was getting cleverer all the time, as if she'd been asleep when he first met her but was now waking up, and while that was quite interesting and just a little bit attractive it was also rather worrying because his past experiences with rapidly accelerated cognition and intelligence expansion in near-human entities had been a bit negative. They tended to do things like go mad and try to destroy causality. Or they wanted to consume all the information in your brain, or they became telepathic and accidentally dominated entire star systems, or occasionally their conceptual mass just ran too hot and they flat out exploded, which was not only dangerous and sad but also disgusting.

A single narrow bridge, just wide enough for a car, spanned the distance from the meadows and fields of Jonestown's farms to this other place delineated by the house. Mr Heidt was standing on the front steps.

He was definitely not the monster, or at least, not at the moment. He was short, barrel-chested and broad-shouldered, and he had a vast, bristling beard.

'Ms de Souza,' he said, very politely, and his voice was a deep, elegant bass, 'a pleasure.' He turned. 'And you, Doctor. Thank you for coming.'

Somewhere beneath their feet, the world shrugged, just a little.

Pah pah POM.

He felt a twinge near one of his hearts, and knew the TARDIS was in real pain now. He looked at Heidt.

'I tell you what,' he said abruptly, 'let's toss a coin.'

Heidt peered up at him. 'I beg your pardon?'

'Let's toss a coin. Not that I don't appreciate the drama. Impossible village, impossible house, giant monster inside the TARDIS. It's masterful. And I have a high standard of evil plots. When I use the word "masterful", it means something. But if you want to be really different, let's skip the banter and games of chess and ridiculous methods of execution and get right to it. You toss a coin, I'll call. If I get it wrong, you win. I die, you leave everyone else alive, because – well, they're not exactly Time Lords or Daleks, are they? They're humans. Or nearly humans. They're small potatoes and you know it. Everyone lives except me. Buuuuut If I get it right, you leave. Everyone lives, even you. No exterminations. No xenocide. Just peace. How about that?'

Not-Christina stared at him.

Heidt nodded slowly. 'It's a very good deal, Doctor.

Unfortunately, I can't take it.'

'Of course you can.'

'I really can't. Because I didn't ask you here to play cat and mouse. I need your help. If you don't help me, I'll die, the temporal mine will fulfil its function, and you and the TARDIS and quite a lot of time and space will cease to exist.'

'But you are the mine!'

Heidt shook his head. 'Not any more,' he said.

Once upon a time, there was a terrifying weapon of high technology and fury. It was one of thousands. It was alive, after a fashion, given intelligence to make it more dangerous. It was adaptive, cunning, and hungry. It thought of itself as Son 11-21.

Son 11-21 was seeded in a remote part of time and space, the littoral plain of a rift, and there it waited and waited for its moment. Opportunities came and went, but they were wasteful, incomplete. It was programmed to optimize its impact, and these small chances were not enough. It was there to strike a decisive blow, to turn the tide of a battle, to immobilise a vital convoy, to capture a crucial messenger.

That was fine. Waiting was something it did well, part of its core identity. It settled into a tiny trapdoor universe spun off from the real one, and it waited.

And then suddenly it had waited too long.

The Time War ended, and was won, was lost. The little trapdoor universe was sucked along with everything else into the lock.

But the enemy was not contained. There were loopholes: fabulously arcane and difficult to create, dangerous to the greater fabric of existence in ways which were painful to think about, but they were possible – just. They could be forced, if one were mad enough, dedicated enough. In consequence, these eruptions when they did happen were always the action of the worst or the best, always the consequence of schemes whose scope and ambition were dauntingly vast. Arks; helix tunnels; alternate realities and paradox engines: the lock was incomplete.

That was intolerable. Son 11-21 watched single entities whisper away into the originating universe. And realised it could follow.

Its position was unique. Creating its trapdoor universe where it had done, it had woven rift energies into the web, and those energies had made the trapdoor less absolute than it might be, less stable. In the originating universe, that had been a flaw which might leave Son 11-21 vulnerable to assault from within its own trap, so it had fortified itself. But now, here, that same flaw could become a doorway. The trapdoor universe might open not out into the timelocked region, but back into normal space.

Son 11-21 reached, tore, and fell.

The passage was appalling. It was not how re-entry should be. It was violent and corrosive. Son 11-21 was compromised, scrambled, damaged. Its ability to create such passages was burned away. It huddled in space, trying to repair itself, and mostly failing. Processors were vaporised, great parts of its mind simply turned to gas and ash. Its consciousness fragmented, had to be loaded into discrete systems to maintain some form of rational thought. It tried to repair itself, but much information was gone and simply could not be retrieved. Amongst which: Son 11-21 no longer knew which side of the war it had been on.

And then the TARDIS came.

The damaged mind within Son 11-21 found that it was in a dispute with other aspects of itself. It argued for patience, for repair, but the self in the weapons system was now hardwired for destruction and was prepared to accept allied casualties in the hope of punishing an escaped enemy. The war had been like that, towards the end.

It couldn't destroy the TARDIS outright, couldn't take it out of the universe and hold it. But it could do other things which would work as well, in the end. It struck, pushing at the TARDIS's own temporal dislocations, unbalancing them, sucking and undermining and buffeting, forcing time to flow differently in and around the vessel, stressing the fabric of it, draining its energy. It was a new method of attack, untested and uncertain, but it was what was available and it was working, if slowly.

In desperation, the mind of Son 11-21 opened a doorway onto the TARDIS and stepped through, only to drag the feral entity from the weapons system along with it. Son 11-21 struggled with his twin as they *rampaged through Jonestown, shattering and smashing, but it was only when the electrophysical presence they inhabited was briefly disrupted with jets of water that he was able to seize control of their shared body and force the feral self temporarily away.*

Heidt spread his hands. 'And here we are.'

'Son 11-21?'

Heidt nodded. 'Yes. Or maybe that honour belongs to the monster, and I'm the aberration.' He paused. 'Do you happen to know, Doctor, which side I was on?'

'No. And there's a fifty per cent chance I wouldn't tell you if I did. All right, what do you want? Can you stop this?'

'Yes. If you repair the mine, I can take control and stop the attack.'

'Give you the keys to the kingdom. The launch codes.'

'Yes.'

Christina raised one hand as if she was at school. 'Or, alternatively, that might all be so much rubbish and you just need a hand to reset your zap gun and when we do it we die and you win.'

'That is possible.'

'You couldn't just tell us how to beat your monster? Or escape?'

'I am precluded from sabotaging my own mission. But I can engage in temporary alliances to restore my own full function. And once I'm back in control, I have discretion over whether to execute my purpose at any given time. You see?'

'We can't trust you.'

Heidt nodded. 'You might look at it that way. Certainly I would, in your position.'

'Right,' she said.

'But he wouldn't,' Heidt added, pointing to the Doctor.

Since the Doctor didn't argue, she supposed he wouldn't, although in her honest assessment his optimism was symmetrical with a somewhat justifiable level of lethal paranoia. Although if he were a little less determined to be gentle with the universe's horrors, she thought, he probably wouldn't have to do appalling things quite so often.

'Well, fine,' she said. 'We'll go back to Jonestown and think about it.' The old puzzle? *If one man always lies and another always tells the truth…* But it was much harder if either one of them might do both.

Heidt twitched slightly. He was looking regretful, even dyspeptic. Had he eaten something that disagreed with him? Well, yes: a TARDIS. 'That may be a problem.'

She glowered. 'I expect we can get a taxi if your nice car is not available.'

'No doubt you could, but my control of this situation is only temporary.' He glanced over at the Doctor. 'I have tried to arrange matters so that you have everything you need. But I'm afraid quite shortly my time will run out. Do not leave the house. There is nothing else on the pinnacle, and my other half has the ability to destroy the bridge at any time.' He twitched again. 'I must leave you. Do please feel free to look around. The library is particularly interesting. And when I return, do bear in mind what I have said.'

When it came again, the twitch was not a twitch at all, but a spasm of the body. Heidt lurched away from her, and she saw his face ripple as if he was made of water. She moved to support him, and found the Doctor's hand on her arm.

'Don't.'

Heidt rolled his shoulders and twisted, and she heard things pop in his spine.

'Thank you, Doctor. If you touch me, Christina, it may accelerate the process. The weapons system might interpret that as a physical attack.' He coughed, hacked and groaned.

The Doctor barely glanced at her, went on. 'You should go. Now. Walk across the bridge and don't look back.'

'No!' Heidt spun in his crouch, flung out his hand. The joints were cracking and the fingers hooked and clawed at the air. 'No, no, no! She has to stay! She has to!' He lurched closer, his rictus face stretching towards them. 'Damn you! I can't say it out loud! You can't send her away or it all comes down like wasps tearing through the web. It's perfect now! Perfect! But if she goes then where's the surprise? You can't make a breakfast without mushrooms.' He shuddered, lowered his hand. 'Don't make her go, Doctor. She has to be here. I have prepared... I can't say more. I can't. It's happening now. I'm leaving. When I come back we'll either all be dead or we won't. Breakfast in the library. Perfectly all right, it's full of spiders. Weavers, webs or woven? Perhaps it's all the same. Go. Look. Five minutes, maybe less. Go now!'

And he stopped. Not just stopped speaking but stopped, stock still and silent, and no longer breathing. His body froze in place. She had expected some vile werewolf transformation, but this was not that. It was eerier, bleaker. He was simply absent, and his absence implied the presence, somewhere nearby, of the other.

Pah pah pom.

Well, that was not unexpected.

Pah pah pom.

Even if it was rather close at hand.

Pah pah pom.

Casual, even. Close and casual and confident. Not in a hurry. She looked out of the window, and saw the bridge in ruins, the house isolated in the middle of the pinnacle. 'Run,' she told the Doctor, and took his hand.

Christina grabbed him and said 'run' and then he heard it: the triple beat of the weapons system, Heidt's other half. She was very fast, he thought. Even if she had anticipated, she was fast. He looked at her hand and saw it flicker slightly, purplish light dancing around the edges. Refraction from the glass chandelier, probably. Probably.

She was right, it was definitely time to go. This house was a puzzle, the library apparently contained the solution. But Heidt couldn't or wouldn't tell him what solving the puzzle would mean, so he had to work that out before he worked out what the puzzle was and how to solve it because otherwise he might be levered into defeating himself.

He looked around. There were three doors: the way they had come in, which led to the shattered bridge; a small door to the kitchens which he suspected would be downstairs, and hence, if Heidt was to be believed, closer to the enemy; and the big, bold double doors to the rest of this floor, including no doubt the library. Heidt wanted him to go there, that was clear enough. He instinctively wanted to go somewhere else, to step outside the game, but if he beat it and it was aimed at the enemy that would be something of a fatal embarrassment. It had occurred to him that he had only Heidt's word for it that Heidt was the nice half of the mine's consciousness, or indeed that there were two halves at all.

In the end, it came down to a choice: trust, or don't. *Heidt knows you believe in trust. He could be manipulating you. But he let you know that he knows. Show of honesty. Show of honesty could be a ruse, can't trust it. If you don't trust it, and he's telling the truth, and you lose.* Round and around and around. Finally, the question is: if you're going to die, do you die believing in enemies or friends? All right, one vote in favour of trust.

And Christina: why was she here? She was a piece of what Heidt intended, obviously. Key. Detonator. Bomb. Hostage. Save her. Save Jonestown. Save the TARDIS. Save himself.

She was tugging on his arm. 'Run!'

He ran for the big doors. For the library. *I am the Doctor. In the end, I choose this: I choose trust, I choose to solve the puzzle, I choose to see what's behind the curtain.*

They went through.

The Library was huge, with more books than she'd ever imagined. They were stacked in shelves, lying around in piles. Some were floating. It was impossible.

She stared. The Doctor was nodding slowly, as if he'd known all along, though she was reasonably sure he hadn't.

He looked over at her with a ghost of a smile. 'Go ahead.'

'It's bigger on the inside!'

'Yes,' he said. 'This is my library.'

The TARDIS library, he meant; so they were back in the TARDIS proper. Inside Heidt's house, the room he sent them to, the room he was presumably protecting, was in the Doctor's part of the TARDIS, the bit of the machine which was still functioning the way it was supposed to.

But if the monster got in here, that would mean very bad things, she was sure. Death and endings.

She realised she despised death.

She felt the monster arrive outside, the appalling power of it. The doors behind them shuddered, but held. The noise was not that neat three-part beat any more, it was a scream, a howl of metal and stress, far too long. The Doctor winced. 'Propulsion,' he muttered. 'And structural integrity fields.'

'That sounds bad.'

'It is.'

'Then do something. Solve the puzzle.'

He seemed to ignite. 'Yes! Exactly. Solve the puzzle. *Allons-y!* That's French, you know.'

Marvellous. Now he was quoting Arwen Jones at her.

But he was moving, too, talking to himself, thinking aloud the way he had before but much, much more faster.

'Library, library, library. He can't say, he's trying to tell us but he can't go right ahead and say it. All right. Full of books. But really full of books. Too full. Can't possibly be a book he wants

171

me to find unless there's a clue because we don't have time to read them all and he has to point the way. What's not where it should be? Ludowig's *Histories of the Dalek Imperium* ought to be there but it's here… no, that was me. This one is… *The Quarry*. (Only signed copy in the universe. He'll be missed.) But not what we need right now… No! Not books… furniture. Chairs, tables, tapestries… can't be! No! Maps!'

He turned left, hurtled down between the stacks, and they emerged into a sort of side chapel, a room formed by the shelves, with a huge table covered in ancient and modern maps. At the far end was a writing table and a very comfortable-looking chair.

'Maps! Maps maps maps, oooh, YES! Jonestown. Never had a map of Jonestown, never knew it was here, so this belongs to Heidt. (Nice penmanship. Mermaid. Other mermaid. Lots and lots of and lots of mermaids, not really the point…) Map. Map is not the territory. Not what I'm supposed to see, just a clue to tell me I'm in the right place. OW!' Another shrieking impact, and this time she saw his foot twist as if he'd put it down, heard the ankle tear. 'She's been shielding me but now she can't any more, she's losing her grip. Aaaah! Chair! Chair!' She guided him to the chair. 'Yes! Chair. Chair is the answer. Oh, you sneaky sneaker! Sit down in the chair. What do we see?'

She could see a plain table with a pen, some writing paper, and no ink. There were stacks of paper around the chair, piled up. A manuscript. And, for no obvious reason, a saucepan full of water. 'What's that?'

'Saucepan! Condensation from the cloud layer in the upper stacks. Always rains on the desk. Doesn't matter where I put the desk, always rains. If I don't have a container here it gets on the paper and then it moulders. And you've got no idea the trouble you get when psychic paper goes mouldy. Mould on psychic paper is psychic mould. Psychic mushrooms all over the TARDIS, and when you think at them too hard they try to turn into what you're thinking about… Ah HAH! Mushrooms!

"You can't make breakfast without mushrooms." Right! Right, what else did he say?'

She struggled. Outside, somewhere, the monster was stalking, testing. She could hear it, feel it. Heidt had made no sense. '"Weavers, webs or woven"?'

'Yes! Here are the mushrooms. Trapdoor universe, the mine's like a spider. Is that the web? We already know that, it doesn't help! Oh. Um. Christina?'

He was staring at her hand where it was resting on the saucepan. She stared too.

The paper below was stained and brown where the water had slopped over. It must have gathered while he was away from the desk – hours? Centuries? Had time flowed slowly here, or fast, in this strange emergency? – because the paper was indeed mouldy and green, and the green stuff was reaching up towards her fingers like a strange sea creature. It touched her skin. Tickled. She smiled. 'Don't worry,' she said, knowing he was, 'it's all right.' She turned her hand, saw the tendrils reaching into her skin. Painless. Natural. And with them: memories. So many. So rich and beautiful and terrible. So sad. 'Oh. Rose. You miss her, don't you? You miss them all.' She drew back, and the column subsided into the paper. 'Sorry. I know that was private. It just came into my head.'

He nodded slowly. 'It would. This is my diary.'

'A psychic diary?'

'Of course. It holds everything I feel, everything I see…' He sighed, then stared at her. 'Ohhh, it can't be…'

'What can't be?'

From his pocket, he withdrew a scrap of cloth – the piece of her coat he had torn off in the car after her accident. If her clothes had healed, she supposed, she had to own that it was somehow part of her, unless everyone in Jonestown wore psychic clothes like the firefighters.

He put the cloth down on the paper and watched as it

stretched out, yearning, towards the patch of mould, and the two of them merged. After a moment, the mould rustled and shifted, becoming a wide patch of the same cloth.

He said: 'Brilliant!'

She said: 'What?'

And saw him smile in sympathy. 'This! This is brilliant. You're brilliant. Ooh, Heidt, you cheeky devil. Yes. Yes. YES! Because I can trust you now, can't I? Now that I know what the deal is. Oh, Christina – you should keep that name, you know, she can hardly complain that you're stealing it – Christina, Christina, Christina! You're amazing. This is why we kept talking about cheese! Cheese means mould. Glorious mould! Unconscious knowledge. And my unconscious knows LOTS. Maybe even more than yours. Ooooh, yes! Here's the TARDIS, caught in the temporal sheer. Massive fluctuations in the flow of time inside the structure. To keep me safe she shunts them all into one place. I don't wake up with one foot ten thousand years older than the rest of me, the sheer doesn't stress her buttressing. Right? Right!'

He was nodding, and that infuriating charisma was pulling her in again and she was nodding along with him.

'Ohh, but there's a side effect. Floating around the TARDIS are lots of little spores of psychic slime mould, because the water here's been dripping onto the paper. And inside the sheer zone, those tiny weenie microscopicy psychic boojums start to evolve! Because they would! I mean, it's billions of years all concentrated in a single instant. BANG! Zap! And in the TARDIS there are echoes of people. People I know, people I meet. Bits of genetic material from everyone I've touched, memories and recollections, psychic impressions, sensor readings. And all those go into the mixture so that all that evolution is directed, pushing towards a perfect functioning dream of humanity. WHAMMO! Jonestown.'

He was holding his arms out to the vaulted ceiling, exultant.

This was what he loved, she thought, more than anything. Wonder. Strangeness.

'And you! Most of all, you! Christina de Souza 2.0! Brilliant! Evolved psychic slime mould in human form. So fast you're starting to see your own thoughts reflected through time, getting just that little but quicker than it's physically possible to be! And you're all part of the same thing! "Weavers, webs or woven"! You're one vast network of interconnected psychic mould! Different personalities sharing a single subconscious, which is why you never get lost, even when you're in a city which was built while you were away, why nothing new surprises you, why you know how to drive even though you've never learned! Ooooh, brilliant! You gorgeous mushroom!'

She punched him smartly in the nose. 'Oi!'

'OW! Yes, all right, fair point, not the best way to put it. No, look! You're still connected to the town! You've got acres and acres of space in there. You're evolving all the time. They are. In there, right now, time's passing again, passing so very fast!'

He was staring into her face, holding her eyes by sheer force of self. It was appalling how much self he had. She could feel it now, the edges of him, the record in his diary.

'No, don't look away, look at me. Think. Think, and write it down. Right. Yes. Here…' He drew her hand to the blotter, and the layer of mould reached for her again. 'Write! Write what you want.'

She wrote. She wanted so much. She wanted calm, and quiet, and Simon back again, and she wanted the Doctor on his way with his ankle better and his aquarium back again. She wanted Heidt's story to end well, even – well, why not? And the monster. Well, not much of a monster, in the end. A scared thing, a fragment of a mind in control of a huge machine. Thought of like that, it wasn't so awful, was it? A rescue cat trying to drive a car. She laughed.

She heard the door open, but she didn't pay attention. There was too much, and she had to get it all down. Music, she wanted music, and art, and drama, and children, and she wanted to go skiing because Simon had always said they would. She wanted life. There was so much inside her she had kept all bottled up, in that vast, quiet place where she put everything she didn't want, the lake.

'Christina,' the Doctor said, 'are you ready?'

'Oh,' she said, a little embarrassed. 'Yes.'

'Good,' he said, a bit muted, and she turned around.

The monster stood directly behind her. It towered over her. Opened its mouth.

She stared at it and realised she had no idea what to do.

And felt the Doctor's hand latch onto hers, grip the paper on which she had been writing and thrust it upwards into the descending maw, so that both of them were engulfed at the same time, swallowed to the shoulder in the vast, vile jaws.

She expected the thing to bite down, wondered if it would hurt very much to be eaten. She felt the Doctor pushed away from her, hurled back by focused time distortion. She was alone with Heidt's twin. She waited for the end.

And felt, instead, a connection. Psychic notepaper pressed to the flesh of the monster and bound at the same time into her skin. Contact. She felt howling, rageful things pour into her mind in a great torrent. Years of war, of concealment, of planning and tactics and ambushes and programming, of victories at great cost and sacrifices and last stands, all of it buffeted her. She hated and feared and cheered and celebrated, and was suddenly cut off in a cold, dark place, cast aside, seeing fellow prisoners slip mockingly away into the night, pursuing. Finding one. Attacking. She would win this time. She would crush, rend. She felt herself fading away.

Jonestown rose up inside her, narrow streets and old women buying fish, barrow boys and taxis and markets giving way to skyscrapers and schools. Women and men went to work, went shopping, went out on the town, went home early for a good night's sleep, went out for a pint of milk and fell in love. Thousands of minds touched her own, calm and reassuring and vastly ordinary. What was all this fuss? That little thing? It was loud and silly and a bit childish. No cause for such a ruckus. There was a place for that kind of behaviour.

She dropped the tiny, squalling awareness of the monster into the black lake in her mind, the place where she put everything which unsettled her, and watched it sink. The oily water swallowed it down. At her back, Jonestown nodded, brushed the dust from its hands, and good riddance.

After a moment, Heidt surfaced and swam awkwardly to the shore.

'Thank you,' he said.

'You're welcome.' She waited. He didn't do anything evil. And, she realised, she could have stopped him, anyway. She began to take note of herself, and of her home and what it had become in the meantime.

'Oh,' she murmured. 'That's... brilliant!' And she laughed.

The Doctor stood in the main street of Jonestown and watched it fold itself up and away, saw the houses unravel and whirl into motes of light, saw the people wave cheerfully and then vanish as if stepping through a door. Arwen Jones the fire chief smiled a dimpled smile and faded, and he thought she blew him a kiss as she went. The skyscrapers disappeared and the road itself shifted and shrugged and became the deck of the TARDIS, plain and clean, and he was in one of the starboard passenger compartments, the one he'd been using as a dry ski slope.

There were three people standing by the door.

'Christina,' he said. 'Mr Heidt.'

Heidt nodded gravely. 'I see you worked it out,' he murmured.

'What? Oh, that. Yes. Well, not so hard, in the end. You made it easy.'

'I certainly tried.'

The Doctor paused. 'I don't think I know this gentleman, though.'

'This is Simon,' Christina said.

'I thought…'

'Yes, he was. But he always continued to exist as part of the town. While one of us exists, we all do. It's a bit complicated.'

He grinned. 'Always is.'

'Mr Heidt is coming with us now, so you don't have to worry about the mine going off or anything like that. You could come too, if you want.'

'But then I can't come back.'

'Well, no. Probably not. But you probably wouldn't want to, either. It's going to be remarkable. It has to do with the trapdoor universe and the—' She stopped. 'You wouldn't understand.'

'Try me.'

'It's been seven thousand years since we last spoke, Doctor. We've come rather a long way. And we fixed the TARDIS for you. She's all shiny and healthy, good as new.'

'Oh. Thank you.'

'A universe where every atom is a universe unto itself. And that's just the beginning. You only travel forwards and backwards through time – don't you ever wonder about left and right? Up and down?'

He smiled. 'Sounds great.'

'It will be.'

'But I'd miss the little things. Earth, and so on. And I don't imagine I could take the TARDIS with me.'

'She would have to be substantially changed. Upgraded.'

'Not sure she'd like that.'

'Sooner or later, everyone grows up.'

He grinned. 'Not me.'

She swatted at him in exasperation, but they were already fading away, and a moment later they were gone.

He went up to the console room and peered at the readouts. Fair enough. Everything as it should be. Copacetic. Interesting thing about the word 'copacetic': no one knew where it came from. No etymology, no derivation. Just appeared in the 1960s, entered the language complete with a definition. Generally agreed, but utterly without predecessors in any human language.

Which was really, really interesting, now that he thought about it.

He wondered what he was missing out on, not going with Not-Christina. He wondered whether he'd regret it, when the time came and he had to regenerate.

A universe where every atom was a universe unto itself. That was quite a lot to turn down.

Mind you, what if there weren't any dachshunds? What if wherever they were going wasn't the sort of place where slime mould grew on soggy psychic notepaper and evolved into Welsh towns?

And then, too: copacetic. You couldn't just leave something like that lying around and not have a look.

I mean, you couldn't.

It was just rude.

Wouldn't do to be rude.

He set the controls for Ojai, California, in 1963, because there was a man there who cooked the best French Toast in the history of the Earth.

SALT
OF
THE EARTH

TRUDI CANAVAN

S mithy lifted his nose above the height of the cabin, giddy with pleasure. The wind rushing past his nose and ears was wonderful. He resisted the urge to voice his excitement; his master didn't like him barking, and would yell and bang on the roof until he stopped.

The wind eased briefly as the utility slowed and Smithy braced his four legs when it changed direction, then as it began again he caught a whiff of something strange. It was a smell both familiar and alien. Familiar because he'd smelled it before, alien because it smelt *wrong*. It always came with a tang of salt, which was common here in this flat place of dried out lakes and ponds.

He whined and hunched down behind the cabin, but after a moment a stray gust brought another scent, and he forgot about the bad smell. Looking over the cabin again, he found the source. Sheep! And not where they were supposed to be. He barked, short and sharp to alert his master, and felt the ute begin to slow. The white shapes were to the side by the time they stopped. Smithy strained at the rope, eager to chase and herd them to wherever his master wanted.

Brown dust surrounded the vehicle as it came to a halt. Now the wind was gone, the heat surrounded Smithy and he started to pant. The vibration in the ute's tray ceased. When his master stepped out of the cabin he came over to scratch Smithy behind the ears, but didn't unclip the rope. His attention was on the sheep.

They hadn't moved. All were facing in the other direction, so they hadn't seen Smithy and his master. All the easier to catch. His master must agree, as he did not hurry to unclip Smithy's rope. Instead he removed the covering around one of his back paws, sighing as stones fell out. Something about the covering caught his master's attention. Not important, in Smithy's opinion, when there were stray sheep to be rounded up.

At last his master slipped the covering back over his paw and reached for Smithy's rope. There was a click as the clip released.

'Git 'em, Smithy.'

Smithy sprang out of the tray and dashed across the brown dirt. The sheep remained still, so he reached them in moments. They'd wandered into a shallow gully, most likely in search of water, but the bottom of it was dry and white with salt. Well, if they'd stayed where they were supposed to they'd have had plenty of good water. Racing around the gully, he barked to get their attention.

They didn't move.

The smell hit him as he came downwind of them. The strange smell, mingled with salt but not enough to disguise the wrongness. The sheep reeked of it. They didn't have the scent of death about them, but they were not moving. He froze, excitement changing to uncertainty.

There was danger here.

The crunch of footsteps reached his ears. He looked up to see his master approaching. Springing into motion, he raced around the gully, filled with a need to protect his pack leader. Circling, he barked a warning, but his master ignored him. His master was the one to give orders, not Smithy.

Following to the gully's edge, Smithy whined as he smelled the strangeness again. His master paused, scratched his head, then took a step forward. Smithy barked and tried to head him off, but was ordered away with gruff disapproval.

The salt crunched under his master's paw coverings. He walked up to the first sheep and reached out to the closest ewe.

He pulled up short with a grunt.

Looking down, his master made a sound of confusion. He leaned down to touch his ankle with his front paw. Above the covering, the skin was slowly turning white.

The same unnatural white the sheep were.

Smithy shivered as the smell of fear began to waft from his master. The man straightened and backed away from the sheep, his gait suddenly jerky and awkward. He made it to the edge of the salty ground and stopped, waving his arms to regain his balance, and looked down.

One back leg was entirely white.

His master straightened and tried walking again, but could only lurch a few steps. Smithy paced back and forth, the instinct to come no closer warring with the need to stay by his pack leader.

His master turned and spoke Smithy's name.

Reluctantly, Smithy slunk to the edge of the salt.

'No!' his master yelled. 'Stay!'

Smithy froze. The paleness was creeping, ever faster, down his master's other back leg. 'Home!' his master ordered. 'Go home.' He made other noises, Smithy did not understand, but in the tone of instruction. Smithy hesitated, confused.

'Go!' his master yelled, angry at Smithy's disobedience. He threw an arm out. Smithy leapt away and ran a few paces, then heard a choked gasp. He skidded to a halt and looked back. His master did not move or speak. His face was now unnaturally pale. He stood as still as the sheep.

But his arm was still extended, pointing towards the place they both ate and slept. Tail between his legs, Smithy raced toward home.

'Here. Put this on,' the Doctor said, handing Jo a bottle of lotion. 'The sun is very fierce out there, you know.'

Jo undid the bottle cap and sniffed at the contents. 'What is it?'

'Lotion. It'll protect you from the sun.'

She looked down at her bare legs and arms, white from too much time spent indoors assisting the Doctor in his lab. 'What would I want to do that for?' Slipping the lotion into her beach bag, Jo turned towards the door.

'Josephine Grant,' the Doctor scolded, picking up the two sun lounge carry bags. 'If I tell you you'll need to take precautions at a destination then you'll need them.'

'Don't be silly,' she said as she pushed open the TARDIS door and stepped out. 'We're not going to some other planet; we're only going to—'

A blinding whiteness dazzled her eyes. Heat surrounded her like a warm hug. She groped in her bag for her sunglasses, remembering belatedly that they were perched on the top of her head. As she did a suspicion began to grow. The ground was suspiciously hard.

'—Australia,' the Doctor finished.

'Australia?' Sunglasses found and in place, Jo looked around. The ground was a shimmering expanse, flat dazzling whiteness extending toward the horizon in two directions, and flat and brown with only the occasional tree to break the monotony in the others. A steady wind buffeted them, hot and dry.

It was not the beach he had promised her.

'Well...' The Doctor turned full circle. 'According to the TARDIS we are in Australia, in the latter part of the twenty-first century.'

'And?'

He grimaced apologetically. 'Just not on the coast. A little fine tuning may be in order.'

Jo sighed and turned back towards the door.

'Still,' the Doctor added, setting the bags down, 'this would do just as well.'

She turned to stare at him in disbelief. He took a pinch of the white soil and dropped it on his tongue. Nodding, he straightened and tapped at the hard white surface with the toe of one shoe. 'We seem to have arrived on a salt lake, which is a bit of unexpected good luck. It's much better than sand, though not as good as the glass plains of—'

'It will *not* do!' Jo protested. 'You said you were taking me on a holiday. Anywhere I wanted!' And then return them to UNIT mere minutes after they had left, so she would not have to apply for time off, and no alien threat to Earth could force her to return from holidays early, as always seemed to happen.

'And you chose Australia, my dear.' He crouched beside the two bags. 'Very unimaginative of you, when I could have taken you anywhere in the universe.' Unzipping the first bag, he began to pull out an odd assortment poles and wheels.

'I said the *beach* in Australia,' Jo corrected. 'Somewhere warm and…' She frowned. 'Wheels? What kind of beach chair has wheels?'

'Beach chair?' The Doctor's looked up and smiled. 'This is something far more entertaining. More than sitting around on a beach doing nothing all day, that is. Which surely you did not expect *me* to do.'

'No, I suppose not.' Jo moved closer, intrigued by the odd contraption the Doctor was assembling despite her disappointment. The triangular frame sat low to the ground with two fat little wheels at the back and one at the front. Heavy vinyl covered the frame, providing a hammock-like seat and an aerodynamic cover. As the Doctor unfurled the next piece she exclaimed in surprise. 'A sail!'

He grinned. 'Yes. This, my dear, is known at this time on Earth as a blokart. A cart with a sail. Or yacht with wheels. A very popular beach activity. Do you know how to sail?'

'Of course. My uncle used to take me out boating when I was a kid.'

'It's the same principle, only with a steering wheel instead of a rudder. Here, help me put together the other one.'

She set down her bag and in a few minutes they had assembled the second blokart. Seeing the gleam of anticipation in the Doctor's eyes, Jo swallowed her lingering objections. Besides, her curiosity had been piqued. Once they'd had a sail – ride – whatever – they could still return to the TARDIS and travel onwards to a beach.

When the sail was in place the Doctor tossed the carry bags in the TARDIS. He held one of the carts still while she climbed aboard and handed her the beach bag, which she stuffed down by her feet with her sunhat.

'Ready?'

She nodded.

'The rope controls the sail. If you feel you're going too fast, let the rope go. The sail will turn edge to the wind. Go slow so I can catch up,' he told her. 'Oh – and you'll need these.'

He handed her a pair of gloves. As he hurried over to the other cart she slipped them on, then took hold of the sail rope and pulled. At once the wind caught the sail, setting the cart rolling. Soon it was propelling her forward, her speed increasing rapidly. It was exhilarating. She let out a whoop.

'I thought I told you to wait for me!' came a shout from behind.

Turning to look back, she laughed as she saw the Doctor grinning as he caught up. He'd stowed his cape and jacket somewhere, and the collar and cuffs of his white shirt fluttered in the wind. Behind him, the TARDIS was already a tiny blue box in the distance, dark against the white salt.

Letting out some rope, Jo let the cart slow a little so he could draw alongside her. Not far ahead the horizon rippled like…

'Water!' she shouted in warning.

'No!' the Doctor yelled back. 'Mirage!'

Sure enough, the illusion retreated as rapidly as they approached it. They zoomed towards it, and eventually it took on a brown tinge.

'We're nearing the edge of the lake,' the Doctor told her.

Soon she could make out brown soil rising above the white

salt of the lake. Time to try turning the blokart. The sail snapped to the other side as she steered it in a wide arc, and soon they were zipping in another direction. She lost all track of time as they wove about, racing back and forth across the salty surface. Eventually they reached the far end of the lake, where the salt was soft and slightly pink, and had to start tacking into the wind to retrace their steps. It was during one of these turns that Jo saw a strange sight.

A man was standing beyond the edge of the lake. He was pointing away from it. She steered closer to the Doctor.

'Is he trying to tell us something?' she called, pointing to the man.

He looked in the direction she'd indicated, and frowned.

'Let's go and see.'

They steered towards the stranger, rolling to a stop at the edge of the lake. Tipping the blokarts on their side so they would not sail away by themselves, the Doctor and Jo headed towards the stranger.

Or rather, Jo soon observed, the statue. The figure hadn't moved since she'd first seen him and as they neared she saw that he was completely white except for his hair, clothing and shoes. He stood at the edge of a small gully, the base dusted with more salt. A couple of sheep sculptures stood nearby, all white apart from their creamy fleece.

'Well, that's an odd place to put statues,' she said.

'Yes,' the Doctor agreed. 'And very strange and unpleasant statues at that.'

Shading her eyes, Jo saw that he was right. The man's mouth was open, frozen in the middle of a scream. The sheep, too, were twisted as if caught in a moment of torment. She took a step down into the gully.

'What are they made of?' she wondered aloud. 'It looks like salt.'

'Stop!'

She turned to look at the Doctor. Deep furrows had appeared between his brows. 'Don't touch them, Jo. Don't touch anything. There is something not right about this.'

A chill ran down her spine. The wind died away suddenly, leaving an eerie silence.

Then it returned in a huge gust, carrying sticks and leaves. She heard a soft crash behind her and turned back to see the human statue's arm had fallen to the ground, shattering into a rough stripe of white powder.

'I think perhaps we should find out what he was pointing at,' the Doctor said. 'Don't you?'

Jo managed a grim smile, and nodded.

Looking up from washing the dishes, Sunny saw the oddest couple approaching her house.

The man was dressed formally in a long-sleeved white shirt with frilly collar and cuffs. Though his hair was white and bushy, his slim frame moved with an energy that suggested he wasn't as old as he first appeared. The woman was younger and shorter – and her face was red, either from sunburn or exertion or both. She was dressed in a miniskirt and blouse in a style of the last century, reminding Sunny of her own love affair with retro fashions, back when she had been a much younger woman.

Placing the last two plates in the drying rack, Sunny wiped her hands, smoothed her short hair and straightened her clothing. Then she picked up the tub she'd set within the sink and carried the dishwater through the house to the front door. The pair had reached the steps to the veranda and stopped as she emerged. She tipped the water onto a potted chili plant by the steps then turned to smile at them.

'How do you do?,' the man said in an English accent. The young woman smiled.

Tourists, Sunny decided. Probably lost. Nobody visited

these parts for fun. Nobody visited it much at all. The sort of 'Outback' people came to Australia to see didn't look like this, all brown dirt and white salt. They wanted the red dirt and monolithic rock formations they'd seen in travel ads.

'Hello,' she replied. 'Need directions?' She looked for a car, but found none. It was probably back down the road, out of sight behind the house.

The man shook his head. 'Actually, I was wondering if you could tell me about the salt statues over by the lake.'

'Statues…' Sunny felt her stomach drop to her feet. Who was it this time? She shivered and looked over to the dog sitting on her porch. The dog that normally stuck to her tenant's side like a shadow. A terrible suspicion was creeping over her. Smithy ducked his head and whined.

The man heard and turned to regard the dog.

'Hello,' he said. 'Who would you be?'

'Smithy,' Sunny volunteered. 'My neighbour's dog.' She pointed to the house on the other side of the road, about a kilometre away. 'Came here three days ago, starving hungry. Not like his owner to leave him behind when he goes away.'

Smithy rose and wandered over to the stranger, wagging his tail a little. Sunny let out a silent sigh of relief at its friendliness towards the stranger. The dog had been uncharacteristically timid and clingy, flinching if she touched him yet sitting by the door and whining when she went inside. The Doctor scratched Smithy behind the ears and gave his rump a couple of firm pats.

'You haven't seen your neighbour for a few days, then?' the man asked, straightening to face her again.

'No,' she replied. She wondered how to ask about the statue without sounding like a mad woman. No, better to stay silent and walk out to the lake later to see for herself.

He smiled. 'Let me introduce myself. I am the Doctor and this is Jo Grant.'

'Sun Williamson. Call me Sunny,' She raised her eyebrows.

190

SALT OF THE EARTH

'*The* Doctor? Not *a* doctor?'

He shrugged. 'A nickname of sorts.'

Medical doctor? Or a scientist? She felt a brief flash of hope. Perhaps someone was finally taking the salt problem seriously. She eyed their strange clothing and changed her mind. More likely they were British tourists who had seen something strange and were curious enough to ask the locals about it.

The man's expression was grim now. 'Is your neighbour about my height, around 50, with light red hair, wearing shorts, short-sleeved shirt and a worn-out pair of boots?'

Or maybe not, Sunny amended.

'That'd describe plenty of people round here,' she replied.

'Does he drive a truck with the license plate DLF1043?'

Her skin prickled. 'Yes.'

He grimaced. 'I think something may have happened to him. Have many people and animals gone missing lately? Have many strange statues appeared out by the lake?'

She stared at him. This 'Doctor' had guessed at an awful lot more than any ordinary tourist would. Though he could be some wacky conspiracy theorist, attracted by the missing person reports and stories the locals had put on the net. She looked from the man to the woman and back again. Something about their earnest seriousness reassured her, and she felt that flash of hope again.

'Some,' she replied. 'You look like you could do with a cold drink,' she said. 'And I'll need something to wet my throat.' She gestured to the battered old chairs under the veranda. 'Sit down and I'll fetch you something from the fridge.'

Jo pressed the cold glass to her face. Once they were off the blokarts and out of the wind, the heat radiating from both the sun and the ground had combined and intensified until she felt as if she was walking in a huge oven. The half-hour walk to the house had left her sweaty and uncomfortable, and even in the welcome shade of Sunny's porch her skin remained hot – as if it had absorbed sunlight and refused to let it go again.

Their host was small and elderly but with a wiry strength to her. She had both Asian and European parentage, Jo guessed. The house looked as tanned and weathered as its occupant, the brick walls camouflaged against the land by a coating of brown dust.

'When did people start going missing?' the Doctor asked.

Sunny shook her head. 'It's hard to say. Talk started about the bad salt about four or five years ago, but people have been vanishing for longer than that. It took a while for someone to find a… a person who'd turned to salt who was still intact and recognisable.'

'The wind removed the evidence?' Jo asked.

'And rain – when we get it. Which hasn't been for a while. We're in the middle of a drought cycle.' She grimaced as a gust of wind sent dust swirling past the house. 'It's getting windier. I should go out and see if it is Sean, before he blows away.'

'We'll come with you,' the Doctor said, his tone gentle. 'We left our means of transport out there. I don't suppose you have an empty jar I could use to take a sample of the salt?'

'I'll see what I can find.'

As Sunny rose, Jo drained the remains of her drink. The old woman took their glasses inside then returned with a small glass jar for the Doctor. She put on a pair of boots in place of the thin sandals she had been wearing.

'The advice we give to visitors is to wear shoes that cover your feet,' she said. 'We say it's because of the snakes, but they'll protect you if you walk on the bad salt, too.'

Jo stared at her. 'Snakes?'

The woman smiled. 'Yes. Don't worry. If you don't bother them they won't bother you. Though there doesn't seem to be as many of them about since the bad salt appeared. I guess everything has its up side.'

'I guess…' Jo echoed, searching the ground as she followed the Doctor and Sunny towards the road, and the salt lake beyond. It was one thing to find she wasn't at the beach, or investigating a strange and alien menace, and quite another to be walking through snake-infested desert.

The Doctor did not seem concerned, however. Jo tried not to jump every time a nearby leaf or twig moved in the wind. The dog, Smithy, had followed them, and appeared unconcerned by snakes or salt.

'So, you're on holiday?' Sunny asked.

'Yes,' the Doctor looked back at Jo and smiled apologetically, 'or we are meant to be.'

'What do you work as?' Sunny asked.

'Oh, I suppose you'd call me a scientific investigator and consultant, and occasional negotiator.'

'Who do you work for?'

'Myself, mostly.'

'Ah. Self-employed.'

'Preferably. Yourself?'

Sunny shrugged. 'Retired. My husband raised sheep for a while. A typical hobby farmer. He died a few years ago so I put everything but the house up for rent. Sean is – was – my tenant.' She sighed and shook her head. 'I doubt I'll find anyone else crazy enough to try making a living out of this land now we're in drought, and without rent payments… well, I don't know what I'll do. I'll probably have to sell everything.'

The dog whined. Glancing back, Jo saw that he had stopped, head low and nose twitching, his attention somewhere beyond the Doctor and Sunny. She could see nothing in that direction but scrubby plants and the salt lake. Except… it was all a bit familiar. Though something was missing…

'Doctor, shouldn't we be able to see the statue by now?'

He checked his stride. 'Yes. I fear the wind has done its work already.'

They continued on in silence, finding the blokarts where they'd left them before they backtracked and located the shallow gully. Smithy hadn't followed, Jo noted. All that was left of the statue was a salt-encrusted pile of clothing. Even the sheep had crumbled away. She shuddered.

Sunny had brought an old broom handle with a hook on the end. She began to poke at the clothing.

'He'd have been carrying his wallet,' she said. Catching a loop of the short's waistband, she dragged it to the edge of the gully. Something was well stuffed inside one of the pockets. As she crouched beside it the Doctor drew closer.

'Don't touch anything,' he warned.

The old woman nodded. 'I know.'

Taking something out of her pocket, she pressed a button and waved it over the garment. It emitted a soft bleep and she turned it over to reveal a small screen showing a man's face, rotating from face-on to a profile. The Doctor edged closer, his face alight with interest. The man's image smiled.

'I am Sean White,' he said. 'I was born on the—'

The voice abruptly stopped as Sunny pressed the button again. As she closed her eyes and let out a long sigh, Jo felt a pang of sympathy.

'I am so sorry,' she said. 'Was he a friend?'

'No, we argued most of the time, mostly about that darn dog barking at night.' Sunny smiled without humour. 'Sean thought the bad salt didn't exist, and people were giving up and leaving because of the drought.' She shook her head. 'Some of those who disappeared... People who had families who weren't the type to abandon them. People who wouldn't just up and leave without letting others knowing they were going.'

'But surely if he saw the people who had turned to salt...' Jo began.

Sunny straightened and looked at Jo. 'He never did. Nobody believes who hasn't seen one. They think the few photos taken of the victims are faked – just statues made by someone with a sick sense of humour. Missing Persons – the police, that is – came out to investigate some of the cases but by the time they arrived the only evidence was a pile of clothing.' She looked down at the shorts. 'Like this.'

Jo looked at the rest of the clothing. 'Shoes,' she said, pointing at the boots. 'He was wearing shoes. You said shoes would protect us.'

The woman reached out with the pole and inserted the end into the closest boot. She lifted it and gently shook away the salt, revealing a hole in the sole.

'Worn out.' She dropped it on the ground. 'Salt must have got inside.'

The Doctor crouched by the shorts and produced the jar Sunny had given him. With a slip of paper from his pocket, he carefully scooped up a little salt and dropped it inside the jar, then discarded the paper. 'Do the locals have any theories as to the cause of the bad salt?' he asked, rising and pocketing the jar.

'Some blame the local salt works.' Sunny shook her head. 'But that doesn't make sense. They stand to lose their livelihood if the bad salt gets into their harvest.'

'And their lives,' the Doctor added. 'Still, if they work with salt they may have noticed something that others have not.' He glanced back in the direction of the blokarts, then back towards the woman's house. 'Do you have a car?'

'Yes.'

'Could we impose upon you for a lift? I'd like to talk to the salt works owners.'

Sunny nodded. 'Sure.'

'Oh, is that a second salt lake?' the Doctor's assistant asked from the back seat.

'One of many,' Sunny replied. 'The land around here is badly affected by salinity.'

'Salinity?' Jo repeated.

'Salt rises up to the surface when it rains,' Sunny explained. 'When people cleared the land for crops a few centuries back they removed the native vegetation. The trees had soaked up the rain, but with them gone the water table rose, bringing up salt in the soil. Some of it was deposited over thousands of years ago when parts of this region were an inland sea.'

'Could you plant new trees?'

'That's one way to combat the problem. It and other methods have been used successfully in salt-affected areas, but so far nothing has worked around here. Even salt-resistant plants die.'

'What happens to them?' the Doctor asked.

Sunny looked over at him. 'Their leaves fall off. Sometimes they go white and brittle. You can break a piece off and it will fall to dust in your hands.'

'It's not dangerous to touch them, then?'

'No. Do you think it's caused by the same bad salt that kills people and animals?'

He frowned. 'Possibly. If it is, then there must be a point where the poison is exhausted or it wouldn't be safe to touch the plant later.'

'Oh! It's quite pink, isn't it?' Jo exclaimed.

Sunny looked into the rear-vision mirror to see the young woman staring out of the car window. Here there was enough water in the salt lake to support life. She chuckled.

'The colour is from algae. The same kind that makes flamingos pink, I believe.'

'Really?' Smithy ducked away from the open window on the other side of the car and licked Jo's face. She laughed and pushed the dog away gently, then winced as she wiped her face. 'My skin hurts.'

'You're sunburned,' Sunny told her. She looked at the Doctor. 'There's some blockout in the glove box. It'll stop it getting any worse, at least.'

'That's fine. I have some, thank you,' Jo said, digging into her bag.

'Don't forget your ears,' Sunny advised as Jo began to apply the cream. She sighed as she remembered that her neighbour's ears were often red from sunburn. Funny how such details stuck in the mind. Did Sean have relatives? She'd never seen anyone visit him. He'd had a reasonable income from an old wind farm to the north on top of raising sheep. What would happen to it now? What was she going to do with Smithy?

'That would be the salt works,' the Doctor said.

Ahead, a row of small, white conical hills had appeared, too perfect to be anything but man-made. Corrugated iron sheds and a large cement board head office building cast hard, short shadows on the ground. This end of the lake was divided into shallow evaporation ponds. She'd always thought they looked like the patches of a giant quilt.

'I guess it makes sense to harvest salt when nothing else will grow,' Jo observed.

Sunny nodded. 'The salt works is a good source of local employment. A lot of people will lose their jobs if the bad salt gets into the lake. It's never been this close before. I'm afraid another local death isn't the only bad news we're going to bring.'

The visitors were silent as Sunny drove the rest of the way to the salt works. From the number of cars parked outside she guessed half the workforce had already gone home for the day. She pulled up outside the head office.

As the Doctor stepped out he patted the roof of the car.

'Very sensible,' he said. He turned to Jo. 'It runs on solar power. On sunshine.'

Jo peered at the car in astonishment.

Sunny smiled. Anyone would have thought they'd never seen a solar car before. 'Yes, you don't see many of these around any more but with water too precious here to use it for running cars and not enough people, stock or crop waste about for much gas production, it's about the cheapest way to get around.' She patted the car. 'It's old and half rusted through but it still works, most of the time, and I can't afford to buy a new one.' As Smithy leapt out, she shook her head. 'What am I to do with you, dog? It's too hot to leave you in the car.'

She led them to the office's glass frontage and told the dog to stay there, in the shade. Whether he would or not she couldn't guess, but he had always obeyed Sean and seemed reluctant to be far from people – he'd been so eager to get in the car with them and she'd felt too sorry for him to leave him behind.

Once inside, she and the two visitors sighed with relief as cool air surrounded them. The reception area was small and fitted out with fairly recent tech. Video of the salt works and the products it made played over a transparent screen dividing the reception desk from the visitor waiting area. Conveyor belts and packaging flickered over the face of the receptionist – the owner's young niece.

'Hi, Kylie,' Sunny said. 'Lou and Sol are expecting us.'

The young woman glanced at the Doctor and Jo.

'Hi. ID?'

The pair exchanged glances. 'Ahh,' Jo began, opening her bag. 'I'm not sure we're carrying any. We're on holidays, you see. I only brought a towel and lotion and…'

'I called ahead,' Sunny told Kylie.

The girl shrugged. 'I'll give them a buzz.' She looked at the transparent screen. 'Call to MD1,' she said. The images of the salt works vanished and Lou's face appeared. She smiled at Sunny, then examined the two visitors.

'Hello. You're the scientists?'

The Doctor nodded. 'I am the Doctor and this is my assistant, Jo Grant.'

'Sorry about the security. We've had some threats and the police suggested we take precautions.' After looking away to speak to someone else, Lou turned back. 'Give them tags, Kylie, and let them in.'

Lou's face vanished. Kylie asked the visitors to speak their names to the screen. She moved out of sight, then a nearby door opened and she stepped out.

'Welcome,' she said. 'Here are your name tags.'

She pressed a finger against the visitors' chests. At once little glowing names and images of their faces appeared, projected onto their clothing from a tiny square stud. Jo was fascinated, tentatively plucking at the device.

'Don't worry,' Kylie told her. 'It'll fall off again when you leave the salt works.'

'Could you put some water out for the dog?' Sunny asked.

Kylie glanced out of the main door at Smithy and nodded. She opened the door she had emerged from and led them through and up a flight of stairs. Sunny had visited the works a few times before for staff birthdays and retirement parties, but had never been in the higher level. A middle-aged woman with a pleasant, round face and a cute bob haircut greeted them at the door of a glass-walled meeting room.

'I'm Lou and this is Sol, my husband and business partner,' she said, gesturing to a slim, well-tanned man with dark, curly hair.

The Doctor shook their hands. 'Hello,' he said. 'I am the Doctor. This is Jo Grant, my assistant. Your receptionist said you've received threats?'

Sol nodded. 'Yes. Half of the locals don't believe in the bad salt, the other half blame us for it.'

'Not all of them disbelieve or blame you,' the Doctor pointed out, nodding at Sunny. 'What have they threatened to do?'

'Mainly to picket the salt works, or to dig up the ponds,' Lou replied. 'We had one bomb threat but the police traced it to a local whose bark is worse than his bite, as the saying goes. We've heard nothing from him since. The worst trouble has been from a few people in a nearby town who reported us to the environmental authority, claiming we'd poisoned the local area. When no proof was found of that or that we'd broken any regulations, the group started trying to scare customers off buying our products by spreading rumours about them being contaminated.'

'It's not made a huge impact on sales,' Sol said. 'The bad salt is a far more worrying threat.'

The Doctor nodded. 'Indeed it is, my dear fellow. What can you tell me about it?'

Sol gestured to one wall, which was covered by a large flat screen. It displayed a map of the region. 'I've done some research this last year. Every dot on this map marks where a bad salt incident was reported or might have happened. The confirmed reports, where someone has seen a human or animal made of salt, are marked with red while the orange ones are where the belongings of missing people were found.'

The Doctor moved closer. 'Have you marked the dates?'

'Touch the dot to see more information.' Sol demonstrated, a small rectangle of text appearing as he tapped one of the dots.

Jo was staring at the screen in amazement, but as Sunny looked at her she shook herself and smiled. Glancing around the room, the young woman noticed several photographs and certificates displayed on the opposite wall.

'Are these of the salt works?' she asked.

Lou nodded and walked over to them, Jo and Sunny following. 'It was harvested by hand at first. Hard, hot work.'

The first photo was a black and white print of several men shovelling salt crystals from the lake's surface. It was a high-contrast image and all the men were dark against the salt, but the distinctive slim silhouette of some of the figures was instantly familiar.

'Are those aboriginal men?' Jo asked.

'Yes,' Lou replied. 'The traditional owners of this land were treated terribly by some of the early colonists.' She moved to another photo, this time in colour, of men standing before farm machinery. 'Later many of them were employed in the industry, but it wasn't until earlier this century, when they were given back some of their lands, that they began to profit from it. One of them was Sol's grandfather. He built the salt works. His son, Sol's father, built it up into a successful business, which was how Sol could afford to go to university.' She smiled. 'That's where we met. He was studying geology; I was studying chemistry.'

Jo drew in a quick breath. 'Are there any aboriginal legends about evil salt that suggest where it might come from?'

Lou smiled. 'That occurred to me when the problem first arose. I asked Sol's uncle, the most knowledgeable of his family, a few years back.' She chuckled. 'He said it was a new problem. *Our* problem.'

'So it's a recent phenomenon,' Jo concluded.

'No more than ten years,' the Doctor agreed. Sunny turned to see him standing, one finger pressed to his cheek, as he surveyed the map. 'The first incidents were here,' he pointed, circling an area, 'then moved outward in all directions. Except here,' he tapped the screen.

'Different geology,' Sol told him.

'How interesting...' The Doctor pointed to the centre of the first area he'd indicated. 'What is here?'

'That's Bracker's Crater.' Sol pressed two fingers to the map and moved them apart, and the map abruptly expanded so the crater took up the entire screen.

'Volcanic or meteor?'

'Nobody's completely sure. It's so old and eroded that you'd never know it was a crater from the ground. Some years back a few city folk dug around in there, hoping to find evidence it was created by a meteor.'

'Did they find any?'

'If they did, they kept it quiet.'

'What's this?' The Doctor leaned closer, looking at a point at the centre of the crater. 'It says "mine entrance".'

'I don't know…' Sol peered at the words. 'Search screen, find Bracker's Crater mine,' he said. At once an image appeared of a hole surrounded by a fence and a sign declaring 'Danger. Do Not Enter' in faded red paint. Beneath it was a paragraph of text. 'It says it's an old salt crystal mine, abandoned for more than fifty years.'

'How interesting,' the Doctor muttered to himself. He straightened and Sunny felt a chill as he took the jar she'd given him out of his pocket. 'Do you have a laboratory here?'

Lou nodded. 'Not a particularly well-outfitted one, though.'

'Well, we'll just have to make do, won't we?' the Doctor concluded. 'I would like to conduct some tests. As a control and comparison, I will need some samples of salt from your works and some table salt harvested elsewhere, if you have any.'

Sol and Lou exchanged a glance, then Sol shrugged. 'Sure, we can get those.'

'I'll assist you,' Lou said. She smiled at the Doctor. 'Follow me.'

Smithy's eyes closed in bliss as Jo scratched behind his ears. He had a broad head, stocky body and long legs, and his coat was a mottled brown and grey. Kylie had come up to ask if she could let him into the reception area after he had begun whimpering, so Jo had gone down to watch over him.

'I had a dog like him when I was a kid,' the receptionist said. 'In fact, it could have been Smithy's uncle or great uncle. Lots of the cattle dogs around here are related.'

'You have a lot of cattle here?'

'No, mostly sheep.' Kylie glanced up at the screen. 'Looks like your boss is coming down to join us.'

The door to the offices opened and the Doctor, Sunny, Lou and Sol entered the room. Jo jumped up from her chair.

'So Doctor, did you learn anything?'

His eyebrows rose. 'Nothing, which is also something. The sample shows no obvious difference between the salt harvested here and ordinary table salt, apart from a few beneficial trace elements.'

Jo frowned. 'So it's not the salt that's turning people into statues?'

'Either that, or the deadly element is removed afterwards or destroyed in the process. I'm afraid the only way we'll find out is to discover some bad salt in the midst of doing its work.'

She shook her head. 'How are we going to do that?'

The Doctor smiled and looked at Smithy. 'I've a hunch *we* won't. But our canine friend here just might.' He turned to Lou and Sol. 'Thank you for the use of your laboratory.'

Sol shook his hand. 'Thanks for taking time from your holiday to tackle our local mystery,' he replied, smiling broadly. 'You are clearly far more qualified than either of us. Where did you study?'

'Oh, here and there.' The Doctor waved a hand dismissively and turned to smile at Smithy. He patted his leg. 'Come, Smithy.' The dog trotted over to him. 'Let's see how good that nose is, eh?'

As Jo followed him out of the door and into the sun, heat surrounded her again. She turned to Sunny. 'The sun here is so strong, it's as if it has *weight*,' she said. 'How do you stand it?'

'You get used to it, I suppose,' Sunny replied, shrugging. 'I'd probably find the cold winters over your side of the world hard to endure.' She got into the car and, once they were all aboard, started it. 'Where to?'

'Bracker's Crater,' the Doctor said.

Sunny hesitated, her brows knitting with doubt for a moment, then shrugged and nodded. She turned on a small screen on the car's dashboard, spoke coordinates to it, and set off down the road.

Surprised, Jo leaned forward. 'The meteor crater? I thought you decided the bad salt was a recent thing? The crater must be millions of years old.'

He turned to regard her. 'Yes, but we can't ignore the fact it is located in the centre of where all the victims, or suspected victims, of bad salt were found, as if the salt has been moving outward from that point.'

'So you might be wrong?'

He turned away 'Not necessarily. I want to investigate the salt crystal mine, and *that* is certainly more recent.'

The air blowing in the partially open window smelled unfamiliar to Smithy. It was oddly uninteresting, too. He'd not caught a whiff of animals or carcasses in some time. Within the car he could smell the complex mix of scents that surrounded people and the vehicle, including the sweet stuff one of the people had rubbed onto her hide and an underlying tang of rust. In fact, so much smelly stuff surrounded him it almost overwhelmed his senses, but not so much that he didn't catch the sudden taint of wrongness.

He stiffened and let out a whine, unsure where it had come from. Sniffing cautiously, he caught another whiff from somewhere below. Somewhere under the surface he was standing on.

Which was much too close for comfort. His hackles rose and began to pace back and forth, barking. The male non-human person beside him spoke sharply, but not to Smithy. As the car abruptly slowed Smithy almost lost his balance and fell into the dangerous hollow in front of him.

He yelped and scratched at the door, desperate to get out. It might not be any safer outside, but from the increasing smell he was certain he was in danger where he was. The male person opened his door and Smithy took a flying leap over him and out, dashing towards an outcrop of rock, which his instincts told him was a good place to be.

The people followed him, which was unusually smart for people. They stood beside him on the outcrop, looking back at the car. Smithy heard a loud, tortured creak from the vehicle. He flattened his ears and whined, and waited to see what the people would do next.

The creaking noises died away as quickly as they had started, yet nobody moved. Sunny's heart continued racing, as much from the possibility that they had just narrowly avoided becoming a set of salt sculptures in a rusty old car than from the effort of climbing the steep, rocky outcrop.

Would they have crumbled away or, sheltered by the car, remained intact long enough for someone to find and identify them? Maybe they'd have lasted long enough to finally prove to authorities that people really were turning into salt statues.

She'd rather convincing them didn't involve her and the nice British pair dying, however.

'What just happened?' Jo asked.

'To be honest, I'm not entirely certain,' the Doctor replied. He looked down at Smithy. 'But it was better to be safe than sorry. Am I right, Smithy?'

The dog sneezed. For a few more minutes they watched the car in silence, then the Doctor bent down to pick up a stone and started climbing back down the outcrop.

'Where are you going?' Jo exclaimed.

'Don't worry,' he called back to her. 'I'm wearing shoes.'

Even so, Sunny held her breath as he stepped onto the brown dirt at the base of the outcrop. She felt bad enough that she had never convinced Sean that danger from bad salt was real. If the advice she'd given the couple was wrong, and the Doctor turned into salt, she'd never forgive herself.

But the man appeared to be fine as he walked slowly, careful not to kick up any dust, back to the car. He bent to examine the paintwork near the underside, where it had flaked away over the years to reveal the rusty body beneath. Except that those red spots were now white, she realised. White with salt.

The Doctor produced a jar from his pocket and, using the stone, scraped some of the new salt into it. He returned to the outcrop, where he plucked a fleshy leaf from a succulent growth in a sheltered crack. He dropped it inside the jar.

They all stared at it. Nothing happened.

'All used up,' the Doctor said. 'I think we must have driven over a patch of bad salt. The tyres kicked it up onto the bottom of the car, and it set to work on the rust. I'll check a few more samples, but I think we'll find it's perfectly safe to drive on.'

He moved between the outcrop and the car, scooping up soil and tossing it aside when it had no effect on the leaf. Jo and Sunny followed. When they finally reached the car everyone came to a stop, no one game to get inside, until Smithy suddenly trotted up and jumped in.

Sighing with relief, they climbed aboard, but as Sunny pressed the ignition button no faint vibration came from the engine. She exchanged a look with the Doctor.

'I think it did some damage.'

He nodded and climbed out again. 'Let's have a look.'

As they opened the panels to reveal the inner workings, it was obvious they would not be going anywhere. Tubes had burst, and rubber seals cracked. Coolant and water had turned to salt.

Sunny straightened and took her phone out of her pocket. As she called the car assistant service to request a tow-truck, she hoped desperately that the local mechanic who took care of call-outs in the district would not suffer the same fate they had, or worse. The usual irritating voice menus were followed by a pre-recorded voice telling her she was the twenty-ninth in the queue, and would she like to hold or receive a call back for a small fee?

She chose the call-back service, more out of a habitual reluctance to run the battery down than impatience. It was never good to be caught out in such isolated country without a working phone.

'So we're stuck here?' Jo was asking the Doctor.

'Not at all,' he replied.

'You can fix the car?'

'Hmm, maybe – but not before nightfall.' He moved to the back of the car. 'But we don't have to wait that long.' He opened the boot and a smile lit up Jo's face.

'The blokarts!'

'Which are made of stainless steel, so not vulnerable to unexpected rusting!' The Doctor turned to Sunny. 'Will you be all right on your own?'

She swallowed rising apprehension at the thought, then looked at the dog. Smithy would know if any bad salt was about. He really was a good dog, she realised. Maybe she would keep him. If they both survived the day.

'We'll be fine,' she said.

'Stay on the rocks, just in case,' the Doctor advised.

Sunny watched as the pair hauled the two carry bags out of the boot.

'Let's get these assembled quickly,' the Doctor told Jo. 'It's getting late and I don't know about you, but being caught in the crater at night doesn't appeal.'

It was only when the two blokarts had disappeared down the dusty road that Sunny discovered the bottles of water she always carried had also turned to salt.

'Don't take too long,' she muttered, directing her thought towards both the Doctor and her phone. Without water, nobody lived long in the outback.

The road was much bumpier and dustier than the salt lake, Jo reflected ruefully as she followed the Doctor. They moved slowly, the wind unpredictable where it encountered the fragmented walls of the crater. Occasionally they hit a still area and had to move the blokarts along by turning the side wheels with their hands, relying on their gloves to protect them from any bad salt that might cling to the tyres.

At last they reached the edge of the crater interior. If Jo hadn't known it was one, she might never have noticed that the eroded ridges around them formed a broken circle. The gap they had just passed through was narrow compared to those further to the north.

The Doctor continued following the road. The surface was corrugated, and as the wind blew Jo along after him a vibration came through the blokart, rattling her teeth. She would have slowed to lessen the effect, but the wind had picked up and the Doctor was pulling away, zooming towards some distant objects half-veiled by the dust kicked up by their wheels and blown ahead of them.

Soon enough the objects resolved into the fence and warning sign they'd seen on the screen at the salt works. Jo pulled up alongside the Doctor. He looked over to her.

'It might be dangerous in there. You should—'

'—come along, just in case something happens,' she finished for him. 'How else will I know if you need help?'

'You can fetch help if I don't come out after, say, an hour. If we're both trapped in there—'

'—Sunny will get help. She's bound to drive down here if we haven't emerged by the time her car is fixed.'

He shook his head, then sighed and began to climb out of his blokart. Following suit, she tipped her cart on its side beside his. They moved over to the fence. It was a simple waist-high barrier of posts and barbed wire. Beyond, the road continued down into the earth, disappearing into a dark tunnel.

The Doctor pushed down on the barbed wire at a point where it was already sagging, and carefully stepped over. He held it down so Jo could follow. They turned to face the cave entrance. He smiled at her grimly, switched on the torch Sunny had loaned to them, and led the way into the darkness.

'Keep your gloves on,' he advised. 'Don't touch anything.'

'I won't.'

The shaft was steep, but straight. Their progress was slow, however, as the tunnel was strewn with rubble, and the Doctor had to light the way for both of them. But only the first twenty paces or so were cluttered. From then on the way was clear except where the old wooden slats and beams supporting the walls had failed and the rock and dirt released had spilled out across the shaft.

It was within one of the hollows left by a cave-in that Jo first noticed a crystalline sparkle. Then the torch beam exploring the darkness ahead bounced back at them. The Doctor paused, and Jo looked at his face, faintly lit from reflected torchlight. His frown set her skin tingling with apprehension. What was it that worried him? She strained to see into the darkness ahead. As he pointed the torch down the shaft again she heard him suck in a breath.

'Ah,' he said, his face alight with eagerness. 'If I am not very much mistaken...'

Jo followed as he approached the source of the reflection. The tunnel walls ended and as the torchlight ventured beyond it splintered into a thousand beams of colour. Each bounced off a surface and refracted again and again until they were surrounded by light. She gasped in astonishment and delight.

They stood at the brink of a huge cave. Crystals encrusted the walls in all directions, some as long and thick as her arm.

'Salt crystals, if I am correct,' the Doctor declared, 'which I almost always am.'

'They're beautiful!' Jo turned slowly to take in the whole cave. 'But why didn't anybody tell us about this?'

'Maybe they don't know.' The Doctor's expression became

thoughtful. 'Maybe the danger the sign warns of is not just old mine walls collapsing. These are, after all, *salt* crystals.'

Suddenly the sparkling crystals were as menacing as they were beautiful.

Jo moved closer to the Doctor. 'Should we take a sample and go?'

'Hmm...' Taking the jar out of a pocket, the Doctor scraped a few of the smaller crystals off the wall into it. He then produced the leaf and dropped it inside. It remained unharmed. 'Still, let's keep our gloves on, just in case, eh? Now, let's see where the cave leads.'

They did not walk so much as climb and slide along the cave, since the crystals covered the floor and were as smooth as glass. At least the refracting of the torch beam spread the light more evenly, so the Doctor did not need to direct it at the ground so they could both avoid obstacles. After a few hundred feet, they reached the end of a cave. There the jagged crystalline wall gave way to something glasslike, smooth and convex.

The Doctor moved over to examine it. 'Well, this doesn't fit. And what is *this*?' He swung his arm in a circle, his finger hovering over a crack in the surface. 'A perfect circle.'

Jo nodded. 'It is rather regular, considering everything else is such a jumble.'

'I don't suppose it is a door... but with no handle and no lock.' He reached into his coat and she was not surprised when it emerged holding the sonic screwdriver. 'Shall we see if we can open it? Stand aside.'

Without waiting for her reply, he activated the device and pointed it at the seam, moving it around the circle. Jo stepped to one side and waited, but nothing happened. The Doctor adjusted the screwdriver, which made an odd low noise. He muttered something.

'What is it?' she asked.

'Ah, it's hard to make fine adjustments when you're wearing gloves. I've gone and switched it to a low fre—'

Another noise filled in the cave, but not from the screwdriver. It was deeper and louder – almost felt more than heard – and it was coming from the smooth section of wall. The Doctor froze, then pointed the device at the seam again. Once again it emitted a low noise, and the deeper sound intensified.

'It's opening,' the Doctor said. 'Look!'

Jo leaned closer. Sure enough, the circular section was now just proud of the rest of the surface. A hiss came from the seam, then a crack, and without warning the circle slid forward, liquid spraying out from the sides. Jo felt tiny drops land on her face and arms, and raised a hand to wipe them away with her glove. The circle flopped forward, revealing a smooth back and a single hinge.

The Doctor, who had been standing in front, remained smugly dry. He grinned, then nodded at the hole. 'See? I was right. A door!'

'What's inside?'

He directed the torch within. Jo crouched beside him. A smooth tunnel of the same material as the door extended for a short way, narrowing a little toward the end, where it was cracked and broken and choked with rock.

'Is it… is it a spaceship?'

'Yes. A crashed ship I think.' The Doctor put away the sonic screwdriver and carefully stepped through the hole. 'There's no floor, and water has accumulated at the front,' he warned as she began to follow.

Moving inside, Jo walked along the curved wall to join him. Without the refractive crystals around them all was dark except what was lit by the torch beam. She looked down at the pool of liquid. The Doctor directed the torch downward and as it penetrated the water it illuminated a pale, shrivelled shape. At one end it had a tail not unlike a whale's, on the other a swelling with thick strands – perhaps tentacles – sprouting from a cavity. She recoiled.

'What is *that*?'

'The former occupant,' the Doctor said grimly. 'Probably died when the craft crashed here. An alien underwater species, from the look of it.'

'So it wasn't a meteor?'

'No. And if this ship made the crater, it must have landed millions of years ago.'

'So you were wrong that the bad salt was a recent threat.'

He chuckled. 'Not necessarily. We don't know if this ship is the cause of the bad salt, yet. If it is, then I'd say the miners disturbed the craft and released something, which still makes it a recent threat.'

Jo rolled her eyes. She raised a hand to scratch her face, which was itchy where the water had touched her. The fingers of her gloves caught on something rough. Taking a glove off, she touched her face again and was puzzled to feel patches of crustiness on her skin. Her arms itched, too. Looking down, she moved them nearer the torch beam and saw white spots on her skin.

Her stomach plunged somewhere below her feet.

'Doctor!' she gasped.

He looked up from examining a panel set into the wall. 'What is it?' The torch beam rose and dazzled her, but as she extended her arms it lowered again. She saw the Doctor's expression change as he saw the spots and knew her awful suspicion was right.

'Oh, no,' he said.

'It was the water that sprayed out when the door opened.' She touched her face again. 'I'm turning to salt!'

'Not exactly.' The Doctor grasped her shoulders. 'It would take immense power to change your atomic structure, so it's more likely it has been transferring the salt in its vicinity into anything organic it encounters. You're not in direct contact with the ground or anything else containing salt. That should… well, it should slow it down at least.'

He rose and moved away. The itching sensation was stronger, but Jo could not tell if that was her imagination or not. Looking down at her arms she was frustrated to find she couldn't see them now. The torch beam was flicking around the interior of the ship.

'This craft must be the source,' the Doctor was saying. 'But why? Why salt?'

Jo realised she was breathing too fast. She sat down on one of the larger rocks that had penetrated the ship's nose so long ago and tried to stay calm, but all she could do was wonder how quickly she would turn into a salt statue, even if the process was slower. Hours? Minutes? Did it hurt?

No, she told herself. Don't think about it. The Doctor will find a cure.

If he had the time.

'Of course!' he exclaimed, and her heart skittered with hope. 'They're not just an alien underwater species, they're an alien *salt* water species. Their life-support system would maintain the brackishness of the water.' He was rocking back and forth on the balls of his feet, as close to pacing as the small space allowed.

'Salt water,' Jo repeated. Something about that resonated through her. 'Make salty.' Her lips tingled. She licked them and tasted salt.

'It didn't shut down when the ship crashed.' The torchlight settled on the cracked walls and rock at the nose of the craft. 'It escaped. The miners or meteor hunters disturbed it. Or the clearing of the land causing the water table to rise, flooding the ship and bringing bad salt up to the surface with the brine… But what is it? It must be small. Bacterial? No, I couldn't see any remnants of it in the lab. Something smaller. Nanobots?

Nanobots! Of course. *Atomically* small.' He rubbed his hands together. 'Nanobots moving salt into any water they encounter. Moving so much that salt crystals form. But how to turn them off? They probably have a binary system. On or off. Where are the controls?' He began to search the walls.

All of Jo's face was itching now. And her hands. And inside her mouth. It was dry. She shouldn't have licked her lips. She realised she was really, really thirsty.

'Doctor,' she croaked. 'Please hurry up.'

The torch beam flicked to her face, then away. 'Don't worry, Jo. The answer is here. I only need to work out how the aliens communicated.'

'If how they appear is any clue, then like whales,' she said, the movement causing a flash of pain as her lower lip split.

'Whales!' he shouted, his voice echoing in the small space. 'Of course! Sonar! Ah! That's why the door opened when I used a lower frequency!' A rustle of cloth followed, then the low sound that had triggered the door. 'That means "open". Chances are, the nanobots will only respond to two sounds. One for on, which they are already set to, and one for off.' He moved closer. 'Hold out your arm.'

Jo obeyed, though her shoulder was oddly stiff. The Doctor directed the torch at a white patch, now as large as her hand. It glistened, and as she stared she realised the edges were moving. Spreading.

He pointed the sonic screwdriver at it and the low sound came again.

'Anything?'

She shook her head with an effort. The sound changed.

'Now?'

'No.' Speaking hurt her throat. She hoped he wouldn't ask anything that required a more complicated answer.

The sound changed again, and continued changing. Suddenly a shock went through her. She tried to tell him, but all that came out were the words: 'Stop make salt.'

'Aha!' he said. 'That did something.' He pushed her sleeve back. Her skin was a normal colour past her wrist, and the white was no longer spreading. He regarded the sonic screwdriver thoughtfully. 'Seems I am constantly finding more uses for this than opening locks.' He looked up. 'How do you feel?'

She tried to move, but all her muscles resisted. Parts of her felt numb. Others were painfully cold. His brows lowered.

'Ah. Well. I wonder if I can make the nanobots work in reverse.' He looked around the ship. 'They probably communicated with the ship by sound, but whatever store of energy they used to power the controls will be long depleted.' He pressed a finger to his cheek. 'If I can find a power source… Surely if they had nanobots for creating salt, they had them for other purposes. Like ship repair and treating wounds and illnesses.'

'Repair,' Jo echoed as he turned back to the control panels, though she had no idea why.

Shock went through her, then. An itch far stronger than before followed. It spread and grew rapidly more intense, and she drew in a breath to cry out … but then it faded as quickly, leaving her tingling all over. Suddenly her thirst was gone and she was no longer cold or numb in places. She moved her arms, taking off her other glove and searching for the crusty patches. She found none.

'Doctor,' she said. 'I think that did it!' As he turned the torch beam on her she held out her arms. The white spots were gone. 'Oh!' Relief flooded her. 'Whatever you did, worked.'

'I didn't do anything,' he told her. Grabbing her hands, he examined her arms closely, then looked intently at her face. 'You are, miraculously, healed.'

'It happened when you said "repair",' she told him.

His eyes widened. 'No, it happened when *you* said it.' He straightened. 'The nanobots – all of them – understand you now. Which must be how the aliens communicated with them.

Nanobots for giving orders to nanobots.' He laughed. Then his expression became wary. 'You must take care what you say now, in case you trigger other nanobots.'

Jo got to her feet. 'But we know how to stop them. I just have to say "stop"!'

'Perhaps. But if I recall correctly, you said "stop make salt" before, when the sonic screwdriver turned off the salt-making nanobots. That's more specific. What if you started another process, but didn't know what it was? How could you tell it to stop?'

'Oh, I guess I'd have to say "stop everything" or "all systems off" or "stop all nanobots" or—'

A vibration went through the ship. The Doctor looked up and around, then at Jo. As they stared at each other the sensation stopped.

The Doctor let out a sharp breath. 'Well that was—'

His last words were drowned out by a loud rumble. The ship began to shake. The torch beam flickered around the interior and for a second Jo glimpsed the pool of water churning. She grabbed the Doctor's arm as the shaking increased and threatened to knock her off her feet.

A loud creak came from above.

The Doctor looked up. 'I think we should leave now,' he shouted.

Jo nodded.

They hurried to the door and slipped out, Jo glancing back at the murky water and feeling a moment of sorrow for the poor alien who had died when the ship crashed. It must have been preserved by the salty water. Pickled.

The cavern was not shaking as violently, but it was slow to navigate and by the time they neared the mine shaft the vibration had increased and crystals began to shake loose from the ceiling. They dodged a few as they staggered the last few steps, but once in the mineshaft the danger increased. Planks holding back the walls rattled ominously and dirt rained down from above. They ran blindly into a cloud of dust, hands extended and coughing, tripping when they met the earlier – or perhaps more recent – wall collapses. At any moment Jo expected to feel the roof press down and around her, soil instead of dust filling her lungs and the weight of tonnes of soil and rock crushing her…

Then they were out, sucking in fresh air and skidding to a halt before the barbed wire fence. The Doctor kicked over a fence post and practically lifted her off her feet to help her over the wire, then they both broke into a run for the blokarts.

As they reached them, a long, slow boom came from behind. Turning back, Jo gasped as the ground beyond the mine entrance sank several feet, and a great cloud of dust billowed up.

As the noise faded, Jo let out a long sigh and turned to the Doctor. To her surprise a statue of brown dust stood before her. It grinned. Looking down at herself, she laughed as she saw she was as well coated with it as he.

'Can I talk now?' she asked as she began to slap at her clothes.

'Yes. You turned off all systems, remember.' As he shook his head a halo of brown gusted outward.

'Oh, good,' she said. 'I'd hate to have to stay completely silent for the rest of my life.'

'Heaven forbid.'

She narrowed her eyes at him, but he only smiled in reply. Dusting off her arms, she was relieved to see her skin was back to its normal colour. The heat of the late afternoon sunlight was rather pleasant now. Which was odd. 'Will you look at that? I'm not sunburned any more!'

'The repair must have included skin damage.'

She touched her face as a scarier thought occurred to her. 'Or are the nanobots still in me?'

'They probably are, but they've been turned off.'

'Could they reactivate?'

He frowned. 'They might. I'll take some blood and do some tests when we get back to the TARDIS. It's also possible the nanobots that escaped the ship are still active.' He took out the sonic screwdriver and pointed it at the ground around them. It emitted a low noise. 'I'll make a device set to the frequency that turns the salt nanobots off and give it to Sunny. Then we can go home.'

'Home?' Jo protested. 'What about the beach?'

He smiled. 'Keen to get sunburned all over again?'

She grinned. 'This time I'll make sure I'm wearing plenty of lotion!'

He chuckled and turned to the blokarts. 'Come on, then. Let's return to Sunny and see if anybody has arrived to fix the car yet.'

Sunny leaned against the side of her neighbour's ute and watched the Doctor and Jo walk away. They were an odd couple, with their vintage clothing and fascination with old technology, but they seemed nice enough. She'd never managed to find out why they'd left the big blue storage container out at the edge of the salt lake, but if the gadgets he'd taken from it did kill off bad salt then she really didn't mind not knowing.

She looked down at the devices. They looked like a small but fancy torch and emitted low noises that Smithy found fascinating.

Looking down at the dog, she smiled. He'd kept her company while she'd waited for the mechanic to come fix the car. She supposed she *would* adopt him. It would be nice to have the company. The tenant who replaced Sean would likely come with his own dogs. Her mood lightened as she realised that it wouldn't be so hard to find someone to take on the farm, now that the bad salt was gone. And, as everyone around here liked to say, the drought wouldn't last for ever. She had half a mind to try running the farm herself, and hire a few locals for the heavy work. Maybe just until the rains returned.

The dog's ears pricked up and he barked. A chill ran down her spine and she began to scan the ground, holding one of the devices at the ready. But Smithy's attention was elsewhere. A mechanical, rhythmic whine reached her ears. A light on top of the blue box was flashing. She pushed off the car and took a few steps forward, worried that it was some sort of alarm.

Then the box slowly, but steadily, faded out of sight.

In the silence that followed, she stood frozen, staring at the place it had been.

Then she shook her head and turned back to the car. Very few people had been able to grasp that something was turning people into statues of salt. Nobody was going to believe she had just seen a blue storage container vanish into thin air.

She shrugged. At least this time, nobody needed to.

All had departed from that meeting of the School of Night but for Doctor Dee and the newest member, one who always wore black. He offered Dee a gift: a black, circular looking glass fashioned from obsidian stone.

'A *specularibus lapidibus*,' explained the dark-robed candidate.

'Yes,' Dee agreed. 'A scrying-glass, and a good one at that. Where didst thou find it?'

'Aztec loot, plundered from a Spanish conquistador. It is said that sublime visions can be conjured by it.'

Dee took the object and stared into it, mesmerised by its smooth black surface. He had always been tempted by the dark arts. He saw his ghostly reflection in the polished volcanic stone.

'One might then see through a glass darkly…' he muttered.

'And I have something else that will help in the scrying,' added the other man.

He produced a lacquered wooden box and slid open its lid. Something twitched within and emitted a fetid odour. Dee peered at a creature inside: a fat, purpled slug that squirmed and shimmered.

'An incubus?' Dee gasped.

'Yes,' the man took it out and held it towards Dee's face.

The head of the incubus began to pulsate. Transfixed, Dee felt his revulsion change to a more terrifying emotion: desire. All at once horror became seduction and, as the aura of the creature invaded his senses, Dee began to salivate. With a quiver it leapt onto his face. He felt it on his beard, against his mouth, wet upon his lips. His neck arched back in a spasm of exquisite terror as it slithered inside of him.

Moving quickly, it lodged itself deep within his guts. The incubus took possession of him. Blood, bile, phlegm, Dee felt it in all his humours, but it made its dwelling place that most vulnerable part: his very soul of yearning. And it took his conscious mind for a moment too, wiping the memory of its visitation from Dee's recollection.

'Something else for the scrying?' Dee asked, looking into the now apparently empty box.

'Here,' the man pulled out a slip of parchment scored with grotesque characters. 'Use this incantation. Call upon the Hieroglyphic Monad.'

Three nights later Dee and his fearful pupil Thomas set the obsidian scrying glass on an alchemists' 'table of practice' amid the vast library of his house in Mortlake. They bowed before this altar of blasphemy draped with a tapestry of cabalistic symbols. The young assistant trembled as his mentor began to mutter a dreadful incantation.

'Sir,' the pupil whispered in protest. 'Is this not the dark art of witchcraft?'

The magus in his black clerical robes and skullcap turned to admonish his acolyte.

'Look upon the black stone,' he commanded. 'The scrying glass will manifest sublime visions. Then we may witness the divine and speak with angels.'

'But what if in our attempt to conjure angels we summon demons?'

The older man shuddered a moment. A flickering, fugitive memory of his own demonic infestation. It had come to vivid life by night in grotesque and lustful phantasms, then had left him oblivious by morning. All that lingered was a hunger for dark knowledge and that dreadful brooding of morose delectation. He felt enslaved by own curiosity.

'Hush!' Dee implored, more to himself than to his assistant. He raised his hands in supplication and began chanting once more. The obsidian mirror began to glow and the outline of a curious symbol formed on its polished surface. 'See!' he called out. 'The Hieroglyphic Monad! The great talisman that can draw down heavenly forces.'

There came a great rush of wind within the library and a ghostly throbbing light that threw wild shadows against the cluttered bookshelves. As the bearded sage stood to greet this apparition, his pupil crouched in terror, his hands clasped in prayer.

'May the saints preserve us,' he begged.

Lightheaded with astonishment, Dee slowly approached the strange blue box that had miraculously appeared within the confines of the great library. 'See what I have conjured!' he declared, breathlessly. 'It appears to be some sort of sarcophagus. Egyptian, perhaps.'

As he tentatively reached out to touch its panelled sides, a door sprang open and a man in brightly coloured garb stepped out.

'What are you doing in there?' Dee demanded. 'Who are you?'

'Well, I could ask you the same question.'

'I'm the Doctor.'

'What?' spluttered the Doctor indignantly. 'That's *my* line. *I'm* the Doctor!'

'Well, you look like a fool in that jester's motley,' Dee retorted, indicating the garish frock coat and yellow britches.

'How dare you, sir! What gives you the right to insult me?'

'I'm the Doctor.'

'You keep saying that! Doctor who?'

'Doctor Dee.'

'Doctor Dee?' the Doctor pondered. 'I've heard of you.'

'Of course you have. Doctor of divinity and of mathematics. Alchemist, astrologist, navigator, I am, sir, Her Majesty's most noble intelligencer. And the greatest mind of our time.'

'Only of *your* time? Well, I can do better than that,' the Doctor boasted.

But Dee ignored him. 'Now my magical prowess is proven,' he continued, touching the side of the blue box once more, 'in conjuring this vessel.'

'This is *my* vessel! So hands off.'

'But do you deny that I summoned this craft?'

'No! I mean, yes, I mean...' The Doctor was momentarily baffled. 'How did you do that?' he asked.

Dee turned to his table of practice. Thomas rose timidly up from behind it.

'First let me introduce my pupil. Thomas Digges, an able mathematician and astronomer in his own right.'

'Honoured to make your acquaintance, sir,' said Thomas with a deferential nod.

'Delighted, I'm sure,' the Doctor answered tersely. Then he clicked his fingers, as if remembering something. 'Oh, yes, *I've* got an assistant too. Peri!'

A young woman in denim shorts and a silver zip-up jacket emerged from the TARDIS.

'What's up?' she hailed them, then turned to the Doctor. 'Where are we?'

'Elizabethan England. Not sure if that's quite the look for this period.'

'Hey, if you would have let me know where we were going...'

'Never mind that now. This is Doctor Dee and Thomas Digges. I present my companion, Perpugilliam Brown.'

'You can call me Peri.'

'An angel!' Thomas declared as he rushed forward to kneel before Peri. 'We have truly conjured an angel. May I?'

Thomas took her hand and kissed it.

'Hey, cut that out, er...'

'Digges. Thomas Digges. Your humble servant.'

'Yeah, right. Look, get up will you?'

'I am at your command,' Thomas stood.

'Listen, Tommy, I'm no angel.'

'But surely you are from some strange land.'

'Well, I'm an American.'

'A wondrous creature of the New World!'

'I guess.'

The Doctor turned to Dee. 'So, how did you manage to make contact with our TARDIS?' he demanded.

'TARDIS?'

'Yes, this vessel of ours.'

'Let me show you.'

Dee led the Doctor and Peri over to his table of practice. He pointed to the symbol that still burned against the black surface of the scrying glass.

'Hermetic wisdom instructs us to gain astral influence through the correct use of talismans,' he went on.

'Yes,' the Doctor nodded. 'A symbolic device that activated a distress signal in the control system of the TARDIS. Let me have a look at it.'

Peering into the obsidian stone, the Doctor could make out that the sign on it was an entwined composite of arcane glyphs representing the stars, the planets, the elements.

'Fascinating,' he remarked.

'It's happened before,' Peri shrugged. 'When we first met, the TARDIS was diverted by that weird symbol from my stepfather's archaeological survey. Right?'

'Another life. So many lives.' The Doctor absently traced the outline of the figure with his fingers.

'Yeah, well, you were kind of different then,' said Peri.

'My fifth incarnation. Never liked that one much. So tediously sure of myself. Now this,' he pointed at the emblem. 'This looks like the Hieroglyphic Monad.'

'You know it?' Dee started, surprised by the Doctor's knowledge and at the quiver of something in his guts.

'What's the Hieroglyphic Monad?' Peri asked.

The Doctor shrugged. 'I suppose it was a Renaissance

attempt at the Grand Unified Theory.'

'Yes,' said Dee with a growing feeling of visceral excitement. 'This symbol encodes a vision of unity in the cosmos. I wrote a treatise on it seven years ago. Unfortunately my commentary is incomplete. I'm yet to decipher it completely.'

'Well, it's best left alone,' said the Doctor. 'Trust me.'

Dee's disappointment was physical, a palpable sinking in his stomach. 'But you have some knowledge of it,' he said. 'Perhaps you are of the School of Night.'

'Perhaps.' The Doctor shrugged again.

'What's the School of Night?' asked Peri.

'A secret society,' Thomas explained. 'A place where freethinking scholars might talk of subjects condemned as heresy. Alchemy, astrology, heliocentricism.'

'Heliocentricism? Like, the Earth going round the Sun?' she asked.

'It is a dangerous belief, my lady,' Thomas assured her. 'Men have been burnt at the stake for it.'

'And the School of Night is where I acquired this talismanic scrying glass. From a new member,' said Dee, turning to the Doctor. 'One much like yourself, sir.'

'Not another doctor, I hope.'

Dee laughed. 'No. The two of us are more than enough, sir. This one has not reached our exalted status. In the secret academy he is between bachelor and doctor.'

Peri frowned. 'This distress signal is kind of strange,' she said. 'Last time that happened it was a trap.'

'Do you know what might have alerted us?' the Doctor asked Dee.

'We have observed a great disturbance in the heavens,' he replied.

'In the constellation of Cassiopeia,' Thomas added.

'Wait a minute,' the Doctor clapped his hands together. 'What time is it?'

'The chimes struck midnight more than an hour ago,' said Thomas.

'The date, man, the date!'

'It's the morning of the third of November.'

'Yes, yes, go on.'

'The year of our Lord fifteen-hundred and seventy-two.'

'Of course! The supernova in Cassiopeia, Earth time 1572.' The Doctor took out the fob watch from his waistcoat and studied it. 'But that doesn't happen until tomorrow.'

'We have seen a strange light distortion in the constellation. Come,' beckoned Dee. 'Upstairs to our observatory.'

They climbed a spiral staircase up into a windowed belvedere on top of the library. By an open casement a brass tripod held a hexagonal wooden column that pointed out into the night sky.

'Behold, our perspective glass,' said Dee. 'A marvellous artifice constructed by Thomas here.'

'It was my late father's invention,' the young man explained. 'He proposed that by fixing lenses both concave and convex within a frame at the correct angles one might view distant objects with greater clarity and increased magnitude.'

'Am I getting my centuries mixed up or wasn't it the seventeenth century that the telescope was invented?' Peri whispered to the Doctor.

'There were many prototypes,' he explained, noting that the instrument was aimed at the great 'W' of Cassiopeia. 'Might I have a look?'

'Pray, be our guest,' said Dee.

The Doctor put his eye to it and hummed to himself for a minute. He stood back.

'There's certainly a distortion somewhere in that constellation. We're looking at the past, of course, but I can't explain it. Unless...' He stroked his chin. 'Unless someone was powering up a massive interstellar transportation portal.'

'What?' demanded Dee. 'A door in the heavens?'

'Something like that. I need to check the instruments in the TARDIS.'

'I would like to see the inside of this TARDIS,' Dee ventured.

'Very well,' the Doctor gestured at the stairs. 'Lead on, Doctor.'

'Please, after you,' Dee rejoined. 'Doctor.'

And with that they both went back down to the library.

Peri had wandered over to one of the windows of the belvedere. It was a cold, clear night. She gazed up at a vaulted cosmos ripe with starlight. Below she could make out the silvered curve of the river Thames and the faint glow of the city beyond. Then she was aware that Thomas was looking at her. She turned to hold his stare.

'Well, what do you know,' she said. 'Your Doctor is as crazy as mine.'

Thomas shrugged nervously.

'I am honoured to have him as my guardian and tutor. But yes,' he agreed, 'a prodigious mind rarely has an even temperament.'

'You're telling me.'

'I was 13 when my father died. I promised that I would continue his work. Doctor Dee has been my second father. My mathematical father, I call him.'

'Your dad died when you were 13? That's weird, so did mine.'

'That is indeed strange. And this Doctor of yours, he is your guardian?'

'Not exactly. We're companions, you could say.'

'Oh.' Thomas looked embarrassed.

'Hey, it's nothing like that.'

'I did not presume, my lady,' he flustered.

'Look, relax, will you?' She gestured at the perspective glass. 'Can I take a look?'

'Please.'

'That's Cassiopeia, huh?'

'Yes. Named for a vain queen who boasted of her unrivalled beauty.'

'Is that so?'

'Yes. Thou need'st not boast of thine.'

'Gee, thanks.'

'No, no, I mean,' he stammered. 'I mean, thou dost not boast, yet thou art beautiful.'

Peri lifted her head from the perspective glass. 'Listen Tommy, take it easy, OK?'

'Perpugilliam…' He enunciated the word with delight. 'An enchanting name. It is Latin for "by a handful", is it not?'

'By a fistful if you're not careful.'

Thomas gave a nervous laugh. 'I have heard it said that the natives of America are quite savage.'

'They weren't kidding.'

'Ah! The proud beauty of such wild nobility.'

'Hey, enough!'

Thomas jumped back a little at the force of Peri's voice.

'Forgive me, lady.' He lowered his head. 'I meant no offence.'

'Yeah, I know, I know. But listen, you don't even know who I am. I'm not an angel or some exotic savage. You might like to know that I'm something of a scholar myself.'

'A scholar?'

'Don't look so surprised. I'm a pretty good one. I've been studying at Caltech.'

'Caltech?'

'The California Institute of Technology. It's a pretty good school. It's in America.'

'Another wonder of the New World.'

'Yeah. The America four hundred years in the future.'

'You are a woman of the future?'

'You better believe it, Tommy. And I like to think I'm pretty intelligent. So am I the only one who thinks that something very fishy is going on here?'

'What do you mean?'

'The TARDIS gets diverted here by some symbolic device that generates a distress signal. The last time that happened was big trouble. And your Doctor Dee and his strange School of Night, that new member he mentioned: "between bachelor and doctor". What does that mean?'

'Well, in the ranks of academia, between bachelor and doctor…'

'Oh no!'

'… is a master.'

'Quick!' Peri ordered. 'Back downstairs!'

'If I'm right,' the Doctor said to Dee as they passed through the library. 'My instruments should be able to detect the size and location of this interstellar portal.'

'Wait,' implored Dee. 'I feel sure that this has been foretold in scripture. Let me see…'

The Doctor sighed heavily as Dee found his Bible and began to quickly leaf through its pages.

'Yes!' Dee pointed at the page he had found. 'Revelation, Chapter Four, Verse One: *After this I looked, and behold a door was opened in Heaven; and the first voice I heard was as if it were a trumpet talking with me; which said come up hither, and I will show thee things which must be hereafter.*'

'Maybe that's it,' the Doctor nodded, inspired by the strange words. 'Perhaps someone on Earth has been communicating with Cassiopeia.'

A servant entered just as Dee was about to reply.

'A guest to see you, sir.'

'At this hour?'

'He is of the School, sir.'

'Then show him in,' Dee ordered and then turned to the Doctor. 'Just as our name implies, we rarely meet in the presence of the Sun. Perhaps it is the one I mentioned.'

'The one you said that was much like me,' said the Doctor as a dark figure appeared at the doorway. 'Wait a minute…'

A man entered, wearing a black coat with a high collar. The sneer framed by his goatee beard was unmistakable, as was the tissue compression eliminator that he held in his hand.

'The Master!' hissed the Doctor.

'Yes,' he replied. 'You are right, Doctor Dee. We are two of a kind. But this one has shown no mercy to his own. I barely escaped the last predicament you set for me and I swore then to return to this, your favourite planet. I scarcely made it. My TARDIS damaged, with all its fluid links depleted, crash-landed by some ancient homing beacon, an old obelisk within the City of London. Now, the key to *your* TARDIS, if you please.'

As he pulled out the key and slowly handed it to the Master, the Doctor noticed Peri and Thomas coming down the staircase behind him.

'So it's you that has made contact with Cassiopeia?' he asked.

'Yes. My communication systems are still operational.' The Master laughed and turned to Dee. 'I have spoken with a higher intelligence.'

'You mean in angelic conversation?' demanded Dee, feeling that curious throb once again in his guts.

'Something like that,' the Master smiled as he noted the look of longing in Dee's face. 'Aren't these Renaissance terms charming, Doctor? I feel quite at home amid these alchemists and sorcerers.'

'Hey!' Peri shouted and the Master spun round. The Doctor lunged forward, making a grab for the tissue compression eliminator but it fumbled from his hands and onto the floor. The Master struck the Doctor with a glancing blow to the head that felled him, then turned to the magus.

'Give that back to me now, there's a good fellow,' the Master implored softly.

Dee, who had picked up the device and was examining it,

stared at the object in his hand. 'What is this curious wand?' he asked.

'It has the power to shrink a man to a homunculus. Give it to me and I'll show you many other powers.'

'But the Doctor,' Dee protested.

'You saw how he attacked me. You were right, we are both alike. But I will tell you secrets that he would never reveal to you.'

'Don't listen to him!' Peri called out.

'Think of what I could teach you. The transmutation of elements, the capacity to converse with angelic forces. I could even show you how to unlock the code of the Hieroglyphic Monad.'

'The Monad!' gasped Dee, feeling the worm of temptation come alive and his own will drawn by it. The incubus inside fed off his hunger for learning and heightened his craving for dark intelligence.

'Yes.' The Master pointed down at his adversary. 'This one wouldn't tell you that, would he? Do you know why?'

'Because it is forbidden knowledge?' Dee asked, now possessed by a fervent lust for transgressive wisdom.

'Perhaps. But also,' the Master grinned, 'he doesn't know. I have seen it all. As a child, I gazed through the Untempered Schism, into the very Vortex of Time.'

'And it sent you mad!' taunted the Doctor, as he struggled up on his knees.

'He is a lesser mind.' The Master stared into Dee's eyes as he spoke. 'Give me that wand and I will give you what you want. I can make you a true magician.'

Dee's body convulsed as the incubus moved inside him, directing his intent, steering his actions, all the time glutting itself on his desperate curiosity. He slowly passed the tissue compression eliminator into the hand of its owner. The Master smiled and aimed it at the Doctor. Peri and Thomas moved forward.

Stay back!' the Master warned them. He kept the weapon aimed at the Doctor as he backed his way to the TARDIS.

'Now Doctor,' he said as he unlocked the door of the time machine. 'I will shrink you to the size of your meagre ambition.'

'No!' screamed Peri and rushed him. In the ensuing struggle she was pulled into the TARDIS with him.

'Wait! Unhand her!' called Thomas, and he followed her through the entrance.

The TARDIS doors slammed behind all three of them, and all at once it began to dematerialise.

Dee helped the Doctor to his feet and the two men looked warily at each other.

'Why on Earth did you let the Master get away like that?' the Doctor shouted.

'Well, I…' Dee shrugged, unable to explain how physically enthralled he felt by the Master's promises.

'He's an extremely dangerous fellow!'

'But he said that he could decipher the Monad whereas you could not,' Dee reasoned. 'He knows more than you, doesn't he?'

'Well…' The Doctor blew through his lips. 'Technically speaking, perhaps.'

'Technically?'

'Yes. He lacks my creative imagination, my flair. Being a genius is not just about knowledge, you know.'

'But he has more knowledge. Yes?'

'Yes,' the Doctor conceded tetchily. 'Now we really must get after him.'

Dee nodded, smarting at a cramp in his innards, an awful yawning emptiness.

'Where have they gone?' Dee asked.

'I suspect the Master has stolen my TARDIS to make his way to Cassiopeia for some reason. But he let slip that he has left his own damaged TARDIS somewhere in London. If we can find it I might be able to repair it. Though I'll need to find mercury to fix the depleted fluid links.'

'Mercury? Why, I have a plentiful supply here.'

'Really?'

'Of course. No alchemist worth his salt is ever without mercury. Now we need to find where he has hidden this vessel of his.'

'An old obelisk within the City of London, he said.'

Dee thought for a moment. 'Of course!' he exclaimed suddenly. 'It must be the London Stone!'

'What did you mean by barging into the TARDIS like that?' asked Peri.

'I wished to save you from that diabolical fellow, my lady,' Thomas replied.

'Well, that's very gallant and all. Now he's got us both.'

They sat on the floor of the control room with their hands tied. The Master had subdued them with the threat of his tissue compression eliminator and he now adjusted the coordinates at the Doctor's console.

'For once, I entirely approve of your wretched interference, Peri,' he told her. 'A couple of healthy specimens from the Cassiopeian's brave new world are just what we need.'

'What does he mean?' Thomas asked Peri.

'Who knows?' she said, recognising the distinctive sound and feel of a TARDIS coming in to land. 'But I'm thinking we're about to find out.'

The Master bade them stand and walk before him as the doors of the TARDIS opened. They had materialised inside the outer rim of a vast spherical vessel several miles in diameter that turned slowly around a central hub. Above them stretched a bewildering labyrinth of walkways and transit tubes that connected great halls and tiered galleries. A group of blue-skinned humanoids greeted them. Their leader stepped forward.

'Hail to the Master!' he declared and the other Cassiopeans echoed his tribute.

Guardian Lex was with the reception committee on board the Mothership when the Master arrived. It was deemed a great honour to be in the presence of the 'Saviour of the Cassiopeans'. Quite a cult had grown up around this miraculous stranger who promised to save them from an impending apocalypse. So many new and strange beliefs had come with the instigation of the Great Selection. But her biologist's curiosity was equally drawn to the creatures that he had brought with him. Pinkish-hued, like himself, these were the *humans* that he had spoken of.

She watched them stepping out of the blue vehicle, stumbling slightly as they adjusted to the artificial gravity generated by rotation of the massive craft. They looked up at the vast viewing panels around and wondered at the cosmos beyond.

Supreme Commander Grell of the Cassiopeian Fleet showed the Master to the control station of the interstellar portal. At a distance, a circle of lights could be seen that marked out an area of space that shimmered like the surface of a great body of water.

Grell gestured. 'The portal. Built to your exact specifications.'

'Now it needs only to be programmed to the correct coordinates,' said the Master.

As they spoke, Thomas gazed through another viewing panel. A vast fleet could be seen that stretched for miles in orbit above a green and yellow planet. Great space stations wheeled slowly in the stratosphere; shuttle craft and supply rockets zipped to and from the world below.

'Ships that sail the cosmos!' Thomas gasped. 'A great celestial armada!'

'Thomas,' Peri tried to calm him down but the young astronomer could not contain himself.

Setting at the edge of the planet was an angry sun that seethed with wild bursts of solar flare. Beyond was the bright pattern of the cosmos: stars, galaxies, gas clouds.

'Look at the stars!' Thomas exclaimed in wonder. 'They go on and on! They are not fixed in their spheres as we thought.'

'The savages from your new territory are quite backward, as you can see,' the Master explained. 'Once I have finished with them you might like to keep them as zoological exhibits. Or exotic curiosities. Is there an examination facility I could use?'

The Commander gestured to Lex.

'Provide all that he requires,' he ordered her, then turned back to the Master. 'Will your excellence join us on the bridge later?'

The Master nodded and they were led away to a transport tube that whisked them away to another part of the ship. They arrived at a gantry that crossed over a great botanical garden.

'It is a short distance to zoology from here,' Lex informed the Master.

As they walked, they could see space beyond the lush flora around them. The Master turned to the Cassiopeian.

'You are responsible for conserving examples of your home planet's life?'

'I am one of the Guardians, yes,' she replied.

'You see, Peri? A fellow ecologist.'

'I don't get it,' Peri protested. 'What's going on?'

The Master pointed at the boiling sun in the sky. 'This star is about to go supernova. All life in this solar system will soon be obliterated. I contacted the Cassiopeians and instructed them on the construction of a great interstellar transportation portal so that enough of them might get away.'

Lex nodded grimly. The 'Great Selection' had begun once it had been revealed to the Cassiopeians that some of their race might escape the coming conflagration. It was a harsh new creed that twisted all that Lex had learnt and cherished. A system of control that ensured that the elite would be saved whilst the masses perished was cynically dubbed *enhanced natural selection*. The desperate craving for survival had corrupted their culture:

their civilisation had descended into barbarism.

They passed into a corridor flanked by a series of chambers containing animals, an astonishing bestiary of creatures scarcely vigilant of the new exhibits come to join them. Lex showed them to a room with a variety of cages and examination tables. She summoned two technicians.

'This great Mothership of the Cassiopeians will preserve their flora and fauna until they reach their new world,' the Master went on. 'Yes, I offered them a fertile planet to colonise. Your Earth.'

'What?' Thomas looked incredulous.

'Don't look so shocked, young man. After all, is your nation not about to embark upon the colonisation of a new world? And from our discussions in the School of Night, Doctor Dee appears to be one of the foremost advocates of this new imperialism.'

'Er, well, yes,' Thomas agreed. 'He has directed his skill in navigation to aid many of our explorers of the Americas. And he does assert our rights to settle in these new lands.'

'Well, there you have it,' the Master reasoned. 'A certain justice, wouldn't you say?'

'I... I don't understand,' Thomas replied.

The Master turned to Guardian Lex. 'The inhabitants of Earth are a barbaric race, fierce and stubborn,' he told her. 'Mercy is quite wasted on them. But there are many ways to subjugate them. Ah yes, time is a continuum of power, a struggle for survival. The endless domination of one force over another. Peri understands this, don't you, my dear? That enslavement and genocide are all part of what we call progress.'

As he glared at Peri, she turned from him. Thomas could not comprehend why she did not defy the Master's words.

'But Peri shows that the establishment of colonies in new lands need not mean subjugation of the native peoples,' Thomas insisted.

'Does she?' retorted the Master with a wry grin.

'Why yes, she is an American from the future! An example

of how developed her people are after four hundred years of colonisation. Might we not thrive as well if occupied by an advanced civilisation?'

The Master broke into a cruel laugh. 'I think we'll start with the male,' he said, gesturing to Lex and the technicians. 'Get him on that examination table.'

They grabbed Thomas and secured him. The Master took out a lacquered wooden box.

'Now, Peri,' he said, carefully picking out a writhing creature and holding in front Thomas's terrified visage. 'Why don't you tell your friend here what happened to the natives of your land?'

Dee and the Doctor walked down to the river and found a waterman who rowed them up to the City. He set them down on a wharf by the Fishmonger's Hall and they walked up towards Eastcheap. The Doctor noticed that at times passers-by would stop and stare, not at himself, but at Dee. By a draper's stall on Candlewick Street a mother pulled her child to her as they passed and muttered a prayer.

'The fame I have acquired by my art hath caused many an ignorant soul to be fearful of me,' Dee explained wearily.

But by then they had come to the London Stone, a rough pillar hewn from limestone with iron bars fixed to its base.

'Some say it is a Roman relic,' Dee said, and then in a darker tone added: 'others, that it is an ancient altar of the Druids.'

'Well, you know,' the Doctor told him, 'obelisks and stone circles are quite often old navigation signals for time travellers.'

'I knew it,' Dee muttered.

They approached the Stone, and the Doctor busied himself by prodding at it. Dee looked around warily. Bystanders had already started to take note of the well-known alchemist and his gaudy familiar.

'Chameleon circuit,' the Doctor noted.

'What?' Dee asked.

'The Master has materialised his TARDIS around the London Stone and used his chameleon circuit to make it look like the obelisk. I just need to find the door.'

A crowd had begun to form around them. The Doctor pulled out a silver object from his pocket.

'What on Earth is that, sir?' asked Dee.

'Multi-dimensional skeleton key. Now, the lock should be somewhere here…' He continued to tap against the surface of the Stone.

'Whatever it is you are doing,' Dee implored, 'pray be quick about it.'

'That's the one who meddles in magic,' someone called out and pointed. 'What's he up to now?'

'The devil's work, no doubt,' came a hoarse reply.

The mob had begun to get restless.

'It's all right,' the Doctor assured Dee. 'I think I've got it… Yes—'

With that the door sprang open, and the Doctor disappeared inside. The mob gasped in collective astonishment.

'He made that man vanish into thin air!' someone shouted.

Dee tried to follow the Doctor but the door had closed once more. He turned and gave an apologetic shrug to his outraged audience.

'Sorcerer!' a woman screamed.

They closed in on him. Dee turned back and banged his fist against the Stone. He could feel them at his back, ready to tear him to pieces, when suddenly the door gave once more and he tumbled within.

'Oh dear,' he sighed as he was safely inside. 'This isn't going to do my reputation any good at all.'

'Isn't the effect of this creature fascinating?' the Master asked Peri, who was now stretched out on the examination table whilst Thomas raved and ranted in one of the cages.

'It is a pleasure parasite, quaintly known as an incubus to those natural philosophers of the School of Night. Once it infests its subject, it sucks upon the particular desires and fixations of the host's body. And as it feeds it stimulates the appetite. I've implanted one in Doctor Dee, who is quite driven by his yearning for hidden knowledge. This one,' he pointed at the young man who drooled and ripped at his own doublet, 'has baser feelings, I think. I do believe he is quite entranced by your helpless form, Peri.'

'You're a monster!' she called out.

'This tedious moral authority of yours,' the Master sneered. 'Your poor young friend was quite taken in by this dream of the Americas that you represent. That lie perpetuated by a land built on slavery and genocide. Now all he feels is honest lust.'

Peri watched Thomas struggle, panting and grabbing at the bars. She recalled how he had swallowed that dreadful creature that now possessed him, the frenzied look of horror that so soon turned to one of bestial rapture. Now his face was an ugly grimace of need. His desperate passion seemed much like hatred. Though in his eyes she saw some flicker of conscience, she was sure of it. Something that peeped out in despair from a malevolent mask.

The Master turned to Guardian Lex. 'You'll find humans easy to manipulate,' he told her.

Lex nodded deferentially, hiding her disgust at what she was witnessing. This was the type of gratuitous animal experimentation that she deplored. So much of scientific practice had degenerated since the Great Selection. And she knew that all of the plans for the great exodus from Cassiopeia would also have terrible consequences. The entire ecosystem of the colonised planet would be laid waste. She had seen secret reports on the estimated devastation of the human species by contamination and disease and the suitability of survivors for forced labour. She looked away and checked a relayed report on the impending supernova from the ship's bridge.

SOLAR DENSITY NOW APPROACHING CRITICAL MASS, it announced.

'The fleet will be preparing to enter the interstellar transportation gate soon, sir,' she told the Master.

'Yes, well this won't take long,' he said as he approached the cage.

Thomas howled.

'How does it feel to be a savage?' the Master taunted him.

'Please,' begged Peri. 'Please stop this.'

'By all means,' he agreed and took out a probe. 'I can draw the incubus out by using the correct frequency.'

He aimed the device at the cage and a faint oscillation could be felt in the air around them. Thomas doubled up in a sudden seizure, his mouth wide in a rasping growl.

'One has to be careful,' the Master observed, putting the probe down and taking up a long forked implement. 'Once agitated like this the incubus goes on the attack.'

As Thomas retched the slug-like thing out onto the floor of the examination room, it bristled and hissed, ready to strike out. The Master swiftly caught it with the forked prongs and held it up.

'Shh,' he implored, and the creature seemed to give out a little sigh. 'That's it, yes. It will calm itself once it knows it is to feed upon a host once more. Now it's your turn Peri.'

She flinched as he gently placed the incubus on her neck. She felt its cold slime as it moved slowly up towards her face.

Lex watched the display that charted the death of her sun.

SOLAR DENSITY INCREASING. THERMAL NEUTRINO LEVELS DETECTED.

The countdown to supernova had begun.

Once the Doctor had replaced the mercury in the fluid links of the Master's TARDIS, he ran a quick systems check on its console.

'Not in such bad shape, really. Have to realign the temporal stabilisers but that shouldn't take too long. In the meantime let's power up the astral map.'

A holographic cartogram of the near cosmos was projected before them. Dee gazed at the seemingly solid images of stars and planets that swam before his eyes.

'Oh, to have such star charts,' he mooned.

'Look,' said the Doctor, dragging the control to focus in on the Cassiopeia system. 'Here's our interstellar transportation portal. See that flicker there? Now, if I just home in on whatever is operating it… There! That's where we're headed. Now, we're looking at a star system many light years away, so we're looking at something that happened many years ago. So we'll have to travel through time as well as space.'

The Doctor set the controls and the TARDIS started up. Dee looked around him in utter incomprehension, trying to adjust to the fact that the space they inhabited was so much larger than the obelisk they had gained entry to.

'The Master said that you would not give me knowledge of certain things,' he said. 'You are forbidden to, are you not?'

'The High Council of the Time Lords are a bit fussy. And they've never trusted me.'

'Time Lords?'

'Yes, the noble order I belong to, for my sins. We're not supposed to interfere with history. Only to set it right.'

'So you will be gone to another time after this? And I will be left in the darkness.'

'My dear fellow,' the Doctor urged, as much to himself. 'We must not give in to the black moods of melancholy.'

They materialised by a control point in the Mothership. The Doctor spied his own TARDIS close by.

'There she is,' he said. 'Dear old girl. Now, the portal's guidance systems should be here somewhere.'

'What are these?' Dee asked, pointing at a row a large capsule-shaped objects.

'They look like life pods, part of the ship's evacuation system. No, this is what we want,' said the Doctor indicating a control panel. 'Hmm…' He examined it. 'I see they're using a tribophysical waveform macro-kinetic extrapolator. Well, that would make sense. Just as well I brought this.' He pulled a small metal box from his pocket.

'What is it?' asked Dee.

'Portable randomiser. They want to travel to your solar system, at your point in history, well, we can send them somewhere else.'

Peri could see the head of the incubus out of the corner of her eye as it undulated over the line of her jaw onto her cheek, its suckers pulling at her flesh as it moved, the tail of it flicking against her throat.

'This is the really interesting part,' said the Master as he watched her struggle against the straps that held her to the examination table. 'The point at which resistance becomes acceptance.'

Peri felt all of her responses to the thing begin to change. Its once foul odour now an intoxicating scent, its slimy feelers finding nerve points to soothe and caress. As the head of the incubus reared up in front of one eye, she saw the surface of its skin mottle in hypnotic patterns.

'It seeks out your pleasure,' the Master explained with an ugly laugh. 'It wants you to like it.'

Peri knew that she had to fight against a growing sense of wellbeing. She tried to hold back the curious wave of pleasure that rushed through her, pulling her wrists against their bonds, making the straps dig into her, to remind herself of pain and discomfort.

A new status report come on screen:

SOLAR CRITICAL MASS NOW IMMINENT. INTERSTELLAR TRANSPORTATION PORTAL ACTIVATED.

'Sir,' said Lex.

'Wait,' the Master insisted. 'This shouldn't take long. What's strange is how close disgust and delight are in the human species.'

'But your presence is required on the bridge, sir. The fleet is approaching the portal.'

'Oh, very well,' the Master sighed. 'All work and no play. I'll see you later, Peri.'

She was only dimly aware of him leaving, escorted by the technicians. Now she was ready to give in to the incubus. It already seemed part of her. She was possessed by a lonely yearning for the parasite, a hunger for the demon familiar. As it slithered against her mouth, she wetted her lips, ready to ingest it. For a moment she savoured its monstrous kiss. Then came a ghastly shriek and she was overcome by a suffocating terror. She felt a sudden and violent wrenching, as if her flesh was being torn from her face.

The Mothership had turned slowly from its orbit and taken its place as the lead craft of the Cassiopeian armada which now manoeuvred into formation at the mouth of the interstellar transportation portal. On the bridge, Supreme Commander Grell observed the immense area of space that rippled before them. All around its edge were satellites, their winking navigation lights marking out its vast circumference.

'Fleet on course, sir,' announced his first officer.

'And how close are we to supernova?' asked Grell.

'Neutrino levels now at optimum. We've detected an iron core forming at the heart of the sun. Solar mass will soon reach critical. We are entering the stellar collapse phase.'

'Check fleet positions,' Grell ordered. 'Prepare to enter portal. Confirm jump coordinates with all pilots.'

The Master entered the bridge.

'The portal is ready?' he asked. 'Have you set the time and space coordinates I gave you?'

'Yes,' replied Grell.'

'Then you should arrive in a high orbit above planet Earth. In their primitive superstition, the natives will take your landing parties to be spirits or angels. Most of their religions have a strong apocalyptic element. You might find it useful to exploit that.'

An alarm sounded.

'What is it?' demanded Grell.

'Something strange has happened, sir,' the first officer announced. 'Interstellar portal controls have been reset.'

'What!' Grell thundered.

'Sensors indicate that someone has put our guidance system on manual override.'

The Supreme Commander turned to the Master, who nodded to himself.

'I think an old friend has dropped in. Take me back to the control room. Have a couple of guards escort us.'

The incubus seemed to hover above her face. Peri frowned, conscious once more of how disgusting it was. It squirmed as it was held in a pair of large forceps. Guardian Lex had pulled it off her face just in time.

'Ugh.' Peri nearly retched, her sense of taste and smell now keenly repelled by the putrescence of the thing.

But as Lex put it in a large specimen jar and sealed it, Peri realised that what made her really feel sick was the dim memory of how fond she had been of the loathsome creature. Lex then began to undo her restraints.

'You're letting us go?' asked Peri.

'The Master said you were an ecologist. Is that true?'

'Just a student but, yeah, I guess.'

'Then you'll know how I feel about what's being done here.'

Lex unlocked the cage and Thomas stumbled out, bewildered.

'What happened?' he asked.

As Peri stood up, she noticed the probe that the Master had left behind. The device he had used to extract the incubus from Thomas.

'What do you remember?' she asked him.

'A horrible dream.' Thomas rubbed at his face. 'I remember the Master saying something about the savages of America. Then I became a savage myself.'

'Come on, quickly,' Lex beckoned them to leave. 'There's some sort of security alert.'

Thomas adjusted his clothes and as he did so he flushed with embarrassment.

'Perpugilliam, I have an awful remembrance of sinfulness,' he told her.

'Try not to worry about it,' she replied.

'A monstrous vision that I became vile and base.' His voice was heavy with guilt.

'Let's change the subject, OK?'

'Very well, then. The Master bade you tell me something. What will happen to the savages of America?'

'It turned out they weren't the savages, Tommy. We were.'

'Who?'

'The colonists,' she replied and caught Lex's eye. 'Can you take us to the TARDIS?' she went on.

'The TARDIS?' asked Lex.

'Yeah, you know, that blue vehicle we arrived in.'

The Doctor installed the portable randomiser into the portal controls.

'This is a mathematical device?' asked Dee.

'Yes, I suppose so. I used to have one in my TARDIS. If I wanted to make sure that no one knew where I was headed, it generated a random destination. With this one, I've adapted it with a failsafe key.' The Doctor reached into his pocket.

Dee frowned. 'But if one following you was able to leap

ahead in time,' he reasoned, 'then they might predict where you are going to arrive.'

'Well, yes. It is always hard to know any process is truly random.'

'Surely, in theory, all events in the universe could be predetermined.'

'Yes, yes, perhaps. Good grief, man, I'm only trying to explain how this thing works in practice. I'm aware that determinists believe that randomness doesn't exist in theory.'

'And they are right, sir. The universe is not left to chance by divinity,' Dee insisted.

'You know, I had an argument with Einstein that was just like this, and he was as stubborn as you are.' The Doctor held out his hand. He opened his palm to reveal two cubes. 'That's when I decided to fashion the failsafe key like this.'

Dee peered at the objects in the Doctor's hand. 'A pair of dice?'

'Yes, rather clever, don't you think? If anything goes wrong with the randomiser, simply roll those two and a final element of chance is introduced into the process. Here, you'd better keep hold of them.'

'Very well, but your reasoning is still flawed.'

'Look, I've used a randomiser before. It always seemed to work.'

'Well, it seems to me that you scarcely know how all of these devices of yours work. It's as if you've merely inherited a box of tricks.'

'That's hardly fair!'

Their argument had become so heated that they didn't notice the Master enter the control room, followed by Grell and two guards.

'I don't see why you're being so critical,' the Doctor protested.

'It is a simple matter of mathematics, sir. This thing is not truly random, merely unpredictable.'

'Unpredictable, yes. I'll agree to that. I'm the soul of unpredictability.'

'Yes,' the Master boomed, making them start at the sound of his voice. 'You're so proud of that, aren't you, Doctor? You like to think of yourself as eccentric and capricious, but you are so boringly conventional. I suspected that you would find and fix my TARDIS. And I knew that, in your arrogance, you would imagine that you were one step ahead of me. Now, stand away from those controls.'

Grell's guards covered them as the Master approached the panel.

'Indeed,' Dee sighed bitterly. 'The Master hath the greater intelligence.'

'Now Doctor, I've a special fate for you.' The Master turned to Grell. 'Prepare one of the escape pods for this saboteur. And have it launch away from planetary orbit.'

'That will send it towards the supernova,' said Grell.

'Exactly. Even you will not escape such a conflagration, Doctor. Once and for all your destruction is assured.'

The guards escorted the Doctor to an escape pod. The hatch hissed open.

'Let me just disconnect this randomiser and I'll come and dispatch you myself. Wait.' The Master checked the panel once more. 'There's a failsafe key. Where is it, Doctor?'

'Why should I tell you?'

'It's a remote manual device, but your hands are empty. So…' The Master turned to Dee, noting his clenched fist. 'Give it to me.' He approached Dee with an outstretched palm, staring intently at him. 'Oh yes, you will hand it over. Think of what I can give you in return.'

'Roll the dice!' called the Doctor.

'A suitably florid metaphor. But no,' said the Master softly. 'Take no heed of him. You took him for a fool at first, and you were right. No, listen to me. Listen to what I can tell you.'

Dee struggled against the incubus that had come alive inside once more of him, but an unconscious will began to take hold.

'All the secrets of alchemy and metaphysics. The key to magic numbers and sacred geometry. The Hieroglyphic Monad decoded, the Grand Unified Theory of the universe,' the Master promised. 'All yours.'

Dee tried to control the hand that held the dice but it made a quivering gesture of its own, reaching out to the Master.

Then an oscillating whine filled the air. The Master frowned.

'Peri!' shouted the Doctor as he spied his assistant pointing something at Dee.

It was the probe that the Master had left in the examination room.

Dee's face flushed purple and his breath came in heaving sobs that wracked his frame. In a violent seizure, he bent forward and spewed the incubus out.

'No!' cried the Master as the creature that squealed and flared up in front of him now leapt at his face.

Dee opened his hand and the dice clattered onto the floor.

'Guidance systems are now locked onto a chance setting,' said the Doctor as he broke free from the guards and came across to where his adversary lay. He took his TARDIS keys from the Master, who now grabbed at the furious incubus that attacked his face.

'See to the Master!' Grell ordered as the Doctor helped Dee and led Peri and Thomas to his own time machine.

'If you'll excuse us,' he said as he unlocked his TARDIS and hustled everybody inside.

'Wait!' Grell called after them.

The Doctor closed the door behind him and the TARDIS dematerialised.

'Electron degeneracy pressure now at maximum,' the first officer announced. 'Stellar mass now confirmed unstable.

Our sun is about to enter its collapse phase. Commence final approach to interstellar transportation portal.'

'But the coordinates have not been corrected,' observed the navigator as she checked the controls. 'They appear to be fixed on an uncertain setting.'

'What do we do, sir?' the first officer asked as his commander appeared on the flight deck.

'There's no time to reset our course,' Grell announced grimly. 'We'll have to take our chances.'

Lex looked back to see the last sunset over her home planet. She wept as she watched the darkening beauty of a dying world, then felt a surge of power as the Mothership was hurled into the unknown.

With a grinding lurch the TARDIS came to a halt.

'What's happened?' asked Peri.

'I hate it when someone else has been fiddling my controls! What's he done now?' The Doctor began to try a sequence of buttons on the console.

Peri looked on impatiently. 'And where are we?' she demanded.

'Oh dear.' The Doctor flicked on a monitor screen above. 'The Master seems to have left some sort of steering lock on. We've only managed to materialise into the space outside the fleet. See? There they go.'

He pointed at the screen. The Cassiopeian armada was streaming through the transportation gate, each ship winking out of visibility as it crossed the threshold.

'Where will they go?' Peri wondered.

'Who knows?' There are many myths of a lost fleet of starships roaming this galaxy. This might have been the beginning of them. Right,' the Doctor said as he flicked a switch. 'That should get us back to London in 1572.'

Nothing happened.

*

As the TARDIS slowly drifted in space the dying sun came into view. The Doctor pointed up to it and turned to Dee and Thomas.

'Now, this is really interesting,' he told them. 'Not every day you get to witness a supernova. This star has achieved a critical mass where it cannot support its own weight. It's just about to collapse.'

'Doctor,' Peri said. 'Get us out of here.'

'Don't worry,' he assured her as he punched in a familiar sequence. 'The Fast Return Switch. That'll get us back to where we last were.'

'You say this star is about to fall in on itself?' Dee asked, gazing at the screen.

'Yes,' replied the Doctor. 'Then, suddenly, it will sort of bounce back, as the force collapsing meets its core energy.'

'Then what happens?'

'A terrific explosion. When a supernova detonates, it can be seen for millions of light years.'

'An apocalypse,' Dee whispered.

'Yes. A great destructive force. But a creative one, also. New stars will form from the vast debris of this holocaust. It is how the universe regenerates itself. It's like a great alchemist's crucible, transmuting elements, hurling great energies across the cosmos.'

'Doctor,' Peri sounded impatient.

'Yes, yes. Don't worry. The Fast Return Switch has been activated.'

Nothing happened again.

'Ah,' he admitted. 'Now we really are in trouble.'

All stared at the screen now as the star began to darken and turn in on itself, its very matter crushed as elemental particles fused and split at its core. A final and terrifying twilight.

'Now a god doth close its eye,' Dee gasped.

'This is it,' said Peri.

She felt Thomas's fingers reaching for hers.

'Might I offer this unworthy hand,' he murmured.

'What? Oh, yeah,' she replied and grabbed hold of it.

'Only one thing for it,' the Doctor told them. 'A percussive intervention.'

'A what?' asked Peri.

'This,' he explained, raising a fist and giving the controls a good thump.

There was a burst of brightness as the fire of a billion suns was unleashed in an instant. A blinding white light flooded everything. Energy, matter, information, all blanked out into nothing.

Doctor Dee felt his mind clear. He felt at last purged of the need for dark wisdom and in place of that terrible hunger a marvellous emptiness. A brightness. This was revelation, he thought. Illumination. Light, yes, light was all. The Creator's first command and his last. Yes, light, the pureness of it. He had at last joined the Elect. Not the School of Night, no, the School of Light! The scroll was now unrolled and he saw at once its parchment bare. He knew everything now. And nothing. He had read the blank page of the universe.

Then slowly, as he blinked his eyes open, the interior of the TARDIS began to come back into focus. No, he thought, not yet. But it was too late. His mind had already started to fill with the tedious details of existence and he felt despair at its complexity. That gnawing hunger for arcane knowledge came back to him. He noticed once more that a TARDIS was bigger on the inside than the outside. How could his feeble mind ever explain such things?

'We made it!' Peri called out.

'Good girl,' said the Doctor, patting the console.

It was dusk when they arrived back at Dee's house. The whole of London was in a clamour at the bright new star now seen burning in the heavens.

'The appearance of this supernova is one of the most important events in the history of astronomy,' the Doctor told them. 'It will challenge once and for all the old beliefs and the ancient models of the universe. It can no longer be seen as an unchanging celestial realm, with the stars set in fixed spheres.'

'Yes,' agreed Dee. 'But it will make some fearful. It is the end of the old order and stability in the cosmos.'

'You and Thomas are part of that change, you know. Your observations of this phenomenon will be very important.'

'Yes, yes. We must start to make measurements. Thomas…' Dee turned to address his pupil, but he had gone.

'I think Thomas and Peri are saying their goodbyes,' the Doctor suggested.

'Must you go so soon?'

'I'm afraid so,' replied the Doctor.

'But you could settle awhile and take some time to study. With my library, observatory and laboratory at your disposal, think of what you could gain from a sustained period of learning and reflection? You always seem to be rushing about in time and space, never taking time to properly understand the universe around you.'

'Yes,' the Doctor sighed. 'It is tempting. But it's not my way, thank you. I trust you have recovered from your ordeal.'

'I fear that I will always be afflicted by a troublesome hankering after dangerous wisdom. I'm simply tempted to learn more than I should, I know that. And this brief adventure has not helped. Of course, it will seem like a dream in a matter of days; certainly no one would believe it if I told the tale. So, I will continue to feel out of my time, somehow belonging to a different era.'

'Hmm,' the Doctor pondered. 'You are much like a Time Lord in many ways.'

'And you sir,' Dee rejoined, 'are much like a magician.'

254

'Doctor,' the Doctor held out his hand.

'Doctor,' Dee replied as he shook it.

'I wish that I could come with you to your time,' said Thomas to Peri.

They walked together along a pathway down to the river.

'Well, you'd love Caltech.'

'It doth truly sound like paradise.'

'Yeah, a geek's paradise.'

'A geek? What is a geek?'

Peri smiled. 'It's what we call people of great intelligence in our world.'

'Oh, how I would love to be a geek.'

'Well, Tommy, I think you already are. But you belong here. You're important for your own time. Your theories and experiments might change the way people think.'

They stopped by the water's edge.

'Perpugillium,' Thomas turned to face her. 'I must apologise for my behaviour when I was in that cage. What must you think of me?'

'Hey, Tommy, you couldn't help yourself, right?'

'But don't you see? That very beastliness is part of my true nature.'

'Look, a guy once said: "We are all of us in the gutter, some of us are looking at the stars."'

'A wise man. But what if the Master is right? That progress brings with it greater destruction and every new craft or intelligence merely increases our capacity to cause suffering.'

'Then we have to make sure that we work against that. That's what I'm trying to work on with my studies.'

'This ecology you spoke of with the Cassiopeian? Forgive me, I know not this discipline.'

'Sure you do. It's like the scientific study of the interactions among organisms and their environment. And how we can hold on to the balance between them.'

'That sounds like the essence of all natural philosophy.'

'Yeah, I think it is. And it's just as important to look up at the stars. Especially our new friend here.'

She pointed to the bright body that hung low in the darkening sky.

'Yes,' Thomas agreed. 'I must assemble our instruments to determine the parallax of that star, to prove it is beyond the planetary spheres. Otherwise some might take it to be a comet or a meteor.'

'Now, do me a favour, Tommy,' said Peri. 'Don't go talking about travelling through space or witnessing a supernova close up, will you?'

'Only if I want to be taken for a madman. No, I will pretend I had my feet on the ground the whole time.'

'And forget the whole thing?'

'Not you, Perpugilliam. How could I forget you?' He nodded up to the heavens. 'Every time I look at the stars, I'll think of you.'

Peri leaned forward and kissed him on the cheek.

'Goodbye, Tommy,' she said and turned to walk back to the house and the waiting TARDIS.

'A restless spirit,' said the Doctor as he checked the controls of the TARDIS, 'with a sense of knowledge beyond his scope. Having seen too much yet not enough.'

'Doctor Dee?' asked Peri.

'Yes.'

'Sounds like another doctor I could mention.'

'I suppose we did have a few things in common. I've a feeling I've not seen the last of him. You seemed to get on well with that young astronomer.'

'Yeah, he was kind of sweet.' She shrugged. 'For a geek.'

'Then you might be interested in this.' The Doctor activated a viewing screen.

There was an image of a diagram with the Sun at its centre and a series of concentric circles showing the orbits of the planets. Outside this solar system was a representation of the myriad stars beyond.

'It's *A Perfit Description of the Caelestiall Orbes*, published by Thomas Digges in 1576, four years after you met him. It was the first time in English that anyone had demonstrated in print the new Copernican, heliocentric, world view.'

'Wow, when it was still seen as heresy.'

'Yes. And not only that. Thomas seems to be the first person on Earth to postulate an infinite universe, that stars were not merely fixed to an outer sphere but went on and on. He's sometimes forgotten in the history of science, but an astronomer from your time said: "Digges' original contribution to cosmology consisted of dismantling the starry sphere and scattering the stars throughout endless space."'

'Well how about that, Tommy? That's pretty cool.'

'It is rather good, isn't it? And, here, this is what he said himself.'

The Doctor pointed to an inscription on the diagram beyond the outer rim of the solar system. Peri read it out loud:

This orb of stars fixed infinitely up extends itself in altitude spherically, and therefore immovable the palace of felicity garnished with perpetual shining glorious lights innumerable, far excelling over sun both in quantity and quality the very court of celestial angels, devoid of grief and replenished with perfect endless joy, a habitacle for the elect.'

Peri felt her eyes brim with tears.

'There's another inscription,' the Doctor added. 'Right here at the bottom. No one's really been quite sure of its significance. Until now. It reads: *Per Pugilliam Pulvis Sidereus*. It means—'

'I got it,' Peri smiled. 'I learned pretty good Latin studying botany, you know. It means: "by a handful of stardust".'

THE BOG WARRIOR

Planet Cashel

The Doctor stepped out of the TARDIS and closed the door behind him. He looked around at planet Cashel. It looked typically standard. Trees. Rocks. Three moons in the sky.

It was dark, beyond the woods was opaque, and high on the mountain a hazy glow on the horizon revealed a village. Despite the distant activity, it was still, hushed, peaceful. The only thing that broke it was the hoot of a distant owl and the rustle of the leaves when the warm breeze blew. There was a sweet boggy earthy scent in the air, not dissimilar to Earth. Yes, he could stay here for a while. He closed his eyes and breathed in.

Making sure the TARDIS was secluded in the wooded area, he went for a short stroll and found a rock to sit on, which gave him an ideal view of the spectacularly star-filled sky, with the three moons shining brightly. He enjoyed the rare moment of peace, content, feeling free, feeling safe.

A vehicle in the distance, the sound of wheels on gravel, stole him from his thoughts, and he leaped into the trees in time to see a horse-drawn carriage appear from round the corner. Two figures disembarked and the Doctor peered with interest to see what kind of creatures inhabited this planet. They were surprisingly human.

'Don't look,' a female said.

'I'm not looking,' a young boy no more than ten years old replied huffily.

The Doctor leaned out a little more and saw the young boy peeking at the young woman dressing and he smiled, but he did the young woman the honour of looking away too.

'OK, I'm ready,' she announced and both the boy and the Doctor turned to look at her.

She was breath-taking. The Doctor had never seen a woman so beautiful. He guessed she was in her early twenties, had cocoa-coloured skin, and was wearing a magnificent ball gown, a charcoal-silver, glittering and brilliant with every inch of the fabric embedded with a mirror-like jewel which was splendid in the moonlight. She twinkled like one of the stars in the sky he had been studying only moments ago. A white mask then swiftly covered her pretty face; a startlingly realistic stern-faced mask that didn't do her natural beauty any justice, with tiny holes in the appropriate places to aid her sight and smell. Her jet-black hair was kept back off her face in dozens of intricate plaits, and carried a blue tint as it shone beneath the moonbeam; however, it too was quickly concealed by a sizeable hood also covered in glass jewels.

The boy stared at the young woman in shock. He tried to speak but stammered, but she was too preoccupied to notice his obvious crush on her.

'Right,' she said, nervously, sliding on white gloves so that not an inch of her flesh was on display, though she was resplendent in her gown, which looked like it had taken a thousand pair of tiny hands, over a thousand hours, to create and finesse. 'I should go now. I'm already late. I'll meet you back in here in one hour?'

The boy nodded, still speechless.

She hurried on.

'Wait, Ash! One more thing.' The boy retrieved a parcel gift-wrapped in burlap from the carriage. He peeled back the cloth to reveal a pair of shoes, dazzling with such brilliance that they threw millions of dots of light onto Ash's mask. He looked at her anxiously, anticipating her reaction, his feelings for her clear in his young innocent face.

Ash gasped. 'Where did you get these? They're stunning.' She handled them gingerly as though afraid she would break them.

'These are the shoes your father gave to your mother.'

The Doctor saw the look of love pass from the boy to the young woman.

'This is them?' She swallowed hard, her voice trembling. 'I heard about these shoes. I thought they were rumour. However did you find them?'

'I was there.' He looked down at the ground, ashamed of his spying. 'In your mother's cell before they took her away. Nobody saw me. I left as soon as he gave them to her. I didn't want to steal their final moment together.'

Ash swallowed hard. 'I thought that if they were true, they were lost for ever.'

'Nothing is lost for ever, Ash,' he said confidently, standing up straight, puffing out his chest.

Trumpet sounds started up behind the Doctor, and he turned, confused that anything other than more trees could be behind him.

'Prince Zircon has arrived,' Ash said, their moment broken as she panicked.

'Good luck,' the boy called as she hurried away with the shoes in her hand. He looked after her with longing.

The Doctor moved further into the trees to see what was going on. He came to an abrupt stop as the trees ended unexpectedly and the ground cut away into a slope. Below him was a deep ravine, cut out from a rocky mountain, which appeared to have been chipped away here and there to reveal a marble floor, a spectacular midnight blue with tiny flecks of silver sediment, which mirrored the night sky. A shimmering grand staircase cascaded into the outdoor ballroom, which was lit by enormous cages of fire. Men were in fine dress, white tie with tuxedos and coat-tails, and the women wore opulent dresses shining with precious stones, like Ash's, which he had never seen the likes of before. The guests' faces were hidden by masks, but it was a masquerade ball like no other as the masks were startlingly human, the faces of men and women etched with wrinkles and scars, some alarmed, some serene, and all the physicality that a human face possessed. It was a disturbing sea of faces and so he concentrated instead on the triumphal procession of the royals who were entering to a great furore. The brass section of the masked orchestra stood to announce their entrance.

The Doctor identified Prince Zircon as he took his seat on a large throne carved from the massive trunk of a bog-oak tree, the chair's back twisted and stretched high into the sky, as did the five other thrones alongside him. Beside him were a couple who the Doctor supposed were the King and Queen. On the opposite side of the stage sat a woman dressed in an exquisite black ball gown with an enormous ballooning skirt, which dazzled under the caged fires, though he couldn't help thinking she looked like a crow with her long black feathers extending from the neck of the dress and up around her face and the back of her head. If Ash was a star, this woman was the night sky. Beside her sat two younger women, one extremely slight and sickly looking, somewhat lost in the oversized bog-oak throne. Dressed in an unbecoming purple, giving her the appearance of being freezing cold, her veins were highlighted by her translucent skin. Beside her sat a rather rotund red-faced young woman with a sweaty brow and décolletage, squeezed into her garish crimson and blood-orange dress, giving the illusion that she was on fire. Entitled to wear their own faces, nobody from the royal party wore a mask. Around them, soldiers were dressed in iron masks and fur capes secured with brooches, with iron protecting their legs and arms. There were at least a dozen more soldiers of the same decree dotted around the exits, standing to attention in a menacing fashion, razor-sharp spears in their iron-clad grips.

Prince Zircon looked uncomfortable. He looked angry. His father, the King, was sweating profusely and he mopped his brow with a handkerchief, while his wife, the Queen, was unreadable. She seemed neither nervous nor angry; she was solid, strong as she stared directly ahead. Knowing his expedition for solace and self-inspection was well and truly over, the Doctor pushed forward a little more to hear what the royal party beneath him were saying, trying not to send rock fragments sliding down the cliff to the soldiers below.

'Who are you?'

He heard the boy behind him suddenly and he jumped, startled.

'Ssh!' the Doctor warned, afraid the soldiers would hear. 'Who am I? Who are you?' he asked playfully, not unnerved in the slightest by the young boy.

The boy assessed him suspiciously.

'I'm a visitor. On holiday,' the Doctor said, extending his hand, anxious to get back to his spying. 'I come in peace, hope not to leave in pieces. They call me the Doctor. Whoever they are. But they do, and so can you, if you so wish. But if you can come up with a better name, I'll take that.'

The boy looked at his outstretched hand warily. He folded his arms in defiance. 'Root.'

'I'll stick with the Doctor, thank you.' The Doctor turned away to face the action once again but kept an eye on the boy. He couldn't help but notice the look of innocence the boy had had when gazing at Ash had disappeared, and he now saw eyes that had seen more than most at such a young age.

'No. That's my name,' the boy said huffily.

'So what's going on here tonight, Root?' the Doctor asked. 'It looks like fun.'

Root fixed him with a look of surprise. 'You definitely are a visitor. You haven't heard? That's King Quartz and Queen Mica of Lindow, our neighbouring kingdom. Prince Zircon is here to meet a wife from Tollund. They are to be married tonight.'

'That's a bit fast, isn't it? Though what do I know of young love? He doesn't look too happy about it, does he? Don't know why, they all look all right from up here. If not a little dazed. And expressionless.'

'That's not their real faces,' Root said, frowning.

The Doctor feigned shock. 'Well, beauty lies on the inside, isn't that what they say? At least that's what I was told, on numerous occasions. Wonder why…'

'If Prince Zircon doesn't take a wife, there will be a war between Tollund and Lindow. Another one,' Root said, annoyed that the Doctor wasn't taking it seriously.

But the Doctor was. He was taking it all in.

'Who are the other women on the throne?'

'Xenotime,' Root said, with a voice of loathing, 'She calls herself the Queen but you'll not hear me call her that. And her daughters. Erbium in purple and Terbium in red.'

'Xenotime…' the Doctor thought aloud. 'A rare phosphate mineral which may contain traces of arsenic. Rare earths Erbium and Terbium are the expressive secondary components.'

The boy studied him.

The Doctor continued his analysis. 'Mica was derived from the Latin word, probably influenced by the word *micare*, which meant "to glitter", which she most certainly is doing in her place on the throne, and quartz originated from the German *quarz*, which came from the Slavic meaning of "hard". Though King Quartz is not quite living up to his name, is he?' The Doctor watched the King mop his brow with an unsteady hand.

The Doctor continued his appraisal of the situation while Root watched on, curious. 'Zircon is a mineral with a yellow-golden tint, among others, and is often a popular substitute for diamonds. Prince Zircon is a handsome blond-haired royal with the ability to prevent a war. He is sitting in that jagged ravine appearing quite the diamond in the rough, isn't he?' He didn't wait for Root to answer. 'And Root,' he finally turned to the boy. 'The base of something, the cause of something…' he studied the boy some more. 'Hmm. Yet to be seen. Yes, I think I'm understanding what's going on here, but I need more.' Curiosity heightened by this planet, he leaned closer to the royals on their thrones.

'Go on, Zircon, ask somebody to dance,' Queen Mica muttered to her son under her breath.

'Dance with me, Mother,' he said, bored.

'Not me,' she said through gritted teeth. 'A woman. Everyone is waiting.'

'They can keep waiting. I'm not moving from this throne,' he said loudly.

'If you do not, there will be war,' she said, urgency in her voice.

'I'm prepared for war,' Prince Zircon said loudly.

The soldiers shifted from one foot to the other, not liking this but unable to act on their eavesdropping of the private royal conversation. Or at least, refusing to act on it at that point. Yet.

'The warriors will annihilate us,' Queen Mica said quietly then. 'You are a fool if you think you have a chance in battle with them. Their numbers are greater and their strength brutal.'

Prince Zircon didn't answer.

'I need a drink,' King Quartz said.

A masked woman brought him a goblet and he looked into it uncertainly. Despite his obvious thirst he set it aside suspiciously. The King looked to his son to get things moving so he could be at peace.

'My son…' Queen Mica lowered her voice. 'This ceremony is merely symbolic. No one is expecting you to *love* the woman. I know you're thinking of… *her*, but you must think of Lindow, of Tollund, of the whole of the planet Cashel, and do what is good for the people. Their lives are in your hands.'

'The whole of the *planet*, Mother. Well, that certainly is putting a great duty on me.'

'With duty comes great responsibility, your actions are

not just about you and what makes *you* happy. And you will discover when you are King—'

'I will *never* be King if this is the sacrifice I must make for our kingdom,' he interrupted. 'And the people of Lindow *and* Tollund are willing to fight. On *our* side.'

'Those you mix with masquerade as warriors but they haven't the fortitude to withstand the kind of war we're faced with.'

'Masquerade. How fitting, Mother. And look at us here, masquerading, for all to see.'

That silenced her.

On the other side of the stage Erbium, the slight lady, turned to Xenotime. 'Mother, when is he going to choose a woman? They're all staring, they don't like to wait, you know what they're like.' She swallowed nervously.

'Keep your mouth closed, Erbium,' Xenotime snapped.

Erbium steamed. Terbium sniggered. 'Oh, have another canapé,' Erbium snapped, throwing food from the display at her sister. Terbium gasped at the pig's head that landed in her lap.

'Girls,' Xenotime snapped and she looked across to the King and Queen with annoyance.

Suddenly Prince Zircon stood and there was a hush in the crowd, but when they realised that he was focusing his gaze beyond them, they all turned to stare at the marble staircase that glistened in the moonlight.

'There she is,' Root whispered and the Doctor watched intently as Ash stood at the top of the staircase.

There was an audible gasp from the guests.

Ash made her way down the steps, tentatively. She did not want to trip, not now, having made such a grand entrance. Prince Zircon made his way down from the royal thrones and the crowd parted, the ladies giggling and fanning themselves as he came near them and he waited for Ash at the end of the stairs, hand extended. Xenotime viewed Ash suspiciously and Erbium and Terbium squabbled about who they thought she was. She seemed to be a mystery to everybody, all apart from Root and the Doctor.

Prince Zircon brought Ash to the centre of the floor and the orchestra started up a new bizarre tune, which sounded to the Doctor like a record being played backwards. They danced. Prince Zircon looked utterly enchanted, the look of revolt gone from his face as they twirled around the room together.

'It's done. I'll be off, then,' Root said, unable to hide his heartbreak.

'It's never easy,' the Doctor said.

'What is never easy?'

'When they leave.' Thinking of all those he had lost, so many memories of so many goodbyes, the Doctor barely registered the boy leave. He watched the couple dancing, in a trance.

'Well, thank goodness for that,' King Quartz said to Queen Mica, with relief, the fear gone, and overconfidence in its place. 'Whatever you said to him worked.' He reached for the goblet he had previously put aside and gulped it down.

Queen Mica didn't look so sure. Her own mask had slipped. The impenetrable solid face now had a crack. Fear. Xenotime, pleased by the connection, was transfixed, and her obvious relief showed that she too had been in great distress. But as she watched the partners swirl around the floor, her eyes seemed to register something that displeased her. Her face twitched, then turned to alarm. She slammed her large bog-oak staff down on the stage three times.

Many guests were startled from their enjoyment of watching the dance and let out surprised yelps. The orchestra's music teetered out and few musicians were left playing. There was confusion whether to continue or to stop, but they decided to pick it up again and endure. Oblivious to the rest of the world, Prince Zircon and Ash persisted with their dancing, gazing into one another's eyes, though not much could be seen of Ash's.

'Uh oh,' the Doctor said, sensing trouble. He looked around and noticed Root had gone. Perhaps it was time for him to make his way to the TARDIS. But something about the scene was captivating him; he felt drawn in, he couldn't leave it. He had to find a way in past the guards.

'Enough!' Xenotime screamed, banging her staff on the floor again three times, even louder this time. She stood.

The music stopped. Everyone was silenced. Prince Zircon and Ash stopped dancing and he held her gloved hand tightly in his, his chest heaving up and down from dancing and, as his adrenalin surged, ready to fight.

'Remove your mask!' Xenotime pointed her finger at Ash.

The guests turned to the mystery woman who had enchanted the prince.

'Reveal yourself!'

Zircon raised his voice. 'She will do no such thing.'

The guests gasped.

'Do I have to remind you, Prince Zircon, that tonight's ceremony is for you to find a woman of the bog to dance with, whereupon you will marry her tonight?'

The Doctor rolled up his nose. 'Woman of the bog?'

'If you do not, our good friends of the Boglands will not be pleased and we will have war in our lands. Blood will be spilled, lives will be lost, and that blood will be on *your* hands, Prince Zircon.'

'I think this is where I should bid my adieu,' the Doctor said, standing up and stretching, procrastinating, as he didn't want to leave. 'I said I *should* leave, but that's not to say I will,' he said, finally seeing a way in. With all eyes on the scene playing out before them, including the soldiers, he made his way as quietly as he could around the perimeter of the ravine. Below him a large rock jutted out. He lowered himself down onto it, sending stones chasing each other down the wall and ducked down to avoid being seen. He was now halfway down. He looked around for the rest of the way down, something he probably should have thought through before sliding down the stockade.

'Who's to say this isn't a woman of the bog?' Prince Zircon replied. 'I've chosen my woman. I want to marry her. Tonight. Now. Let's proceed with the ceremony,' he said grandly.

There was a gasp from the guests. A little twitter of excitement was quickly killed by Xenotime as she thumped her staff down again.

Three thumps. She always thumps the staff three times, the Doctor thought waiting for the second and third. On the second, he jumped; the third hid his yelp as a rock sliced his shin.

'She must reveal herself before you marry,' Xenotime repeated.

'I don't believe that was part of the plan, Xenotime. I'm offended you would question me. A Prince. A *future King*.'

'I am *Queen* Xenotime and you will address me as such,' she shouted.

'Can't she speak for herself?' Erbium called out.

'Yes, mystery woman,' Terbium joined in smugly. 'Reveal yourself and prove your prince right that you are a woman of the bog. Save him from his most certain death for if he is lying to the Queen…' She tutted and wagged a ruby-wielding finger.

The Prince looked at Ash and swallowed hard, his confidence waning.

'Very well,' Xenotime announced breaking the chatter that was beginning to grow in the crowd. 'Lift the hem of her dress.'

There was confusion, among the people, not to mention among Ash and Prince Zircon. Ash straightened her spine, raised her chin, prepared for anything, and then she lifted her hem.

Xenotime screeched, 'Seize her!'

'Run, Ash,' Prince Zircon urged her but she wouldn't let go.

The Doctor was suddenly beside them. 'I'd take his advice, Ash,' he said. 'Come with me. I'll help.'

Prince Zircon took in the Doctor, immediately found cause to trust him but gave him a look of warning. The Doctor nodded, an assertion of his word.

'Go with him. I'll find you.' Prince Zircon pushed Ash away.

The warriors descended the steps from their posts at the exits. Prince Zircon produced a sword. The Doctor grabbed Ash's hand and pulled her through the panicking crowd who were all also running toward the exits, bundling together in terrified screams that even the soldiers were finding it hard to keep the crowd at bay. The crowd managed to break through the exits and moments later, panting, the Doctor and Ash arrived at the meeting place with Root.

Ash circled the empty space where Root and the carriage had been, in a blind panic. 'He said he'd be here.'

'He wasn't expecting the party to end so early,' the Doctor said. 'In here.' He led her to the area he had hidden in first.

She looked at him, unsure, her body starting to tremble in shock over the events of the evening.

'Trust me,' he said, holding out his hand.

Soldiers were approaching. She gulped, took his hand and he led her into his hiding place. He stepped back out to the road, and braced himself for the warriors. Instead of the army he expected, there was one lone soldier, wearing a pointed skin cap of sheepskin, which stood out from the others, perhaps making him a leader of some kind.

'She went that way,' the Doctor told him, pointing in the wrong direction.

The eerie iron mask stared back at him. The soldier took a moment to take him in and assess whether he was lying. The Doctor gave him the best innocent face he could muster. The warrior reluctantly took the route the Doctor had advised him, and he also redirected the army that way.

'Thank you,' Ash said, stepping out from the trees. She started to run in the opposite direction.

'Ash, wait!' the Doctor called. 'I promised Prince Zircon I would keep you safe!'

'You've done enough.' Her voice trembled. She stumbled in her shoes, ripping the hem of her dress as she fell. She pulled one shoe off and then looked around for the other that had tripped her. Unable to find it and knowing she had no time to spare, she let out a sob for all she had lost that night and continued running. Then she was out of sight.

The Doctor looked from the direction of the TARDIS to where Ash had run. There was no question of where his loyalties lay. A glint in the trees up ahead caught his eye and he spied the shoe Ash had left behind. He tucked it in his overcoat and ran in the direction of the town in the distance.

Tollund Town Square

The Doctor was breathless and had an aching chest by the time he reached the medieval-looking village, with cobblestone alleyways, charming shop fronts and delightful balconies overlooking a small square. If they weren't on the cusp of war, he would have taken time to take more of it in. Instead he was greeted with panic, as people darted around in every direction. Market stalls were being shut up, some being dragged into buildings, doors and shutters were banged shut and bolted, locks were abundant and loud as the townspeople barricaded themselves inside.

'Excuse me, I'm looking for a young woman—'

A door banged in the Doctor's face. An elbow jabbed him in the stomach, a hand pushed him in the back. People were running and disappearing down alleyways, into buildings, into cellars and basements. Nobody would look him in the eye, pushing him away or ignoring him, wanting absolutely nothing to do with this stranger who had no doubt brought trouble. Within thirty seconds, the Doctor was isolated in an empty town square, all shops and homes boarded up with wood, shutters closed, doors locked tightly, lights out.

In the distance he heard footsteps approaching, the stomping of angry warriors who had realised they had been wrongly directed, the ground almost vibrating from the numbers. He spied a winding staircase in the far corner of the square and he ran to it and upward, but when he reached the top an iron gate shut in his face, and a weathered old woman glared at him, as though it was he who had brought this on them all. At a loss for places to hide, the Doctor felt resigned to his inevitable capture and who knew what after that. He had enough experience to know that calm explanations of truth didn't always yield positive results, especially when the truth was that he was an alien man who travelled the universe in a blue box.

He saw the warriors' shadows on the ground encroaching on him, and felt the ground beneath him shake. *How many were there?* He swallowed hard, knowing his capture was certain, and looked around for a place to hide the shoe. He took the shoe from his overcoat and made a quick decision as the soldiers were close to penetrating the town square. They breached it just as the Doctor ducked into the shadows, and he was so surprised by what he saw, that he froze.

'What? What?! What??!!'

The soldiers had discarded their masks and what was revealed beneath was frightening: rotten, dark-brown polished faces of skeletal men and women; some had hair, which hung in a long lanky mucky rope-like manner in patches on their cracked and dirty skulls. Their eyes, which he'd thought originally had been black and empty were, in fact, just not there at all. Their sockets were hollow, their teeth wobbled in their mouths, for those that had them, and were covered in decay, plaque, mud. Their arms were long and gangly and, like their legs, had rotten flesh hanging from them, flapping in the breeze as they ran, though it didn't look like flesh – it was like leather, unusually polished, shiny, preserved.

But it was the smell that truly upset him. The smell of rotting, a stench so vile it filled his nose, throat and chest and made his stomach churn. The power was so overwhelming it stung his eyes, like onion vapours pervading his senses. He felt dizzy, hot from the suffocating power of it, and he suddenly understood the reason for the citizens bolting their doors and windows, not a crack available for person or scent to drift through and hide in.

The Doctor hid in the shadows as best he could, while they spilled into the square. With an intense dread coming over him, he identified the soldier he had lied to, with the sheepskin cap on his rotten head secured under his chin with a hide thong. Like the others, this corpse man didn't have eyes but the Doctor knew that he had been seen, and that he was being stared at in his hiding place in the shadows. The soldier stood still while his ghoulish compadres inflicted chaos around them, banging on shop fronts and homes, using hammers and axes to break through the wood and windows, while those inside cowered and screamed, and the brave fought back. The Doctor fully intended to help the people, and so he turned away from the soldier and began making a plan. But two things happened. Firstly, from the corner of his eye, he saw the soldier come towards him, and secondly the Doctor felt his legs give out. Then he felt no more as his head smacked against the ground and everything went dark.

Tollund Tunnels

When the Doctor woke, the sirens were still ringing and people were screaming; he couldn't have been out for very long. Lying on his back he could see up through slits in the ceiling as barricades were broken down, windows were smashed and people were dragged from their homes, their feet dragging along the slits he spied from, sending sand and dirt falling onto his head and body. Villagers tried to defend themselves but were ultimately powerless against the soldiers with their spears, shields, axes, hammers, swords and lances.

The Doctor attempted to lift his head, but intense pounding made him rest it again. Assuming he was a prisoner, he was surprised when he could move his hands, and his legs. A little more movement in his fingers and toes, he rubbed his aching back and became more aware of his surroundings. The room he was in was hot, it smelled of smoke; something was burning. He checked to see if there was any part of him on fire. He tried to get up again.

'I wouldn't do that if I were you,' came a voice from the shadows. It was deep and low, hollow, as if it had to travel a very long way to get to him.

The Doctor squinted his eyes to see. The figure came forward and he saw him, the soldier, his captor with the unusual shiny rotten skin. He was wearing the skin cap.

'I really did think she went the other way,' the Doctor said, in his defence.

'I didn't believe you.'

'Well, then, why did you go that way?'

'Maybe I wasn't trying to find her.'

'Well, then, *I* don't believe *you*.'

They stared each other down.

'Who are you?' the Doctor asked, scrambling to his feet. '*What* are you?'

'I should be asking you that.'

'I'm a visitor. I've done nothing wrong. I arrived to this mess. Nothing to do with me, and I don't know anything either so if you'd be so kind as to let me go...' He expected the soldier to challenge him, leap at him, spear him, eat him, *anything*, but he didn't move.

The soldier sighed and his weariness was evident. 'You have

the shoe, that's all we need. Give it to us, then you can be on your way. Go back to wherever you came from. Never come back.'

The Doctor frowned. Surely there was more to it than that? But he never had been one for backing down. 'Shoe? What shoe?'

'He knows about the shoe,' Root suddenly said, in the distance. 'Sorry I wasn't here when you woke up. Hope Mossy didn't scare you. I got you this.' He walked towards him and handed him a goblet. 'It will help your headache. Sorry about that, by the way, I only had enough time to grab your legs and pull.'

The Doctor looked upwards, saw the people being lined up. He wasn't sure if he had been saved or set up. He disposed of the water, suddenly very unsure of the boy.

'You pulled me down here… Why?'

'To save your life. You're welcome, by the way.' Root struck a match and lit a candle and a makeshift home was revealed.

'A root,' the Doctor said, aloud but to himself. 'Typically lives under the ground.'

'Are you crazy?' Mossy said to Root, reaching up and extinguishing the flame with his rotten fingers. 'They'll find you.'

'They,' the Doctor noted. 'Aren't you on *their* side?'

'No. He's one of us,' Root said.

'Us? I'm not even one of you,' the Doctor said, rubbing his pounding head.

The sirens and mayhem ended suddenly. The Doctor and Mossy set aside their squabbling to see what was happening outside. Xenotime led the way as warriors dragged a beaten and bloodied Prince Zircon through the square. They pulled him up onto a stage for all the villagers to see. There was the sound of distant drumming.

'What's that?' the Doctor asked.

'The rest of the army are on the way,' Mossy said.

Xenotime took centre stage. 'Somebody out there has something that I need. They know who they are. I know that he is here, now, in this square. If anybody is harbouring a stranger, then you will be killed.'

The Doctor saw that the old woman who had slammed the gate on him was the only person not to be lined up. She'd given them what little information she knew of him. Survival.

'If what I want is not returned to me by midnight, Prince Zircon will be killed.'

'She'll kill him anyway,' Root said angrily, and Mossy shushed him.

'Midnight,' Xenotime stressed, and she turned and glided out of the square, her gown skimming the cobblestones as she was escorted out by her soldiers, followed by her nervous-looking daughters, who attempted to maintain their pride despite the change of mood. Prince Zircon was tied up in the town centre, guarded by a team of rotten corpse men.

'Harbouring a stranger...' Mossy looked at him. 'Who are you, Doctor?'

'I'm a traveller. Simply passing through.'

'What timing,' Mossy said, trying to digest that.

'It's always about timing,' the Doctor replied.

'Oh, this is hopeless,' Mossy said, suddenly seeming to become weak, and collapsing to the floor, knees hunched up, head bowed.

'Don't say that, Mossy. It's not hopeless. We can do this.' Root knelt by his side.

The Doctor lowered himself to Mossy's level. 'What, may I ask, are you planning to do?'

'Stop Xenotime's rule of terror,' Mossy said tiredly. 'To send us back to the bogs where we came from.' And then as if suddenly realising it was a monumentally impossible task, he laughed.

'Mossy is a chieftain and now a leader of Xenotime's bog warriors,' Root explained. 'He was sacrificed in a ritual in his time and buried in the bogs. Xenotime used her witchcraft to convince the King of Tollund to marry her, and when she became Queen she used her witchcraft again to bring the dead in the Boglands back to life. Xenotime uses the men and women from the bogs as her slaves – the strongest men and women as warriors for her army, the others for peat digging, working the land and everything else she needs. But the people of the Boglands decided to rise against her; they didn't like their place in the kingdom, they wanted their own power. There was a small uprising. Many lives were lost,' he said sadly. 'My parents died. Xenotime came up with the idea of marrying Prince Zircon with one of the royal bog women. That way they would have representation on a higher power. They would be happier with better conditions but she could still maintain control of Tollund with the bog people as her followers.'

'Prince Zircon has to marry one of you?' The Doctor scrunched up his nose, looking at Mossy. 'Well, that was never going to happen.'

'It could have, if he hadn't been in love with Ash, Xenotime's stepdaughter. King Tollund's daughter.'

'Ahhh.' The Doctor said, understanding. 'And where are Ash's parents, the King and former Queen of Tollund, dare I ask?'

'Xenotime had them killed,' Root said, angrily. 'She convinced King Allanite that Queen Amethyst was a traitor. It wasn't just him – the entire kingdom believed it, even Ash. That was before Xenotime turned. Before that she had been a doctor in the village, a witch doctor, but she had helped people. Her story was credible. King Allanite left his wife and married Xenotime. Then she started getting crazy. She raised the bog people, she locked the former Queen Amethyst up in a cell, condemned Princess Ash to slave labour, turned all of the bog warriors against King Allanite so that he no longer had any power. She sent his supporters into the peat tunnels. She is extremely powerful. Her witchcraft has us all scared.'

'Witchcraft?' The Doctor shook his head. 'No, that's what she wants you to believe.'

'She is very powerful.'

'No she's not. It's not magic that preserved the bodies. The acidity of the water, low temperatures, and lack of oxygen combined to tan the bodies' skin and soft tissues of the bodies in the bog. The skeleton disintegrates over time as we can see...' He looked at Mossy. 'But the bodies are remarkably well preserved, with skin and internal organs intact. This is not witchcraft. It's simply nature. Science. Whatever you like to call it. Them coming back to life again, I'm not altogether sure how she did that, I'm guessing she didn't at all, that nature played into her hands, that's it was merely magnetic forces of the planet interacting with the natural elements...' He was pacing up and down.

'Doctor, what are you saying?' Mossy was beside him now, urgency in his voice, the fatigue suddenly gone.

'I'm saying Xenotime has no magical powers. In fact, no power at all other than her soldiers, but then, aren't they on your side?' he questioned Mossy.

'Some. Not all. My plan does not appeal to all warriors. Look at me. You can barely stand the sight of me. Do you think I want to live like this? Do you think most of the bog people want to live like this? As slaves? We have lived already. Now we want to rest. Those who wish to live on are dangerous and must be stopped. The others want power; I want peace.'

'We'll get you your peace, Mossy,' the Doctor said, feeling a rising anger on behalf of all those whose lives had been ruined. 'And she won't have power for much longer.' The Doctor reached out his hand to Mossy. 'I want to help. I'll join you.'

Appreciating the gesture, Mossy went to take his hand. He

stalled. 'You have what Xenotime is looking for?'

The Doctor nodded. He didn't intend to give the shoe to them yet, not until he knew what it was about the shoes that Xenotime wanted so much. They were best hidden for now. 'They're in a safe place.'

They shook hands.

The Peat Tunnels

'When did King Allanite realise he'd made a mistake about his wife?' the Doctor asked, as they made their way through the hot tunnels below the city.

'As soon as she was locked up to be sacrificed to the bogs,' Root replied.

'Sacrificed to the bogs?'

'Thrown in the bog and drowned,' Mossy explained. 'And before you ask, she wasn't raised from the dead. Though I don't know why – Xenotime would have enjoyed parading her around in front of everyone.'

'Because she couldn't, that's why,' the Doctor said, sure now that Xenotime had absolutely no power. That whatever had occurred in the bog had been a natural phenomenon, which she had cleverly disguised as her own doing. 'Tell me, what is the importance of the shoes? Root, I overheard you tell Ash that they were a gift from the King to the Queen whilst she was captured.'

'The King visited the Queen before she was taken away to be killed,' Root explained. 'I was there. Well, down here in the tunnels. I saw them together in her cell. Mossy sneaked him in to her. The King gave her the shoes. I didn't hear what they had to say, I didn't think it would be right to watch their final moment, but some believe he gave them to her for her afterlife. The bog people used to be buried with their clothes, sometimes wearing them, other times with their clothes folded beside them.'

'Is that what they left for you?' the Doctor asked Mossy, but was duly ignored. 'I understand your theory, Root, but *a pair of shoes*? And diamond ones at that.' The Doctor frowned. 'Seems unlikely she'd need them in an afterlife. It must have been a message of some sort. They must have a significance.'

'I agree,' Mossy said. 'There is something more to it.'

'It's my fault all of this has happened,' Root said. 'If I hadn't given the shoes to Ash to wear tonight, Xenotime wouldn't have seen them, then Ash and Prince Zircon would be married.'

'Ash appreciated the gesture, Root,' the Doctor said. 'But whatever it is about these shoes that we don't know, it has made Xenotime very angry. And afraid. And if she's afraid then they are our weapon against her. So let's find Ash first, and find out more about the shoes.'

Mossy led the way as they ventured further into the underground tunnels, protecting them from the other warriors who were searching, pretending the Doctor and Root were his captives. As a senior warrior in Xenotime's army, they respected him and didn't dare question him. The smoke began to thicken the further they went.

'What is this place?' The Doctor stopped, caught in a fit of uncontrollable coughing. The heat was so intense he had to lose a layer of clothing.

'It's the Tollund heating system,' Mossy explained. 'We dig the peat from the bogs and then we dry it for fuel, we also burn it to get bog iron. At least, Princess Ash and her people do. The fire is just this way, these tunnels lead into the vents in every building which is why Root here knows pretty much everything about everyone. There's no place this lad can't get access to.'

Root looked proud of himself.

Finally the tunnels opened up and the Doctor found himself in an enormous cavern. It was suffocatingly hot as the workers burned peat from the bog iron, and it was loud with the sound of metal being beaten into shape for weapons. It was also where the peat was dried for fuel. A domineering fire, too hot to even look at, rose from a hole in the ground and dwarfed the room. The Doctor found himself having to hug the walls unable to bear the extreme heat.

'Princess!' Root shouted, spotting Ash hard at work. She was a far cry from the woman the Doctor had seen a mere hour earlier. Gone was the glamorous dress and instead she wore a crop top, revealing toned midriff and torso, and worker's trousers. She was covered in dust and ash, and smeared in sweat and grime and looked more like a warrior and less like the typical princess. This was a princess condemned to hard labour.

'Root.' She gave him a hug. 'I'm so glad you're OK. What are you doing here?'

'We came to rescue you.'

'Rescue *me*? I'm fine. Everybody here vouched for me that I was working all night. Including Mossy, and for that I'm grateful,' she thanked him. 'I know helping us is dangerous for you but it worked. When Xenotime took one look at me in here she knew I couldn't have been the woman at the ball. I'm just sorry our plan for me to marry Zircon didn't work. It was stupid of me to think it would.'

'It wasn't stupid. Everything is worth trying for your freedom,' the Doctor said.

'You,' Princess Ash said, noticing the Doctor. 'You helped me earlier. Thank you.'

'And I'm not finished yet. The other shoe, Ash, tell me you still have it,' the Doctor said urgently.

'The gift of shoes from my father to my mother? It's nonsense. Xenotime's jealousy soars every day, and for what reason? She killed them both, what more can she do to keep them apart?' Ash asked, her anger rearing. 'I told her I had no idea what she was talking about but I gave it to Coalette, one of her servants, she's on our side. Coalette just put the shoes back in Xenotime's shoe room so she will find them eventually, I'm sure.'

'Oh no, Ash,' Root whined.

'They're just shoes, Root. I appreciate all you did to share them with me but she has taken every material possession of Mother and Father away from me. They are no longer important. I've learned to preserve my parents' memories in my head. Those, she can't touch. And where is Zircon? Please tell me he's safe.'

The Doctor and Mossy left them alone for Root to reveal recent events to her.

'Tell me what you know about the shoes,' the Doctor asked Mossy.

'Not enough. Queen Amethyst was granted permission to choose her own clothes for her execution. King Quartz had the shoes specially commissioned whereupon he brought them to her cell days before her murder. That is all we know.'

'We need to find the person who made the shoes. Do you know who that is?'

'It would have been King Allanite's most trusted friend and adviser, Professor Lanthanum.'

'Lanthanum,' the Doctor said, pacing again. 'It's a chemical element with the symbol La and atomic number 57. It's a silvery-white metallic element, malleable, ductile, a soft metal that oxidises rapidly when exposed to air and has numerous applications as catalysts.' He stopped pacing. 'Catalysts. Yes, we must find him.'

Ash interrupted them, eyes wild with fury for her lover's predicament. 'Xenotime promised me he was safe!'

'She is playing you, Ash, and we must go,' Mossy said suddenly. 'They are approaching. I fear your friends' loyalty will be questioned.'

'I'm sorry,' she whispered, looking around at her fellow

workers who had gathered. Those who worked alongside her were her father's greatest, closest and most loyal men and women. They had served alongside him and as punishment for their loyalty were forced to work in the peat cavern, facing scorching temperatures as Xenotime's slaves. 'I can't lose Zircon too. She will have taken everyone from me.'

'I believe that you have an army of your own, Princess Ash,' the Doctor said, noticing the workers slowly gathering closer to Ash. 'And they appear ready to fight, for you and with you, in the name of your father and mother and of all those who have been lost. Am I right?' the Doctor asked them.

The workers stood to attention, united, and raised their shovels and work utensils in the air and cheered. Their force and strength was enough to send a shiver through the Doctor.

Xenotime's Castle

'Princess, I'm sorry but I can't let you in.' Coalette's big brown eyes stared back at them, fearful and apologetic, from the hatch in the door that led from the tunnel to the castle. 'She has invited the royal bog men and women from the party to the castle to apologise for the disastrous night, security has been increased everywhere, none of us can move without questions. She's worse than ever.'

There was a disappointed silence from the three.

'You mean *masked* men and women will be arriving in numbers at the castle, any moment?' the Doctor asked.

They all looked at him.

Twenty minutes later, the Doctor and Ash were dressed and masked and ready to enter the castle under the guise of royal bog people. The only problem was the attire wasn't quite what the Doctor had intended.

'A dress?' he hissed, pulling at his chest uncomfortably, as they made their way through the corridors of the castle, away from the large crowd who had just entered.

284

'It was all Coalette could find,' Ash whispered leading the way, checking around corners before she resumed again.

The Doctor huffed, still unhappy with his predicament. He tripped over the hem of the dress as he shuffled after her. He wondered whose dress he was wearing, the too-cold sister or the too-hot one. It felt too tight and he was too hot. He could barely breathe behind the mask. And the wig was irritating him. He itched and pulled on the corset as he followed her.

A bog warrior was up ahead. 'What are you ladies doing here? No one is permitted to be in the royal residence.'

'Queen Xenotime has asked for her cape,' Ash explained. 'She is cold. We are her dressers. If she does not receive it immediately, there will be trouble.' Ash did a good job of playing the part of the nervous humble slave.

'Very well. Proceed.' He watched them suspiciously, then his eyes fell upon the Doctor. 'Hello, lovely.'

The Doctor adopted a high-pitched giggle and hurried away, shyly.

The soldier laughed and walked on.

'You're wearing my lady-in-waiting Oakly's face by the way,' Ash said sadly. 'She always made every man turn to stare.'

'What do you mean, I'm *wearing her face*?'

'Didn't you know? Before execution, Xenotime makes a cast of their face, for it to be worn after their death, as a reminder to all those who try to rise up against her.'

The Doctor shuddered. 'I've had many faces in my time, but at least they've all been mine.'

Ash looked at him confused.

'Never mind.'

'Through that door is her laboratory, where she does her witchcraft,' she whispered pointing to a door painted black. 'Nobody goes in there.'

'Not nobody,' the Doctor said, immediately heading towards it.

'Doctor, don't! It's dangerous.'

He ignored her and turned the handle. He peeped his head inside and smiled. 'I knew it,' he said to himself.

The room was empty. Xenotime's power was all smoke and mirrors, nothing but an illusion.

The Doctor quickly returned to Ash's side outside a large double door. They had reached Xenotime's bedroom and, as she was downstairs entertaining, they knew they were safe for a few minutes. They made their way through the plush suite, Ash pausing to look around.

'Are you OK?'

'This was my parents' room. I used to be afraid of the dark. I used to creep in at night and sleep in between them.'

They stared at the large double bed. The Doctor put a comforting hand on her shoulder and tried to respectfully remind her that they had little time to spare. With Prince Zircon's midnight execution looming, they needed to move quickly. With recharged energy for their task, they hurried to Xenotime's dressing room. It was a long corridor of pure white, floor-to-ceiling glass shelves lit up. The Doctor had to blink against the white light. There were hundreds of shoes.

'This shouldn't take long,' the Doctor said confidently. 'All we have to do is find the lone shoe.'

'They're all lone shoes,' Ash said, devastated. 'Her paranoia is even worse than I thought.'

It was only then that the Doctor noticed that on the left-hand side were the left shoes, and on the right-hand side were the right shoes. He didn't want to let Ash see his disappointment; they had less than an hour to go until midnight.

'Let's get to work.'

Ash sat down while the Doctor carefully brought her every single right shoe that remotely resembled the sparkling shoe he had found in the trees. He was gentle handling them, afraid he would activate the weapon hidden inside. His task was not easy as so many of the lone shoes resembled the gift from King Quartz to Queen Mica; it was as though, in her wild state of mind, Xenotime had made duplicates of the rumoured shoe in order to protect herself, or had scavenged the kingdom for lookalikes. Down on bended knee, the Doctor slipped shoe after shoe onto Ash's delicate foot. And finally, thirty right shoes in, the shoe clicked into place.

The Boglands

Mossy led them through the tunnels in the direction of Professor Lanthanum. Eventually, the tunnels could only take them so far and, as the town came to an end, they were forced to emerge outside. The Doctor was thankful for the fresh air but it meant they were in worse danger. Since Xenotime's discovery of her raided shoe closet, they were now searching for Princess Ash *and* the Doctor, while poor Coalette had been captured.

The Doctor was unsure why they were headed out of the town and towards the countryside, to the Boglands, if they were searching for King Allanite's trusted adviser. 'Why is he living here? I thought the bog people lived separately from the... humans.'

'We are human,' Mossy said, defensively, then, too tired to debate, he dropped it. 'Professor Lanthanum was seen as a traitor because he wouldn't declare his loyalty to Xenotime, so she killed him and buried him in the Boglands.'

'But then she regretted it,' Ash continued. 'Professor Lanthanum is the cleverest man in all of the kingdoms, and so she brought him back to life again as her slave. He simply refused and no torture would change his mind. His punishment is to live here.'

'A fate worse than death,' Mossy said, the weight of the world on his shoulders.

The Doctor swallowed, but it was further proof of Xenotime's failure. If she was truly powerful, she would not have raised Professor Lanthanum from the bogs; he was too large a threat to her.

They walked through the deserted village. Hundreds of bog people were living as peasants; men and women, who didn't fight, were sitting around their fires with their children in foreboding silence after word spread of another terrible war. Unable to age, unable to live properly, they were like shadows waiting for an end that they couldn't control. Those that saw Mossy nodded at him respectfully.

Professor Lanthanum's house stood alone, on the outskirts of the bog community. It was sixteen metres long, with mud and wattle walls, with a low-sloped peat roof to prevent the peat from sliding off. The door was made from oak panels, and when Mossy knocked it was immediately opened by an old bog man, dressed in civilian clothes.

He looked at Mossy, then at Ash. 'I've been expecting you.'

They sat squished together inside the cramped conditions. The house was divided into three aisles lengthwise by the two rows of oak poles that carried the roof. The floor was earthen apart from where they sat around the fire, which was compressed mud.

'So finally the shoes have shown up. I wondered if they would ever be recovered.' Professor Lanthanum's voice was low and gravelled. The Doctor had a hard time focusing on his face. Lanthanum hadn't been dead for as long as Mossy and his people and for that he had decomposed less, but it meant he was more difficult to look at, as he was closer to how he had looked originally; there was more flesh which had changed colour and hung in strips, more visibly rotten.

'I found them,' Root said. 'I took the shoes from Queen Amethyst's cell after they took her away. Xenotime found out that the King had visited her. As punishment to both of them, the soldiers took her away early, without the clothes she'd been promised. She didn't even have time to prepare.'

Ash swallowed hard, listening to this.

'The warriors had seen the shoes and were to come back for them, along with her other clothes but I got there first. I was keeping them for a special occasion for Ash. I knew that if Ash had them, she would have nowhere to hide them and Xenotime would take them away from her but I didn't know that she would recognise them tonight.'

'And if you hadn't taken them, they would surely have been lost for ever,' Lanthanum said. 'And I haven't the means or wherewithal to recreate them.' He smiled sadly at Ash. 'They were a special design for your mother. Commissioned by your father and thankfully the perfect fit also for you, Ash. Your father was not to be allowed near your mother during her… death, and so he wanted a way for her to protect herself. To annihilate all of the bog people. He could have done it himself but he felt her opportunity would be greater.'

'Annihilate the bog people? No!' Root objected. 'You can't kill them! Not Mossy. Not the good people. Not you, Professor!'

Mossy reached out to him, and Root fell into his arms sobbing.

'I can't lose you, Mossy, you're all I've left. Who will look after me?'

Ash reached out to pat the boy's head comfortingly.

'I have watched you become a man over this short time, Root,' said Mossy. 'You don't need me now. It's time for us to go now and when Tollund is saved, you can live as you should, with the people you should be with.'

Professor Lanthanum held his hand up to silence them. 'We have no time for that now, boy. I need to show you how to use the shoes. Where are they?'

Ash took the shoe she and the Doctor had retrieved, from her satchel and handed it to the Professor.

'Just one? Where is the other?'

They all looked at the Doctor.

'Ah. Well, um. That's the thing. I put it in a very safe place. At the time. It seems to be, now, quite the centre of things.'

Tollund Town Square

The Doctor, Ash, Mossy and Root watched the square from their hiding places in the tunnel.

'You see, there it is.' The Doctor directed their gazes to where he had hidden the shoe.

Seeing it, Mossy glared at the Doctor who was biting his lip and looking sheepish. 'Oops.'

In the centre of the square was a bog oak structure. On the Doctor's arrival into the town, he hadn't yet known of the bog people, and it had looked like a statue of a skeleton tree family reaching out to a woman and child. The faces were haunting and didn't depict the peace it was attempting to portray. The sparkling shoe peeped out from the cape worn by the bog man, yet nobody had noticed it. It was now the centre of activity. Prince Zircon was on display, in cuffs, surrounded by dozens of warriors, who were making a cast of his face for one of Xenotime's trophy masks. Beside them Xenotime sat on her throne overseeing her prisoner and watching the crowd. The people had been forced onto the street to watch his execution. There was ten minutes to go to midnight.

'How are we supposed to get to it?' Root asked.

Mossy fell back and the Doctor could sense his confidence waning. He took him aside from the others.

'Mossy, you said that you were a chieftain in your time.'

'Indeed.' He raised his chin proudly. 'The finest.'

'And you were sacrificed to the bogs for the gods?'

'For the sake of the others, for all the good that did any of us. I've brought us to this point, Doctor. I've battled with all my might, but I'm... tired. We're all tired. My people, we live as slaves in constant pain and deterioration. This is not a life. This is no way to live. If we can't have death, how can we appreciate life? I've led these –' he looked at Ash and Root – 'children, to this point, put them in grave danger, and I don't even know if I can do it myself. Putting them at risk will all be in vain.'

'But what if your sacrifice wasn't in vain, Mossy, what if it was so that you could be here, on this day, so that you could save so many? What if this is your fate and the gods are watching you? What if this is your moment? Don't give up.'

Mossy suddenly transformed. He straightened up, adjusted his cape. 'Sphagnum is in my command, and he is my friend. I know he is uncertain of Xenotime's plans and he will protect me. He is the warrior standing on guard closest to the shoe.'

'Mossy, you can't,' Ash said, trying to stop him, but she was too late. Before anybody had any time to think about it, Mossy was striding through the square. He walked with authority to the statue, retrieved the shoe and swiftly hid it under his cloak.

Sphagnum was the only person to see him. 'Mossy,' he said, looking around nervously. 'What are you doing? Is that the shoe Queen Xenotime is searching for? You must tell her at once.' He looked up at Xenotime. As if sensing trouble, her eyes moved to them instantly.

Mossy started walking away.

Sphagnum raised his voice. 'Where are you taking it?'

Mossy turned to him, his voice low so that Xenotime wouldn't hear. 'We must do the right thing, Sphagnum.'

'What are you talking about?' Sphagnum said, nervously. 'We have given her our word to protect. When this prince marries among us, we will have more powers. There will be no war. None of us want another war.'

'You are a fool if you believe her. She is going to kill him, Sphagnum. What then? We lose even more.'

'She is just trying to lure the girl in. This is just a trap.'

'You really believe that?'

Mossy tested the waters, slowly turning away from his anxious friend, whose eyes were searing into him, torn by his loyalty to his friend and loyalty to his Queen.

'Stop!' Sphagnum said, raising his spear to his friend. 'Hand it over, Mossy.'

Mossy quickly threw the shoe in the direction of the Doctor. The Doctor leaped out of the shadows and caught the shoe, hoping it wouldn't explode in his hands. As the Doctor helped Ash put her shoes on, Mossy did little to fight his fellow soldier and friend. He was stabbed in the heart and staggered to his knees.

'Mossy,' Sphagnum said, watching his friend fall to the ground. 'What have I done?'

Root was inconsolable and rushed to his friend's side, doing his best to help keep him alive. Mossy, on his deathbed, turned to Ash. 'Do it now,' he forced out.

Seeing the commotion, Xenotime immediately called her soldiers into action. 'Kill Zircon *now*!'

'But there is ten minutes left, Mother,' Erbium said, looking at her sister nervously, realising things were getting terribly out of control.

'I don't care. Kill him!' Xenotime ordered a warrior.

Seeing Sphagnum grieving over their leader, the warrior hesitated.

'Very well, I'll do it myself,' she shouted, trying to grab a spear from a warrior, in panic.

The warrior fought her.

'Xenotime,' Ash called loudly to her stepmother and the square went silent.

Xenotime froze at the sound of her stepdaughter's voice.

Ash's footsteps were loud on the cobblestoned ground. Xenotime saw the shoes on Ash's feet, the sparkle of the millions of diamonds, mismatched with her smeared, peat-stained worker's clothes. The fire was burning brightly in Ash's eyes and she stood, strong, bravely against her nemesis, the woman who had destroyed her family.

'This is for Zircon.' Ash put her hands out, like a gymnast, to balance herself and went up on the tip-toe of her right shoe, keeping her heel off the ground, then she went up on the toe of her left foot. Two small clicks could be heard.

'This is for my father.' Ash went down on her left heel, then went down on her right heel. There were two more clicks. Everybody watched, mesmerised.

'And this, dear stepmother, is for my mother,' she growled. Ash jumped in the air, as high as she could go so the shoes would get the full force of her body as she connected with the ground.

'No!' Xenotime shouted, but it was too late. The shoes had been activated, and their force against the cobblestones caused the ground to vibrate and sent waves of light so powerful and so bright that they blew Ash backwards and winded her as she slammed against the wall.

The ripples of light, worked their way across the square, disintegrating each bog person it touched, so that they exploded in a puff of ash and then disappeared.

Then it reached out beyond to the countryside where men, women and children sat together in their homes holding hands, hugging, waiting for their freedom to come.

Professor Lanthanum stood alone at the open door of his house, eyes closed, breathing in and out slowly, awaiting his fate.

Then the light struck them all, leaving only the townspeople, Xenotime and her daughters, without their warriors to protect them.

Mossy was gone and, despite their victory, Root grieved the empty floor of dust beside him. The Doctor comforted him, while Ash ran to free her love, Prince Zircon. Once on the stage before the people, they cheered for her.

Xenotime looked around in panic.

'Where is your witchcraft now, Xenotime?' the Doctor called to her.

Her eyes searched the crowd for the source of the voice and they fell upon the Doctor. He smiled at her, knowing her time had come to an end. The King and Queen of Lindow marched into the square with their army. Xenotime, Erbium and Terbium were seized at once and the people chanted for their execution.

Ash raised her hands to silence them, at home in her new role as leader of Tollund.

'We will not kill Xenotime, Erbium and Terbium,' she called to the people.

They were shocked and, before their rage could overtake her power, Ash continued.

'We will treat them with the same kindness and respect as they have treated *their* family and the people they led. They will be stripped of their titles, their castle and their possessions.' Her voice trembled with the emotion. 'I condemn them to work in the peat tunnels for the rest of their lives, doing hard labour just as they forced their slaves to do.'

The people cheered, punching the air.

'Mother,' Erbium moaned. 'Why don't you use your witchcraft.'

'Yes, Mother,' Terbium sobbed. 'Use your powers to kill them all. Do it, Mother.'

Xenotime looked at her daughters in wild panic.

'Do it, Mother,' Terbium said through gritted teeth. 'What happened, have you lost them? Or did you ever have them at all? Were they just another of your lies?' she screeched.

'You don't have any powers, do you?' Erbium said weakly, realisation dawning on her, before she collapsed, leaving the soldiers to carry her weight.

Ash continued to address the people. 'My family is not complete. Root, where are you?'

The boy, who was still on the floor where Mossy had fallen and then vanished, looked up at the Doctor. The Doctor winked and urged him on. The people parted for him as he made his way through the crowd and up to the stage.

'This is Root,' Ash said, putting her arm around his shoulder as he stood in between her and Prince Zircon. 'He taught me that nothing is lost for ever, and that includes hope. He may not have the blood of royals but he is the peoples' prince and I would kindly ask you to treat him as such.'

The people applauded.

'Many people helped us achieve peace and freedom today, and I must thank them.' She looked at the Doctor and he placed a finger over his lips.

She nodded her gratitude, and the Doctor smiled, proud of her. And then as the celebrations began, he slipped away and returned to his TARDIS with a welcome phrase ringing in his ears.

All is never lost. Not least, hope.

THE LONELINESS OF THE LONG-DISTANCE TIME TRAVELLER

JOANNE HARRIS

I

The Wellness Parade had just ended, and the fireworks were starting again. A ghostly swipe of shooting stars in a sky the colour of vanished time. For a moment the Queen remembered a rhyme she'd learnt when she was a child.

Star light, star bright, wish I may, wish I might…

But she knew better than that, of course. Wishing was too dangerous. Survival was keeping her eyes on the ground and leaving the stars to scratch their messages unseen against the mirror of the sky.

Her name had been Alice – once, in the days when people still had names. Now she was simply known as the Queen, although she had no subjects left. No subjects, no story, no wishes, no dreams. Dreams could be fatal. Wishes could kill. And tears – tears were even worse. She'd learnt that lesson the hard way.

Now the Parade was over, the Villagers were going home. The Baker, in his white hat; the Postman, with his satchel; the Milkman, in his clean blue smock, swinging his crate of empties. All of them were smiling, of course. The Wellness Code demanded it. But there was a look in the Milkman's eyes – a look that she had seen before. His face was flushed; his hair was wild; he looked like a man in the grip of some deadly intoxication. The Queen knew the signs only too well. And she knew the price of interference. But she had to do something, she told herself: after all, she *was* the Queen.

The Milkman, too, had once had a name. She tried it now, in an urgent hiss. 'Patrick. *Pat.*'

The Milkman flinched and shifted his crate from one hand

to the other. His eyes rolled like ball bearings. In a loud and ringing voice, he said, 'That was a great parade today! One of the best we've had, I think. Not that the others were bad, no. The others were all *wonderful*! But *this* one –' His voice had reached desperate pitch. 'I do love fireworks, don't you? Fireworks are my *favourite* thing. Except perhaps for toys. But – you know what I wish? *You know what I wish?*'

'Patrick, please.' She kept her voice low. Over the sound of the fireworks, only he could hear her. Above, a daisy chain of stars trembled in the darkening sky. 'Relax. It's going to be all right. Go home now. You're looking tired.'

He gave her that look again. 'Tired? Tired? You must be joking. I'm full of life. I'm happy. *Very* happy. I mean, who *wouldn't* be happy here? We have everything we want. Everything's perfect. Everything's good.' He lowered his voice. His eyes rolled. 'Was that all right? Did it sound OK? For God's sake, did I sound *happy?*'

The Queen put her hand on his arm. She said: 'Patrick. Please. You need to rest. How long is it since you slept?'

He started to laugh; a dreadful sound. 'Sleep? Alice, how *can* I sleep, knowing that monster's watching me? Knowing that she sees everything, hears everything that's happening? You're the Queen. You can stop her, I know. Go and see her. Talk to her. Please, Alice, *I don't want to die!*'

For a moment, the Milkman's voice rang out, too loud in the sudden lull. The Postman, the Baker, the Villagers all turned to look at him. The silence was cavernous; immense.

The Milkman looked at the Queen in appeal. 'Please, it's only a word,' he said. 'I didn't mean to say it, I swear!'

But it was too late; a rushing sound was gathering, like dust on the wind. A grinding, throbbing monotone, like a double heartbeat –

The Milkman dropped his crate. There came a sound of breaking glass.

'No,' he said, and started to run haphazardly down the Village street towards the tail of the Wellness Parade, where a couple of floats still lingered. A phalanx of clockwork Dragoons turned their heads to watch him go, standing to attention. A herd of pastel Ponies – mostly pink, but some eggshell-blue; pale-green and lemon-yellow – scattered as the Milkman ran from the thing that pursued him, the thing that was opening in the sky like an inverted funnel of stars –

The Queen averted her gaze. It was, strictly speaking, against the rules, but she'd seen the Gyre in action before, and she didn't need to see it again. The rest of the Villagers raised their eyes – their faces shone silver, then crimson as the Gyre did its work. For a moment, they saw something genuinely astonishing – a Milkman ascending into the sky, his legs still pumping desperately – and then he was gone in a shower of stars, and everyone clapped and chorused:

'Ahhhhhhh.'

Only the Queen did not clap. She was not above the law, but her rank did give her some privileges. Instead she kept her eyes to the ground and her hands in her apron pockets as the sound of the Gyre faded at last, and the light returned to normal. A few moments later, a Milkman's cap dropped from the sky and rolled for several yards until it finally came to rest beside an object that had not been there a few moments earlier – a large, blue cuboid topped with a flashing light and a sign that read: POLICE BOX.

The Queen's first thought was Patrick had somehow summoned it. But Pat had not been capable of reining in his unruly tongue, let alone of summoning such an important item as this. Someone else, then? But who? *Who?*

As she watched, the light went off. The police box stood silent and immovable, as if it had always been there, and had not just popped into existence moments earlier. Then, the door swung open and a man – a stranger – emerged. She had expected a Policeman to come out of a police box, but this man, in his velvet coat, with his exuberant shock of white hair, looked more like a stage performer – a hypnotist or a magician – than any kind of official.

She also thought he looked unwell; his face was almost colourless, his movements those of a clockwork toy. He looked at her with bloodshot eyes.

'Sarah? Sarah Jane?' he said.

Then he collapsed at her feet.

II

The Doctor rarely dreamed – in fact, he had always assumed it to be an almost exclusively human habit – but this time his dreams had consumed him. The radiation generated by the blue crystals of Metebelis III can have a number of unpleasant effects, including headaches, nightmares, delirium, muscle spasms, contact burns, deep-tissue damage, lapses of consciousness and finally, inevitably, death.

It had been a calculated choice. His actions had saved much more than Earth from servitude to the Spiders. But the price had been very high. He had a few hours left; maybe less. His head was already pounding. His extraordinary senses were already starting to fail; his cells breaking down, one by one. Of course, he'd encountered death before. He would, most likely, regenerate. But during his long exile on Earth, he had made a number of friends there – Sarah Jane Smith, Jo Grant; all his colleagues from UNIT. He didn't want to vanish, not without at least letting them know. Or so the Doctor told himself. The truth was more prosaic than that. He didn't want to die alone.

Now, as the TARDIS bore him home, the Doctor considered the loneliness of the long-distance time traveller. Every Time

Lord had their way of dealing with the problem. His own way had been to recruit suitable companions – it had seemed like a good solution once, but something had happened to him over the years, and the roles had shifted. Once, he had been a teacher to his human companions, revelling in their admiration and his own superiority. Now, he could see how wrong he had been. Contrary to all expectations, these primitive, small-minded beings had turned out to be more capable than he had ever imagined. And now, he himself had fallen prey to that most human of failings – pride.

Yes, it was pride, he told himself, that had first taken him to Metebelis III. Pride, vanity, and that Messianic tendency, that drove him to save the universe over and over again – as if he were at the centre of it; immortal; indispensable.

Thank all the gods for the TARDIS, programmed to take him back to Earth, where Sarah Jane was waiting. It would be good to see her again, one more time, before the end. Because, although Death, in his case, was a natural process of change, whatever survived of him after that would forever be different.

Now, as the TARDIS rematerialised, her central control array dimming once more, the Doctor hauled himself to his feet. It was difficult, but not impossible. His metabolism was slow enough to combat the cellular degeneration for at least a few minutes more. Time to explain things to Sarah Jane before he was no longer himself.

There was a tolling in his head like that of a bell; his vision swam. The tolling grew louder. He realised that he'd heard the sound before; it was the TARDIS's Cloister Bell, an alarm he hadn't heard in years. Some kind of a malfunction? Perhaps. There were no signs of trouble. In ordinary circumstances, he would have checked before going outside. But his time was running out. He would have to take the risk.

His coat was crumpled; he straightened it, along with the ruffles of his shirt. He took a moment to steady himself. His vision doubled; he almost fell. And then he opened the TARDIS door and staggered out into the night, where a woman was waiting for him.

'Sarah? Sarah Jane?' he said.

The sound of the Cloister Bell filled the world. And as he collapsed at the woman's feet, a line from John Donne followed him into a vortex of darkness; a line from Meditation 17, *Devotions Upon Emergent Occasions*:

> Send not to know for whom the bell tolls –
> It tolls for thee.

III

It was light when the Doctor awoke, feeling drained, but lucid. His memories of the previous night were interspersed with broken dreams of crystal caverns and falling stars, but at least his head had stopped aching. He was lying on a bed, covered in a yellow quilt. From a half-open window came the sound of birdsong.

There was a woman sitting close by. Mid-thirties; bobbed, dark hair; hazel eyes that seemed older than her years.

'Good, you're awake,' she told him. 'I didn't think you'd last the night. We only have one kind of medicine here, and I wasn't sure how well it would work.' She indicated a large, cartoonish bottle that was standing on the mantelpiece. A handwritten label said: MEDICINE.

The Doctor put a hand to his head. 'Young lady,' he said. 'That's impossible. I am currently suffering from exposure to a lethal form of radiation. My condition is incurable.'

The woman gave an unwilling smile. It had been some time since anyone had referred to her as *young lady*. 'I know it's hard to understand. Just try to rest. I'll make some tea.'

The Doctor went to investigate the bottle on the mantelpiece. 'Excuse me,' he said in his sternest voice. 'But this is rose-hip syrup. Soothing for sore throats, and surprisingly good with a scoop of ice-cream. But—'

'Is it?' said the woman, sounding rather distracted. 'That sounds lovely. I'll just make that tea.'

Left alone in the little room, the Doctor took in his surroundings. There was, apart from the bed, a chair, a table with a single stool, a vase of flowers, a mirror, a rug. He checked his face in the mirror to make sure he was still himself: it had occurred to him that perhaps he had regenerated overnight, which would plausibly explain the absence of his symptoms.

But the face in the mirror was still the one with which he was familiar; craggy, strong-featured; silver-crowned. The Doctor was unsure of whether or not to rejoice at this: the whole situation was unreal, and not a little puzzling.

Behind a blue bead curtain he could see into the kitchen, where the woman who had taken him in was making tea in a large brown pot.

'I don't think I caught your name,' he said.

'They call me the Queen. We don't have names. And you?'

'I am the Doctor.'

She put down the pot without looking at him. 'That's not a word we use,' she said in a low and careful voice. 'You might want to choose another.'

The Doctor raised an eyebrow. 'Do *you* have another name?'

'Told you. We don't have names around here.' She paused, then looked at him curiously. 'You called someone's name last night. Sarah Jane. You thought I was her.'

'Did I?' The Doctor looked thoughtful. 'Yes, I suppose I might have done that. You look a little like her.'

Something in the eyes, perhaps. Something in the tilt of the head; a kind of quiet defiance. This woman was older than Sarah Jane, but she had the same expression. And there was a kind of sadness akin to resignation in everything she said and did; this woman, young as she was, he thought, had already suffered tragedy.

He saw she was wearing a wedding ring, but there was no sign of anyone else in the tiny cottage. Only a photograph, mottled with age, in a frame on the kitchen wall. It showed a little family group – two parents and a young child – and although the faces of father and child had faded with the sunlight, the woman's face was still recognisably that of the Queen: smiling; happy; radiant.

There was a mystery here, he thought. Perhaps a personal tragedy; perhaps a more complex situation. In any case, he told himself, he couldn't leave without knowing more. The curiosity that defined him (and which had almost led to his death) had taken hold again. There was something wrong here; the Cloister Bell had told him as much. But there was no sign of anything, except for that nagging certainty that he was missing something big –

'Where *are* we, exactly?'

It *looked* like Earth. In fact it looked like Oxfordshire: rolling hills and little fields and flocks of fat, fair-weather clouds. The inside of the cottage was equally familiar: the radio; the carriage clock; the oval mirror on the wall; the vase of tulips by the bed. And Earth was where the TARDIS had been programmed to return him – but Earth where? Earth *when*?

The woman who called herself the Queen handed him a cup of tea. She didn't look much like a queen, he thought, in her flowered apron and blue jeans – and yet, she didn't strike him as being at all delusional. And she was human, without a doubt. The Doctor had been around humans for too long to mistake one for anything else.

'This is the Village, of course,' said the Queen, pouring milk into her cup.

'Does the Village have a name?'

She shrugged. 'It doesn't need one. It's the only Village there is. It has everything we need. But tell me. Why are *you* here?'

It was an excellent question. 'I must have got lost in the Time Vortex. Some minor calibration. The TARDIS hasn't been herself over the past few centuries.' He interrupted his monologue to take a mouthful of his tea. 'This is very good tea, by the way. But what exactly do you mean by *this is the only village?*'

The Queen gave a sigh. It always fell to her, somehow, to explain the Village to newcomers. Some took it better than others. Some – like poor Patrick – never really took it at all.

'You'll see soon enough. When you've had breakfast, I'll show you around. But – there are rules. If you stick to them, everything will be all right. Don't worry, I'll look after you, at least until we know who you are.'

'What do you mean, who I am?'

'Well, you can't be the – *Doctor*,' she said, lowering her voice at the word. 'There are no Doctors allowed here. I thought, when I saw your Police Box, that you could be a Policeman. But you're not, are you?'

'No.' He smiled at her. 'I'm not.'

'So – what are you?'

'A traveller. I came here in the TARDIS: what you saw as a Police Box.'

She gave him an anxious look. Of course, it was not unusual for new arrivals to be a little disoriented. But this man was different; she'd known from the start. And now this talk of travelling –

Had he come here on his *own*? How was that even possible?

'If you know a way to leave, then use it. Use it, soon, before…'

'Before what?'

She shook her head in agitation. 'It doesn't matter. You need to be gone. If you arrived here by accident, it could be that it's not too late. You could get away from here!'

She broke off, and the Doctor saw she was close to tears. 'My dear,' he said gently. 'Don't you think you should tell me what's going on? I may be able to help, you know.'

Once more, the Queen shook her head. 'You can't. But maybe *you* can get away. Get back into your Police Box before—' She stopped herself from going on. She was privileged, of course, but there were things that not even the Queen could afford to say aloud. 'I think I should show you the Village now,' she said, in a brittle, cheery voice. 'I think you'll like it. But please…' She paused. 'Don't ask questions, don't complain, don't use the D-word, and most of all, *never wish for anything.*'

'The D-word?' said the Doctor.

'You'll work it out,' she told him. 'Now. Let me show you the Village.'

IV

It was the most perfect English village that the Doctor had ever seen. Rows of cottages, some of them thatched; a lane that was bridal with apple-trees. Every garden was in bloom: tulips, daffodils, wallflowers filled the warm air with their scent. A cat sat curled on a nearby wall. Washing hung on a clothes-line. In the distance, church bells rang a joyful carillon.

Beyond was open countryside; green hills vanishing into the haze. The Doctor, with his acute sense of smell, could identify forty-two different Earth flowers, as well as the scent of candyfloss; of wood smoke from a chimney; of cut grass and warm hay and the good smell of horses. It was wholly idyllic – and yet, there was something missing.

Checking his fob watch, which contained a hidden TARDIS compass, the Doctor frowned at the display. There seemed to be two readings there; almost as if the TARDIS were in two different places at once.

Of course, he might have misread the signs. So much of the TARDIS's function was intuitive, rather than technical, that even he could not always be sure of what she was trying to convey. But ever since his arrival here, even in the cottage, he had been increasingly struck by the essential *wrongness* that ran like a dark thread through the fabric of this reality.

A Postman with a satchel passed them on a bicycle. He gave the Doctor a curious look, but called out a cheery greeting. The Queen raised a hand. The man cycled on. The whole of the little scene was perfectly timed, like a clip from a movie.

'Hurry,' said the Queen. (*Queen of what?*) 'There's a parade in the Square at noon. The place will be full of people. If you want to find your box…'

The hard part, she knew, would be going unseen. The Queen had special status. People noticed what she did, although it had been a long time since she had lived in the Castle. Now she tried to be ordinary; nevertheless, she was still the Queen. The Doctor, however, was different. Alien to this environment, his every move was an offence. The longer he stayed in the open, the more likely he would attract the wrath of the Gyre.

'This way,' she told him, leading the way. 'And please – leave any talking to me.'

Turning onto a cobbled street, they came to a row of little shops: a grocer's; a sweetshop; a post office; a bookshop; an ice-cream parlour; a toyshop; a baker's; a pet shop; a florist's; a church. All of them were quaintly perfect in their detail. The bookshop had a fine display of illustrated books for children; the sweetshop, a collection of old-fashioned glass jars filled with sweets of all different kinds; the toyshop, a window filled with dolls, bricks, kites, bears and boats.

A Grocer in a striped apron was standing in his doorway. 'Who's this? The new Milkman?' he said, indicating the Doctor.

The Doctor was about to reply, but the Queen interrupted him. 'Just a visitor,' she said. 'No need to ask questions, is there?'

The Grocer flinched. He was a small, nervous man with eyes that moved incessantly. He'd been a friend of Pat's, she knew; back in the days when people had friends. Nowadays, it was easier not to be too close to anyone. She'd seen three Grocers come and go; for some reason they seemed to be more susceptible than Postmen, Butchers or Milkmen. This one was already showing the unmistakable signs of stress; it wouldn't be long before it all became too much for him to handle.

'Lovely day,' he said at last, his mouth contracting into a smile. 'Looking forward to the Parade?'

'Yes, of course,' replied the Queen, before turning back to the Doctor. 'Not far now,' she said. 'Come on. The Square's at the end of this street.'

It was an oblong square of grass surrounded by flowering cherry trees. All around, there were houses and shops all built from the same mellow stone; a fountain with statues of dragons and swans and a squat little church with a weathervane perched atop its pointed spire.

The Queen was standing in the place where the TARDIS had appeared. But nothing remained to indicate that anything had been there at all, except for a square patch of pavement surrounded by confetti. For a moment she stared at the ground. Then she turned to the Doctor.

'I'm so sorry,' she told him. 'Your Police Box isn't here.'

She had expected him to show distress, alarm, or at the very least, surprise. But the Doctor just looked thoughtfully at his watch and murmured: 'Yes. I thought so.'

For a moment she waited for him to react. Some people took it badly. Some took days, even weeks, to accept that this was reality. Some went insane. Some tried to escape. She shivered at that memory.

'You have to get indoors,' she said. 'The Wellness Parade will be starting soon.' That meant crowds of people; floats; toys; horses; majorettes. People asking questions. 'Come *on!*'

It would be quiet in the Church. The Vicar had left a long time ago. Now, only the sound of the bells existed to remind them. She took the Doctor's arm. 'Come on. I know a place where we'll be safe.'

The Doctor said nothing, but followed her. An idea was starting to form in his mind. But to explore it in full, he needed the Queen's assistance, and she was far too anxious now to give him her cooperation. She led him into the Village church, a cool and pleasant building filled with rows of oaken pews, where light through the stained-glass windows formed a kaleidoscope on the flags. A number of hand-lettered panels hanging on the stone walls said: *Happiness is in our Hearts*; *Trust in Me* and *All Shall Be Well*.

'What's a Wellness Parade?' he asked.

'We have it every day,' said the Queen. 'When you see it, you'll understand. It's a way of reminding ourselves how much we have to be happy for.'

The Doctor raised an eyebrow. 'I see. Forgive me for saying so, my dear, but you don't *seem* very happy to me.'

She shrugged. 'You're wrong. We're all happy here. It's the only way to be.'

He looked at his fob watch again and frowned. 'What date is it?'

She gave a sigh. 'It's Saturday, April 8th,' she said.

'And yesterday?' said the Doctor.

'Saturday, April 8th.'

'I see. And how many April 8ths has it been?'

'More than I want to remember,' she said.

'I understand,' said the Doctor. In fact, he was only beginning to see the picture that was emerging. The ringing of the Cloister Bell; the erratic behaviour of his TARDIS compass; and now, this village, suspended in time – all pointed to a paradox in the Time Vortex. Could this be a ploy by the Daleks to draw him into one of their traps? It would not be without precedent. The Doctor's most relentless foes had once used their Vortex magnetron to bring about the same effect – although the thought of Daleks here seemed absurdly incongruous. And yet, *something* had diverted him, against the TARDIS's programming. The Time Lords, then? He doubted it. This was no Time Scoop procedure, but something far more elegant.

'My dear young lady,' he said to the Queen. 'I think we need to talk. Don't you?'

She gave him a look of pity. 'Not now. The Wellness Parade is beginning.'

V

They heard the Wellness Parade long before it finally came into view. The distant sound of a marching band, with trumpets, horns, fifes and drums, approaching along the main street. Then at last the band appeared; marching in perfect formation, smart red jackets, capes and hats, buttons gleaming in the sun. A dozen majorettes followed them; batons twirling; heads held high. Then a pair of kettle-drums and a piper in full livery.

All around the little square, the Villagers had come out of their shops and houses to watch the Parade go by. The Doctor, too, watched – through a grille cut into one of the big church doors. The angle was excellent, covering most of the square, as well as the approach from the street. He saw the procession arriving; heard the sound of applause from the crowd. But there was something rather odd about both the procession and the applause; as if the whole scene had been staged to be part of a larger performance. There was something too perfect about those majorettes in their pleated skirts, the band in their scarlet uniforms. The music was almost too precise; not a single wrong note or missed beat. Even the bystanders seemed part of the show; the Baker in his impeccable whites; the Butcher in a striped apron; the Postman he'd seen only minutes before, now shouting and throwing confetti as the first of the floats came into view.

A collection of giant Toys were sitting on a giant heap of bricks. There was a Bear; a Clockwork Clown; a Doll; a sad Pierrot; a Mouse. The figures were larger than human beings; perfect in every detail: the Doll, pink-cheeked and golden-haired, was scattering handfuls of wrapped sweets; the Clown was turning somersaults; and the grinning, capering Pierrot was throwing confetti into the crowd.

'Extraordinary costumes,' the Doctor said.

The Queen smiled, but did not reply.

Next came a troop of pink Ponies, trotting in time to the music. Their manes were plaited with multicoloured ribbons; their flanks were marked with rainbows and hearts. Next came another of the floats: Soldiers standing to attention, occasionally breaking formation to shoot streamers into the crowd. Next came a troupe of dancing Dwarves, dressed in Arthurian costumes. Next, a magnificent pirate ship, with a crew of ragged, drunken Pirates.

The Doctor watched in fascination as the Parade unfolded. It had taken him a few moments to realise what he was seeing, but now the picture was becoming clear. Through the grille, he could see the giant Bear and the clockwork Clown moving between the Villagers, handing out sweets, throwing streamers and marching alongside the Soldiers. It occurred to him that a child would love this colourful and eccentric Parade, and yet, among all the onlookers – a hundred people, maybe more – he could not see a single child.

'Where are the children?' he said to the Queen. 'I don't think I've seen any here.'

She shook her head. 'You won't,' she said, and the sadness in her eyes stopped him from asking more questions.

Besides, on further inspection, he thought that maybe the entertainment was rather too sinister for a child. The Bear's jaws opened in a grin, revealing rows of vicious teeth. The Clown's eyes moved like machine-gun sights. The Doll, with her golden ringlets, sat on the flower-decked float and smiled. Her teeth were small and even, like the teeth of a circular saw. Her eyes, which were cold and cornflower-blue, gleamed in hungry merriment.

'They're not costumes, are they?' he said.

Slowly, the Queen shook her head. At last, she told herself with relief, he was beginning to understand. If she could help him survive the week, then maybe he might have a fighting chance. If she could find him a place, somehow – something that would allow him to fit neatly into the community –

Suddenly she had an idea. 'You could be the new Vicar!' she said. 'There are clothes in the vestry. You could live in the Vicarage. No one would guess you were from the Outside.'

The Doctor frowned. 'My dear girl. Do I *look* like a vicar?'

She tried to explain. 'But you'd fit in. You could be safe.'

He smiled. 'You'll have to do better than that, I'm afraid. I'm rather fond of my bow ties, and I don't care much for dog collars. Not to mention the TARDIS, of course. The old girl's been with me for a long time, and I'm not about to abandon her now.'

She sighed. 'You're being very difficult.'

'You're not the first person to notice, my dear.'

The Queen thought deeply for a while, her face constricted with anxiety. Finally, she came to a conclusion.

'All right,' she said. 'I'll show you. There's a door at the back of the church. We can get out without being seen. After that, it's a walk through the fields.'

'That sounds remarkably simple,' he said.

'Trust me, Doctor,' she told him. 'It's not.'

*

VI

They left the church as she had planned. The Wellness Parade was well under way. The band was playing Souza, and the sound of drums and marching boots reached them from the Village square as they crept through the back streets. The air was filled with carnival scents; candyfloss and horses and waffles cooked by the roadside.

Polly had always loved carnivals. Recalling, the Queen was surprised at how much pain the memory still caused her. Was she watching the Parade? Very probably, she thought; though she rarely appeared in person. But once, she had lived among them like any other Villager; feeding the horses; stroking the cats; running through the meadows. Once, she had been their little Princess, the darling of the Village.

Of course, the world had been larger then.

She glanced at the Doctor, who seemed to be slowing down. 'Are you all right?'

He nodded, but she thought he looked paler than he'd been before. The rose-hip elixir in which Polly had once believed so implicitly was starting to lose its potency. The illness that had afflicted him when he had arrived in the Village would not take long to return, she thought. Was it a sign of worse to come? And could they have already been seen?

The Doctor himself had been aware of the change since he had entered the church. The symptoms of the Metebelis radiation – the sickness, the physical weakness, the sweats – had started to manifest again. Not as badly as they had on Metebelis III, but he guessed it was just a matter of time before his condition reached a critical stage. All the more reason to get back home as soon as possible, he thought. He looked at his fob watch. The reading gave the location of the TARDIS as being in fourteen different places at once; all less than nine miles away.

314

He gave the watch a little shake. Now, according to the display, the TARDIS was in two thousand different locations.

'Please. We need to hurry,' said the Queen in a low voice. 'I'm supposed to be at the Wellness Parade. If anyone notices I'm not—'

'Why?' interrupted the Doctor.

The Queen sighed. In all her time in the Village she'd never met anyone so full of questions. 'We're *all* supposed to be there,' she said. 'It brings the community together.'

The Doctor thought of the carnival floats; of the giant toys so lifelike that they seemed almost to breathe; of the clockwork soldiers whose guns shot streamers rather than bullets. The similarities with the Autons had already crossed his mind, although he was inclined to think that this was something different. But what he suspected was so strange that he was hesitant to articulate it, even to himself. Best to wait and see what the Queen was so eager to show him.

A cloud of multicoloured balloons, released from the Village square, pixelated the sky above. The Queen looked uneasy.

'Balloons,' she said. 'This is the first time we've had balloons.'

The Doctor looked unmoved by this, but she had grown suspicious of change. The cloud of balloons moved gently downwind, scattering across the sky, and it occurred to her how easy it would be to use them to spy on the Villagers; reporting unauthorised movements; objects and people who didn't belong –

'We have to hurry,' she told him. 'Something's going to happen.'

Please, don't let it be the Toys, she told herself as she scanned the streets. Toys were supposed to be comforting; cuddly; nostalgic – even the Toys in the Wellness Parade – but that had changed. Like everything else.

The lane that led out of the Village went into a little valley. A stream ran through it; shallow and bright, dotted with little stepping stones. Beyond that, there were woods and fields bordered by hawthorn hedges. But just as she and the Doctor approached the boundary of the Village, she saw a human shape detach itself from the shadow of a nearby house.

It was the Village Policeman; tall in his dark-blue uniform; buttons bright; helmet cocked; barring their road into the fields. He alone was not obliged to attend the daily Wellness Parade; instead he patrolled the Village streets in search of irregularities. It had probably been he who had reported the TARDIS and arranged for its removal. Perhaps he hadn't wanted to share his privileged status with anyone.

'Allo-allo-allo,' he said. 'What's all this? Not at the Parade?'

To the Doctor he looked like a caricature of every Policeman he'd ever seen. Stolidly British, from his moustache (rather like the Brigadier's) to the soles of his well-polished shoes. His words, too, seemed taken from a script; under the brim of his helmet, his eyes were keen and questioning, and, the Doctor thought, quite insane.

The Queen said: 'Let us pass, please.'

'I'm afraid I can't let you do that, ma'am. Duty calls. You know that.' He turned his gaze onto the Doctor. 'You're going to have to come with me and answer a few questions.'

'I'm giving you an order,' said the Queen in her most imperious tone.

'Sorry, it's my duty, ma'am. Now if you'll just step out of my way—'

At that, he lunged at the Doctor. But the Doctor was quicker, evading him with a series of moves adapted from Venusian aikido – a twist a feint, and a forward roll that brought him to his feet again right *behind* his adversary, allowing the Doctor to utilise his extensive knowledge of human pressure-points and to paralyse the Policeman without causing any permanent harm.

'He'll be all right,' he assured the Queen, rolling the

unconscious Policeman into a nearby privet hedge. 'Just a little trick I picked up – oh, somewhere or other. And now – I think we have company.'

It was one of the toy Soldiers from the Parade, just rounding the corner of the street. For a moment his inhuman, shoe-button eyes blinked at the irregular scene. Then he raised his rifle.

For a moment the Doctor was unaware of the danger in which he stood. He'd seen the Soldiers shoot streamers, not shells – and besides, the thing was just a toy –

There came the click of the safety release. Then, a crack of gunfire.

'*Run!*' shouted the Queen.

The Doctor obeyed. There came another gunshot, and the ricochet of a bullet from the wall of a nearby house. The Doctor felt a fragment of stone whip past his cheek, almost close enough to graze the skin.

'*Not* just streamers, then,' he said, as he and the Queen found shelter behind the corner of a building.

The Queen looked bleak. 'Not even close. We're going to have to run for it, before it brings the others.'

Already the Soldier had been joined by several of its companions, as well as a sugar-pink Teddy Bear, made sinister by its yellowing teeth, the blonde Doll from the carnival float, and the grinning clockwork Clown. The Soldiers fired again, and the Queen flinched away as the bullets struck stone just inches from her head. The little alley was fast becoming a sniper's gallery, and there was nowhere left to run that wouldn't take them back to the Square –

The Bear dropped to four paws and began to prowl towards them. Behind him, a phalanx of Soldiers; rifles raised, began to march. They could be on them in moments.

Surrender was no option. She knew what would happen if they were caught. She'd seen it with the Milkman, and his crime had been far less severe. Pat had been unlucky, she thought. If everyone who lost control was banished to the Gyre, she thought, then no one in the Village was safe. But an open act of defiance – well. *That* was something different.

She glanced over her shoulder at the open fields beyond. The Soldiers were slow and cumbersome. Their weapons were best at close range. But even so, to risk a dash of several hundred yards on foot would be a virtual suicide. Unless –

She turned to the Doctor.

'Can you ride?'

VII

It was a risk. He knew that much. But time was getting increasingly short. He couldn't afford to linger here. Quite apart from the fact that his very presence was a crime punishable by summary execution, another death sentence awaited him, one pronounced by the Great One back on Metebelis III.

But the Queen's idea might work, he thought. It was worth a try, at least, and in any case it was better than getting shot as they ran through the fields. The difficulty was getting back around the posse of Soldiers. The Queen knew a way through the tiny streets – some of which were so small they barely counted as streets at all. Edging their way through a narrow divide between two little cottages, the fugitives managed to double back towards the body of the Parade.

The square was filled with people. To the Doctor, it looked like the living deck of a game of Happy Families. There was a Farmer in a smock, chewing on a corncob pipe; a Farmer's Wife in an apron, hands still floury from making bread; a fat Chef with a curly moustache; an Italian Tenor. There was also a Gardener with a spade; a Milkmaid with a bucket; a Flower-Girl in a straw hat; a Grandmother in a rocking-chair. All rubbing elbows with jugglers; clowns; dancers; acrobats; living Toys. A scene from Breughel, with the cast of an Enid Blyton storybook – and still, not a child among them.

But there was no time to waste; already they were attracting looks. The Queen had a smear of blood on her face where a chip of stone had cut her cheek; both she and the Doctor were dusty and dishevelled.

A Delivery Man with a peaked cap and a brown-paper parcel under one arm hissed at the Queen: 'What's going on? I heard shots.'

The Queen shook her head. 'Not now. Let us through.'

She could see half a dozen ponies following a float that was made to look like a confectioner's window; on it, a giant Pastry Chef reclined on a bed of cream cakes. Taking the Doctor's arm, she led the way through the milling crowd. The Villagers parted to let them pass; murmurs and side glances followed.

At last they reached the ponies; their soft flanks dappled in ice-cream shades. The Doctor selected a strawberry-pink; the Queen a baby-blue one. By then their presence was causing alarm; passers-by looked at the Doctor with expressions of superstitious fear; some drew away or averted their eyes.

Murmurs followed in their wake.

Who's that?

Don't ask questions.

Part of the Parade, maybe?

No. He's from the Outside.

The murmurs grew and multiplied. Now the Doctor and his companion could have only seconds before they were seen by the Soldiers patrolling the far side of the Square. So far, their backs were mostly still turned; a row of giant keys stuck out from between their shoulder-blades, revolving thoughtfully as they marched.

Who winds the guards? the Doctor thought, as he carefully

mounted his Pony. Beside him, Alice did the same, trying not to make any noise. Polly had always loved horses, though she had never learnt to ride. Alone of all the creatures that made up the daily Wellness Parade, the pastel Ponies had never become frightening or sinister. And now, as danger threatened once more, the ponies might be her only chance –

There came a cry from across the Square: '*Halt! Halt or I'll fire!*'

But the Queen knew that the Soldiers would not risk firing into the crowd. Beside her, the Doctor urged his mount on back the way they'd first come; the Ponies were sturdy little things, and although his was ludicrously disproportionate to his height, it carried him surprisingly well.

Of course, the Queen knew that any escape was only a temporary reprieve. But the Doctor's unshakeable certainty that he could retrieve his TARDIS had strengthened her resolution. He might be insane, she told herself. They might be riding to their deaths. But, as she kicked her Pony's flanks and felt the sudden wind in her hair, the Queen felt a surge of emotion so pure and unexpected that it took her a while to identify the sensation.

It was hope.

VIII

From a distance, the Gyre had seemed like a bank of bluish haze. But as they came closer, they both began to see it as it really was; and to hear its voice; that throbbing sound, like a double heartbeat. Closer still, it became a thunderous wall of white noise and agitated particles, which girdled the horizon in a broad and lethal curve.

'This is the Gyre,' said the Queen, raising her voice to compete with the sound. 'It used to be much further away.

Now, you can't go further than this.'

The Doctor watched in silence. They had left the Ponies beyond the last ridge – the gentle creatures had become increasingly nervy as they approached – and come the rest of the way on foot. Now the Doctor stood at the last boundary of the Village and stared up at a living wall; a wall that, according to his watch, seemed to consist of the subatomic remains of innumerable carbon-based forms – plant, animal, human – as well as that of the TARDIS.

'The Gyre,' he repeated softly, and quoted Yeats's lovely words from *The Second Coming*:

> Turning and turning in the widening gyre
> The falcon cannot hear the falconer;
> Things fall apart; the centre cannot hold;
> Mere anarchy is loosened upon the world.

Except that in this case, the centre *did* hold; the anarchy and chaos contained. He'd seen time storms off Gallifrey, and sandstorms on Aridius. He'd travelled the Time Vortex from Alpha IV to the Eye of Orion, but never had he seen anything quite like this. A rapidly rotating electromagnetic field, charged with chaotic particles, moving at incalculable speed and rising high into the air like a tornado's funnel. The Village and its surrounding countryside were in the eye of the matter-storm, which rose so high above them that only the blue of scattered light remained, giving the illusion of clear skies above.

At a guess, the diameter of the eye was something close to ten Earth miles, which made the comparison absurd – no tornado was ever so vast – but that was what it looked like. An artificially controlled tornado in the Vortex, encircling, of all things, an English country village.

The Doctor's compass now showed the TARDIS as being in a hundred and fourteen million different places simultaneously.

'How very singular,' he said. 'A perfectly controlled linear environment, contained within a single oscillation of the space-time Vortex. What an elegant and simple solution to Faust's existential dilemma. The best of both worlds. Heaven and hell. The beautiful moment, suspended in Time, potentially, for eternity.'

'What?' said the Queen.

'Goethe,' he said. '*Man errs, till he has ceased to strive.* Faust. He too was a Doctor. Yes, I'm beginning to understand.'

'*I* don't understand at *all*,' said the Queen.

The Doctor assumed a modest look. 'Well, Goethe *was* an acquaintance of mine, rather a long time ago. *Everything transitory is but an image.* Rather a nice phrase, if I say so myself. And, if you're exploring the nature of Time, it helps to make friends with a Time Lord. Of course, for the most part, he was drunk, and thought I was the Devil—'

The Doctor broke off, with some regret. Now was not the time for reminiscences. If his theory was right, then he was in far worse danger than he had ever been on Metebelis III.

He took out his sonic screwdriver and fiddled with the settings.

'What's that?' said the Queen.

'Just a multipurpose tool,' said the Doctor absently. 'I've found it useful in the past. Now, if I calibrate it to focus on the last temporal oscillation, then reverse the polarity of the field, I should, in theory, be able to collect and reassemble matter from the Vortex.'

He waved the sonic screwdriver at the circling dust cloud, looking to the Queen even more like a stage magician. 'By this method, we should be able to reverse the effect of the atomic dispersion and – *Voilà!*' He made a theatrical gesture.

The Gyre began to react to the pull of the sonic screwdriver.

'No!' said the Queen. 'It's dangerous. You don't know what the Gyre can do!'

The Doctor remained unperturbed. 'My dear young lady, there's nothing to fear. I know *exactly* what I'm doing.'

The Gyre increased its unearthly howl. A smaller funnel within the cloud now began to open. Ropes of lightning tethered it to the body of the Gyre, which spat and howled its growing rage in a frenzy of turbulence.

The Doctor shouted above the din: 'Nothing at all to worry about!'

And the Queen stood frozen, helplessly, as the vortex yawned and writhed; releasing a thing half-lily, half-snake, rearing monstrously over them...

The Doctor made a final pass with his sonic screwdriver. At the same time, the Gyre released a sudden, apocalyptic flare of light.

The Queen flung herself to the ground.

The Doctor shielded his eyes with his hand.

There came a sound like a cracking whip, the tip of the sonic screwdriver fused into a meaningless blob, and at the same time, the secondary funnel was reabsorbed back into the Gyre, leaving behind it a familiar shape against the sullen matter-cloud –

'Ah,' said the Doctor.

The shape began to move feebly.

'Patrick. *Patrick*,' said the Queen.

The Doctor gave a wry smile. 'A minor miscalculation,' he said. 'I have to confess, I was rather hoping to reconfigure the TARDIS. Instead, we appear to have configured... a... a rather dishevelled Milkman.'

He looked at the sonic screwdriver. The damage was not irreparable, but until he was able to replace the fused component, it was more or less useless. He would have to find another way to bring back the fragmented TARDIS. The Gyre, too, seemed to be under the influence of some kind of violent disruption. Lightning stitched its surface; waves of rogue energy rose and fell within the circling matter-storm.

The Queen threw her arms around Patrick. 'I thought you were gone for ever,' she said. 'This man brought you back. Oh, Pat – how is that even possible?'

The Milkman stared at the Doctor. He was pale, but seemed otherwise unhurt. 'I don't remember anything,' he said. 'Except for the Wellness Parade, and the fireworks.'

'That's probably for the best, old chap,' said the Doctor, patting his arm. 'Now why don't you and your friend the Queen start from the beginning?'

IX

'Once upon a time,' said the Queen. 'There was a beautiful Princess. But she was under a terrible curse, put on her by an evil enchanter. The King and Queen, her parents, were heartbroken when they heard the news. They promised their daughter that they would find a way to help. They called every wise man and specialist, and promised them their heart's desire if they could break the enchanter's curse. But try as they might, no one managed to find a way.

'Meanwhile, the Princess had to live in a distant tower. She took all her toys and her books with her, and for a time, she was happy. But soon she grew lonely. She wanted her friends. She wanted to be like the other girls. She grew impatient, then angry.

'Her parents tried to give her hope. But the curse stayed unbroken. The young Princess began to feel that no one really cared for her. She grew tired of wise men and specialists who were neither wise nor special enough to understand how to cure her. She grew tired of promises that never came to anything. And so she looked for a way to escape. And then, one day, she found it.'

The Queen paused in her narrative, and the Doctor saw that her eyes were wet. 'You have to understand,' she said. 'It wasn't the Princess's fault. But she was so young, you see. And afraid. She didn't know what she was doing. She was only trying to live. And then – there was an accident.'

Once more, she paused. The Doctor could see how hard she was trying to find the words. He did not for a moment believe that this was the real story, but in his experience, fairy tales often contained a truth deeper than mere reality.

'What kind of an accident?' he said.

The Queen shook her head. 'A Bad Thing. One that changed everything.'

The Doctor pondered that for a while. 'I think I understand,' he said. 'Tell me, this Princess – is she still here?'

Silently, the Queen nodded.

'Can you take me to see her?'

'No. No one sees the Princess. Not even the Queen. Not since—' She stopped.

'Not since what?' prompted the Doctor.

The Queen glanced uneasily at the Gyre. 'No. It isn't safe,' she said. 'You're asking too many questions. She's everywhere. She watches us. She could be watching us, right now.' She took the Doctor by the hand. 'You should have stayed in the Village with me,' she said. 'We could have dressed you in the Vicar's clothes. We could have sat by the fountain, eaten candyfloss, and watched the end of the Wellness Parade. There'll be fireworks tonight. It's a good life. You get used to it. Just as long as you follow the rules.'

The Doctor smiled. 'Ah, yes. The rules. *Don't ask questions, don't use the D-word, and most of all, don't wish for anything?*'

The Queen and the Milkman nodded. They looked like children lost in the woods.

'You don't attract attention,' said the Milkman, looking at the ground. 'Just try to fit in and be happy.'

The Doctor gave him a little smile. 'I'm afraid I'm not good at fitting in.' He glanced at the ridge behind them, where his keen vision had detected movement a few moments before. Now, he could see them approaching, slowly but relentlessly: clockwork Soldiers with guns that shot real-life, lethal bullets; Teddy Bears with steely claws; baby Dolls with laser eyes; and Clowns with long, carnivorous teeth.

It wouldn't be long.

The Doctor gave a broad, and curiously sunny smile. Death in front of him, Death at the rear, and the blue death of the crystal cave consuming his body from within. His favourite odds had always been those in which he was outnumbered. Now, in spite of the fever that crawled like spiders over his skin, he felt as alive as he'd ever been. He said: 'I am the Doctor, and I wish to talk to the Princess.'

'Don't,' said the Queen in a whisper.

But the Doctor simply raised his voice and repeated: 'I am the Doctor, and I wish to talk to the Princess.'

'You don't know what you're doing,' said the Milkman in a low voice.

'Oh, but I do,' said the Doctor. Then, raising his voice even further, he roared: '*I am the Doctor, and I wish to talk to the Princess. Right now!*'

There came a moaning from the Gyre. The instability he'd first detected seemed to be getting more pronounced. The single oscillation that had kept the Vortex in check had become irregular, tugging in all directions at once. Lightning crawled like veins beneath the darkening skin of the matter-cloud.

The Milkman turned and started to run.

The Queen stood her ground, but her face was white. 'You have no idea what you're doing,' she said.

'Actually, I think I do.'

Above them, the narrowing curve of the Gyre was reaching

out in readiness. Bolts of untethered lightning swam within it like circling sharks.

The Doctor watched as something – a shape – began to appear from the turbulence. It looked like a face a storey high, with eyes as dark as tunnels and hair like whips of lightning. It was not a projection, but something three-dimensional; a giant Head carved into a cliff of living, speaking energy.

'*How dare you make demands of ME?*' The voice was a thunder that ran through the ground. '*How dare you break My commandments?*'

The Queen took a step. 'Ignore him,' she said. 'He's only here by accident.'

'*What kind of an accident?*' said the Voice.

'It doesn't matter,' the Doctor said. 'We need to talk. Just you and I.'

'*You can't tell Me what to do,*' said the voice, childish in spite of its resonance.

'Oh yes, I can, young lady. And it's high time someone did. The centre cannot hold for long. The Gyre is contracting. One day it is going to collapse. And when it fails, this reality will disappear, and you, and all the people in here will die.'

The Queen shook her head. '*No,*' she mouthed.

But the Doctor was watching the face in the cloud. Emissions of fugitive plasma lashed across its features.

'*No one dies here,*' said the Voice.

'Oh, but they do,' the Doctor said. 'Yeats understood what happens when the natural order of things is disturbed. Goethe did, too. Anarchy. Tell me, what was the Bad Thing? Did someone die? Is that why you're here?'

The voice gave a wordless wail, and within the Gyre, the turbulence began to increase. A wave of plasma swept over the face, obliterating the features. The sound of thunder was now so loud that the Doctor's eardrums buzzed. Soon, they would burst with the pressure.

The Queen said: 'Please – she'll kill you!'

The Doctor shook his head. 'She won't.' Then, addressing the Gyre, he said: 'I think I can help you. I think I know what's happening. But you have to let these people go. The Queen. The Milkman. Everyone. You have to let them go before this world collapses on itself!'

The static in the air increased. The howl of the Gyre was like the sound of atomic storms from the heart of the Sun. A rope of lightning lashed out at him, and he lunged aside. He felt the hiss as the plasma dispersed into the ground beside him, and felt the skin scorch on the back of his hand.

'Stop that *at once!*' the Doctor snapped, sounding more like an irritable schoolmaster than a man in fear for his life. 'Haven't you done enough damage? I said, I think I can help you. But you have to *let these people go!*'

Incredibly, the volume decreased. The pressure on his eardrums was gone. A sob of cosmic proportions resonated through the Gyre.

'That's better. Thank you,' the Doctor said, readjusting his ruffled shirt. 'This is one of my favourite shirts. And scorch-marks never, *ever* come out.'

He smiled. It was a disarming smile, though Sarah Jane – if she had been there – would have recognised it immediately. It was what she liked to think of as the Doctor's 'Vegas smile'; the expression he always assumed when he was about to take an impossible risk.

'Now,' said the Doctor. 'Shall we talk?'

And with that, he took a running jump and threw himself into the Gyre.

X

Time is infinitely flexible. A second can sometimes last thousands of years; an ice age can pass in a second. In this case, the actual time was no more than a couple of nanoseconds, and yet it lasted long enough for the Doctor to realise he'd made a mistake.

The Time Vortex is a toxic environment, in which neither the common laws of physics, nor the laws of Time apply, and to enter it unprotected is to risk far worse than death. As a child on Gallifrey, he had looked into the Untempered Schism and glimpsed the heart of the Vortex in all its cosmic insanity. This was infinitely worse – to be physically immersed into that hostile intelligence. And yet, he'd taken the risk with his eyes resolutely open. If he was correct, then this was only a tiny antechamber of the Time Vortex; contained within the conscious mind of a single individual –

Not that it mattered at this point. His own mind was preparing to shut down. A surge of blue light washed over him, and he heard the voice of the Great One, the Matriarch of the Spiders, and her screaming, metallic laughter. He'd always known it would come to this. Pride and self-assurance had always been his downfall. And yet, he'd been so certain he'd guessed right; so certain his gamble would pay off. He'd been wrong.

The blue light dimmed into darkness. The Doctor waited for the end. There were still so many wonderful things that he had never seen; so many alien galaxies that he had never visited. Time was so short – even *his* time, which, after all, had been longer than most. But all good things must come to an end. He hoped Sarah Jane would understand.

Besides, it was almost pleasant to drift; like a little boat moving downstream into a tunnel of darkness. Death was a great adventure, he thought. Who better than he to conquer it?

He opened his eyes to find himself lying on a stone floor. He blinked at the unexpected light; raised a hand to his aching head.

'You wanted to talk,' said a childish voice. 'Welcome to the Castle.'

XI

The Doctor struggled to his feet. He was in a hexagonal room, like something from an Earth fairy tale; surrounded by narrow windows, with pointed arches and panes of irregular, mullioned glass. Beyond that was nothing but fog; a swirling, heaving mass of it stitched through with threads of lightning. He realised they were still in the Gyre, though there was no sign of the Village.

The room was mostly bare, except for a large four-poster bed, draped with muslin; a bookcase filled with children's books and a multitude of paper stars that hung from the ceiling on pieces of string. And there, at the window, stood the Princess, wearing a long pink dress and carrying a star-tipped wand.

She looked to be about 8 years old, with hair the colour of cowslips that fell into ringlets to her waist. A child. And yet, if his theory was true, this was a child with more raw psychic power than any being he'd ever encountered; the power to warp Time itself and to remake the world to meet her needs, borrowing from the vast archive of the space-time continuum to create a unique reality.

Of course, he'd heard the story – or at least, the Queen's version of it – a story filtered through fairy tale, but at the heart of which lay truth. He doubted this child was a Princess. But he could readily believe that she lay under a terrible curse. He found himself thinking of Faust again; of Margaret's little soliloquy:

I'm still so young, still so young too!
And already I must die!
I was pretty too, and that's the reason why.

The Princess extended a small, pale hand. The Doctor bent down to kiss it. 'Your humble servant, your Highness.'

She looked at him gravely. 'You're funny,' she said.

'I'll have you know, young lady, that some people consider me *dashing*,' said the Doctor, adjusting his bow tie. It had suffered a number of indignities back on Metebelis III, and he feared it might never recover. Still, he reminded himself, there was no harm in making an effort.

The Princess watched him curiously. Her eyes were dark, like the Queen's, and as sad.

'You don't look like a Doctor,' she said at last. 'Doctors wear white jackets, and masks, and stick needles in your arm. And none of it ever helps. So there.'

'I'm not that kind of Doctor,' he said. 'But I *am* here to help, if I can.'

She gave him a doubtful look. 'You are?'

He nodded. 'But first – why April 8th?'

'That's my birthday,' said the Princess. 'The three of us went to see the Parade. I got a Princess dress and a toy village. I wished the day would last for ever and ever and ever.'

The Doctor thought of the Village and smiled. It all made sense, he told himself. The place was a lonely child's fantasy. Living toys; pink ponies; things that only a child could love. Every day was a carnival; every day a holiday. Her very own model Village; its people, model Villagers, each with their individual role; safe; simple; predictable.

Except that something had happened; something that had made her retreat into that fantasy world for good, taking a whole community of unwilling followers with her. Parents, friends, shopkeepers – all of them trapped in a psychic hell, unable to rejoin reality; all of them trying to survive as their artificial world grew ever more demanding, subject to rules that must be obeyed, or face the gravest consequences.

'Tell me about the Bad Thing,' he said.

She shook her head. 'We don't talk about that.'

'Today,' said the Doctor, 'we have to.'

The Princess took on a stubborn look. Her expression darkened. Outside, the Gyre responded in kind, sending feathers of lightning to drift past the mullioned windows.

'I won't, and you can't make me.'

The Doctor sighed. He was unused to dealing with children, even at the best of times. Even discounting his impending death, this was not the best of times.

He tried again. 'What's the D-word? Is it *Doctor?*'

She shook her head. Face red, arms crossed, she looked like a vengeful pink angel.

'Princess, I can't help you unless I know what happened.'

The child took a deep breath and held it. Her face went even redder. The Doctor wished that once – just *once* – his life could be simple, for a change. What could have happened to alter a child's game into a nightmare? Why had she retreated into a world of make-believe? If it wasn't *Doctor*, then what in the Worlds was *the D-word?*

Then it came to him, finally: a sudden inspiration. A memory of the photograph he'd seen on the wall of the Queen's little house. Three figures, their faces faded with time. A game of Happy Families. Who was missing?

The Princess… The Queen…

The King is dead. Long live the King.

'You lost your temper, didn't you?' he said. 'And then a Bad Thing happened. I think you made a wish. Am I right? *I wish you'd leave me alone*, perhaps? Or was it *Daddy, I wish you were dead?*'

The Princess gave a howl of anguish. The mullioned windows behind her pulverised into a cloud of glass. The Gyre, which had been a misty grey, flared an ominous scarlet. Tentacles of lightning writhed into the little room.

'I didn't mean to do it!' she wailed. 'I didn't mean it! *Daddy!*'

For a moment the Doctor thought he'd gone too far; that the unstable Gyre would collapse, consuming them both in its giant maw. For an instant, the whole of that reality seemed to shrug – a prelude to wavering out of existence – and then the Princess flung her arms around the Doctor's waist and sobbed; no longer a vengeful entity, but a frightened, exhausted child.

The Doctor waited patiently for the eruption to subside. Finally, it did. The Gyre returned to its natural colour; the lightning withdrew into the cloud.

He said: 'You know, it wasn't your fault. Power like yours is unstable. You were too young to understand. But you can't hide away for ever, Princess. Sooner or later, you have to go back.'

She looked up at the Doctor and said: 'Could *you* bring my Daddy back? You said you were here to help me, and I saw you bring back the Milkman.'

The Doctor shook his head. 'It doesn't work that way,' he said. 'Not in the real world, I'm afraid.'

'So why did you come here at all?' she said.

The Doctor gave a rueful smile. 'I'm here for the same reason you are,' he said. 'I'm here because I'm dying.'

XII

Death was always more tragic, he thought, when it came to the very young; and yet the ancient clung to Life with equal desperation. Perhaps it was because he himself was so close to extinction, but the Princess's story seemed to chime eerily with his own. Both of them were lonely. Both of them craved adventure. And both were in possession of powers far beyond their control; powers that allowed them to fling open the doors of perception –

'What do you mean, you're dying?' she said.

The Doctor started to explain about the crystal cave, then stopped. 'That's not important, is it?' he said. 'The important thing is, I don't have much time.'

'Stay here,' said the Princess simply. 'No one ever dies here.'

The Doctor shook his head. 'I can't. Time has a habit of marching on. Whatever we do; whatever games we play with it. An old friend of mine, by the name of – oh, well, you wouldn't know him – wrote a story about a man – a Doctor, in fact – who made a pact with the Devil. It went like this: the Devil would give the Doctor everything he could possibly want; but if at any moment, he was *truly* happy, if ever he wanted to stop Time, then the Devil would have the right to drag him down to Hell.'

The Princess assumed a mutinous look. 'I don't believe in Hell,' she said.

'Neither do I,' the Doctor replied. 'Though I suspect my friend would have disagreed. But if I did, maybe stopping Time would be a good way to get there.'

For a moment he paused, and thought of how often *he* had used the Time Vortex for his own ends. There was a reason the Time Lords had guarded their knowledge so jealously. The power to manipulate events throughout Time and Space was a drug that had too often proved fatal. He himself was far from immune. And the Princess was a child – albeit a child with psychic powers far beyond anything he'd encountered before – a child who desperately wanted to live.

'They couldn't cure you, could they?' he said. 'All those doctors and specialists. They promised, but they couldn't; instead all they wanted was to study you, to find out *how* you do what you do. They kept you in their hospitals, tested you in their behavioural labs, made you read cards and run mazes. And so, you escaped. To the Village. A place where *you* were in control and you could do just what you wanted.'

The Princess nodded, suddenly looking so much older than her years that for a moment the Doctor glimpsed the woman she might have grown up to be – the mother; even the grandmother – if Life had been fairer.

'It doesn't work, does it?' he said. 'Even in a dream world, Reality gets in the way. What's your name, my dear?'

'Polly,' she said. A single tear ran down her face.

The Doctor took her hand. 'All right. Polly, let's go home.'

XIII

He'd expected a dangerous journey back through the intricacies of the Vortex. In fact, there was no journey; merely a strange little shift in Time, as if the controls had been reset.

He blinked, and found himself in a room much the same as the one he'd left. Here was the bed, draped with curtains; the bookcase filled with books; the stars hanging from ceiling. A plush bear lay at the foot of the bed; brown, with button eyes.

The only real difference was that the bed was a hospital cot, and that the drapes were not flowing muslin, but hypoallergenic plastic. And there was a little girl on the bed, surrounded by tubes and diagnostic machines; thinner than her coverlet; skull like a piece of Delft china; eyes shut; barely even breathing. Gone were the roses in her cheeks; the cowslip curls; the pink dress. And yet, she was the Princess – Polly as she might have been in another, better life.

The woman who looked like Sarah Jane was standing by the door, looking dazed. And right beside her, the TARDIS, once more intact and ready to go –

'Doctor,' said Alice. 'You brought her back.' Her eyes shone through a kaleidoscope of tears.

The Doctor glanced at the chart on the bed. Earth diagnostics were primitive; but even so he could tell that Polly's condition was as incurable as his own. Yes, he'd brought Polly back, he thought – just long enough for her to die.

There was a chair by the bedside. Alice went to sit there. She took Polly's hand in hers; it looked like the bones of a tiny bird.

The Doctor felt in his pocket for his TARDIS key. His sickness had been kept at bay by the medicine from Polly's world, but here, it had returned in force. Nausea assailed him. His skin was laddered with radiation burns. His vision was dimming. Soon, it would fail. There was no further reason to stay; he'd saved the remaining Villagers. Polly's mother was with her now; surely the only thing to do was to leave them both to say their goodbyes.

On the bed, Polly opened her eyes. For a moment her unfocused gaze rested on the TARDIS.

'You got your box back, then,' she said in a voice that was almost a whisper.

'Yes,' said the Doctor. 'Thank you. And now—'

'Don't,' said Polly. 'Stay awhile.'

She sounded weak, but lucid. The sad dark eyes were galaxies in which the stars were fading. He knew he should leave – his time was short, and Sarah Jane was waiting – but he found himself unable to refuse a frightened, dying child's request.

He put the key back in his pocket. 'All right.'

'Tell me a story,' Polly said. 'One of your adventures.'

The Doctor smiled. 'A story?' he said. 'I'm not very good at stories.'

'But stories are worlds,' Polly said. 'New worlds for us to visit. In stories, we live for ever. That's what Mummy told me.'

The Doctor looked at Alice. Tears were running down her face. For a moment he understood the helplessness of motherhood; the love; the pain; the terrible joy. *Oh, these humans,* he told himself. *They look so insignificant, but – they're bigger on the inside.*

Then, he had an idea. 'Can you walk?'

Polly shook her head.

'Then I'll carry you.'

They must have looked quite a pair, he thought, as he carried her into the TARDIS. But perhaps the familiar surroundings had lent him a little extra strength. It took him as far as the console. There he laid Polly; in his embrace, the child felt like an armful of birds; but her eyes were wide and excited.

'What *is* it?'

'This is the TARDIS,' he said. 'She's been with me a long time, and she knows *all* the stories.'

The big eyes widened still further. 'You mean it's *alive?*'

'Alive? Oh yes – and much more.'

He knew he could never explain what she was; not to a scientist, let alone to a child barely 8 years old. He himself could barely predict her moods and inconsistencies. But the TARDIS had brought him to Polly's world, against his own instructions. *Had* that been Polly's influence? Or had it been *the TARDIS herself,* somehow sensing a deeper need, an existential imperative?

He'd had so many adventures; he'd taken so much for granted. His appetite for life was undimmed, even after three incarnations. But Polly would never live to see a double sunrise on Betelgeuse; or run from Daleks on Skaro; or see the spider orchids bloom on the garden planet Chimeria. She would never go to school; or hear an opera; or fall in love. But stories are worlds, she'd told him. Stories make us immortal…

He patted the TARDIS's console.

'This is Polly, old girl,' he said. 'I'd like you to tell her a story.'

He took one of Polly's hands in his and pressed it to the console. He knew that already the interface between TARDIS and child had begun; a process so infinitely complex that not even he understood it.

The TARDIS console began to glow; not its usual ice-blue, but the pink of a summer sunrise.

Polly said in a wondering voice: '*Oh! It's full of stories.*'

'Is it?' said the Doctor.

He, of course, could not be sure of what the child was seeing. The TARDIS would give herself willingly – if she gave herself at all. But *something* was happening, he could tell; some kind of psychic transfusion. All the tales a Time Lord could gather over three lifetimes – memories; experience; joy; every colour of story – all of it conveyed in a link that lasted only seconds.

The rose light faded. Polly lay on the TARDIS console. Her eyes were filled with stars; her face, radiant with happiness.

The Doctor picked her up again – she seemed even lighter than before – and carried her back to her mother's side.

'Here. I think she'll sleep now.'

Alice smiled at him through her tears as he stepped back through the TARDIS door. She wasn't sure what had happened inside the Doctor's funny Police Box, but *something* had changed. A wheel had turned. A weight she'd carried for so many years that she'd come to think of it as part of herself had suddenly been taken away.

The light on the TARDIS began to blink. There came a grinding, throbbing sound, like a double heartbeat.

Alice glanced up at the window. Night was falling; the first stars were coming out against the blue.

Polly said: '*Star light, star bright, wish I may, wish I might.*'

Then she smiled and closed her eyes.

In seconds, both she and the TARDIS were gone.

CHAPTER ONE

The Doctor looked up, frowning. 'Did you hear that, Zoe?'

'I did, Doctor.'

They both waited, silent, then it came again, a long, low drone, followed by a higher screech.

'You know what that means, don't you?' the Doctor asked.

'I do,' Zoe answered, although she did not turn away from the long page of equations she was scribbling in her notebook.

The Doctor picked up his book, turned a page and, before he'd read half a line, was startled by an even louder screech. 'Does he do it deliberately?'

Zoe worked on her calculations, seemingly oblivious to the Doctor's increasing irritation.

'I'm talking to you, Zoe.'

'Yes, you are,' she looked up from her notebook, 'And no, I don't suppose Jamie chooses to irritate you, any more than you deliberately interrupt my calculations every time I work on them.'

'We have a computer for that kind of thing, you know.'

'And you keep saying my upbringing was too reliant on technology. Look.'

Zoe held up her notebook, where she was working on five different calculations, in an almost 3-D pattern.

'Ah, Minkowski's spacetime theorem applied to the motion of the Eagle Nebula. Very good,' the Doctor said. 'But you'll find the differential you're after in the third line, second column across, is out by zero point two three five eight…'

'But I—'

'Squared.'

Zoe looked at her calculations and saw immediately that the Doctor was right. She turned the page and began again, and the Doctor tried to temper his usually brusque tone. 'I wasn't telling you off.'

'I got it wrong. Now I'll get it right.'

There was silence for a moment, until the screech sounded again before reverting to a drone, and the Doctor groaned.

'Patience, Doctor,' Zoe said, 'It's how he relaxes. I work on calculations, you play your recorder, Jamie plays the bagpipes.'

The long, low drone in the distance began slowly to morph into a tune of sorts, though not one either the Doctor or Zoe recognised.

'There are other ways to pass the time, Zoe – interacting with your fellow travellers, for instance. What you're calculating is already known deep within—'

'The TARDIS. Yes. And I'll check my answers against the TARDIS's data.'

The Doctor shook his head, raising his voice over Jamie's bagpipes, even louder now. 'There's more to astronomy than the distance between places. It's about the places themselves, the histories. It's not just about the… the…'

'The music of the spheres?' Zoe finished the Doctor's sentence, laughing, and opened the door as Jamie marched in, bag under his arm, chanter in his mouth, cheeks puffed out to blow. He finished his tune on a long, low note and bowed, then he backed out of the door and returned with a tray holding three bowls of steaming porridge.

'Breakfast is served.'

The Doctor and Zoe exchanged glances; they'd had Jamie's porridge before.

'Sugar and cream?' Zoe asked hopefully.

'Sacrilege!' Jamie answered. 'Proper porridge is soaked

overnight and made with salt, never sugar.'

'Sorry, Jamie,' the Doctor interrupted him, 'but salt's not good for the heart, and I need to worry about that more than either of you.'

'You're not that old, Doctor,' Jamie said, winking at Zoe.

'I didn't mean my age, I meant…' The Doctor shook his head. 'It's neither here nor there, now that the porridge is very much here.' He looked at the tray Jamie was holding, the congealed mess in each bowl looking even less appealing as it cooled. 'I'm just not very hungry.'

'I've spent all this time…' Jamie was crestfallen.

Zoe stood behind the young Scotsman looking directly at the Doctor. 'Be nice,' she mouthed.

The Doctor opened his mouth to complain, then he saw the droop of Jamie's shoulders, the possibility behind that of his raised temper and a bad day ahead for all three of them. 'Fine. But not a big bowl. As I said, I'm not very—'

'Hungry, I know,' Jamie said, smiling. 'So I'll give you the middle-sized bowl. I think you'll find it just right.'

The Doctor reluctantly took the bowl held out to him, and as he did so another noise began. A noise that brought a light to his eyes.

'Ah, in that case, I'm afraid we'll have to shelve the porridge. I've no doubt it will be just as good when we get back.'

'But it won't be hot…'

'As I said, just as good,' the Doctor answered. 'Put the tray away – and your pipes, we don't want them damaged if it's a tricky landing. Zoe, notebook down, eyes on the screen. Jamie, stand steady, we're coming in to land.'

Zoe watched the man she often thought of as tired beyond his years, hopping nimbly around the console, stowing Jamie's bagpipes here and the porridge well out of view over there. He was almost smiling, or at least his frown was now gone. He'd been bored, she realised. A couple of days with just her and

Jamie for company, and the Doctor was edgy and impatient. Now, the TARDIS pumping out its landing noises, a sound Zoe herself welcomed with excitement and trepidation, she saw that the Doctor was awake, alert, fully himself. Other people might believe it was better to travel than to arrive, but not the Doctor.

A few moments later the TARDIS was still and Zoe brought up the outside world on the scanner screen. A high blue sky fell to a deep blue sea, a tall lighthouse marking the point where the land ended and the sea began.

The Doctor clapped. 'Alexandria! And by the look of the lighthouse – solid, little salt damage – I think we'll find the Musaeum still standing and the collection in its prime. Now, Zoe, I'm certain there are several astronomy scrolls you'd like to see, and Jamie, the Musaeum of Alexandria was founded as a compendium of all the world's knowledge, they possess every scroll in the world, and usually the original – they're not fond of copies here. They're bound to have a porridge recipe we can all stomach.'

CHAPTER TWO

After the cool quiet of the TARDIS, the heat, noise and smells of Alexandria were almost overwhelming. Everywhere she looked, Zoe saw something she had only ever read of: a spice she had imagined but never smelt, or an animal that had featured in childhood storybooks, and then only just – for Zoe childhood had been brief, the period of learning longer and always intense.

Everywhere he turned, Jamie saw another preacher or street politician, touting their faith, declaring their truth, insisting their cause was the cause of right. He was sorely tempted to find a soapbox and step up to harangue the English, until the Doctor pulled him away with a stern whisper that if he was going to shout at anyone for invading Scotland, he'd have to shout at Romans now, and that Alexandria, just a century since Mark Antony was in Cleopatra's passionate embrace, probably wasn't an ideal time to decry the notion of empire, not without a full army.

They walked on, following the Doctor's lead, past stalls promising remedies for everything from broken bones to bad breath, others laden with sweet pastries, dense with nuts, dripping in rosewater and honey syrup, a fishmonger's stall that assaulted Zoe's nose; the synthesised foods she'd grown up with had had scent but no smell, and certainly not the rich tang of just-caught fish. Poor Jamie took one look at the pile of fresh, silvery herring and was desperate to buy up a load there and then to take back to the TARDIS and smoke into kippers –

maybe that would be a breakfast the Doctor would approve. He turned to ask the Doctor and found the older man trying on a round, red, boxy hat, with a silky black tassel hanging from it.

Jamie shook his head. 'It's not you, Doctor.'

Zoe joined in. 'Not you at all.'

'Another time perhaps,' the Doctor said, with an apologetic shrug to the stallholder, as he took off the fez, putting it back down on the table.

They were forced to edge their way around a crowd five-deep at one stall, and Jamie hoisted Zoe onto his shoulders so she could see what was worth such attention. She looked past the clamouring hands with fistfuls of coins to a stall piled high with silks in a dozen different reds, clashing with the oranges alongside, the purple beneath indigos and yellows, the stallholder holding up a green fabric shot through with so much blue that it appeared to change colour as he ran his hand beneath the fine cloth.

As they pushed through, and the morning sun climbed higher, light reflecting from every kind of copper pan and pewter bowl, the Doctor explained the enthusiasm for silk. 'No one knows how it's made.'

'Silkworms—' Zoe began, and the Doctor shushed her furiously.

'Only the Chinese know that yet. It's highly profitable to them and to the traders. Right now, silk sells for more than gold.'

'But we've been synthesising silk for centuries…'

'Yes, Zoe, when you come from, you have. But as you noticed at the fish stall, there's a difference between real and synthetic. Here, take this.'

He pulled out his own pocket handkerchief, and tied to it was another, and then finally a long measure of the same blue-green silk the stallholder had been touting.

'How did you get that?' Jamie asked.

'I paid,' the Doctor replied, 'if that's what you're suggesting.'

'But you were beside us all the time.'

'Not while you were showing off, lifting Zoe onto your shoulders. Now, Zoe, I'd like you to feel my own perfectly pressed handkerchief, then the synthetic one.'

Zoe felt both pieces of fabric. The Doctor's own was soft, but the second piece of cloth was entirely different.

'It's so...'

'Real,' the Doctor declared. 'Yes. Synthetics are extremely handy when you can't get hold of the real thing, or when the old one is worn out, but a facsimile will never have the depth of the original. Now, my friends, here we are, at the original Musaeum.'

The Doctor had been leading them down an alley away from the market. Now they turned a corner, and there, dazzling in the sunlight, stood the Musaeum of Alexandria itself. Imposing though elegant in line and symmetry, it was a complex of walls within walls, buildings within buildings. It was beautiful. And yet –

'What on earth's that stink?' asked Jamie.

'Ah, that's the Zoo. The Musaeum of Alexandria was famed for its wide collection of animals from all over the known world. I believe we're at the western entrance.'

As a spray of water from an elephant's trunk beyond the wall hit Jamie full in the face and chest, the Doctor nodded his head. 'Yes, the western entrance.'

CHAPTER THREE

They made their way up the wide marble steps to the main entrance. The doorkeeper studied the Doctor and Jamie, noting their odd attire. He had seen kilts before now – the Musaeum was well-stocked with any number of national costumes – but the Doctor's baggy trousers and bow tie were both new to him. He was, however, well versed in the eccentricities of the academics who studied at the Musaeum, and the Doctor was no doubt just one more. Zoe did not pass so easily.

'No women,' the doorkeeper said, holding up a flat palm to stop her entering.

'What?' Zoe asked.

'Explain to your girl,' the doorkeeper replied, nodding to the Doctor and pointing a dismissive thumb at Zoe.

'You could speak to me, you know,' Zoe stormed in response.

The doorkeeper shrugged and went back to his post. 'Rules are rules, love.'

The Doctor took Zoe aside. 'Use his rudeness as an opportunity. He's hardly even looked at you, so you can…'

'Oh, yes,' Zoe answered, her fury evaporating as she saw the meaning behind the Doctor's words. She whispered, 'I'll be back as soon as I can find a toga and a haircut.'

With that she ran off back to the market. The Doctor was about to call a warning to take care, but she was gone. And besides, there was music coming from inside the great hall that lay beyond the doorkeeper's post. Glorious music that called Jamie and the Doctor, both men suddenly wanted nothing more than to follow the music drawing them inside, to find it and play it and join in. They left the great doors behind them and went deep into the heart of the Musaeum of Alexandria.

They walked through the palatial entrance hall, painted and gilded, garnished with mosaics, and dotted with sculptures of famous generals and fine thinkers. Wide corridors led off the hall, and stairs rose to more rooms and deeper chambers. Above each corridor a symbol was carved in relief, indicating the collection the corridor led to.

The Doctor peered up at each of the finely carved panels, noting the spheres that indicated the Hall of Astronomy.

'Zoe will love this,' he said to himself.

Jamie stood impatiently alongside him. 'Doctor, this way, the music's coming from this corridor, come on.'

The Doctor nodded. Jamie was right. The music was indeed glorious, swelling and peaking, still for a moment, then rushing back at them almost as a wave. He smiled when he saw the carving above the corridor: nine women in a semi-circle, each holding an object, each one beautiful and enticing. Just as he noticed that the women appeared to be real, if miniature, all nine sprang to life, animations in stone, beckoning them down the corridor. Then just as suddenly as they had started to move, they stopped.

'Doctor! Did you see that? The carvings?' a startled Jamie asked.

'I did indeed. Hero!'

'Who is?'

'Hero. Brilliant man. Created the first robotic cart. Sadly, they went on to use it for war, of course, but all the same, an astonishing mind. I'd quite forgotten he worked here. It appears he has created an entire set of Muses to welcome us. If I'm not mistaken, they'll be part of the glorious sounds we hear from within. Now,' he said, turning at the clatter of sandaled feet running up behind them, 'Who do we have here?'

Zoe ran across the entrance hall, her short bob scraped across her head and plastered down with oil, and dressed in a tunic that barely scraped her knees, held at her waist with a leather belt.

'You don't look any different,' Jamie said. 'How did you get in?'

'I didn't need to look different,' Zoe answered. 'There was a crowd of Roman lads, astronomy students, here on some kind of exchange trip. I got in the middle of them and joined in their conversation. They're badly informed on the mineral compositions of Mars and Saturn, though. I very nearly set them straight…'

'Zoe, you didn't!'

'Of course I didn't, Doctor,' she said. 'But I certainly wanted to.'

'They'll learn in their own good time. Now, come along both of you, if the stories of Hero are correct, this is going to be a hugely entertaining trip.'

Chapter Four

The sight that greeted them was indeed entertaining. In a room that was twice as long as the entrance hall and double its height, a wide mezzanine running all around it, stood five women, each on a raised dais, the better to show that she was both beautiful in her own way and utterly different to the other.

'Oh,' said Zoe, 'so they let women in if they're beautiful.'

'It's not beauty that makes them stand out, Zoe.' The Doctor looked around. 'The others must be about somewhere.'

They stood at the back of a crowd before the first woman. She was very tall, her skin a rich black, her thick hair trained in cornrows from her scalp and falling to her waist. As her hand moved across the stone tablet she held, it carved letters out of the very stone.

'She can't be real!' Jamie whispered in shock.

'She is and she isn't,' the Doctor replied. 'Calliope is the muse of epic poetry, and everyone knows poets write in exaggerated beauty to get at the truth beneath.' Not a tall man himself, he stood on tiptoe to see the people in the front rows. 'Don't get too close, either of you, look there.'

Looking over the crowd's heads themselves, Zoe and Jamie saw what the Doctor meant. Those closest to Calliope were writing furiously, counting out meter with their feet or clapping with a free hand. Some wrote on parchment, others on scrolls, the walls, the floor, whatever they could get their hands on. One elderly man was so desperate to write that, having no quill of his own, he grabbed the quill from the young man beside him, jabbed it into his own finger until blood flowed out and used the blood to write on his toga. None of them seemed to notice there were others scribbling just as frantically, each one was so caught up in his own grand tale of love, loss and heroism.

Beyond Calliope was another crowd, this one even more animated. The Doctor told Zoe and Jamie that she was Erato, as indicated by the cithara that she strummed as she half-sang, half-chanted her lyric poetry.

'Sappho,' the Doctor said, half to himself, as Erato's lyrics came to him above the clamour of the crowd around her. 'Interesting choice.'

The poem she recited was all about dying for love, and those around her were in paroxysms of passion.

'Looked at that way, love does seem extremely foolish,' Zoe whispered to Jamie. 'Jamie?'

But Jamie had made his way into the crowd. When the Doctor and Zoe pulled him back, they were horrified to see their friend distraught, tears rolling down his cheeks.

'How I loved her. She was from another village, but it might as well have been another world, centuries-long fights between our clans. We'd meet in secret, far from prying eyes. She'd golden hair and deep green eyes, and her voice, so sweet. And just as strong was her feeling about the English, matching my own, we were matched by nature, and held apart by our stars.'

The Doctor and Zoe had seen Jamie in a temper often, and sometimes in dour dark moods, but this was new, not like him at all.

The Doctor pulled him further from Erato's music, and just at the point that Erato's voice was as loud but no louder than any of the others, Jamie came to himself, horrified when he realised what his friends had heard him say.

'But I never speak about... I never... Doctor?'

The Doctor shook his head. 'I don't know, Jamie. We need to be very careful about getting too close to these Muses. They're inspiring all sorts of extremes in people, some very enjoyable, I'm sure. Speaking of which, this will be Thalia.'

He looked to the other side of the room where a red-headed woman held the mask of comedy, giving ventriloquist's voice to it, stories and jokes flowing between her and the mask. All around, people were laughing, united in mirth, and the Doctor found he desperately needed to know what was so funny. He took a step closer and before he'd heard what Thalia had said, he found himself chuckling. Then, when he was within hearing distance, he heard the mask speak a punchline, the nub of a Gallifreyan joke he'd once loved and long forgotten. He took a few more paces closer, ignoring both Zoe and Jamie, one more step and without warning, the Doctor was bending backwards and a massive guffaw broke from his startled mouth, and then he was truly laughing, holding his sides in the exquisite joyous pain of hysterical laughter.

The Doctor's uncharacteristic laughter was infectious. Even as she frowned at it, Zoe felt herself giggle. She took a step back to get away from something that was clearly odd, but the crowds around the other muses were moving closer to them, lyric ecstasies combining with the hysterical laughter made her even more worried.

Speaking through tears, his laughter clearly as painful as it was enjoyable, the Doctor pointed behind Zoe and Jamie. 'Ter-Ter- Terpsichore!' and then collapsed laughing again.

Terpsichore stood just behind Jamie, playing her lyre. 'I know that tune, it's from my village, I know it, she's playing my reel!'

And then Jamie began dancing, skipping and leaping to the music. Zoe found herself twirling with him, believing she knew the steps, sure that it might be possible to know the steps and never have learned them, until a tap on her shoulder brought her to herself.

Zoe turned to see an older woman, holding a globe in one

hand and a sharp compass in the other. She had none of the frenetic behaviour of the others around them and her calm intensity drew Zoe in.

'I am Urania, I have truths to tell you…'

Then all Zoe could think was yes, this was what she had wanted for so long, someone who knew more than she did, knew the what and also the why, the very depths of the secrets of space itself. Zoe looked into the black eyes of the small woman, and it was like looking into the eyes of every grandmother who had ever watched life unfold around her. And this grandmother would tell Zoe everything she had yearned to know, since she first started learning.

While Jamie danced to Terpsichore's music, and Zoe was deep in conversation with Urania, the Doctor lay twisting on the floor. He was laughed out, yet his body bent and contorted still, trying to make him laugh.

CHAPTER FIVE

The Doctor was not laughing now. Slowly, he dragged himself across the marble floor, back towards the centre of the room. He knew that if he could get himself far enough away from Thalia's influence, the agonising laughter that was wracking his body would stop. Casting about to try and focus on anything but the laughter that still bubbled up inside him, he looked down at this own hand. Here, this cool piece of white marble he was dragging himself over. It was similar in texture and colour to the building material for the great lighthouse of Alexandria; it was possible the two had been quarried from the same place.

'Good,' he thought. 'That's a start, more like that.'

He forced himself to think harder about the marble, the way it had none of the give of wood, none of the brutal edge pieces of a mosaic floor. This marble was solid and smooth, quarried in big slabs, in Italy perhaps, or Greece, it had been laid with care and precision. Millennia ago it had been simple rocks, and heat and pressure, metamorphism, had turned it into this precious material, had changed crystal structures and chemical composition while the rocks themselves had stayed solid. They remained both their original selves, and the more precious quarry of pure white marble.

The Doctor was far enough away from Thalia now to stand. He pulled himself up, patting the marble in gratitude. The hall was in disarray, people shifting attention from one muse to another, a flow from anger to love to loss to laughter. The Doctor knew that the tricky thing would be not to stop the

Muses, but to persuade his young companions that they did not want to dance a reel or discuss astronomy for all time. Standing in the centre of the maelstrom, the Doctor realised there wasn't a great deal of time left. He had counted five Muses so far, which meant there ought to be another four. He craned his neck to look over the dancing, laughing, chanting, riotous crowd that now filled the hall, and thought he could just make out the veiled figure of Polyhymnia, muse of hymns. Which meant that Clio, muse of history, and Melpomene, muse of tragedy, couldn't be far behind. The Doctor had no intention of waiting for it to end in tears.

He saw Zoe edging away from Urania. 'Good girl,' he thought to himself. 'She must have spotted it too.'

He held out his hand and Zoe seized it, allowing him to draw her close to him.

'That was astonishing,' she said. 'I had no idea there was so much else to know. But it's not right, is it, Doctor? There's something strange about them.'

'There certainly is…' he began, his voice a low murmur beneath the cacophony all around, trying not to draw attention to himself.

He needn't have bothered, for suddenly all the attention in the room was on Polyhymnia.

The veiled woman raised her arms at the far end of the room and immediately there was a hush in the incessant noise, and out of the sudden silence first one person, then another, then more joined in, until the whole room sang in harmony and unison. The Doctor felt the soft music wrap around him, even as he tried to shut it out, the sound – and more, the feeling of sound – welling up within him. It was quiet yet full, a gentle chant, clearly in praise of something.

'What are they singing about, Doctor?'

'I think the better question is not what, Zoe, but who.'

The Doctor was about to explain when, from behind the

now-united hymn-singers, came a new sound.

'Oh no,' he muttered. 'Not that.'

'Not what, Doctor?' asked Zoe.

'Can't you hear it?'

Zoe listened, although the hymn also made her want to exult in song with unknown words forming in her mouth, and there it was, a single, fine, perfect note held behind the singing. One note, played over and over. One note from an instrument she thought she recognised.

'Doctor, that sounds like…'

'Yes Zoe,' he frowned. 'I'm afraid it does. It sounds remarkably like a recorder. It's an aulos, and if I'm not mistaken that means it's being played by Euterpe, Giver of Delight. Oh dear, if the punchline from an old joke had me in paroxysms of laughter for ten minutes, it doesn't bear thinking what this will do.'

Even as he spoke, the note itself became more insistent, yet simultaneously more pure, and then it seemed that everyone in the room was now playing an aulos, part-flute, part-recorder, all lovely.

'I'm sorry, Zoe, I know I shouldn't,' the Doctor said, reaching into his pocket as he spoke. 'But there's something about being part of a thing larger than oneself. I have to – I need to play too.'

The Doctor had his recorder at his lips, and Zoe saw a dreamy quality overtake his face as he took a light breath and pursed his mouth to blow. Then he suddenly stopped, looked around, and shook his head, shaking himself free of the hold the music had over him. 'Where's Jamie?'

CHAPTER SIX

Jamie had followed her, impossible not to, the glorious young woman who had suddenly appeared in the room and taken his hand in the dance. Other than Zoe and the Muses, she was the only woman in a room full of reeling men, the reel that had made him forget entirely the loss he'd sobbed over just moments before. Even now, running through a corridor that must have taken them from one end of the Musaeum to another, and then hurrying up a spiral staircase, even this pace felt like a dance, like horses galloping to music.

'Hurry,' she called over her shoulder. 'Faster still.'

And though Jamie was thinking he had never run so fast or climbed so high since he was a boy, training hard in the hills, he was able to keep going, to leap up the seemingly never-ending steps.

And then they were there. She put up a hand to stop him, a wide door lay ahead, she held a finger to her lips, then took both of Jamie's hands in hers.

He thought she was going to kiss him, thought his heart might burst from the running and the dancing, all anger run out, danced out – and then he stopped thinking as the hand she brought to his face pinched a point on his temple. He stopped thinking because the pain was so intense, because she was bringing him to his knees with pain, because all he could see were the stars in his eyes, and then nothing. All was dark.

When Jamie came to, it was on the other side of the big door, in a bright room, white marble floor, white stone walls, beneath a dome of fine alabaster, letting in a pure, diffuse light. Jamie was strapped to a table, arms, legs, head and body pinned down. There was a strong smell of cloves and of lavender and something else that he didn't recognise.

'It's turmeric.'

Jamie heard the young woman's voice and turned his head the fraction the binding would allow.

She stood to one side, grinding something with a mortar and pestle. 'Turmeric, lavender, cloves, comfrey and a few others I don't think you'd know, even if I knew your native words for them. They'll help with the pain.'

'Good,' Jamie said. 'I could do with some help with the pain. I could do with getting up off this table too.'

She smiled and carried on grinding the mixture.

Jamie tried again. 'If you're not going to let me go…'

'It's not up to me.'

'No, of course not,' he said. 'Then do you not want to give me that mixture? My head's pounding from whatever you did at the door, and my back and knees aren't doing too well after all that dancing and running either.'

She shrugged and came closer to the table, close enough for Jamie to see how beautiful she was, how beautiful and yet now – how frightening, as she smiled and said, 'This isn't for the pain you feel now.'

'No?' he asked, not looking forward to the answer.

'It's for the pain you're going to feel.'

Jamie, who had feared it might be something like that, decided discretion was the better part of valour, closed his eyes and began breathing deeply to calm his fear. The Doctor and Zoe were bound to be on their way to rescue him, weren't they? Then he pictured Zoe deep in conversation with the astronomer, the Doctor rolling helplessly on the floor, crying with laughter. And he pictured himself, laid out on the table, a worse pain promised, no one coming to his rescue.

CHAPTER SEVEN

At first it seemed as if the people had come to their senses. Young men straightened dishevelled robes, old men smoothed wild beards and tried to assume their usual wise faces. For a moment it appeared that the hold of the muses was over. Then Polyhymnia began to sing again, and the people joined in with her, much slower now, as they deliberately and calmly turned, forming a circle around Zoe and the Doctor.

'Doctor?' Zoe asked under her breath.

'Stand close, and don't give your full attention to Polyhymnia. I think they need to fully get our attention before they have power.'

The Doctor whispered a few more instructions to Zoe, who was struggling as much as he was to keep herself calm.

She nodded at his advice and began calculating light year distances, whispering to herself, 'If Proxima Centauri is four point two two light years distance from the Earth, and the year now is AD 60, then the distance that Proxima Centauri has moved in relation to the Earth, between this year and my own time is… is…'

Zoe felt herself drifting off, her eyes desperate to lift to Polyhymnia's own, her heart crying to sing with those now only an arm's reach from her, closing in, closing tighter. She tried harder to think for herself. 'Something simpler. OK, if… if… one light second is two hundred and ninety nine million, seven hundred thousand hundred… I mean, seven hundred thousand, no, I… I mean…'

Zoe burst into tears, the pressure too much for her and, pushing the hymn singers aside, she ran from the room, back the way they had come in.

It was so unlike Zoe to cry in public that the Doctor didn't know what to say as he called after her. 'Zoe! Come back, you don't know... this place... Zoe!'

But even as he called, the Doctor felt his feet turn back, felt the song rise in his breast, felt his arms lifting and his whole spirit wanting to join in with those now standing tightly around him as they sang to Polyhymnia. He opened his mouth to join the song, and Polyhymnia stopped them all by raising her hand, a single movement that shushed the crowd immediately. They settled themselves on the floor, snuggled up to each other, and before a minute had passed the Doctor could hear light snoring all around.

'That's a good trick,' he admitted.

Polyhymnia pulled back the heavy veil that covered her head and most of her face, speaking as she did. 'I will teach you some time, my friend.'

Hearing the masculine voice, the Doctor looked up sharply, and where just moments before he had seen a statuesque woman, a strong and powerful conductor leading a crowd in passionate song, now he saw a small, wiry man, shorter than himself and apparently a good decade older.

'Hero?' he asked, incredulously.

'One and the same,' the older-looking man bowed. 'How do you know me?'

'You are famed, of course,' the Doctor replied. 'Your inventions.'

'Ah yes, my "inventions",' Hero answered, looking around at the sleeping crowd. 'The people are so gullible.'

'You're not Hero the great inventor?'

'I am. But perhaps not the inventor you have heard of, the one who makes fountains shoot hundreds of paces into the sky...'

'Oh.' The Doctor was disappointed. 'You didn't?'

Hero weighed his hands in the air. 'Forty paces, fifty. Supplementing the skill of invention with the magnificence of illusion is an ancient Egyptian trick, one the old Pharaohs' magicians knew well.'

The Doctor's face lit up. 'You're a conjurer.'

'I am an artist,' Hero sternly corrected him. 'These people believed they were in the presence of the Muses. They believed it, and so it felt as if they were. Even you, my foreign guest, who arrived so certain of himself, even you were rolling on the floor in agony with laughter, an agony merely suggested by me, one which your own mind created entirely for itself.'

The Doctor rubbed his aching ribs. 'My mind has done worse things.'

'But we jump ahead,' Hero said. 'You know who I am, you have enjoyed my little show, yet I have no idea who you are…?'

'I am the Doctor,' he said, bowing.

'I see.'

'Do you?' the Doctor asked. 'Perhaps you do. But is "enjoyed" the right word? Engaged, enjoined perhaps, that would be more appropriate.'

Hero smiled. 'I saw you arrive, you know.'

'So you were waiting for us?'

'Not waiting, exactly, I'd planned to work with my Muses today anyway, and Alexandrians are a gullible lot, they'll turn up at anything if you promise them a spectacle.'

'A spectacle like this?' the Doctor asked, looking round at the dozens of people now sleeping soundly on the cool marble floor.

Hero took the Doctor's arm and pulled him towards the far corridor, 'Enough of these layabouts, tell me about your machine, you were not there, and then you were. I'm anxious to learn your secrets.'

The Doctor pulled his arm back. 'And I yours. So perhaps

we might trade secret for secret? You tell me where my young friend is, and I'll explain the rudimentary elements of time travel.'

'Time, is it?' Hero's face lit up. 'I might have known. Oh yes, this will be wonderful. I've read every scroll in the Library for these secrets and found nothing I could make sense of, and here you are to give me the truth. So how is it powered? Do you use the Sun? Optical instruments?'

'Both, in a manner of speaking, yes. But first – my friend?'

'The Hibernian lad? Feisty, isn't he? He's enjoying my hospitality at this very moment, I hope. Do come along. Secret for secret, as you say...'

The Doctor shook his head and, against his better judgement, followed Hero, muttering to himself. 'Never follow, always lead, that's the way you must succeed, never follow, always lead, still there's time for a nasty deed...'

Chapter Eight

They walked down the long dark corridor, through a courtyard that was a lush and scented hanging garden, then west beneath a deep portico, south through another corridor, up a flight of wide steps, and across a bridge spanning the gardens of the Musaeum Zoo below.

As they walked, Hero explained what the Doctor had just experienced.

'An experiment in thought control. I am famed for my mechanical expertise, but there's only so far one can go with inventions. A creator can only work with what he has to hand. The finest tools, the richest materials, come through our port day in, day out. And everything on every ship is checked by Musaeum staff. Our great Library only exists because there is not a book or scroll in existence that is not held here – either the original that comes into the city, taken to be copied and that copy is given to the owner, or originals smuggled from other nations beneath priests' robes or between the folds of babies' swaddling. There are scrolls here where each letter of a foreign alphabet has been painstakingly copied and the copier himself with no knowledge of the letters his hand forms. It is all available to me. And yet I've grown tired of making carts with neither horse nor driver, fountains that flow down as well as up, weapons that need no soldier to guide them. I have discovered it is possible to bend a man's will, to make him believe something impossible, absurd, and to believe it with every fibre of his being. And I have found that it is easier to make a crowd believe rather than an individual, that where one might be merely swayed, a dozen will be certain, a hundred adamant.'

'And a thousand?' the Doctor asked.

Hero turned and smiled. 'A thousand would be an army, would they not?'

They had reached a high-walled, domed building.

'But the Muses?' the Doctor asked. 'They seemed very real.'

'I'm glad you thought so. They are mechanical, of course, but there is one element that makes them seem so very alive.'

The Doctor wasn't sure he wanted to hear the answer, but at the same time he couldn't stop himself asking. 'In addition to the thought control?'

'Thought control is part of it. If I assure the people these are the Muses, if I plant the possibility that they might experience the inspiration they've wanted all of their lives, then I find they are more than likely to believe me. They want whatever my Muses offer them.'

'But the loss? There were people bemoaning real loss,' the Doctor interrupted.

'Have you never wallowed in loss, Doctor? Never taken the time to grieve a terrible fate and felt afterwards – if not better, then perhaps purified, elevated – to have given it the attention it deserves?'

The Doctor knew only too well the losses he grieved, and he was not prepared to discuss them with Hero. 'I'm sure we've all had reasons to want to tear out our hearts from grief. But my young friend – you were going to take me to him?'

'I have,' Hero said, opening the door before them and leading the Doctor towards a large circular room ahead. 'And how clever of you to consider the possibility of losing one's heart. Every artist knows the Muse does just that: takes his heart.'

Hero stepped aside and now the Doctor saw Jamie, strapped to a table, a range of medical instruments on a smaller table alongside, and beyond Jamie, six of the Muses now standing against the wall. As he watched, first Calliope, then Erato, then Thalia, Terpsichore, Urania, and finally Euterpe reached down a right hand and twisted something on her left hip and, pulling back, revealed the mechanical workings inside. Liquid flowed through hollow tubes turning wheels and screws, mechanical levers and pulleys. Each Muse, seemingly real on the outside, was metal and wood on the inside. Metal and wood and...

'That's...' the Doctor looked on, horrified.

'Yes, it is,' Hero agreed, bouncing at the Doctor's side. 'As I said, only a Muse can truly steal a man's heart.'

Inside her chest cavity each Muse revealed a real, human, beating heart.

The Doctor turned to Hero. 'Why would you do that? Why do they need that?'

Hero frowned. 'I tried for many years to make them truly live. And I failed. But you will understand, as a doctor, that we learn from our mistakes. With every failure I came closer to realising that in order for my Muses to appear truly human, they needed to also hold something truly human.'

'You killed people to remove their hearts?'

Hero shook his head. 'No! How can they be said to be dead if their hearts still beat? I have not killed them, but granted them immortality in a far more powerful form, the perfect blend of art and science.'

'So why us?'

'Doctor!' Jamie shouted from the table. 'Stop chatting and do something!'

The Doctor waved away Jamie's anger and turned back to Hero. 'I am interested. Why us?'

Hero nodded, enjoying explaining his work. 'Good question, very good. I've found there's no point using any old heart.'

'Oh, great,' Jamie muttered.

'I need hearts that are frenzied, passionate, animated. To animate a true Muse, one I can employ to create my life's work, the heart must be full, wild, reckless even. Your young friend fulfils those criteria marvellously.'

Hero clapped his hands and Erato and Urania closed up their bodies, and came at his bidding, to either side of the Doctor, ready to take him away.

'This life's work, what would that be?' The Doctor was clearly stalling for time now.

Hero shook his head. 'I have no idea. Yet there are three of you, three passionate beating hearts, and when I place them in my Polyhymnia, my Clio, my Melpomene, I have no doubt I will find out. Nine Muses, each ready to grant me all possible inspiration.'

'Three of us?' the Doctor asked, worried that Hero had already captured Zoe.

Hero smiled, as the two Muses grabbed the Doctor's arms and began walking him to an antechamber. 'Your other friend will turn up. I saw through her disguise immediately, and one of our guards will eventually find her. I can't think that a young girl will outwit all of the Musaeum staff. I will have three of you. Then, with all nine Muses fully animated, fully alive, what might I not imagine and create?'

'Wait,' the Doctor went on. 'I have yet to tell you the secrets of time travel…'

But Hero smiled, 'What is time travel compared to all knowledge, my friend? Time is but one component of truth. When all nine Muses work for me, I will have all the secrets there are. I don't think I need to keep you around just for that, do you?'

CHAPTER NINE

While Hero was assuring the Doctor that Zoe would be found, Zoe herself had just slipped past the third Musaeum guard and finally found the display room the Doctor had been talking about when he'd whispered the urgent instructions that had her pretending to run away crying. In reality she was trying to get as far away from Hero as possible, and to collect the piece the Doctor sent her to find.

The room was filled with hundreds of musical instruments. Lyres made of outlandishly shaped gourds, pipes of bone and wood. If any people had ever made music, the instrument was here, careful annotations in Greek and Latin alongside telling the visitor where the piece was from and guessing the date that it might have been created.

Zoe scanned the shelves closest to her and, thanking her education in astronomy for providing her with classical Greek and Latin, passed shelves for Egypt and Ethiopia, those for Byzantium and Asia, and finally found the instruments of Greece. There, tucked away, long ignored, she found what she had come for. It was as the Doctor had said, a small, plain, double pipe. As she picked it up, Zoe felt an overwhelming urge to play it, but the Doctor had been very clear: 'When you have it, do not, under any circumstances play it, not until you find Jamie and me. Do you hear, Zoe?'

Shaking herself, Zoe grabbed a fold of cloth from a shelf behind her and wrapped the pipe in it, then hurried from the room. The Doctor had told her to avoid the main parts of the

Musaeum, to stick to back corridors if possible, and to find the way to Hero's workshop. He hadn't known what Hero was up to, but he was certain that the secret of the Muses lay with the inventor. Most of these back corridors were empty, but eventually she came across two young Greek men in furious – and utterly inaccurate – discussion about the properties of the Sun.

Lowering her voice and scuffing one foot on the ground, she aped Jamie at his most laddish and asked, 'Know where I can find Hero? Got a message. Delivery at the front gate.'

Neither of the young men bothered to look up from the parchment they argued over. One of them waved an arm in the direction of a high walkway. 'Follow that over the Zoo, domed building, can't miss it.'

'Nutty old man's always in there,' his friend added. 'Tinkering away, no idea of what really matters.'

'Thanks,' Zoe said, and then she leaned over and whispered, 'It's actually more hydrogen than helium. Helios is a bit of a misnomer.'

Then she ran on up the spiral staircase, all the time holding the joined pipes close to her side, hoping that she wasn't too late.

In the antechamber the Doctor sat among half-formed mechanical shapes. Some were almost complete as Muses, but for a face missing, or limbs that appeared to have ripped themselves from the torso, others were mechanical skeletons. All were prototypes for the Muses. All now lay inert and foreboding, a message from Hero's journey to this moment, a journey littered with mistakes and misshapes.

Jamie lay on the operating table as Hero took the ground-up paste his beautiful young assistant had made and added water to it, ready for Jamie to drink.

'Open wide, and swallow this down. You won't feel a thing, I promise.'

Jamie, opened wide, screaming at the top of his lungs, 'Doctor! Zoe! No!'

And for the second time that day Jamie was knocked out. This time, Hero had no intention of him coming round again.

Zoe rounded one corner of the walkway and stopped dead in her tracks. Directly in front of her were two guards.

'You can't come this way, lad,' said one of the guards. 'The old man's experimenting in there, not safe.' He pointed towards the domed building.

'But I'm meant to give him something... for the experiment,' Zoe said. 'He needs it right away.'

The guards shrugged, and as one of them explained rules were rules and there was nothing he could do, the other peered at her a little more closely. 'Where're you from, lad?'

Zoe began backing away. There was no time to risk being uncovered as a girl.

The guard took a pace closer. 'Let's get a look at you.'

'It's fine. I'll take it round the long way.'

Zoe raced back down the spiral staircase and, instead of heading into the corridor again, where the young astronomers were still puzzling over the Sun, she ducked around the base of the staircase and came smack up against a wall, twice her own height.

From above she could hear one of the guards. 'I'll check which way she's gone. If that's not a girl, my old eyes are worse than my wife says they are.'

Zoe knew that the walkway had led over the Zoo towards the domed building. Now she had no choice but to cross the animal enclosure. She tucked the pipe into her belt, and began to climb the wall, stone by stone. The guard was already puffing his way down the steps. Zoe was at the top of the wall as he reached the bottom. Not waiting to check out the lie of the land, Zoe dropped straight down on the other side. Just as Zoe noticed three baby hippopotami alongside their intensely protective mother, the mother hippopotamus let out a long, stinking roar, its mouth wide and teeth gleaming in the Alexandrian sun.

Zoe grabbed the pipes, ripped off the cloth she had covered them in for safe-keeping, deftly throwing it to land square in the furious mother's face, covering its eyes. In the moment of the creature's confusion, Zoe sprinted across the enclosure, running for all she was worth.

By the time she reached the other side of the compound and flung herself up another wall, there was small crowd gathered on the walkway above, and another on the viewing platform, all keenly watching the snarling hippopotamus as it shredded the cloth with its massive teeth. None of them noticed the young girl, climbing a distant wall, pipes in one hand, and a mantra playing over and over again in her head: 'Let it not be too late, let it not be too late, let it not be too late.'

CHAPTER TEN

Perhaps it was too late.

Zoe had climbed the wall, and found herself on the edge of the wide alabaster dome. She made her way around it, keeping low so that her shadow did not show through to those inside. Eventually she found a narrow opening in the alabaster, and levered herself in. Inside there was a narrow ledge, circling the inside of the dome, Zoe crouched down to keep herself hidden. When she looked below she saw Jamie strapped to a table, his shirt pulled open, and Hero selecting a knife to use on her friend.

She was about to scream out, when she heard a thin whistle. Hero must have heard it too, for he looked around, confused.

Zoe saw the Doctor first, directly below her, a Muse guarding him on either side.

'What are you doing?' Hero asked.

The Doctor had his recorder in his hand. He spoke quietly. 'My friend here, I appreciate he will live for ever in the Muse, but I'd like to play a little tune for him, if I may? A Scottish tune?' The Doctor nodded at Erato and Urania on either side of him. 'My new friends understand the power of a funeral dirge in its place.'

Hero frowned. 'The problem with these Muses is they have no idea how much I've done for them. Very well, but quietly, I need to concentrate.'

Hero picked up a thin knife and, as he did so, the Doctor looked up and winked at Zoe. Clinging to the edge of the dome opening with one hand, Zoe held the double pipe in the other, and despite her precarious position and never having played before, she felt certain she would be able to play sweetly, perfectly.

As she took a breath and Hero made his first nick in Jamie's skin, the Doctor let out a belter of a blow into his own recorder. Zoe brought the double pipe to her lips and blew.

Nothing happened. There was no sound.

The Doctor played his own recorder again, and again Zoe tried with the double pipe. No sound.

Hero looked away from Jamie to see what was going on, and what he saw had him drop the knife and back away to the far wall, away from the Doctor and from Zoe above.

The Doctor turned to see what had so scared Hero and he too looked startled, but he looked up and said to Zoe, who couldn't see what Hero and the Doctor could see, 'Keep playing, keep playing!'

And so, teetering on the edge of the dome, Zoe continued to play a sound she could not hear, a tune that no human ears would ever hear. She played the tune that called the Muses – the *real* Muses – from their home, the planet Helicon, renamed Mount Helicon in the myths that humans had created to explain the astonishing power of the alien women they rewrote as 'the Muses'.

Below Zoe, the mechanical Euterpe snapped to attention. Her body shifted and grew, seemed to take up much more space. As did Urania and all of the other Hero-made Muses. Then the misshapes emerged from the antechamber, and they too ranked themselves alongside their fellow Muses. They kept coming, half-made limbs, and talking heads, eyes rolling animatedly across the floor, mouths speaking, though no sound came from them. All of them were more alive than they had ever been, more alive than Hero could ever make them.

And then Euterpe reached up her arm, an arm that seemed to extend itself without elongating, to reach without changing shape, and she plucked the pipe from Zoe's hand.

Zoe grabbed the dome opening with both hands now, and carefully, trembling, she crouched down, sitting on the lip of wall at the edge of the dome.

Now Euterpe played the pipes, her own pipes, the original aulos, the prototype recorder stolen from her eons ago, and eventually forgotten. It had been traded, transported, and finally arrived, its precious origins unknown, conserved on a dusty shelf in the depths of the Musaeum.

When Euterpe played, everyone could hear the music. It was more than beautiful and it took only moments for Hero to be weeping at his own foolishness, at the enormity of his presumption in thinking he might recreate a real Muse. The music was beautiful enough to rouse Jamie, who woke neither annoyed nor angry, but grateful to be lying there, to feel the music running through his body, in time with his still-beating heart.

Finally, when Euterpe's music had called in the original Muse to each of the other Hero-made Muses, she played a long, pure, high note that shattered the alabaster dome, shards miraculously falling clear of Zoe.

It was Melpomene who took Hero to task.

'I was once Muse of Singing, just singing, did you know that, Hero?'

Hero shook his head.

'And when it was understood that the voice is the way to all feeling, and all too often to the feelings you humans run from, they made me Muse of Tragedy. Now I stand before you, you tragic figure, and I wonder, how should I inspire you now? Your arrogance has brought us back to this tedious Earth, where all you ever do is moan and complain and beg us to visit…' She was warming to her theme now, prowling the room, the other Muses and pieces of Muses nodding and clapping, tapping half-made fingers and toes on the marble floor in applause and agreement with her. 'Whining, "Oh Muse visit me", "Oh Muse, I can't create without you", "Oh Muse, help me, help me, help me"…'

Melpomene paused and took a breath, her body and voice suddenly vast. 'Do you not think we grow tired of HELPING?' she demanded, looming over Hero. 'And even more insulting,' she added, back to her original size, 'when you demand we attend you, we have to pretend to be men to get in.'

The Muses and the many mechanical half-pieces tutted and shook what heads they could as Melpomene closed her argument. 'We, who are the essence of all that is inspiring in women, inspiring of men and of women, have to pretend to be men, because you demand we arrive. When the whole point of being a Muse – the whole point,' she thundered, 'is for YOU to wait for US.'

She looked at Jamie who was gazing at her in adoration, at Hero cowering before her, and at the Doctor, who was leaning against the wall, a quiet smile on his face.

She glared. 'Do I amuse you, Doctor?'

'No Melpomene, you enthuse me – as you always have.'

Zoe thought she saw a fleeting smile cross Euterpe's lips at this, and she was certain Clio and Erato winked at each other, but Melpomene didn't so much as blush.

'As I should,' she said, holding her hands out to the Doctor. 'As I should.'

CHAPTER ELEVEN

That evening, after Hero had promised never again to demand the Muses' attention, after the nine sisters had used their combined power to breathe life back into those who had died in Hero's attempts to recreate them, and after Jamie had stopped complaining of the small nick to his chest – not least because Terpsichore had taught him the original ninesome reel that Jamie's own eightsome reel was based on – the Muses, content to enjoy an evening in Alexandria, put on a show for everyone in the Musaeum's theatre, the chorus played by Hero's mechanical puppets and masks.

Long after the show, the Doctor sat in deep conversation with Melpomene, Urania and Zoe discussed astronomy, and Jamie danced for hours with Euterpe and Erato. Hero himself sat happily with Thalia, chuckling at her jokes as he tinkered with his new project. Having given the Muses a solemn promise to stay away from creating people or anything in their guise, he was now working on a prototype animal, starting small, modelling his new invention on one of the many wild dogs that roamed the city, building what he believed would be the first mechanical canine.

It was just before dawn when the Muses took their leave. They stood beneath the shards of the shattered dome, waiting for the stars to align their way.

Urania turned to Zoe. 'You didn't happen to see an old cloth near the pipes, did you?'

'Ah, why?' Zoe asked, frightened of risking her new friend's wrath.

'After Euterpe's aulos was stolen, I found I'd also lost something in the theft.'

'Oh?'

'An embroidered cloth. I'd done the work myself.'

Zoe remembered the cloth in which she had wrapped the aulos, the small bumps of embroidery on it, soft with age. She took a deep breath. 'Oh. And... was it a pretty picture?'

Urania screwed up her face. 'As if I'd bother embroidering a picture. It was a star map. Took me millennia to get it right. Quite a few galaxies I don't think even your own people have discovered yet.'

'Oh no, that's awful, I'm so sorry,' Zoe blurted out.

'Well, you were in a hurry. Saving your friends is far more important than looking for a map you didn't even know existed. Never mind, I've done without it for this long. Fare you well, Zoe.'

Jamie and Zoe collapsed exhausted the moment they were back in the TARDIS, both sleeping an easy sleep that the Doctor envied.

Just before setting the TARDIS off again, he looked out once more at the Alexandrian sky, now a deep rose in the dawn light. 'Precious city,' he said softly to himself.

The TARDIS whirred and rose and took off in a blaze of its own light, while down below in the Zoo a mother hippopotamus and her three babies snuggled into a nest made infinitely softer with a thousand ripped shreds of an ancient, Muse-crafted star map.

About the Authors

A.L. Kennedy has twice been selected as one of Granta's Best of Young British Novelists and has won a host of other awards – including the Costa Book of the Year for her novel *Day*. She lives in London and is a part-time lecturer in creative writing at Warwick University.

Jenny T. Colgan has written sixteen bestselling novels as Jenny Colgan, which have sold over 2.5 million copies worldwide, been translated into twenty-five languages, and won both the Melissa Nathan Award and Romantic Novel of the Year 2013. Aged 11, she won a national fan competition to meet the Doctor and was mistaken for a boy by Peter Davison.

Nick Harkaway won the Oxfam Emerging Writers Prize at the Hay Festival in 2012. He was also awarded the Kitschies 'Red Tentacle' (for the year's most intelligent, interesting and progressive novel with speculative elements). He is the author of three novels – *Tigerman*, *Angelmaker* and *The Gone-Away World* – and a non-fiction book about technology and human social and political agency called *The Blind Giant*. Before he began writing novels he was a notably unsuccessful screenwriter and a truly hopeless martial artist. He likes red wine, deckled edges and most of Italy, and lives in London with his wife and two children.

Trudi Canavan lives in Melbourne, Australia. She has been making up stories about people and places that don't exist for as long as she can remember. While working as a freelance illustrator and designer she wrote the bestselling *Black Magician Trilogy*, which was published in 2001–2003 and was named an 'Evergreen' by *The Bookseller* in 2010. *The Magician's Apprentice*, a prequel to the trilogy, won the Aurealis Award for Best Fantasy Novel in 2009 and the final of the sequel trilogy, *The Traitor Queen*, reached #1 on the UK *Times* Hardback bestseller list in 2011.

Jake Arnott was born in 1961, and lives in London. His debut novel, *The Long Firm*, was published in 1999 to huge public and critical acclaim. *He Kills Coppers, Truecrime, Johnny Come Home, The Devil's Paintbrush* and *The House of Rumour* have followed to equal acclaim. Both *The Long Firm* and *He Kills Coppers* have been made into widely praised TV dramas.

Before embarking on her writing career, **Cecelia Ahern** completed a degree in journalism and media studies. Her first novel, *PS, I Love You* was one of the biggest-selling debut novels of 2004 and a number one bestseller. Her successive bestselling novels are *Where Rainbows End, If You Could See Me Now, A Place Called Here, Thanks for the Memories, The Gift, The Book of Tomorrow, The Time of My Life, One Hundred Names, How to Fall in Love* and *The Year I Met You* and have collectively sold 23 million copies. *PS, I Love You*, starring Hilary Swank and Gerard Butler, became an international box office success, and *Where Rainbows End* was adapted to *Love, Rosie* starring Lily Collins and Sam Claflin. Cecelia also co-created the hit American television comedy series *Samantha Who?*

Joanne Harris is the author of *Chocolat* (made into an Oscar-nominated film with Juliette Binoche and Johnny Depp), and twelve more bestselling novels. Her work is published in over fifty countries and she was appointed MBE in the 2013 Queen's Birthday Honours list. Born in Barnsley, of an English father and a French mother, she studied Modern and Medieval Languages at Cambridge and spent fifteen years as a teacher before (somewhat reluctantly) becoming a full-time writer. She lives in Yorkshire with her family, plays bass in a band first formed when she was 16, works in a shed in her garden, likes musical theatre and old sci-fi, drinks rather too much caffeine, spends far too much time online and occasionally dreams of faking her own death and going to live in Hawaii.

Stella Duffy was born in London, grew up in New Zealand, and now lives in London. She is the author of seven literary novels, including *The Room of Lost Things* and *State of Happiness*, both of which were longlisted for the Orange Prize. *The Room of Lost Things* won the Stonewall Writer of the Year 2008, and she won the Stonewall Writer of the Year 2010 for *Theodora*. She is also the author of the Saz Martin detective series. She has written over 45 short stories, including several for BBC Radio 4, and won the 2002 CWA Short Story Dagger for 'Martha Grace'. Her ten plays include an adaptation of *Medea* for Steam Industry, and *Prime Resident* and *Immaculate Conceit* for the National Youth Theatre (UK). In addition to her writing work she is an actor and theatre director.